I0653464

CONFESSING TO THE CEO

Iona Rose

SOME BOOKS

Author's Note

Hey there!

Thank you for choosing my book. I sure hope that you love it. I'd hate to part ways once you're done though. So how about we stay in touch?

My newsletter is a great way to discover more about me and my books. Where you'll find frequent exclusive give-aways, sneak previews of new releases and be first to see new cover reveals.

And as a HUGE thank you for joining, you'll receive a FREE book on me!

With love,

Iona

Get Your FREE Book Here:

https://dl.bookfunnel.com/v9yit8b3f7

Chapter 1
Scarlett

On principle alone, I don't run.

For anyone or anything.

But the moment Sophie called with that strain of pain in her barely audible voice, I found myself running through the city, and hailing down taxis to get to her.

"He's gone, Scar," she whispered in an awed voice. "I think he's really gone. Please come over. I'm in Queens. Flushing Meadows Corona park."

I knew she was scheduled to meet her wedding planner and caterer at an event this evening, along with her fiancé Jerald. So, the fact that this was happening was alarming, to say the least. As I rushed to her, I realized I couldn't recall the last time I'd seen her distraught, and I grew even more worried.

She'd never burden anyone with her pain unless it was quite literally so intense everyone could feel it and queried about it. The closer I got to her, the more anxious I became.

I spotted her sitting alone, her shoulders slumped, at a

table in the big hall, facing the tall windows. The sun was already setting, and the view through the garden beyond was breathtaking.

"Sophie," I called. She was so lost in her thoughts that even though my voice echoed through the nearly empty hall she didn't hear me.

"Sophis," I called even louder, a touch of panic in my voice.

She turned then, and I stopped in my tracks.

My God, she looked devastated. Her face was pale and pinched, and her eyes were red and swollen. Of course, I knew she'd had her doubts; I saw it once or twice in her eyes when they'd argued, but she had never shared them or complained.

"Bastard," I muttered as I squatted in front of her and held the sides of her arms.

She shook her head. "Don't blame him. He's having a hard time. He's just lost his mom. I understand, I do, it's really hard for him. They were so close..."

She could say whatever she wanted, but as I watched my twin, the person I loved most in the world, look so dejected and sit in front of me, as though everything she was had been sucked out of her, I couldn't help but feel hurt and furious at the same time.

Somehow, I managed to compose myself and rein in my emotions so that I could show up for her as she needed, not as I wanted.

"What happened?" I asked.

She managed a trembling smile. "You had your presentation today, right? How was it?"

"Are you kidding me?" I asked incredulously. "You're talking about that now?"

She wiped away tears from the corners of her eyes to prevent them from falling. "I don't want to talk about it yet. I don't know how to even get up from this chair. I don't know how to survive the next second, so I've just been sitting here..."

"Did he give you a reason?" I asked.

She inhaled deeply and released it slowly. "He did, but it made no sense. I mean... it did, but it's not enough. I can't accept it. We've been together too long."

She shook her head. "I love him and I hate him at the same time."

My brows furrowed at this. I truly didn't want to rush her. I just wanted to be here to listen, so she could speak as slowly as she wanted. However, I truly wanted to get something out of the way.

"He didn't cheat on you, right?"

She lifted her gaze to look at me blankly. "I don't know."

My face immediately darkened. "Do you suspect it?"

"I have no clue," she said. "But I don't think so. I just think he's a bit sad and lost. He's lost the only parent he had."

She paused again.

"To be honest, I'm not completely surprised. The signs have been there for the last seven months. I was just hoping it would pass. Then we got engaged, and I was sure that all was well, but now..."

"He was supposed to meet me here, but he called and said he needed time away. From me... from everything. To think, to understand, to digest the loss, because since then, he hasn't been able to see anything clearly without his grief tainting it. Even me."

"Okay, that's not so bad. He just needs time, then. I can understand that," I consoled.

She nodded. "I do as well, but it doesn't change the fact that I've been abandoned mere weeks before our wedding. The invitations have gone out, I've been with him for nearly seven years of my life. Was all of that just a waste?"

More tears escaped from the corners of her eyes.

"It can't just have been a waste. I love him with my whole heart. I still..." she stopped herself. "God, I feel so pathetic. I really can't believe this."

"Did he give any indications that he'll come back?" I asked, and she let out a dark scoff.

"He didn't give any indication of anything whatsoever, the freaking asshole."

A smile tugged at the corners of my lips. It was just so funny to see her curse. She rarely did. She was the complete opposite of me, and I'd always teased her for it.

"What did you say to him?" I asked.

She went silent for a few seconds. "What could I say?"

"Maybe what he needed... " I paused. "Maybe what he needs is someone to talk some sense into him. Maybe you've coddled him a bit too much, and so he's just wallowed and completely rotted in his grief... no offence."

"So you're saying this is my fault?"

I sighed. "You know that's not what I'm saying."

"So what are you saying?"

"He's always loved you because of your temperament. He loves how calm and considerate you are, but maybe during this time in his life, that's not what he needs. Maybe he needs someone to be like a bucket of ice-cold water dumped over his obtuse head. Maybe that's what he needs to see clearly."

She smiled a little, and it was such a relief that I almost didn't know how to contain myself.

"I mean it though," I said.

She nodded. "I know what you mean, and I tried that, trust me. It didn't work. Nothing worked. He just... he just seems broken and destroyed, and once again, I'm not a monster. I do understand, and this is the most frustrating part. Now, I'm almost kind of wishing he cheated on me so that I'd have a very valid reason to vent and scream. As it is the slow loss is just so quiet and deep and excruciating. There were no fights, no big blowouts... those at least, could be addressed and resolved, but this is just so quietly insidious. A simple phone call to inform me that he needs to be away from me, leaving me to do whatever I want as a result."

"So you didn't curse him out at all?" I asked, shocked. Boy, I would have turned the air blue if someone had pulled that on me so near my wedding.

"Not this time, but I did two weeks back," she replied. "We fought about the way he didn't seem to care about our wedding." Her brow creased. "Do you think that was the reason why he broke things off today?"

I was surprised to hear this. "You? You lost it with him?"

"Yeah," she replied. "He... he has a six-figure bakery. I couldn't wrap my head around the fact that despite this, he didn't care who would handle our cake or pastries. I showed him some photos, and he was so disinterested. He just wanted me to contract it out to whoever."

"What?" I frowned. "Sophie, I love you, and I'm sorry for

saying this, but are you sure his grief is what has him acting like a complete tool or could there maybe be something else going on?"

She was silent for a while, then she shrugged. "I really don't know. That's what's killing me in all of this. I really don't know. I always felt like I understood him deeply, like we were on the same wavelength but... now he feels even more distant to me than a stranger."

Maybe this was for the best, then, I thought, but I didn't dare say it out loud. She looked at me then as though she could read what I was thinking – this had been the case numerous times in the past.

"What?" I asked.

"I want to still try... I can't give up this easily."

I immediately started to shut this down, but then once again held back. She kept staring at me.

"What?" I frowned.

"I know what you're thinking."

I didn't deny this possibility.

"Okay," I replied, and her face weakened as though she was about to cry again.

"Sophie, come on."

She reached forward and hit my shoulder. "I need you to be on my side right now."

"That's why I'm not saying anything," I replied.

"So, do you think I should?"

"Should you what?" I asked, hoping that she would quickly abandon this horrendous notion.

"Do you think I should give up?"

"He wants you to," I replied, and tears filled her eyes again. I leaned forward then and pulled her into my arms.

"You know what Mom always used to say," I said. "Time resolves all problems so..."

"You think I should give it time."

I was hesitant to say this as well, so she leaned away to look at me.

"You never liked him."

"It's not just him I don't like," I said.

She sighed.

"He's okay, but you, I love, so I say, take the time off and let's see how you feel."

She pulled away from me. "I can't take the time off right now."

"Why not?"

She picked up her purse, and we began to leave. "Things are hellish at work, and my boss doesn't understand what excuses are. I can't leave."

"What do you mean your boss doesn't understand what excuses are?"

She shrugged in response, and we walked on to catch a taxi. One stopped almost as soon as we reached the stand. Inside she turned to me.

"What?" I asked.

She narrowed her gaze at me but didn't say a word. Then she shook her head and looked away.

I wondered what gears were turning in her head, but knowing her, I knew she primarily wouldn't spit it out until she had thought it through properly.

"We still look alike, right?" she asked out of the blue, and the question startled me.

"What?"

"I asked, we're still identical, right? Indistinguishable."

"I have no idea," I said, "but we haven't been mistaken for one another for a long time."

"That's because your style changed in college. Your makeup is bolder, your hair's a bob, your outfit..."

I grinned. "You mean I'm hot? Yeah, I get it."

She smiled, but her gaze began to rove over my face in earnest.

"What are you thinking?" I asked worriedly.

"You know what I'm thinking."

My eyebrows nearly shot up to my hairline, and I began to shake my head. "No... no... no..."

"Oh please, Scarlett. Can you?"

I watched her. "You're serious?"

"Why not? We've done it so many times."

"That was when we were kids," I stated, still shaking my head.

"No, we did it in college and during your internship, at that first company you worked for. I did it because you needed my help. I did it for you. Will you do it for me?"

I kept staring at her, then I looked away.

I heard her sigh. "It's okay if you don't want to do it? We haven't been too close these past few years, have we? Because I instead invested all my time with that jerk."

"We're twins," I said softly. "Even though we drift apart sometimes, we'll always have each other and no one else."

She smiled then and leaned against me, resting her head on my shoulder. She remained silent for a few blocks further, and then she brought it up once again.

"So..." she said. "Do you think you can pull it off?"

I considered her request. It felt too strange to be her

after all these years. We were not kids or in college anymore.

"Are you able to leave your current job?"

"I always can," I replied. "That's one of the benefits of going the freelance route."

"When was your contract due to end?" she asked.

"I still have a month and a half left," I replied.

"Oh..." she said, her voice forlorn.

"Don't worry," I told her. "It's not hard for me to find another place. I'll help you out. Just tell me that your current workload is not much. What do I have to deal with this coming week?"

She smiled at me and told a blatant lie. "Not much at all."

I narrowed my gaze at her and she looked away quickly.

Oh my God! I knew that look. It was going to be a mad week.

"Whatever it is, I'll handle it. But wait, where is your company located? In Manhattan?"

She bit her bottom lip. "Yes."

I sucked in a breath through my teeth.

"A bit too far from Soho?"

"A bit," I replied.

"I can pay for your taxi for the week?" she suggested.

"You don't have to do that."

"It's no trouble, I know you hate the subway, plus Montgomery pays quite handsomely, so it's not a problem."

"Montgomery?" I asked, and she nodded.

"My boss. His name is Lucien. Montgomery is his surname."

"Ah, so that's where the company name Montgomery Holdings comes from?"

"Yeah," she replied.

"And he's filthy rich, right?"

"Net worth is just under two billion."

"Wow. How ancient is he?"

"Thirty-two years old," she replied.

My mouth nearly fell open. "What?"

"Young, huh?"

I nodded. "Way too young. I was hoping he was an elderly boss who could barely see. Then it would be most likely that we could get away with this."

She thought about this, parted her lips, but closed them back.

"What?" I asked.

"He acts quite aloof like he doesn't know anything, but sometimes I'm able to listen to his conversations, and I'm actually amazed by how much he knows. About the company, about everything. Like we're situated on various floors, and sometimes I hear what is going on just by listening to him. I low-key think there's a spy somewhere in the office that silently feeds him information; otherwise, I have no clue how he literally knows everything happening at a given time."

"So he's nosy?" I asked.

"Not nosy but vigilant, I think is the appropriate word. His day has to be completely organized, and he has a huge client he's planning on signing this week," she said, stopping at the realization of the magnitude of her workload.

"Wow," she said to herself as she thought. "This is truly a

bad time to leave. I'll wait for the week to run out, maybe some other-"

Suddenly her phone began to ring, so she got up and pulled the phone out of her pocket. She, however, didn't respond. Instead, she stared at it until I was forced to check who it was. Montgomery was written as the caller.

"Is that him?" I asked.

"Yeah," she said, and then to my surprise, she passed the phone over to me.

"What?"

"Answer it," she said. "Our voices are similar, but I think my pitch is slower than yours. Let's see, first of all, if he'll notice the difference."

I stared at the phone as it continued to ring, all the while she urged it toward me.

"Answer it," she said, but I hesitated. Eventually, I sighed, but just as I accepted it, it disconnected.

I started to hand it over, but she stopped me. "He'll call back. He wouldn't be calling if it wasn't important."

"That's good, at least he doesn't disturb you."

"Oh no, he does. He doesn't call me late because he doesn't have to. I'll probably be in the office working late with him."

"Oh no," I wrinkled my nose. "You have to work late a lot?"

"Usually, but the bonuses are insane, plus lately I've been glad to be anywhere but home," I stared at her and couldn't help but feel saddened by her words.

"We've really not been as close as we should be? I should know this?"

"We talk a lot, just not about these things, plus I didn't exactly want to tell you about Jerald either."

"You're right," I nodded, "It's all your fault."

She smiled, and just then the phone began to ring again.

"Speaker," she said. "Try it out."

I nodded and responded.

"Sophie, where's the shares division proposal?" came the cold, quiet voice.

For a moment, I was a bit startled as I listened to him because I had expected a boisterous tone. However, he sounded so calm like the undulating surface of the ocean.

"Hello?" he called again.

I turned to look at Sophie, who was thinking.

Eventually, she figured it out and raised her hand. "It's on my desktop," she whispered.

"Sophie!" he called again, and though his tone wasn't loud, I could still feel the annoyance in his tone.

"Oh, sorry," I replied.

Sophie mouthed the next set of instructions to me. "Sorry, sir."

"What?" I mouthed back.

"Sir," she whispered fiercely, and my frown deepened even further.

"Sophie?" he reminded again, and she nudged me.

"Sorry, sir, it's on my desktop."

He went silent briefly. "You didn't print it out? You said you'd leave the documents on my desk."

I watched the worry flash across Sophie's face. Then she began to nod, and my attention focused on her lips. "I did, sir, but I think I left that one out."

Once again, he went silent.

I expected him to hang up then or scold her and get someone else to do what he wanted, but he dished out new instructions over the phone.

"I need those documents now," he said.

I frowned again before I could tell him to figure it out himself, but in more colorful words, Sophie nodded vigorously at me while whispering, "I'm almost there, sir."

I was forced to repeat the words, and afterwards, I set the cell phone down.

"You're almost there?"

"I'm his assistant," she told me. "He has others, but I'm the only one with complete access to him. Others are restricted in one way or another, and I'm the only one with a hefty salary and additional bonuses."

I still wasn't convinced, however, she wasn't interested in trying to convince me. "I want to build a long-term career there; you don't, so—"

"I know, jeez, don't rub it in."

"So, will you go?"

"Wait, what?" I asked, taken aback.

"It's just to give him some documents, let's do this as a test run."

"But... we look so different," I pointed out.

She assessed my appearance and nodded. "Yes, we do, but that's quite easily fixed."

I couldn't help but admit that I was curious about her boss.

"He doesn't know you have an identical twin, does he?" I asked.

"Nope. He knows almost nothing about me," she replied. Then she stopped herself. "Wait, as I said earlier, he always seems to know more than he lets on. So maybe he does know, hence the need for a test. So if he asks who you are when you go there now, you can make up something like I'm on my way, and if he doesn't ask, then the coast is clear."

"And my hair?" I asked. "How do I explain why I suddenly have a bob rather than a bun and different clothes for that matter?"

She looked at me. "Don't worry about that. He wouldn't notice if you went in with a bikini."

"As if," I scoffed

"I've been working directly with him for over three years, and there hasn't even been a tense moment between us."

"Is he gay?" I asked.

She smiled. "Absolutely not."

"What makes you so sure?"

"You'll see," she said, with a secret smile. "But on second thought, and just to be safe, I'm not looking to lose my job. Let's exchange clothes. We can explain away the haircut, but clothes for sure will be much harder."

I perused her dress shirt, buttoned up almost to the collar, her pencil skirt, and flats.

She smiled again. "You look absolutely disgusted."

"Why do you dress like that?" I asked "You look like Aunt Theresa, only a hundred pounds lighter. Maybe this is why there hasn't been any tension."

"And I am extremely keen for it to remain that way." She gave me a look.

I brushed her concern away. "Don't worry, I wouldn't dream of seducing your boss."

Chapter 2
Lucien

Her hair was suddenly short. At first, I was startled by this, but ultimately uninterested. However, when I looked at her again, I couldn't help but notice that a few more buttons than usual were released from her shirt. Her breasts were pressing against the fabric, and I couldn't help but wonder what it was I was missing.

I looked at her face, and I realized that within the space of a few hours, she seemed to have turned into a different person. She, however, seemed to be more guarded, as though she were guilty of something because she didn't meet my eyes.

"Here is the report, sir," she said and stood before my desk. She placed it on the surface, and once again, I looked up, wondering what was happening and why she was acting so out of character. So I looked up from the document I had been perusing and leaned back against the chair to watch her.

"My hand can't reach that far," I said, but she just stared at me. Eventually, though, she seemed to understand what was wrong. "You want me to bring it to you?"

I didn't know how to respond to this because it wasn't even a valid question. Of course, I was expecting her to bring it to me just like she had for the last three years; however, now it was suddenly as though she didn't want to come within a year's distance of me.

I didn't have the time to give to any of these sudden changes and peculiarities, so I took the document and began to go through it.

"I'll be leaving then," she said, but it didn't register until she was heading toward the door that she had just said she was leaving. I raised my head and watched her, confused.

"Are you alright?" I asked, and she stopped in her tracks. She turned around to meet my eyes, and at the swish of her bob, it hit me, she was completely different. I almost wanted to call out her name, certain she wouldn't answer, but that would seem crazy. I would seem crazy.

I turned and checked the time. It was just after nine pm, and working until the later hours of the night was nothing new to me, so why was I suddenly feeling so off-balance?

"What do you mean?" I heard her ask and returned my attention to her.

At the confusion on my face, she clarified the question. "Why are you asking me if I'm alright?"

I didn't respond. "Wait a bit," I told her. "I need you to send this to the Chief Financial Officer."

"Is he still here?" she asked, and I didn't miss the surprise in her tone.

Once again, my gaze shot up, and then I cocked my head. Now, it just felt like she was playing with me; otherwise, why else would she be asking me if the finance director was here?

This time, I ignored her, and she went on her way. I couldn't, however, help looking at her once more as she pulled the door open, and it was then that I noticed yet another thing that seemed off. In the space of a few hours, she seemed to have added a bit of weight.

"Sophie," I called, however, she didn't turn around. "Sophie," I called again and this time, she stopped in her tracks. It was almost as though she only realized then that I was calling out to her.

"Yes," she turned around, and yet another thing was off. Her voice and the way she addressed me. It was much coarser and much less polite. I had been so used to her calling me 'sir' that now that she wasn't, it stood out to me like a sore thumb.

And so I stared at her face properly; however, despite her different haircut, I couldn't detect anything off.

"You cut your hair?" I asked, and to my surprise, her eyebrows shot up.

Of course, she was surprised; I usually didn't engage in personal questions, but I truly needed to understand why everything suddenly felt so different.

"Yes, sir, I did," she said.

"Is that why you left work early?"

Her lips parted several times to speak, but it was as though she couldn't quite decide on what she wanted to say. Needing the brief break, I straightened and leaned against the chair to wait for her response.

"I had an appointment with my wedding planner," she said. "I... think I told you about this."

She had, however, I decided then that I wasn't interested any further.

I still had a mountain of things to handle, so I nodded and returned to work.

Chapter 3
Scarlett

I couldn't breathe.

My heart was pounding so hard against my chest that the moment I exited the office and shut the door behind me, I needed a few minutes to recover. And so I leaned against the wall with my eyes shut, trying to catch my bearings. Until my phone, or rather Sophie's phone, finally rang again.

I was nervous, I realized, as I prayed that he wouldn't be the one calling. So, when I saw my name on the screen instead, since Sophie was using my phone, I let out a deep sigh of relief.

"How did it go?" Sophie asked as I placed the phone against my ear. I started to walk, not knowing if he was watching me through the cameras or something.

"Where are the cameras here?" I asked.

"Why are you asking that? Did something go wrong?" Her question made me laugh.

"Even if something went wrong, why would I be asking you about the cameras?"

"Who knows, to make a hidden escape or something," she replied. I rolled my eyes.

"First of all, tell me where the CFO is and why your boss was so startled by the fact that I wondered if he was still at work?"

"Oh no," she said, worried. I wondered what the problem was.

"The CFO is a bit peculiar in that he likes to come in later in the day. He comes in at about two pm, so he usually leaves late. He's not a morning person."

"Ah," my mouth slightly fell open. "Well then, shit."

"Not shit," she said. "How exactly did it go?"

"Well, going by the question I just asked, there were, as you could imagine, a few blunders."

"Oh no," she said. "I knew we shouldn't have done this. Holy shit."

"For someone who is supposedly heartbroken, you sure do have the energy to still panic," I said.

"You want me to be single and unemployed?"

"Relax, Sophie, it's fine. As long as he has no clue you have a twin, none of my blunders or his suspicion will cause any damage. He'll just chalk it up to you probably being off due to some personal issues. And if he's as nonchalant as you claim he is, then he shouldn't care at all."

"Yeah, yeah," she said. "He's nonchalant about personal business, but it doesn't mean he doesn't notice stuff. And he hates being lied to in any form. That is the one thing sure to get me fired. Maybe I should just ask for some time off. It will be paid. He'll be upset with me, and I truly don't want to disappoint him since this is a client we've been trying to sign for more than a year but..."

"Isn't this supposed to be a week of rest for you?" I asked, and she went silent.

She sighed, "Yeah."

"So what makes you think you and your hero complex abandoning this work so abruptly will bring you a shred of peace? We haven't been caught, and I'm sure we won't be, so just stop panicking and tell me where the CFO's office is."

She listened to me and managed to calm down. "It's on that same floor, a few offices down. Just go to the end of that corridor and then turn right; his office is the first door on the right. His name is David Bernard."

"I got this," I said and started to walk. "Corridor though?" I said with the phone against my ear. "That's putting it lightly. This is like a runway. This place is huge. And all these paintings? Are they real? They look expensive."

Suddenly, a few people came out of nowhere, and the impulse to turn away to hide nearly made me twist my ankle.

"Sophie," two out of three of the group immediately caught me. "What are you doing here? I heard you left early for the day."

Just as I was trying to avoid their eyes and think of a response, the only woman amongst the two shot her eyes wide open.

"You went to meet your wedding planner, didn't you? Don't tell me you finished the meeting and came back to work. Oh my God, Sophie."

"I didn't come back because I love work so much," I replied much to her amusement. "The boss called me back."

"Oh oh," one of the men said. "You usually always defend him. He must have royally pissed you off today."

I smiled at this and nodded, even knowing that Sophie was going to kill me. "He did."

"Finally, we're on the same page. Anyway, get going. You're going to David?"

Thanks to Sophie, I now knew who this was. "Yes," I replied and held up the folder in my hand.

"Alright, we're heading home now. See you tomorrow."

"See you tomorrow," I said and turned to watch them all disappear into an office at the opposite end. They were all so impeccably dressed with not a hair out of place.

I looked down at the phone then and saw, to my surprise, that the phone was still connected.

"Hey," I called as I placed it against my ear once again. "Did you catch any of that?"

"Yes, I did," she said.

"How did I do?"

"You did way too much. Went over the line in fact but..."

"But what?"

"You have a bob. My hair's usually in a bun and my make-up minimal. Why didn't they notice that?"

"Do you know who they are?" I asked as I turned the corner.

"No, I couldn't tell from their voices."

"Then they probably never noticed your hair before since it's always tied back. Or they probably don't care. They look like the type not to really care. Is everyone in your office dressed so stuffily?"

"What do you mean stuffy?" she asked just as I arrived at the CFO's office. "Buttoned-downs buttoned all the up, fat neckties, calf-length skirts."

"We mean serious business there, Scar," she said. "Lucien doesn't mess around."

"Apparently," I said. "Look at how cold this interior is."

"What do you mean cold? It's sophisticated."

"No, it's dark. There's no warmth and color."

"Scar, I'm not doing this with you. Go in to see David and hand the document over. Oh no, first of all, confirm what it is."

I did as she asked and observed the file.

"Revenue share between shareholders," I said.

"Oh alright, I know what that is," she said. "He'll probably not ask you any questions, and if he does, just say you'll get back to him."

"Sophie, you're forgetting that I work in this fold too, and my boy might not be a billionaire, but we deal with serious business as well. So, whatever questions he asks, I'm ready to answer."

"Okay," she said just as I knocked on the door and headed in.

His secretary was still available, and she immediately smiled at me as I came in.

"Hey Sophie," she greeted, and I smiled back.

"Can I go in? Delivery from Lucien."

"Sure," she said, but then she stopped for a moment and looked up from her screen.

"Are you alright?"

"Yes," I replied, and her eyes narrowed. "Your voice is coarser than usual. Are you sick?"

"Um..." I started to think of an excuse to give for why I didn't have my sister's soft dulcet tone, but then she caught yet another massive difference in me.

"Holy shit, you cut your hair," she stood up then and started to march toward me.

I felt ambushed and extremely nervous, but I managed to stay in my place as the elderly lady came over.

"I saw you this morning, and you had your usual bun, and your hair was brown. Now it's a bob and pitch black? What happened? Are you trying out styles for your wedding?"

There were so many questions being asked that I didn't know how to respond or where to start, but thankfully her landline began to ring, so she momentarily forgot her interrogation and hurried back to her desk.

"Sir?" She answered and kept her eyes on me, studying me. I lowered my gaze and looked around.

"Yeah, she's here. Oh. Alright, I'll let her in."

She ended the call and smiled at me. "He's anxious, and you know how he gets. He's waiting for the file."

"Sure," I replied, and she smiled broadly at me.

"When you're done, stop by and tell me all about this haircut. I'm thinking of going shorter too. Is it your usual hair salon or somewhere else? I need all the details."

I stared at her for a moment, nodded, and then headed to the office. Chating—now this was the part I didn't like. It was one of the perks of not working in any place too long because it meant I didn't need to pretend to be sociable or social. I could do my work, keep the chatter to a minimum, and immediately be on my way. I was attending law school later at night, so during the day, I needed to conserve my energy as much as possible.

The CFO was just as old as I'd expected, something to do with giving zero fucks by the time he came into work.

And he surprised me with his accent, which was hardcore British. It made me wonder how he found his way all the way here in the Big Apple. Perhaps he was scouted.

He barely looked at me or noticed me. All he did was take the document from me and then began to peruse it.

"Thanks," he said, and after acknowledging this, I turned around and went on my way. Their office was gorgeous, much more sophisticated and luxurious than ours was, but that was expected for the location smack in the middle of Manhattan.

I was nervous, I realized, and for this very reason, I was excited. Hopefully, I didn't end up costing Sophie her job at the end of the day, but it had been such a long time since I had felt this excitement when it came to going to work. And so I decided right then that I was most definitely going to take this gig.

Chapter 4
Scarlett

"Absolutely not."

A few hours later, I was lounging in Sophie's hanging reading chair and watching as she laid out clothes across her bed for me for the week.

"You're going as me," she said. "You can't dress to draw attention."

"I also can't dress in a way that will destroy me inside. Absolutely not, Sophie."

"What's wrong with button-downs?"

"They're just button-downs and beige, tan, green? Jesus."

She sighed then and collapsed onto the bed.

"You're supposed to be letting me rest, not stirring up my emotions for no reason."

"I've told you multiple times to rest. I don't need to wear your clothes, plus I am busier than you are. I'll tone it down but I'll keep my style. Trust me, it'll do your brand wonders."

"And then after you leave?" she asked.

I shrugged, and she gave me a dark look.

"It's just clothes, Sophie," I said. "No one really cares what anyone wears. I just want to look my best, conservatively speaking, of course, so that I can feel confident enough to handle all the shots that might come at me. Trust me, from the little preview earlier today, I'm expecting there to be many, many more. I don't want to feel like an imposter; I want to feel like myself, and if I do, then I'll be unflustered."

She watched me again and then collapsed against the bed.

We were both silent for a while as I returned my attention to my book, but from time to time, my gaze went to her.

"Are you okay?" I asked.

"Yeah," she replied. "What did you think of my boss?" she asked.

"Lucien?"

"Yeah," she replied. "What did you call him?"

"Well, I haven't called him directly by name yet. What do you usually call him?"

"Lucien," she said, and I nodded.

"At least he's not a tool about titles."

"He's not a tool about most things; he's just very conscientious. And as I told you, this is a very important week. The more I think about it, the more I'm truly glad that you're filling in for me. I'd hate to disappoint him."

As she spoke about the man I'd met earlier, I also couldn't help but bring him to mind. One thing was for sure, and that was the fact that he was incredibly attractive. If I hadn't been so nervous about being found out, I would have taken a bit more time to appreciate just how attractive he was at first sight. But I guessed that within the next few days, I would have more than enough time to do so.

"Is he married?" I asked, and she looked at me in surprise.

"Do you know absolutely nothing about him? He's pretty popular for being so financially successful at his age."

"So he's not married?"

"Of course, he's not."

"Oh," I said, while she narrowed her eyes at me. "Don't go loosening the screws in his brain. Whatever damage you cause, I'm the one who has to clean up when I get back there next week."

This made me laugh, however, I wasn't quite sure how to respond to it just yet. Of course, I wouldn't get involved with him. If I did, then this would severely affect Sophie's work, so I put him out of my mind before it started to shine all its light on attention for him.

"Do I have any wearable clothes here?" I asked. "I don't want to have to go home in the morning."

"I'm sure you do," she said. "How are you going to handle things with your job?"

"I'll take a couple of sick days. I'll tell them that I suddenly came down with something."

"They'll allow this?" she asked.

"Not if I take it for a week at a stretch," I replied. "At first, it'll be two days and then a little bit more till the week runs out."

"What if they don't tolerate that and you get fired?"

"I'll get another job. It's not a permanent position, and

unlike you, I'm not looking to build a career there. I'm flexible and I don't get attached."

"Alright," she said, and our agreement was put in place.

Chapter 5
Lucien

For some reason, she came to my mind more than once. It had never happened before, but there was just something so different about her from the previous day that I couldn't put my finger on. I was sure it was just a distraction. However, as I stood before the mirror in my closet and selected a tie, I couldn't help but think of how different she seemed.

Just then, my phone began to ring, and shaking off the thoughts, I focused more on the goals for the day. We would be going through our presentation for the client to be given later that evening in a conference call, so I thought about all the points I wanted to include. On the way to the office, I jotted them down on my phone and instantly sent them to Sophie so the team could begin implementing them immediately. Afterwards, I shut my eyes, and soon enough, we were at the office.

"I'll be heading out later this morning again," I spoke to Michael. "What time did you arrange with Sophie?"

Michael stared at me, lost for once, and I wondered what was happening.

"What's wrong?"

"I wasn't aware that you'll be heading out again this morning, sir," he said, and I was taken aback. Even I recalled that I had a business panel to speak at, so why didn't Michael know, and more importantly, why hadn't Sophie informed him and made preparations like she always did?

"I was about to ask you if Sophie remembered to get Mr. Cuban a gift to take on the way, but I guess she forgot everything altogether."

At this, I shut the door and walked into the building.

I was greeted in every direction by the staff and managed to respond, but by the time I got onto the private elevator that led to my office at the top, I couldn't hold back at the very unusual error. And so I called her phone, and to my surprise, she didn't pick up.

This, too, had never happened before.

I called her again, and she didn't pick up, and by the time I walked in, I was fuming.

It was made worse by the fact I also didn't see her at her desk, but what I did see was her phone and my missed calls.

I turned toward my secretary, Larry, and he seemed to instantly understand what I wanted.

"We didn't have the cream that she wanted on this floor, so she went down to the lower floors."

I didn't even want to understand what any of that meant, so I just turned around and went into my office.

A few minutes later, there was a knock on the door, but I didn't respond.

However, to my surprise, it came again, and I was

forced to look up from my desk. She never knocked. And more importantly, when she did, which was only when I had company, she knew to come in immediately. She had access to all aspects of my life.

The knock came again, and I got even more mad. Eventually, I was forced to respond before I was driven crazy by the distraction.

"Come in," I said, and the door was pushed open.

She was gorgeous.

This was the first thought that crossed my head, and it startled me so much that I was lost and caught staring at her until she arrived before my desk. She had on a leather high-waisted dark skirt with a jacket over it. However, the buttons were open, so it was quite difficult not to notice the full swell of her breasts peeking out from the top. And then her lips were a bright red.

In all the years I had worked with her, I realized now I couldn't even recall if she had worn makeup. But now, the all-black attire, dark hair, and red lips made it impossible to look away. Something had to have happened between the previous day and today. She almost seemed like a different person, yet not at the same time.

She seemed a little startled at my outright gaze, and only when she lowered hers did I realize what I was doing.

"What is it?" I asked a bit more hostile than usual.

What I didn't expect, however, was the slight anger that flashed in her eyes, and once again, I was taken aback. She'd never had any look of defiance with me, and this was one of the reasons why I had felt so safe with her over the past years. She did her work well; she was a bit shy and just generally soft enough for me to let my guard down.

Now, however, as I gazed at the annoyance in the brow of the woman before me, I wondered again if I was looking at a completely different person.

"What is it?" I asked again, and she gave me a very strained smile that I most definitely did not recognize.

"You asked for me earlier? Larry said you asked where I'd gone."

"This was true. Michael isn't aware that we're heading to the panel soon?" I asked, and she went still. I watched the sudden alarm that came into her eyes. "You are aware?" I asked.

Usually, I would continue with my work, not even bothering to look at her, but now it was as though I was studying her every move.

She cleared her throat, and I understood instantly that she was about to cook up some lie.

"Um... I'm aware," she stuttered.

"Then why isn't he?"

"He probably just forgot," she said, and I narrowed my gaze at her. Shaking my head, I returned my attention back to work. I had wanted him to fetch me some food before I had to go for the panel, but now I had no interest in eating, so I remained silent as she exited the office.

Chapter 6
Scarlett

I had quite a few less-than-polite words I wanted to send Sophie's way the moment I returned to her desk, or rather my desk now. However, when I returned and tried to call her, she didn't pick up. She had fallen asleep in the living room, watching movies to take her mind off her woes, but I was certain that she should be up by now. She hadn't drunk any alcohol besides ordering a huge batch of junk food the previous night. Still, it wasn't enough reason to be in a stupor.

And so, I called and called until eventually, she answered the call.

I was pissed.

"Miss Ma'am," I began my complaint with a lowered tone so that the secretary Larry from across the room wouldn't hear me. "I'm going to need you to be on call and available at all times. It's my first day, and anything could go wrong."

I immediately heard the flow of pee down into the toilet bowl, and I sighed.

"Sophie."

"Sorry," she croaked. "I'm fucking exhausted. What do you need?"

"Well, apparently, he has a panel this morning that you were supposed to tell the driver about, but didn't. He sent some messages and a voice note this morning about changes that needed to be made in his presentation."

It took her a while to process all of this, and then she yawned.

"Yeah," she said. "Right, that's true. Wait! He sent messages."

"Yeah, I found them in your phone on my way this morning."

"Oh, we need to work on that then, his panel is in an hour. You saw my calendar, right? You saw the note?"

"Yes, I did. Now, please focus and show me where they are. If we want this thing to work out, we need to be on top of things. I already don't like the way he stares at me. It's as though he's a hawk zeroing in on its prey."

"He stares at you?" She asked, surprised.

"Yeah, so is that normal?"

"Absolutely not!" I heard the panic once again slightly rise in her tone. "Damn, he's getting suspicious. I mean, I knew he was vigilant, but not this vigilant?"

"He might have suspicions, but he'll never be able to figure it out as long as he doesn't ever become aware that you have a twin."

"Alright," she said. "At this point, I almost don't care. I stayed up late and slept in for the first time in forever, so if he finds out and wants to fire us as a result, then I'm almost happy."

This made me smile as I perused through the rest of his activities for the day.

"So now you're praying to get fired?"

"No, I'm just realizing that I've been too rigid with my life. It's time to let loose a bit."

"Honey, we live in New York," I reminded her. "Unemployment in this pocket drain is not it."

"Yeah, but then what's the point in being scared when you have a twin sister you can leech off of?"

"I have to pay my law school tuition," I said. "You're the one who's going to have to support me soon, so you better work hard to keep this job. Alright, back to business."

"Yeah," she said and went silent again.

I sighed because I knew just how easy it was for her to fall in and out of sleep. She was probably dozing off on the toilet seat again.

"Sophie," I gritted my teeth, wanting to yell with all my might yet being unable to. She woke up then.

"What? Oh yeah, sorry."

I sighed. "You really needed this break, didn't you?"

"Honestly, more than I realized. I'm starting to feel aches and pains that have been the norm begin to soothe out. I haven't felt this light in years."

"Sophie, work," I groaned as I checked the time.

"Oh yeah, right," she said. "Go to my folders in the downloads section, and you'll see everything related to his company there. It's all organized, so just navigate through the documents and then go to presentations."

I did exactly as she asked and followed her guidance, and in very little time, work was underway. I went through the slides to understand what he would be talking about and what his focus would be so I could facilitate improvements and prevent delays. Eventually, with about fifteen minutes to spare, I was able to look up and take my AirPods out of my ears.

Once again, the feeling of completing a task was incomparable. I stretched and took a few moments to bask in the sense of accomplishment. Unlike Sophie, who had slept like a baby, I was missing some sleeping hours from having to complete some law school reading for my class later that night.

I wondered if they had sleeping pods in this office, which was one of the things I immensely enjoyed about my previous job's office. For a few moments, I got lost in that until the phone on my desk began to ring, startling me. I immediately picked up when I saw that it was the boss himself.

"We'll leave in a few minutes," he said. "You're not going to bring the slides over for me to take a look at?"

"I sent it to your email, sir," I said, and to my surprise, he hung up on me. Once again, I was irritated by his sassy behavior, and in defiance, I remained seated for a few minutes longer as I sent Sophie a message informing her of his attitude.

Me: Is he usually this much of a diva?

Sophie: He isn't. He's probably just a bit upset because of all the looming deadlines and activities for the week.

Me: So he can't handle stress? He's a billionaire and he can't handle stress?

Sophie: I don't know what the problem is, maybe it's you and the fact that you keep forgetting things and making his life harder.

Me: You mean me or you?

Sophie: Scarlett, focus. It's almost 11 a.m. Have you called Michael?

At her words, a gong seemed to strike against my head.

Me: Who?

Sophie: Holy shit! The driver. You didn't inform him beforehand to come and pick you up? You have to leave soon!

Me: What did you save him as?

Sophie: Michael.

I found the number and placed my office phone against my ear to continue messaging Sophie.

Me: What's there to be worried about? Isn't he his driver? Shouldn't he be available at all times?

Sophie: Yes, but during the day, he runs errands all over the city, so if journeys aren't scheduled, he might not be available.

The phone began to ring, and then he picked up. The moment I heard the noise and honking of vehicles in the background, however, I had a very eerie suspicion that I had made a mistake.

"Hello, Michael, this is Scar-" I quickly corrected myself. "This is Sophie speaking. We have to leave for the Carlis Hotel in about fifteen minutes. Where will you be waiting?"

"Fifteen minutes?" He exclaimed, and I nearly pulled the phone away from my ear, wondering what the problem was and why he was shouting.

"Yes," I replied.

"I'm in Brooklyn right now," he said, and panic began to set in.

"Why are you in Brooklyn?"

"I had no clue you had a panel this morning with the boss," he said. "He mentioned it earlier when I dropped him off, and I thought you'd call immediately to clarify with me, but you never did. So I went over to Brooklyn to complete the task you gave me earlier. I'm still in his tailor's shop. They'll have his new suits ready soon."

"Holy shit," I cursed under my breath.

We were both silent for a moment as the magnitude of what was about to happen overwhelmed me. Eventually, though, and from experience, I was able to calm down to ask the right questions.

"Is there any possibility at all that you could get back here within the next fifteen minutes?"

"No, it's almost lunch hour, and the traffic is horrendous."

"Right,' I said. "Thanks."

I hung up the phone and instantly shot to my feet.

The first thing was to revise the slide with him, so I sent a quick message to Sophie to help me out with handling the matter of Michael and our transportation, and then I headed to his office.

Once again, I knocked, and he didn't respond, so I waited aggravated until his secretary spoke.

"He doesn't usually respond, you know this, right? Just go in."

"Right," I said and pulled down the handle. "Sure, I forgot."

I headed into the office then and realized that I was quite nervous to see him.

As our eyes connected, I was once again struck by how

handsome he was. He was impeccably dressed in a pinstriped waistcoat and a crisp white shirt, and his hair was neatly brushed away from his face.

His green eyes were almost hazel and even the glint of annoyance in his gaze was just dangerous enough to add to his appeal.

Though I told myself this wasn't the reason why I was nervous around him.

No, it was because Sophie's job was at stake, and so far, I wasn't doing my best to keep it. So many mistakes were already made, and I foresaw with the way things were going that it wasn't about to get better.

"What is happening with you?" he asked as I arrived before his desk. "Why are you suddenly so slow and sloppy?"

He wasn't trying to be rude or abrasive. He genuinely seemed curious as to why I wasn't as efficient as before, but he couldn't know the truth either, could he?

"I'm sorry, sir," was all I said, and then I went around his desk, deciding to be a bit more assertive. I truly was acting like I was a stranger and knew nothing about him, and this wasn't the case at all.

I got this one right because he wasn't startled at all about the proximity. He took the iPad from me to flip through the slides, but by the time we got to the end, he frowned in confusion.

"Where are the edits I asked you to include this morning?"

I stared at him. "I included them," I responded and began to flip to where I had indeed edited the points; however, he didn't look away from me.

"Those are the ones from the list, what about the additions in the voice note?"

Holy fucking shit.

I was frozen then, and for the first time in a very long time, I was stumped because I had no response for this.

"Uh..." I straightened then and took a few very embarrassing steps away from the scorch of his gaze. "I'm sorry, but I think I missed it."

He didn't say a word. Instead, he stared at me as though he couldn't quite believe what I had just said. And then he returned to his work without further word. I immediately turned around to exit the office, and it took everything in me not to run because truly we were out of time. I slipped my AirPods in and began to listen and soon enough, I was able to get the gist of his changes. I immediately started to implement them. I did wonder why Larry wasn't the one handling this but when I saw that he was hard at work at his desk I couldn't complain. Eventually, the clock struck eleven, and like clockwork, he came out of his office. I almost cried out in frustration. He didn't say a word to me, but I could feel his gaze as he put on his jacket and then meant to head out.

I immediately disconnected my laptop from the desktop, grabbed my phone and purse, and was on my way. I slowed down when I met him waiting in the elevator lobby and decided to wait for the next one so that I could continue my work in peace. However, when he got in and kept waiting for me, I had no choice but to comply.

He now seemed thoroughly annoyed, but I managed to take my mind off this so that I could concentrate. Soon we arrived on the ground floor and strolled past the reception until eventually, we were outside. However, as we met an empty curb, it hit me then that the issue with his transportation was still not resolved.

He looked at the curb and then looked at me, yet I had no answers. I was saved by the bell because just then my phone began to ring.

The moment I pulled it out of my pocket I saw that it was me calling, I briefly walked away and picked up.

"Car service will be there in a few minutes," Sophie said. "Are you two outside yet? Find a way to delay him."

"Yes, we're outside," I replied as low as possible, and then I ended the call when I saw him turn to me.

"Where's Michael?" he asked, and for a few seconds, I was stumped, wondering how to answer this question and get myself out of this mess.

"Uh... Brooklyn," I replied. "He went to get your suits."

"Is he close by?" He asked, and I shook my head.

"No, he isn't, but I've hired a car service."

"And when will they be here?" He asked.

"A few minutes," I replied. "Not more than five."

"You want me to wait out here for five minutes?" He asked, and then he nudged his head toward the skyscraper. "I own the building."

I didn't know how to respond to this, so I simply lowered my head. "I'm sorry, sir, but it's just a little delay. We can head back in to wait if you—"

He left and headed over to the curb. I watched in confusion as he lifted his arm and in a few seconds, a taxi driver pulled up. He got in, and I was almost ashamed to do the same but I didn't exactly have a choice so I got in as well, and to my surprise, he didn't stop me.

I didn't apologize. Instead, I opened up my laptop and by the time we arrived at the venue more than half an hour later, I was done. I saved it into a flash drive, stored my laptop safely in my purse, and then airdropped the updated document to his phone. He was speaking to a bunch of people when he received them, and for a moment, I was scared that he was going to reject it, but he received the document and from time to time, I watched him glance down to go through it.

I didn't stay close enough to warrant him having to introduce me whenever someone new came over to speak to him, which by this point felt like it was every second. But I did stay close enough for his gaze to always catch me when he needed something.

I got him water and some refreshments and disappeared, and then eventually it was time for his speech on the genius business acquisition, scaling, and management in the current times.

After setting up the slides, I of course took charge of aligning it to what he was saying.

For the first time for what felt like that morning, I could relax and so I listened to him speak and he was completely unflustered. I admired him I realized because after looking at his calendar and in that head of his I was sure was a million spinning bottles yet he seemed as calm as a monk. From time to time though I couldn't help but notice that his gaze lingered on me, however, it wasn't in a good way whatsoever. Somehow I noticed it but I could see the immense disapproval in his eyes and it made me wonder if I had messed up some part of the slides.

So far, all seemed to be going well, and I simply ignored

him and his gaze until it was over. He didn't spend any time afterwards, despite the horde of people eager to talk to him. He acted as if he had somewhere urgent to be, but I knew that the next thing on the agenda was simply lunch. Not exactly willing to monumentally mess up again, I quickly called Sophie, asking where he usually preferred for lunch so that I could recommend the place or at least ensure that he got what he wanted from it.

"I've handled it," she told me. "Michael is waiting out front with his lunch."

I was immediately alarmed. "How exactly did you handle it?" I asked, "I'm with your phone."

"And I'm with yours," she replied. "Don't worry, I just told him that I ran out of battery and I borrowed someone else's phone briefly."

"Oh, alright," I said and was about to put the phone away when she stopped me. "Oh, and I was trying to get everything in order since we've been so sloppy and I realized that there was one thing we did miss that Lucien's sure to be pissed about, and he does hold a grudge, so I apologize in advance."

As I looked ahead and watched Michael open the door for the man, I suspected that I was finally able to understand perhaps why he had been grumpy with me all morning. "And what is that?" I groaned.

"There's a man there that Lucien highly respects, Matthew Cubain, and he always goes to this panel solely for him each year."

"And?" I asked quietly as I got into the car as well, but this time I made sure to stay in the passenger seat. Michael gave me a sympathetic look, and I heartily accepted it.

"Well, we didn't get a gift for him. Actually, I did order it two weeks ago, as I usually did, but because of all the issues I've been having with Jerald, I forgot to check on it, and now I realize that it's been stuck in transit for a couple of days. For no reason, I might add. I've been trying to call them now to get it all resolved, but it's not working out."

I shut my eyes then as I took in her words.

"Whether you resolve it or not, it doesn't matter much. Does it?" I grew furious.

"I'm sorry; I know you're mad."

I ended the call then, but I wasn't done seething, and so I included a scathing comment and sent it to her.

Me: The more the day goes by, the more I suspect that you threw me into this den this week so you didn't have to deal with any of this stress.

Her response was just as lethal as I knew she could be.

Sophie: You're right. I really couldn't handle any of it this week. And I'm sorry. I've been making a lot of mistakes this week.

I sighed and sent her another message.

Me: It's my misfortune that I look like you hence I'm available to cover up your mess, so you'd better rest well with the time you have.

Sophie: How are you going to handle this mistake with Lucien?

I was almost tempted to look back to gaze at him.

In a way, I regretted sitting where I was because it was all too easy for me to imagine that he was glaring so hard that there was a hole boring through my head. Regardless, I took a deep breath and considered Sophie's solutions for resolving things with him.

He didn't go to lunch like he usually did, which meant he was truly totally pissed. So the moment we arrived back at the office, I arranged to take his lunch from Michael and knocked on his door. I didn't wait for him to invite me in this time around, and when I went in, I found him once again without his jacket. This time, though, he wasn't seated at his desk. Instead, he was standing before the tall glass-to-ceiling windows, overlooking Manhattan, and he had both of his hands in his pockets.

I stopped then as I took in his impossibly tall and built physique. He looked like he dominated both himself and the entire world, and my heart couldn't help but race a little faster. This was a man who was totally in control, and I was ready then to accept whatever scoldings coming my way for essentially messing up his morning.

"Sir?" I called, but he didn't respond.

I expected as much, so as Sophie had instructed, I placed the meal on his table, got him a beverage from his refrigerator, and then started to take my leave. However, just before I exited the office, he addressed me.

"What is going on with you?" he asked.

I stopped in my tracks. I remained silent for a little while and then I apologized. "I'm really sorry, sir."

"Where's the gift that was supposed to be given to Matthew?" I shut my eyes and lowered my head. It was truly unfair that I was being chastised like this for someone else's error, but she was my blood, so I had no choice but to take this.

I couldn't reasonably apologize again, so I proffered the solution I had agreed on with Sophie.

"Sir, the gift got stuck in transit and I wasn't aware of it.

I take full responsibility for it. I want to assure you, though, that I am monitoring every movement of it, and the second it arrives, I will deliver it personally to Matthew."

He remained still then, but despite his lack of response, I knew that I couldn't leave until he addressed me.

"What's the use in giving it to him then?" he asked. "Are you not aware that he usually doesn't accept gifts? Doing this at the conference was a great excuse and has been a great excuse for the past several years. So why did you make such a grave error this time around?"

I truly didn't know what to say, and then he turned around and faced me. Not much affected or intimidated me, but his gaze at this moment was not easy to pretend to be unfazed by. He continued to match me, and then I decided, like all sisters do ultimately, to throw Sophie under the bus.

"I didn't mean to give any excuses, but—"

"You better have one," he said. "And it better be a good one, or else you'll have to go looking for another job."

I stared at him, somewhat in shock, but I didn't blame him either. I sighed.

"My relationship ended yesterday," I told him.

He stared at me, his brows furrowing, just as I had expected because he obviously couldn't understand why I was telling him this information.

"My fiance ended our upcoming marriage yesterday, so I have to admit that I have been thrown off lately. Before yesterday, there were a lot of problems to deal with, but now that it is over and concluded, I'm going to go back to being prompt and focused. Mistakes like what has happened recently will not happen again. I assure you of this."

He continued to watch me, and never had I come as close to squirming as I felt like in that moment.

"Is that why you suddenly cut your hair?" he asked, and I was a bit surprised to hear this. So in the end, he was paying attention?

"Yes, sir," I replied.

He continued staring at me, and he made it no secret that he was perusing my body and taking in my frame and any further changes he could find.

He was sure to find something for sure because even though I had a similar form to Sophie, I had a bit more meat on my bones than she did. For one, she was a casual vegetarian, and even though she allowed herself to indulge in meat from time to time, she was more often than not usually feeding on vegetables.

I, on the other hand, ate everything and worked out, so I was more on the curvier side and less petite than she was. Plus, there was the fact that our styles were completely different. She stuck to lighter colors and pastels, while mine were dark, bright, and bold.

The breakup, however, should be an acceptable explanation worldwide for the change, so I wasn't too worried.

He continued to watch me, and then eventually he returned to his desk. There were no further words to say, so I released a deep sigh of relief and turned around to leave.

"Remember the presentation we have tonight with Charles Nioly."

"Definitely, sir," I replied.

"There were additional corrections added in the voice note I sent to you. You won't miss those again, will you?"

Truly, he was beginning to sound quite condescending,

so I didn't bother looking back as I replied, "I won't, sir. I'll be heading down now to collaborate with the project team to ensure that everything is in place and ready for tonight."

He didn't respond, so I made sure to roll my eyes as I took my leave.

Chapter 7
Lucien

I watched her leave and couldn't quite understand my recent tolerance and reaction to her and her blunders. Usually, I wouldn't have even bothered to chastise her for this because she rarely made mistakes, and I knew that whenever she did, she immediately corrected herself. But today, it was as though I was purposefully mad at her because I couldn't figure out the sudden changes in her.

Now that she had explained her breakup, a few more things explained themselves; however, it still didn't change the fact that her body seemed to have changed overnight.

Sighing, I shook my head to brush all of these nonsense considerations off, especially as I checked the time and saw that it was quickly ticking away. More importantly, I needed to meet with our CFO once again to make more preparations for tonight.

This occupied my time for the next several hours until seven approached, and all preparations were complete. I put on my suit jacket and couldn't help but feel slightly nervous. It had been a long time since I had felt this much excitement with projects, but Charles' business was a multi-million-dollar beast that, on its own, was sure to beat out the performance of the last two quarters. I had been trying to get him to hand over his business for the past two years while he'd been hinting at and trying to get me to meet his daughter and go to dinner with her.

More than offensive, it was a bit amusing to me that his hope that a relationship could somewhat form between us was the key to getting his business but I had absolutely no complaints.

I arrived early to once again go through the slides, but then at the final minute, Sophie hurried in. She came over to me, and the first thing I noticed was the smell of her perfume. It was different from usual, and it made me stop for a moment to stare at her curiously. She was slightly taken aback by my sudden reaction, but as our eyes met, I didn't exactly care to explain. She smells good enough for me to notice, and once again, it struck my curiosity at the sudden changes in her.

I couldn't help but notice the slight peek of her cleavage through the sheer blouse, and against my will, it affected me. Perhaps it was my slight nervousness at the upcoming meeting, but regardless, all was welcome.

"What is it?" I asked to kickstart her brain.

"I just got a call from Charles," she began, and the moment I heard the name, all of those feelings immediately dissipated. Annoyance and immense irritation took their place because I already knew exactly what she was going to say.

"He cancelled?" I asked, and she shook her head.

"Um... not really, he just said that something came up, and he had to be in London immediately. He said he'd be back soon for his daughter's birthday celebration so he'll be available then."

I was pissed off, but given the multitude of staff present, I tried my best to contain my expression and countenance.

"When is his daughter's birthday?" I asked, however, she seemed startled.

I cocked my head, wondering why she wasn't aware of this. "You don't know?" I asked, and she straightened, then looked around at all the eyes in the room currently on her.

For a moment, I watched her almost become self-conscious and cower, which was the norm, but then she straightened and stared at me defiantly.

"I don't but I'll find out now."

I turned to her in surprise. "You arranged a date for us a few months ago to meet that I refused to attend. You didn't have the information stored somewhere."

And just like that, she seemed lost again, but she quickly recovered.

"A lot of dates to take note of. It's been a tough few months."

At her words, there was slight laughter across the room, but I wasn't amused. Still, I glanced curiously at her once again, but there were more urgent things to worry about, so I brushed it off.

I got up then without a word, and she came with me.

"Should I arrange your car home?" she asked and I stopped to frown at her.

"Why the hell would I go home? You heard him; he has

to be in London and he never stays long there. Soon enough, he'll be in Russia, and this meeting will take another two years to hold. We're going to London right now. Make the preparations and ensure we're ready to leave in an hour."

With this, I turned around and went on my way.

Chapter 8
Scarlett

London in an hour? After working for nearly twelve hours? I didn't even wait until I got to my desk to call Sophie.

"You really did this on purpose, didn't you?" I asked.

"What do you mean?"

"Your boss is a slave driver."

"What do you mean?" she grumbled again.

"He just told me to arrange to fly out to London right now after working all day."

"Well, that's the norm," she said. "And that's one of the reasons I've been able to work with him for so long. I've been very flexible regarding his schedule, so he's always been able to count on the fact that whenever he needed me, I was available."

I listened to her and couldn't believe what I was hearing.

"I have law school tonight. I'm already late for my lesson."

"Isn't it only online?"

"Online or not, I don't want to miss it."

"Well, you can listen to it on the plane?"

"What plane?" I asked, trying to control my frustration. "How does he expect me to find a flight to London within the hour?"

She was quiet for a moment, as though trying to process what I was saying, and then she got it.

"Oh, I get where your frustration is coming from," she said. "It's pretty easy to arrange the flight because he has his private plane. I'll send you Levi's number right now, and he'll get the jet ready. Then you need to call Michael as well to come pick you both up. His passport is in the safe in his office, and you... well, you need yours as well. Where is your passport? I'll go get it. You can't leave the office because you're supposed to have your passport with you at all times. I'll get it and have it sent to you within the hour."

Slowly, and through my exhausted brain, I listened to all she had just said, then dragged my notepad over to jot down the things I had to do to prepare for the trip we were apparently taking to London in the next hour.

I didn't see how this could be possible, but knowing that Sophie could have and has easily pulled this off in the past, I decided to give it my very best, so I succumbed.

"Alright," I told her as I noted my to-do list. "Call Michael to come pick us up..."

"Actually," she said. "You need Michael to, first of all, drive you to Lucien's apartment so that you can pick up some toiletry essentials for him. He might decide to stay in London for a few more days, so it's always nice to be prepared."

I really couldn't believe her, even as I packed up my stuff.

"I enjoy working with him," she said. "It's because of him I've considered eventually starting a social media agency. His methods are novel and genius, and his work ethic is unparalleled. I've already watched him put out so many fires. Anyway, it's worth the extra time and constant availability, plus my bonuses are ridiculous. I have no complaints."

As I gathered my things, ready to hurry out the door, I had very few complaints either, since I would be flying private for the very first time.

"He has a private jet?" I asked as I headed to the elevators. "Why didn't you tell me that?"

"Sweetie, when did we last have a proper conversation? And if we did, why would my boss and his wealthy toys come up?"

"It's not exactly a toy."

"Well toy or not you're about to get on it so have a blast. Pack a dinner attire of some sort because even though he goes for business sometimes he might end up using the opportunity to see some other contact or the other. Not only will you be stuck wherever he is for a couple of extra days, you might need to accompany him to dinner or other meetings. Pack light, but well."

"Wow," I said just as I arrived at the reception and headed out of the building to meet Michael, waiting for me. "We basically do the same job, but now I know that mine has been a joke compared to yours," I said to Sophie,

"It's probably because you keep jumping around," she says. "I didn't gain access to all of this from the very first day. That being said, did you get his apartment key from the office?"

"What?" I stopped in my tracks in the middle of the street.

"You need the key to get into his apartment to pack his suitcase. He usually has one ready to go, but you need to include some of the suits Michael collected today, as well as some casual clothes. He has none of that in the office since he didn't have a trip upcoming until next month."

Sighing, I hurried back into the building and was almost sprinting back to Sophie's desk to retrieve his key. "Remember to collect all business materials from the development team," she shouted into my ears, and I nearly gave up then. The moment I got into the elevator, I instantly retrieved my flats from my purse and exchanged them for heels. I felt a bit more relaxed and able to handle all the challenges heading my way.

We drove to his apartment, which was thankfully nearby first, and through a video call, Sophie was able to show me where everything was. For a long second, I was shocked by the size of his apartment and the views. Only a few warm lamps were on, but the panoramic view of the skyline overlooking Manhattan and Central Park was something that I needed a few moments to process.

"Why the heck aren't I rich?" I complained, and she laughed.

"Don't worry, you will be someday, but for now, let's try to prevent the rich guy from firing you, I mean, me."

I headed to his walk-in closet, found his suitcase under her direction, and in a little time, I was done. "Bathroom toiletries," she called, and I hurried to pack those as well. In fifteen minutes, I was walking out, and Michael was ready to take me to my apartment. He was a bit surprised when I gave him my apartment address instead of Sophie's.

"You moved recently?" he asked.

"I'm staying with my sister for a little while," I explained, and thankfully, he didn't ask any further. I hurried to grab my clothes and passport put away the casserole I made earlier that morning to be consumed for dinner and was on my way.

We arrived more than twenty minutes late, but by then, I didn't care because I was dodging the chaos. We got word that he was already on the plane waiting, so Michael drove me straight to the tarmac, where I was assisted in carrying all the materials and belongings. It was a gorgeous plane, quite sizable, and as I saw it, I couldn't help but feel somehow excited about this entire adventure.

Even better was the view I was met with. What caught my eyes first was the warm, polished wood and leather interior of the cabin. The entire cabin reeked of exorbitant wealth and I couldn't help but feel somewhat envious. Speaking of the man himself, he seemed rather relaxed. He had long taken off his coat and tie and had a few buttons opened.

There was a long sofa on the right, where he had settled in for the night. He had a leg crossed over his other knee and was casually scrolling through his phone.

It was my job, and I appreciated every bit of it thus far, but I really wanted to be the one finally getting to relax while everyone else ran around to make sure my life ran smoothly. Sophie didn't mind this kind of service-related work, but unless there was ridiculous money involved, then a part of me always felt a little bit resentful.

Quickly, I ensured everything was out in its place, and then finally, I got to settle into one of the single seats in the cabin. There was a table in front, and I wanted to lay my head down, but I couldn't until he had retired to bed and was no longer in the vicinity.

"Did you collect all the needed files for the presentation from the team?" He asked, and I nodded.

"Yeah, sir," I did.

"What about Nioly?" He asked. "Have you contacted him to inform him that since he couldn't come to us, we would be coming to him?"

My heart nearly stopped in my chest as he mentioned it, and so, for what had to now be the umpteenth time in one day, I became sheepish and afraid to meet his gaze.

"You haven't contacted him yet?" He asked, and I truly didn't know how to answer it. For one, I could give the excuse that I had been busy trying to get everything ready for the trip as he had asked, but I couldn't exactly say this because the basic essential quality of a good personal assistant was not only your ability to multitask but your ability to handle the most common sense of things without being asked or reminded.

The fact that he was even mentioning it to me was quite embarrassing, and so my options were either to apologize once again or to fabricate something. After all, there was no way he could check until we were back on the ground.

"I have, sir," I said, and he cocked his head at me.

"You have?"

"Yes, I contacted his camp and they're in the process of

facilitating this. He stared at me for a moment but didn't say a word and I didn't care. There was Wi-Fi readily available, and so, although doing my best to appear as flustered as possible, I texted Sophie to handle this.

She knew everything I didn't know about the man and his company operations, so all I had to do was make her understand the gravity of the situation with Lucien being on my ass, and she got her ass out of bed, but of course not without complaining first.

Sophie: You're the best PA I thought I knew, but so far I haven't enjoyed this benefit in the slightest. Are you really as good as you say you are?

I wanted to kill her, but I contained my temper and put the phone away.

Being in such close proximity to him was disconcerting, to say the least, but eventually, given just how much reading I had to do in the materials I had received, I focused my attention on working, and soon afterwards he got up and disappeared into a cabin.

I called Sophie immediately.

"How's it going?"

"He's been made aware of the intention, but final approval and a set appointment time have not yet been given."

"That's a lot of bogus words," I said, and she sighed.

"I'm supposed to be resting, Scarlett," she said, and I almost shot back, but once again I held back.

"Sure, go rest, but please stay on this. Lucien is waiting for a final response."

"I will," she said. "I know how important this is; we've been working on this gradually for about a year now."

I continued to peruse the documents, and soon dinner was served.

It was quite exquisite with a serving of pecking duck, noodles, and fried rice. It was all so delicious and even though I tried to contain my hunger to appreciate the meal, I still ended up nearly licking my plate clean at the end.

Sighing I nodded in appreciation and sent a word of thanks to Sophie via text.

Me: Thanks, this flight should almost be enough compensation for the torture this week is going to be.

She almost immediately responded.

Sophie: Please stop complaining and get back to work.

This made me smile but I did comply.

I turned off my wifi and began to read the reports once again in preparation but I was too detached now from the day's business to concentrate.

I struggled for about an hour and right in the midst of it all, I got bored and fell asleep.

Chapter 9
Lucien

I never quite could sleep very well on planes or flights.

Earlier on in my career, I had focused on reading and catching up on work, but now that there was nothing to do, I found myself restless in bed.

Lying dormant in that way pointlessly and for hours at a time frustrated me to no end, so I eventually got up and headed out.

It was easy to tell myself that I wasn't also curious about how she was faring or what she was up to because that would be an outright lie, and this was confirmed when I arrived in the cabin and saw her head resting against the window.

She had a can of cola open by her side and her laptop as well, and I couldn't help but worry that her hand was going to swing while asleep and her motherboard would be fried. And so I headed over and as quietly as was possible pushed both out of the way. My gaze couldn't help but go to her then and it lingered.

This had never happened before but I couldn't help it.

She wore a bit more makeup than usual I realized.

The thick line that extended past the corner of her eyes and the slight pink shimmer all over it was quite interesting to see. And then there was a soft shade of pink on her lips and her flushed cheeks.

As though sensing my presence or scent, she stirred, and I was forced to quickly move away, before I could completely, however, her eyes came open. I didn't intend for her to notice me or to give an explanation. Instead, I took the Coke along with me and instantly rejected it.

Especially when our male flight attendant Samson got up and came over to retrieve it from me.

It wasn't even empty which made me all the more certain that I had done something very unnecessary but I couldn't overly chastise myself for this so I headed to the bathroom to get my bearings back. I was exhausted, but I knew that only exercise could get me the rest I needed, so I simply headed back to the cabin and picked up my laptop for work.

She kept drifting in and out of sleep, trying to find the most comfortable angle until eventually I couldn't stand it any longer.

"Why don't you go in to sleep properly?" I said. "You know how you usually are with jet lag and right now is the perfect time to rest up. We'll get to Heathrow at nine am and you'll be refreshed for the rest of the day.

She stared at me then as though she couldn't believe my offer and then she straightened and turned her face away.

She began to type then on her phone, and a few minutes later she looked up at me. Once again I noticed this even though I wasn't looking directly at her, but when she did it a few more times I decided to save her the misery and me the distraction.

"The offer's still valid. Please go ahead to sleep."

Her lips froze open for a few seconds and then she replied quite sheepishly.

"Sure sir, thank you," she said. She got up then and headed into the bedroom.

The cabin was much quieter after she left, but I could visibly feel myself relax more, which was a good thing. The change, though, once again made me all the more curious about my unusual interest in her.

Chapter 10
Scarlett

I t was awfully nice of him to offer his bedroom to me. I would have preferred to be a little more cool and not accept, but I was struggling way too much with sleep to in any way prioritize my pride. Accepting his offer was a less hard fight and so the moment I got into the space, I immediately collapsed on the bed.

I expected a big bed, I realized, after all, he was sure to get busy here sometimes, however, he probably despised how cramped the space would have been as a result so it was more or less slightly bigger than a single. It could contain two moderately sized people, but any more and someone would be tumbling to the floor.

I took a quick look around, realizing that the sheets looked quite unused, which made me wonder if he had just sat on the recliner by the side or if he had actually rested.

Regardless, I kicked my shoes off, opened up a few of my buttons, unclasped my bra from behind, and was about to fall asleep when I recalled that I still had my make-up on. Groaning, I got up again and headed out to retrieve my things. I started to head out however just as I pulled the door open, I stopped at the doorway when I realized that he had on dark-rimmed glasses as he worked ever so diligently.

He looked quite different from earlier, and so I didn't blame myself for taking a few seconds to admire him. He looked almost casual with the tails of his shirt now out of his dark slacks and a few buttons from the collar unbuttoned. The folded sleeves up his arms revealed glowing skin adhered with muscles and my heart couldn't help but race just a little bit faster at the sight.

Somehow his shoulders looked even broader than usual, and I couldn't help but wonder just how I would fit in them. Shaking my head at the outrageous thought, and especially as he finally noticed my gaze, I turned away and continued on my way to the cabin.

I didn't need to explain to him what I was doing there and he didn't want an explanation either, so I focused on bringing down my luggage. However, it was quite heavy, so it was with much difficulty that it finally came down. This resulted in me turning around to catch my footing and as a result, I faced him fully, my grasp on the luggage. Our gazes met and then his eyes lowered down my body. I didn't think anything of it and almost even sent him a smile in apology for distracting him from his work, but then when I felt the unusually cold air across my chest. I understood that I had unbuttoned my shirt. As I looked down, more than half of my cleavage was out, so I immediately shot up, my hand going to it. He gave me a look and then returned his attention to his work, and I felt like burying myself on the floor. Opening my luggage then, I grabbed my toilet essentials and was out of there in no time.

As I arrived at the bathroom, I closed my eyes and leaned my forehead against the mirror because there was no way he wouldn't think I did that on purpose to taunt him. What else was the reason I would have stood before him in such a way?

I imagined he shook his head at the sight of me and it made me smack a hand against my forehead.

"It wasn't intentional. It wasn't intentional," I recited, but I couldn't quite convince myself to go out, so I pulled my phone out of my pocket and called Sophie. She didn't pick up. She was most probably asleep, of course, while I was losing every shred of dignity I had by the minute.

It did make me realize, though, that I was quite unhinged around him. I had started numerous new positions like this at the whim of a hat and had never had many problems adjusting or getting along with my bosses, but this time around, it was as though I just couldn't find my bearings.

Me: I think I just showed your boss my boobs!

I hit send. I didn't expect her to react instantly, but when her call started to come in, I knew I was in trouble and that she hadn't been asleep.

"You ignored my call the first time?" I asked, and she went silent, unable to defend herself. "You brat," I scolded. "It could have been an emergency."

"Sorry," she apologized. "Your adjusting has caused me more stress than relief today, so I was taking the time to decompress. Anyway, what do you mean by you just showed him your breasts? Is this an established condition between you two? Please end it, I'm begging you. I won't be able to carry on with it if you start it." Her words were quite peculiar to me.

"I know, I know," I calmed her down. "Don't overreact."

"Oh no, I need to," she said. "This is a freaking big deal.

"Just relax," I told her. "It was a mistake, and I'm sure he doesn't care."

"Well..." she seemed more calm. "You have a point there."

I rolled my eyes. "I'm happy you're relieved, but I'm also offended."

"Girl, where are you having this conversation?" She asked. "Can't he hear you? The plane is not that big."

"I realized then that she was right and lowered my voice.

"You're right. Okay, I'm going back to bed."

"Bed?" She shrieked, and I nearly had to pull the phone away from my ear.

"What is it?"

"Why are you in his bed?"

"He offered," I said. "He saw I was tired and told me to go over."

"I have been tired multiple times in the past several years and not once have I ever ended up in his private bedroom ma'am!"

I was a bit surprised to hear this. "Really?"

"It's the boobs," she lamented. "I knew you were going to be a problem."

"I couldn't take any of this seriously, instead I was quite amused and shook my head.

"It's fine. You'll be fine. Whatever happens. The important thing is that even after a day of fuckups he doesn't seem to hate me, so that's good."

"Yeah I guess," she said. "But don't make him like you too much either. I can't keep up with that."

"Sure," I said and ended the call.

I took my time in removing my makeup and washing my face. Even though I was sure I looked okay without it for the first time I doubted my appearance. I was reminded by Sophie's words that it shouldn't matter, I washed my hands and returned to the cabin.

As I headed past him I kept my head slightly lowered and just as I had predicted and Sophie had hoped he didn't look up, so I was able to return to the bedroom in peace.

As soon as I collapsed spread out like a starfish on the bed I realized it smelled like him. Other people's smell wasn't anything to indulge in but he truly smelled amazing. Like tobacco and citrus and vanilla all in one. It was intoxicating as I hugged the pillow more than was necessary. I was asleep in no time.

Chapter 11
Lucien

London used to be quite an exciting city for me to visit when I still worked in investment banking. However, due to recent miscreancy, I had tried my best to avoid it at all times. This hotel, however, the Connaught, remained one of my favorites.

I was still somewhat awake when we arrived, so I immediately headed in for their breakfast, since it was quite early.

Everything was fresh and tasty, and while I was seated, I indeed received a call from Charles Nioly, confirming the meeting that we were going to be having later that day.

I was impressed because I had been sure that Sophie had been lying to me when she said she had it handled. After all, she absolutely didn't seem like she did. But in all honesty, I wasn't surprised because she was usually quite efficient. The breakup must have really done a number on her the previous day, but I hoped from now on she would be her usual self.

I had no idea where she had gone the moment I had handed over her room key. She, as usual, had free reign to do what she wanted until it was time for our business, so I simply ate alone and headed up as well to rest.

I really wanted to take a swim before I slept, so despite how unideal this was, I couldn't resist, and so after changing, I headed down to their stellar indoor pool.

Given the time, there were very few people making use of it, but it might as well have been empty because the space was so large I was able to swim as fast as I wanted to. There was a swimming pool back in my penthouse in New York, and the ability to have the luxury here as well so I could be completely worn out enough to instantly fall asleep was priceless.

A little while later, I lifted my head from the water at the end of my lap and saw her.

She had just strolled in, dressed in a bikini with a sheer fabric covering over her.

It covered a lot, so by all accounts, she was quite decently dressed. But then, when she found a lounging chair for her things and set it down, I couldn't look away.

I had to admit then, sadly, that I was curious about her body because there was a change, and even though my head didn't want to accept it, the fact was that within the last two days, she had caught my attention because of it.

It only took a few seconds for me to see what I wanted to see, and in the end, I felt myself go hard underneath the water. She was more gorgeous and endowed than I could have imagined.

Her waist was slim, her breasts full and barely able to be contained in the scrap of material attempting to cover them, and her ass as she turned around was something that I couldn't stop myself from vividly imagining rubbing my cock between.

My thoughts were completely out of control making me understand that I was completely out of control as well however I didn't want to leave just yet so I continued with my lap.

A few minutes later, however, when I brushed the hair out of my face, I found that she was nowhere to be seen. She had probably seen me as well and took her leave, which was good. So, I got out of the pool. The ache was good and I felt ready to go right to bed, so I grabbed my towel to head out. My gaze couldn't help but sway once again to the part of the pool where she had been, and just then, a little distance away, I found arms flailing. She tried to call for help, or perhaps she didn't want help, completely fine. But from where I was, I was sure she was the one who was struggling.

And so I called out her name.

"Sophie?"

She didn't respond.

"Sophie?"

She nearly completely disappeared then, and without thinking, I jumped into the water. In no time, I was close to her, and when I dove underwater and saw just how close her feet were to the bottom, I understood that she had either been very close to trouble or was in the midst of it. Yet she didn't call out for help and was still trying, or foolishly confident enough to think that she could handle it.

Soon enough, I caught up to her, grabbed her by the waist, and pulled her up. At first, she struggled to find her balance, but eventually, she gave in, exhausted, and completely leaned against me. I could feel every part of her as I pulled her with me to the steps, but most importantly, I could feel my heart slightly racing at the alarm.

I knew she would be fine, but when I brought her out and laid her flat on the ground, I suspected that it would take a while before she would be.

Her eyes were hazy as she opened them slightly, and I couldn't help but notice that a part of her bikini top had come loose, and one of her nipples was slightly exposed. There were no lifeguards currently on duty, so no one came to help, but we didn't need it. Eventually, she opened her eyes, but I deeply suspected it was due more to embarrassment than anything else.

Her eyes were green, I realized, and for a moment, it felt as though I were looking at a stranger. I didn't think I had ever looked this closely into her eyes before or realized that they were green. Once again, I was beginning to notice more about her than I wanted, and I still didn't know how to feel about it. What I did know, though, was that I was immensely relieved that she was alright.

"Can you speak?" I asked, to which she simply nodded, and this made me smile despite myself.

"Say something?"

She looked as though she was thinking about it and then her eyes went down my body. At the same time, they glimpsed hers as well and her eyes nearly popped out of their sockets.

"Holy shit!" she shrieked as she finally noticed her loosened bikini top and her near completely exposed left breast.

"What the fuck is happening"

I knew then that she was perfectly fine so I rose to my

feet. I couldn't however resist taking one last look at her gorgeous, full breasts and the desire to have them in my mouth was nearly overwhelming. Once again her gaze went down my body and when it lingered on my groin I knew that she could see just how very simulated I was.

Sighing at how eventful the past two days had been I grabbed my things and returned to my room.

Chapter 12
Scarlett

At this point, he had seen my boobs so many times that I truly didn't even see a reason for covering up around him anymore.

I was so embarrassed, especially as he left me lying flat on my back that I refused to move. Not until a woman came out of nowhere and squatted by my side.

"Are you okay?" she asked, and I immediately shot up, my hand covering my chest.

"I'm fine," I smiled at her, and she nodded. However, my throat ached, and I was still terrified. For a moment, I truly thought I was drowning.

However, knowing my boss was right there, I had gone into the deep waters solely to stay out of his line of sight. I had tried to save myself until it almost became too late. Shaking my head, I wrapped my towel around myself and found my way out of the pool area.

I was so embarrassed and shaken that I didn't know what to do, so I headed back to my room to process all that had happened. I wanted to call Sophie, but she worried so easily about everything, and since I was technically safe, I didn't bother.

I did, however, plan on meeting up with my former closest friend from college, who was a single mom with a baby. So when she called to confirm our brunch appointment, I almost cancelled until I realized that she was suggesting to meet at night.

"Oh no, I have a work meeting," I complained, and she replied, "But my mom is babysitting tonight so I can be out later. Trust me, I haven't had a late girls' night out in what seems like years now, so you have no idea how excited I am. Just let me know when your meeting ends and conserve your energy so we can have as much fun as possible."

I nodded then because, given the recent events of the morning, I just wanted to hide in my room and not go anywhere. As I replayed the earlier events over and over again, my shame began to fade into the background, and instead, the extreme attractiveness of his body came to mind.

I couldn't vividly recall all of it, but one thing that had left a lasting impression was the bulge between his legs. Perhaps it was because he was noticeably excited or because it was just so that impressive, I hadn't been able to look away.

I wondered now if he had noticed, but given that he almost completely saw my breasts twice, I felt no remorse whatsoever.

And so, on the one hand, it would be good if I never had to see him again on account of my embarrassment at literally having to be rescued. On the other hand, just how much he was packing kept me up for longer than I needed to be.

Thankfully, I eventually fell asleep and woke up with just enough time to spare. So, by the time six pm rolled around and our meeting with Charles Nioly was due, I came out of the room with our briefcase and materials in hand, completely ready.

I, however, didn't know where he was, so I sent him a message, and he promptly replied, "Already in the lobby," and I began to panic. There was no way I was late. I was almost ten minutes ahead of time, so I couldn't help but check again. I saw that everything added up, so it only meant that he was just extremely early.

I told myself not to hurry as I headed down, but Sophie had mentioned to me just how punctual he likes being to everything, and given the current traffic in the city, I saw a reason in this, so I headed down as quickly as possible in four-inch heels.

It took a little while to find him, but eventually, I met him seated and formally dressed with his phone in hand, and I had to stop in my tracks. One of the staff had pointed me to where he was, which was in a seat obscured from public view by a tall palm plant, so he had indeed been difficult to find.

I wished truly that I could scold him as I approached, but I behaved myself and had a smile ready for him as soon as I arrived and met his gaze.

"Sir," I greeted, and at first, he didn't look up. But when I repeated the greeting, he raised his head and finally acknowledged my presence.

Was he doing this on purpose? I wondered. Being a jerk or was it just the boss's syndrome?

If I was new to being a personal assistant, I would have assumed that all bosses were this way, but this was not the case at all. I understood now that it was based on choice and character because I've had the most considerate of bosses in the past.

But this one, however, was a bit frigid. When I recalled, though, that he had saved my life just a few hours earlier, I sighed and rolled my eyes. Gratitude and patience were the way to go, then, so I managed a smile as I stared at him.

He looked at me in return, and it was as though he was studying me. For a moment, I wondered if there was something on my face until he rose to his feet, and I realized he was just being mysterious as usual. I wondered if he did this on purpose as well.

I was particularly wondering about a lot of things concerning him, I realized, and I wasn't particularly happy about it.

He looked impeccable, though I couldn't help but admit as I watched him walk ahead of me. He was a bit more casual than usual today; instead of a suit, he had on a tweed dark green blazer and a stark white shirt opened at the collar. I had packed for him but hadn't paid attention to this, I realized. In my hands, they were just clothes, but on his body, they looked like a piece of art. They hugged every bulging bicep and complemented his frame so deliciously.

I wasn't surprised now, though, that he looked the way he did given just how powerful he had swum through that scary pool. Most CEOs who worked as hard as he did focused more on their work to the exclusion of everything else, but it seemed he had the time set aside for his health, and it was something to admire.

I, on the other hand, was dressed extremely formally. I had read up a bit on the investor we were going to meet and was told to be in line with the formal attire, needing to prove oneself and importance in every way. So he was going to be in a suit, and I had to reflect the same level of seriousness.

I'd gone for a white pantsuit paired with a waistcoat and the double-breasted matching jacket over it. I wore dark heels and tied my hair back in a bun, but for color, I painted my lips a stark red. I looked great and it made me feel confident, despite the beating my ego had received earlier from my encounter with Lucien at the pool.

There was a car waiting at the entrance to the hotel, and Lucien got in. However, when I started to pull the passenger door open, he stopped me with a command.

"Ride in the back with me."

"Alright," I replied and did as asked. Soon, we were both settled in and making our way to the office in London's evening traffic. It was brutal, but I wasn't concerned since we had more than enough time to spare. It did mean, however, that I was forced to spend more time near him. I had very few complaints, but his sexual appeal was becoming impossible to ignore.

My gaze kept going to his hands. They looked strong, capable, and toned. He had on a very expensive Patek Philippe watch on his wrist that glistened in pure mesmerizing gold, and his scent, once again, was something that I couldn't stop myself from savoring. It was expensive, masculine, elegant... gosh. I was becoming obsessed, and it truly made me wonder, no offence to Sophie, how she had been able to keep her full attention on her fiancé Jerald all these years.

Unable to curb my curiosity, I picked up my phone and sent her a message.

Me: I need to know how you did it.

She immediately responded. She was obviously nervous about the upcoming meeting and had promised to stay ready and available at all times.

Sophie: How I did what?

Me: Worked so closely with this man for years and didn't jump his bones?

She sent a few laughing emojis.

Sophie: Should I be worried about you?

I couldn't resist glancing at him. He was staring out of the window, deep in thought, hair brushed neatly away from his face and with his hand holding his chin.

She most definitely should, but I couldn't exactly say this.

Me: Have you seen him without clothes before?

She sent a barrage of knives and angry stickers.

Sophie: What the fuck? You saw him naked?

Me: No, but close and I need to know if I'm the only one who knows what he is working with.

Sophie: How did you see him without his clothes on?

Me: Swimming pool. I almost drowned.

Sophie: Oh.

Was her response but then her brain seemed to scratch to a halt and her second message followed quickly.

Sophie: What do you mean by you almost drowned?!

Me: Inconsequential. I'm exaggerating. I'm perfectly fine. Answer the question about his crotch.

Sophie: Yes, Scarlett I have seen him without his pants on and yes what you're referring to is very hard to miss.

Me: Goddamn! He's not dating anyone?

Sophie: Scarlett!

I could almost hear the motherly tone of voice she always used when addressing me like this.

Me: What?

Sophie: None of this is your business. You only have a week there with him, remember?

Me: Exactly!

I could almost sense her freaking out internally like she usually did.

Not willing to drag this out any further, especially since I knew that she wouldn't tell me, I helped myself out and went to Google.

Lucien Montgomery girlfriend, I searched. And, to my errant surprise, there was almost no information whatsoever.

I could see his company, see the media companies he managed, see other investments he had made since he started at such a young age, but barely any mention of a girlfriend.

I glanced at him then, even more intrigued, but since it was clear that I was short on my luck for the day, he caught my eye.

I instantly snapped my head away, startled by being caught. The jerky movement had my phone flying out of my grasp. I immediately tried to catch it, and just like that, it flew over to his side.

I froze in place, with my hands in the most awkward and athletic position in the air and with his stern and almost exhausted-looking gaze on me.

I didn't know what to do then, but the goofiness in me came out and the corners of my lips tilted in a smile.

"I'm sorry," I said.

He didn't respond.

Instead, he started to reach for the phone, and I was immensely relieved. However, when he turned the screen around and I saw his gaze go to what I had been looking at, my heart for the second time in the same day stopped dead in my chest.

Lucien

Lucien Montgomery Girlfriend

For a moment, I didn't truly understand what I was reading, but as I stared at the words on the phone longer, I eventually realized what it was. I glanced at her, and this time around, she held my gaze. However, she looked just as mortified as I had expected.

I was almost amused but given that my thoughts were

more focused on what I was headed to do, I pushed the debacle aside and handed back her phone.

She took it and immediately slipped it into her bag while I continued with my thoughts.

Charles was a very tricky man because I was already well aware that this project and his decision to work with us had been finalized.

His making me come all the way to London was for one reason and one reason only, and that was for the chance for me to meet his daughter. No doubt the spoilt brat had refused to come to New York, and thus he had orchestrated this. But so as not to disappoint me to my face, he had made up this entire faux of having some emergency in London.

I was extremely offended, but unlike her, I didn't come from money, so I knew the value of his business in the long term. However, what he wasn't aware of was the fact that I was also judging him because his behavior in this meeting would let me know if, at the end of the day, I cared to even work with his companies at all or if I'd rather take the loss and move on to the next client with a brain and manners.

Soon we arrived at their Pimlico offices, and I strolled in along with Sophie.

She remained behind me, which was one more peculiar thing because usually she was ahead and clearing the way, but I guess she was still embarrassed about the whole fiasco in the car. I didn't care or at least for now, I didn't. Not until after all of this was over. And so I kept my focus on our directions until soon we arrived at their offices.

I was received well and made to wait no longer than five minutes before a tall, slim Russian girl came out. At first, she seemed reluctant and bored as she looked around, but then her eyes settled on mine, and her eyebrow shot up. I watched her intently as she headed over to me, and the biggest smile spread across her face.

She held out her hand, and it was only then that I got up.

"Mr. Montgomery?" she greeted, and I returned the pleasantries, but I sure hoped to hell that Charles wasn't handing this meeting over to her.

"Yes," I replied.

"I'm Polina. It's very nice to meet you. I've heard great things about you."

I hadn't heard anything about her beyond the fact that she was a popular socialite, so I immediately asked the question I wanted to know.

"Where's your father?"

"Oh, he's already waiting for you in the meeting room," she answered. "He was extremely pleased by the lengths you took to ensure he had this meeting, so he's been hard at work all morning doing a final review of your agreement." I was pleased to hear this but kept my gaze stoic and simply allowed myself to be ushered forward.

Her gaze for a second lingered on someone behind me, and I couldn't help but notice the instant change. It was as though her expression changed and darkened, and that was so incredibly startling until I recalled who was standing behind me.

I glanced back at the gorgeous woman behind me and understood. She had been sized up and felt intimidated. I didn't blame her whatsoever. Even I was impressed. Over the last few days, something had happened to her—a drastic change in her aura and appearance, and I still couldn't explain it. Between that and her increased clumsiness and strange new interest in my personal life, was interesting, to say the least.

She followed calmly behind, and soon the meeting began. It wasn't a presentation whatsoever like had been arranged in our office.

Rather, we went straight to Charles, who had a few of his advisers in his office lounge. Everyone took their seats, including his daughter. However, I soon noticed that there was a problem. I looked over because right at that moment, Sophie had been about to take her seat beside me to assist me in sorting through and presenting documents when requested.

Polina, however, had taken that place, and so a very strange and uncomfortable atmosphere filled the room.

"Polina can assist," Charles Nioly said with a smile. "She will be collaborating most of the time with you, so it would be nice to get her started with familiarizing herself with the material."

I was a bit irritated at his words, and when I looked at Sophie, I couldn't help but note her irritation as well.

I expected her to just hand over the folders to Polina since I knew her to be non-confrontational and generally agreeable; however, she didn't give her attention to Charles and his words.

Instead, she turned to me and asked, "Is this what you would prefer, sir?" she asked, no sense of amusement in her tone.

And once again, the room was a bit taken aback by how she sounded. She was unshaken and confident, getting straight to the point, and I couldn't help but be impressed.

"No," I replied, especially given the fact that she had worked on this for so long. I wasn't about to push her to the side for some heiress, rather than see the outcome of her effort over the last few months come to fruition.

"I'd prefer Sophia to be the one to assist me. We've been building this for a very long time, and she knows more than anyone else the ins and outs of our proposal to you."

"Oh, there's no need for a proposal," he said, further irritating me. "Your track record is impeccable, and your working style is commendable. You didn't let me run away to London and instead hopped on your plane immediately to get here. You're wealthy enough now to be comfortable and let things slide, but I can see now that you still take nothing for granted and you're as vigilant as ever, so I have full trust in handing our companies over to yours. Before you arrived, we had a meeting and we perused your projected increase in market share and engagements over the next year, and I am excited to see that you pulled it off."

I stared at him digesting his words and then I sighed quietly. I couldn't exactly be furious at the man for preparing much more than what was needed, but based on the level I had reached thus far, I couldn't argue that I was surprised. I was never romantic about the process anyway, so I took the win and rose to my feet.

"That will be all then," I said, and he seemed a bit surprised.

"What? Why the rush?" He laughed. "I expected we would have some dinner together and get to know each other better. The business is concluded, but you should know that everything else is more important."

"Actually, the business is more important," I replied.

'Everything else, though interesting, falls short in the face of results or disgrace. I appreciate your offer, but I'm going to turn you down. In my diligence to conclude this deal with you, I haven't rested as much as I'd have liked to, and I'd like to get to it."

"You'd prefer to rest than have dinner with me?" he asked, the smile fading from his face as though he was daring me to continue with my stance. I'd never want to cancel a deal more in my life. I would have if not for the wasted time and the list of benefits and bonuses this brings to my employees.

He stared at me, and I slipped my hands in my pockets, waiting. Eventually, he let out a huge smile, and I knew that he had been humbled.

"I like you more than I ever thought I would," he rose to his feet and held out a hand. "When we meet again under better circumstances, I'll be sure to host you for dinner. Polina, will you see them out?"

I didn't bother acknowledging or rejecting this. Instead, I turned around calmly and exited the room. I was truly exhausted, but sleep was what I needed. Due to everything happening concurrently, it was not sleep but a release. For a second, as Polina escorted both me and Sophie over to the elevators, I considered her. It was my policy never to mix business with pleasure, but with the googly eyes and coquettish smile she was throwing my way every chance she got, I couldn't help but once again revisit all the charm and disadvantages of this.

When my attention, however, returned to the woman going ahead of me, not the elevator, in a gorgeous ivory suit that hugged her curves yet hung so elegantly off her body, I was instantly aware that Polina was absolutely not the one that piqued my interest.

Going along with the flow might guarantee future positive business relations, but if I set that precedence of attention for her at the beginning, then it would continue, and nothing was worth that. So, I refused her further desire to escort me to the ground floor, and afterwards, I got in the vehicle with Sophie.

Chapter 13
Scarlett

I had been really quiet recently. More quiet than I ever thought was possible for me, but embarrassing moments had a way of humbling you like nothing could. All the politics and nepotism in the office had been annoying, but in the face of him seeing my phone screen and search earlier on in the car, nothing mattered.

I couldn't help but watch him a little bit more closely than usual and seeing how he had handled the overbearing Charles Nioly and his daughter couldn't help but make me like him even more. And yes, I had decided that I liked him. His somewhat dismissive nature had put me off from the start, but thus far, I had come to realize that he had to be one of the smartest men I had ever come across.

The way he handled people and ignored situations that he should was incredibly impressive and I couldn't help but admire him quite immensely for this. And so, I felt a little more calm in his presence than usual and more than willing to be led by him. Soon we got into the car and were quietly on our way back to the hotel. He didn't talk much and I didn't much care for conversation earlier, but he was beginning to grow on me or maybe it was all my cumulative shame. I did, however, have something that I wanted to say.

"Um..." I began and couldn't believe the words that had just come out of my mouth. I had long made it a point to remove filler words like 'um' and 'like' from my vocabulary, but yet here I was starting a statement to him with 'um.'

He didn't turn, didn't even acknowledge I was trying to strike up a conversation, but I wasn't offended. So I tried again.

"I wanted to thank you for helping me earlier," I said. "I didn't realize just how deep that end was. Actually, I did, but I guess I had way too much faith in my skills than made sense."

He turned to look at me then, but this time around, and for the first time, he looked at me with interest. His eyes moved all over my face, and I truly wondered what he saw. I mean... darn, I was forgetting once again that I was Sophie and what he saw was his assistant and nothing more.

And so I sighed and leaned back against the chair.

"What do you want to eat?" He asked. "Let's have dinner."

I wasn't surprised; however, it wasn't strange for a boss and his assistant to have dinner together, especially when on international trips.

I nodded immediately, eager to spend some alone time with him, but that was until I remembered my date with my friend for later on. I really didn't want to cancel, yet I couldn't pass up the chance to be with Lucien in a much more casual setting.

Me: I'll be having dinner with my boss. Drinks later?

I sent the message as soon as we arrived at the restaurant. Before I could put the phone away I received a response letting me know her daughter was sick and she wanted to take a nap before leaving so it was all working out.

I slid my phone away just as we were shown to our seats.

The restaurant was so gorgeous; however, it was so romantically lit that I wasn't quite sure what to feel. This was for sure not a date, especially given how I was dressed, but he was looking delicious. All I could think about was him earlier, packing dangerous in those swim shorts.

Shaking my head, I pleaded with myself to wipe the image out of my head so that I wouldn't get Sophie fired, but he was just simply becoming impossible to resist.

"Order whatever you want," he said. "We've been hard at work at this for a long time, and though the way it panned out is unsatisfactory, the result is impressive."

"Yeah," I nodded and pulled my menu open.

However, I could feel him staring at me.

It took a while to build up the courage to check, but eventually, I did and indeed caught his eyes on me. Once again, his gaze was boldly roving down my body, and I couldn't help but wonder if this was the way he looked at Sophie as well.

"Was my outfit inappropriate?" I asked, and he returned his gaze to mine.

"There's a change to you," he said. "I've been trying to place my finger on it without much success."

I was immediately nervous, and my eyes lowered from his. The thing was that he always seemed as though he knew more than he was letting on, and so I didn't even realize currently if he was baiting me to reveal the truth since he had already discovered it or that he had no clue and was genuinely curious.

I, however, chose to keep things simple. "It's the breakup," I explained. "You know what they say? It usually changes a woman completely. Most times her appearance."

He didn't respond and instead continued reading the menu. I had so many questions about him and for him, but I couldn't well ask any of them because having been his assistant for so many years, I was supposed to know, right?

I sighed, suddenly unable to wait for this week to be over.

The waiter came over then to take our orders, and once again, he continued to watch me as I spoke. It was quite disconcerting, but nothing, however, could have prepared me for what he said afterwards.

"You're into rebounds?" He asked, and my entire body went still.

For a few seconds, I didn't know how to react. I considered acting as though I hadn't heard him. In fact, I was almost sure that I hadn't heard him.

"You can decline," he said as he lifted his glass for a sip of water. "We've worked together a long time. I'd understand if you couldn't handle it." I was about to respectfully decline until he made that statement, and then I stopped once again and gave him a look. For a moment, I was sure a blink of mischief flashed across his eyes, but I couldn't tell if he was taunting me on purpose with that comment or if he was being deadly serious.

"First of all, I could handle it, I just don't want to, and secondly..." I stopped then because I realized that I truly didn't have anything else I wanted to add.

"Secondly?" He asked. I watched him and thought of Sophie. Although the instruction was to outrightly reject him, I needed to know if he had ever made this same advance to Sophie before and if and how she had rejected it.

He raised his eyebrows in question as I continued to stare at him until eventually, I was forced to lower my gaze to avoid his intense look.

"It's a no," he asked, and truly, I felt ambushed.

"Why the sudden proposition?" I asked.

He shrugged.

"You're available," he said, and once again, I was up in arms.

"Um, available?" I asked in disbelief, and then I scoffed. Looking around the bar, there were countless other girls, any of them would jump at the chance to be with him in seconds.

"You're a billionaire. You could have any young woman you wanted. It'd be easy for you." I told him. "I know it seems that I'm easy because I'm your assistant and I'm right here, but..."

"No," he interrupted. "That's not the reason."

I was curious then because I couldn't think of any other reason.

"So what's the reason?" I asked.

"You're available now," he said. "You never were before."

I was quite startled by this response.

"So you were interested in me before?"

"You're a beautiful woman, Sophie, and you've always been, plus your temperament has always been especially agreeable with mine. However, because you weren't available, that never crossed my mind. Now that you are, I'm making this proposition."

This made sense to me, and as a result, I was no longer offended, but I would never knowingly risk Sophie's job.

"You're not worried it'll affect our working relationship?"

"That's why I mentioned your inability to handle it," he said, and I was annoyed all over again. He was so damn cocky, and although he had a reason to be, it didn't make him any less irritating.

"I can handle it if I wanted to," I said, and he nodded.

"So you don't want to?"

I didn't know how to respond to this, so instead, I got up then and excused myself to the restroom. My head felt like it was coming loose, seated in his presence, and I needed the space to think, plan, and recollect my thoughts.

Chapter 14
Scarlett

I headed over to the bathroom, and the first thing I did was call Sophie.

"Hey! Have you ever at any point in time felt any attraction whatsoever between you and Lucien?" I asked.

Afterwards, I stared at my reflection in the mirror while waiting for a response. I was a little wide-eyed with shock as I caught my reflection. That was mostly because this was something I had never even allowed myself to want. I had been banned from wanting it, yet here I was being handed it on a platter, and I had absolutely no clue what to do.

He was so direct, and I loved that even more. I wasn't surprised, and this also transferred to my expectations of him in other areas. The buzz between my thighs throbbed even harder in anticipation and expectation, but all of that was until my sister sighed.

"Do you know how many times you've asked me this within the past twenty-four hours?" She asked, "Or mentioned it or alluded to it?"

My smile was sheepish even if she couldn't see me.

"I didn't ask this particular question," I replied and heard her sigh.

"I get it, he's hot, but can't you just ignore this and do your job like everyone else?"

That had been my exact plan, but now things had changed, and I wondered about it. If I were to reject him, would this even bode well for our relationship? Would it be awkward? I knew I had to tell her about the proposition because I couldn't truly imagine doing this behind her back.

"Sophie," I called, but she didn't respond.

I continued anyway, "That was my plan, but he was the one who asked me."

Her silence extended for so long once again that I truly thought the line had disconnected. However, when I pulled the phone away from my ear, I found that she was still on the line.

"What?" she asked.

"We're at dinner. The meeting with Charles Nioly is done, and he asked me."

"What do you mean he asked you?" She asked. "Lucien would never do that. He doesn't mix business with pleasure."

I didn't know how to respond until she began to growl at me.

"What the heck did you do, Scarlett?"

"Okay, you need to stop accusing me," I said. "It's making me feel bad."

She ignored this. "It's your cleavage, isn't it? You couldn't just keep it in for one week."

This made me snort in laughter, but truly none of this was a joke whatsoever. She sighed again.

"First of all, let me confirm again that he asked, and this is not you just trying to seduce him?"

"You're offending me," I said. "Why would I do that when your job is at stake?"

"Honey, you do that just like breathing. This is why I told you to wear my clothes and be-"

"Dreary?" I shot back.

"Yes, dreary," she snapped. "What's wrong with that for one week?"

I was beginning to get mad.

"You know what, whatever," I said, ready to end the call.

"Whatever what?" she said. "This matter isn't solved, aren't you still at the restaurant with him? Have you rejected him?"

"No, I'm in the bathroom, but don't worry, your dreary little head, I'm going back now to reject him."

"What's the point in doing so?" she asked. "The bullet's left the chamber. It's not as though you can bring it back."

I went silent, determined not to speak to her until she got her head screwed back on.

"I'd truly like to say that rejecting him wouldn't be a problem because he knows how to separate business from pleasure, but before this very moment, that was also what I'd thought about him, yet now this is happening, so I don't know what to think about him anymore.

"I'll find out," I started to leave the bathroom, especially as some women came in, but Sophie stopped me.

I halted in the hallway and leaned against the wall to stare at the gorgeous painting of candelabra and calla lilies positioned at the end.

"I don't know," she said. "I think you can ask him if this will make things awkward—"

"I already did," I replied.

"And what did he say?" she asked.

"He said it would be fine."

"Of course, he'd say that."

"You don't believe him?" I asked.

"I do believe him," she replied. "It's just... I would prefer none of this happened. But on the other hand, we're talking about him. Will you survive it?"

I scoffed. "This might only be a one-time thing. Who knows if it'll even be any good? And I'm incredibly good at ignoring what or who I want to ignore, so I'm not worried about myself."

"And what about me?" she asked. "Give me a reason why I shouldn't worry as well."

"Because when you return, you won't have the memories. So if you trust that he can remove that from his mind, then you won't have to worry about any awkwardness. We could see it as some sort of business negotiation."

"Well, if it is a business negotiation, then it must have a start date and an end date, right?" she asked.

This made sense to me.

"I don't want him expecting after you leave in a week and when I return that we will continue from where you two stopped."

"Eww," I said, and she agreed.

"Exactly. So if you're doing this, then ensure that it ends on Sunday and that you both agree. After Sunday it's never, ever to be brought up again."

"Alright," I replied, feeling much better. I wanted to

thank her for being flexible, but my ego wouldn't let me, so I hung up the phone instead and formulated my question clearly.

Afterwards, I returned to the hall and our table, ready to accept and negotiate. I felt so excited that I was nearly wobbly on my knees, and this fire only ever seemed to burn even harder as I approached and watched him. I couldn't take my eyes off him, and unable to help myself, I undid a button of my waistcoat.

Unfortunately, he lifted his gaze to mine right then in the act. I was once again so deadly embarrassed that my cheeks flushed pink, but I didn't fix my now very provocative appearance.

Walking was hard, but when I lowered to take my seat, I felt his eyes go to the opening and feast on my breasts.

I was so turned on it was impossible to breathe, but seeing that our food and wine had been delivered, I managed to compose myself.

He, on the other hand, was outright with everything he did, and it was a while later before he finally lifted his gaze to my face.

"Am I to assume by your button that you've decided to take me up on my proposal?" He asked.

I cut a piece of sirloin and nodded as I put it in my mouth. I made him wait until I finished chewing, and then I replied.

"Yes," I replied. "But there are conditions, and I have questions."

"Sure," he said and kept eating.

"First of all, why are you just asking for this now?"

"What do you mean?" he asked.

"Have you ever found me attractive in the past? Why now?"

He stared at me and then he set down his cutlery, giving me his undivided attention. It was a bit unsettling, but I tried my best to remain unfazed. It didn't work internally, but I could only hope that externally it did.

Chapter 15
Lucien

She usually wrung her hands when she was nervous. This time around however and as my gaze lowered I could see she was as composed as ever. Once again I couldn't help but question this shift in her which was the undeniable reason why I had proposed this offer. It was dangerous.

I usually didn't fuck where I worked but just speaking to her right now and smelling her perfume was making me so rock hard that I almost didn't know what I wanted to do with myself. I wanted my cock in that pouty red defiant mouth of hers and I want her milking me till my knees shook. I wanted to empty my load down her throat and watch her savor every bit of it and then I wanted to lift her legs across my shoulders and eat her out till she lost all the strength in her legs.

I was just so fucking attracted to her and I couldn't explain it.

"You're not planning to dispose of me now are you?" she

asked. "I can't help but wonder if that's why you're asking now intending to let me go when we get back to the States."

I was startled as I heard these words so I couldn't help but lean back against the chair to watch her wondering where this nonsensical thought would have come from.

"What exactly are you saying?" I asked.

"Are you planning on keeping me working for you for the long term? Will this... hinder that?"

"Why would you think that firing you was my intention?"

"I don't know," she replied and continued eating. "I haven't exactly been on my best behavior recently."

"It's incredibly strange for you to say that," he replied. "Especially after working for me for three years. It's as though after all this time you truly don't seem to know or understand me at all."

She truly didn't seem to comprehend or understand what I was saying either but since I couldn't currently think beyond imagining my cock ramming into her wet, lush walls, I decided to quickly handle whatever misunderstandings were currently in our path.

"No Sophie," I answered. "My intention is not to fire you. You can sign an agreement afterwards guaranteeing your salary for the next year no matter what. It's mainly because when you had a fiancé I never looked at you in that way. There was no point in admiring anything much about you but now that you're single once again, I couldn't help but notice., I have eyes and I am a man with dire needs."

"Once again you can get whatever woman you want?" she pointed out but I refused this.

"No, I need someone I feel comfortable with enough to

not hold back from, and amongst all the women in my life, that's you. You know this."

She continued to stare at me and then she nodded. Then she picked up her glass and took a sip from her wine.

"I'll consider the proposal," she said. "But I have some conditions. Terms and such I mean."

"Sure," I leaned back against the chair and folded my arms across my chest. I was all but about to bust a nut with anticipation and so I needed this to be dealt with so that we could get the fuck out of here.

"Okay," she said, as she set her cutlery down as well.

She looked me in the eyes and I loved that. It was one thing about her improved mannerisms after this breakup that I loved. He boldness and directness. I truly couldn't wait now to see what terms she would proffer.

"First of all there needs to be a start and an end date that neither of us can cross," she said.

"Alright," I said. "Tonight then."

She started to speak as though she didn't hear me but then my words registered and she was taken aback. "What do you mean by tonight?" she asked.

I was perplexed by her question. "What do you mean by what do I mean by tonight? Were you expecting this to be longer?"

"Uh.. no I just... hm."

She stopped, completely at a loss for words and it made me smile.

I leaned forward then and linked my hands. "If we fuck once we'll be able to move past this more easily I believe. But if we continue to do it then that's where the complication will arise."

Her brows furrowed in what I guessed was annoyance but truly and these days with her I couldn't tell. She was no longer as easy to read had she once had been and this both concerned and thrilled me at the same time.

She looked away then to give this further thought and then she nodded. "Alright," she agreed. "This sounds... okay. One night, nothing more nothing less. I mean if we both keep to our understanding of not making this into something more."

She sounded a bit sarcastic but I couldn't even get mad or irritated. I had always been this way with her. Was always able to let my guard down and this was one of the reasons I believed that sex with her would be amazing.

"Let's start with one night," I said. "Tonight. I want to know how you taste. After that, we can deal with whatever comes next."

"That is not very reassuring," she smiled nervously. "But alright, deal."

She held her hand out for a handshake then and I couldn't help but smile again. I accepted it and we went on with our meal.

It went faster than it probably would have but still, it all felt too slow to me until eventually I threw my cutleries aside and looked at her.

"Want to get out of here?"

"Not without dessert first," she said as she took another sip of her wine. "Their menu looks amazing and they have the chocolate lava cake. It's their most famous dessert and I've always wanted to try it but couldn't."

This was a peculiar statement to me. "You've been here before?" I asked.

"Yes," she replied. "When I was in coll-"

She froze mid-sentence and I cocked my head wondering what was going on.

"When you were in college?" I asked. "You told me you've never been here before."

I could almost see the gears in her head moving as she tried to navigate her way out of this. I didn't think I'd ever caught her in a lie before, in all the years I'd worked with her and this was the reason why I had slowly been able to let my guard down enough to trust her but given the current situation, something suspicious began to roil in the pit of my stomach.

"Um..." she said. "I did come here with my fiancé later on. On one of our vacations."

This sounded reasonable, so I nodded and accepted it however that suspicious feeling didn't go away and it made me a bit thoughtful. It had never steered me wrong before so I had learned to listen, so how was it that in the case of this woman that I mostly trusted it was going off?

Chapter 16
Scarlett

I had nearly been caught.

That slight blunder had kept me quite quiet for the rest of dinner and even now as we rode back in the car and returned to the hotel I could still almost hear my heart pounding in my chest.

Close call... close call, and so I reminded myself to keep my mouth shut.

Soon we arrived but I didn't even notice because I was still lost in thought until my door was suddenly jerked open. I was startled, but as I lifted my gaze and saw the incredibly dashing and handsome billionaire staring down at me with the backdrop of the starry skies behind him I felt my heart skip several beats.

"We're here," he said and I nodded. He stepped back so I could step out of the car, however before I could get my bearings he curved his hand around the back of my neck, and pulled me to him.

It was as though that move alone turned me pliant and completely decrepit of self-will, so more than anything I fell into him as he slanted his head and kissed me.

He tasted like liquor. It was sweet and exotic and incredibly intoxicating. And then he tasted like lust as well. Filthy, unhinged lust and it nearly blew my mind. His tongue weaved expertly in and out of my mouth while sucking with just the right pressure on my lips and it made my knees so incredibly weak.

By the time we parted, my eyes were still shut and it was a while before I reopened them. I stared into his gorgeous gray eyes then and realized that I was gripping his shirt hard for dear life.

"You okay?" he asked and I absolutely was not. I was full of breath, yet out of breath at the same time and whatever this fire was that was licking at my insides I needed more of it. I needed to be flat on a surface, any surface at all, and I needed him slamming into me so hard that I forgot about everything else.

"Let's go," I said and I could almost feel his smile behind me. I didn't give a fuck. Tonight, had absolutely nothing to do with ego. It was the time to let loose and to fuck this man that I would probably never see again after this week, unbeknownst to him.

I was so excited I almost didn't remember the way to our room or where we were going. Eventually, I made it to the lobby and just stood in wait for him. He soon came over to my side and then he looked at me.

"How about a swim?" he asked. "There's a private pool we can use. It's heated."

This sounded wonderful however I wasn't exactly keen on drowning once again especially not on the same day.

As though he could read my mind, or perhaps he just couldn't pass on this chance to mock me, he replied. "I'll keep you safe and above water," he said. "Trust me."

This was most definitely a jibe but I wasn't even offended.

"Sure," I said as the elevator arrived. We got on and I shut my eyes to further savor his scent and presence. I was so fucking intoxicated that I wanted to kiss him once again, but I couldn't quite find the courage to ask for it so I managed to behave myself, and soon we arrived back at our room.

"Five minutes?" he asked and I nodded.

I was almost certain that I wouldn't need more than that so, I headed in and quickly began to tear off my dress.

In all honesty, it was clear to me that a part of me had been expecting and even somewhat looking forward to this early on. Therefore, I had been prepared. It didn't take me much to freshen up and then I changed into the skimpier bikini I had brought along. I grabbed a beach transparent dress and a towel to remain somewhat, decent until we got to wherever we were going.

Just then, there was a knock on my door and I grew so excited that for a few moments, I came close to hyperventilating. I was able to stabilize myself internally after a moment and when the knock sounded again, I hurried over to the door.

I opened it with more difficulty than was needed on account of my shaky hands, and there he was.

He had changed into a pair of shorts but still had his linen white shirt on from earlier. However, all of its buttons were opened and I wanted to lick every part of his body on show. It was glistening and gorgeous and I just couldn't fucking stop staring. This had to be the hottest man I had ever known and whether it was due to just his looks, or maybe as a result of his influence, power, and money, probably a bit of everything, I was excited.

"Ready?" he asked, and he didn't have to ask me twice.

Nodding I shut the door behind me and we were on our way.

Chapter 17
Lucien

I had seen her body before, but knowing where we were headed and what we were about to do I couldn't help but anticipate this even more.

The sheer dress she had over her bikini covered her up pretty decently but it wasn't difficult to still be provocative with all that she had underneath. I wanted to rip it from her body from the moment she came out of her room but I exercised patience until finally we were alone. I ordered a private food service on the way and some liquor and by the time we arrived the charcuterie board and champagne had been delivered.

It was a smaller pool than we had been in earlier and much more private and I loved it. The water was warm so as soon as we arrived, I took off my shirt and shorts leaving me with just my briefs and then I dove in. After dunking my head underneath to feel the warmth I came back up and it was just in time to see her pulling the dress over her head. In the process, one of the coverings of her breasts slipped, and just like that the full heavy mound with its perfectly hard tip was exposed. She didn't notice but when she eventually did and instantly freaked out that was interesting to me. I was the only one present and in a few moments, I was going to be sucking on them so I didn't understand what her nervousness was about.

It was endearing though and it made me even more impossibly hard, I couldn't complain. I also couldn't help but watch as she came around and got into the pool as well.

She came toward me and that bikini she had on didn't hide very much.

The moment she was within distance, I caught her around the waist, unable to wait any longer. I pulled her toward me and once again my tongue was in her mouth. I loved kissing her I realized and especially loved the heat radiating from her body in waves as I pressed her frame against mine. Her breasts pressed against the hardness of my chest as I licked into her mouth and by the time we parted I didn't waste a second in lowering my mouth to them. I plumped them in my hands and loved just how endowed she was because they were so wonderful to the feel and sight.

She was busty and gorgeous and the little moans she made as she threw her head back nearly did me in. I traced my kisses back up to her neck, tasting her skin and then I sucked on the flesh of her lips. I pulled her nipple into my mouth one pink peak after the other and she cried out, holding onto me even more tightly.

She couldn't stop writhing her hips and grinning against my hardness and I loved every moment of it. I couldn't hold back so I reached down and slipped my hand into her thong.

I met her, wet, juicy, and ready and the moment I began to stroke the engorged bud of desire between her thighs I felt her leak even further onto my hand.

She was so turned on that it drove me wild to watch her.

Her parted lips, her heaving chest; she was just so fucking sexy, and as I leaned forward once again to kiss her as though I were starving, all the prior concerns and suspicions of her dissipated into nothing.

Chapter 18
Scarlett

I was losing it.

Slowly, but surely complete mental incoherence was sure to come sooner or later. The way he took his time with me as though he couldn't appreciate my body enough was overwhelming. As though he had no inhibitions... like I belonged to him and he had all the time in the world.

I couldn't believe it or him.

I loved every single fucking moment of this and couldn't wait for him to devour me till I lost my mind.

There was just something about the grip of his hands and how they touched and held me, as well as the viral gorgeous strength that I felt with every flex that turned me on so immensely.

I could barely catch my breath, but then when he lifted me and set me on the surface beside the pool it was even harder to regulate my emotions and movements.

I knew what he wanted to do and I was beyond ready. However at first, I felt self-conscious but then when I reminded myself that I wasn't Sophie and so I didn't have to deal with working so closely with a man that had seen every bit of me after the present week had passed, I completely let loose and lowered onto my back.

He didn't even bother pulling my thong down my legs. Instead, he pulled the tiny black lace aside and I was fully exposed before him. I felt so wet and so heated that the moment he lowered and covered my mound with his lips, I nearly combusted. The heat, the fire of his suction... the pressure of his naughty expert tongue, I cried out. Nothing was stopping me, nothing holding me back and I just couldn't contain myself.

I was sure I called out his name, but not till he slid two fingers inside me and then sucked on my clit at the same time did I truly hear the volume of his name falling from my lips.

Lucien... Lucien I call out again as I rocked onto his fingers and mouth.

It didn't take long for me to come. I was writhing so hard against the floor, my toes curling and my hand caught in my hair, pulling trying to contain the unbelievable sensations of unhinged lust.

I moaned and thrashed around almost unable to bear it as I was dragged to the edge. Eventually, and with his persistent technique, I was thrown off the cliff and I gave in to the waves. It was beautiful. My eyes were wide open but I could see absolutely nothing above me. "Fuck," I swore but he didn't even let me recover.

He caught me once again and before I could register anything that was happening, I was pulled back into the water and was being kissed senseless. I could taste myself on him and it was filthy but the way it mixed with his essence and mine, was unbelievable. I threw my arms around his neck and he kissed me even harder. I could do this forever I realized and I continued to writhe against him, but all too soon he pulled away and I nearly cried.

Nearly truly cried and it was so embarrassing that I was startled for a moment.

"You good?" he asked as he turned me around like I weighed nothing more than a rag doll, and I didn't know what to say. I did nod though, preferring this to admitting outrightly that the railing at the edge was the only thing keeping me standing despite the fact we were in the shallow part of the pool.

I responded with all of me, and held back nothing, ensuring that all the effort he was putting into making me perhaps have the best sex of my life was incredibly appreciated.

He was fast and yet slow at the same time, close and yet far and it all just seemed unreal. As though I was in some sort of trance.

My full ass was pressed against his cock then and I couldn't help but grind into it. He grabbed me by my waist and I nearly melted.

Then he whispered into my ear, his voice coarse and smooth.

"Are you on birth control?" he asked.

It took a while for the question to register but when it did my eyes shot open.

"I am," I replied but I was still a bit hesitant.

He seemed to feel this because he proceeded to ask. "Would you prefer I used a condom?" His warm breath washed over me. I shut my eyes and gave this some serious thought or as serious as I could as he began to rock his cock between my cheeks.

"You're clean right?" I asked.

"I am," he replied. "You?"

"I am," I said.

"Don't worry," he said as I felt his hands go to the string of my thong. He began to pull it down and I was so excited that I could barely stay still.

"If anything goes wrong I have a lot of money to compensate you."

This was amusing to me.

"You're willingly advertising yourself as a prime lawsuit candidate?" I asked and I could feel his smile as he kissed me.

"Whatever it takes to feel all of you," he said as he grabbed my cunt, hard.

My spine instantly weakened at the onslaught of pleasure. His words were reassuring to hear but also kind of scary. But he was a no-nonsense man and given how he had rejected the blonde woman from earlier I just couldn't help but feel completely relaxed with him and his ability to control himself when needed.

This assumption however was severely shaken in the next moment as he whispered in my ear. "Would you take it in the ass?"

My eyes popped open.

I couldn't believe the question. It wasn't that it was strange, after all, it was previously and personally explored territory. What was strange was that even though it was something I was open to and most definitely wanted this was our first time and I wasn't still convinced that it was the better orifice of entry. Even with this concern I didn't bother holding back.

"Yes,' I replied. "I would. But, it's not exactly ideal here or for the first time is it?" I asked.

"It's not," he replied. "But later on, I'd love to fuck all your holes."

I nearly came right then at his absolutely filthy mouth but pretty soon my attention was divided as he parted the wet lips of my sex and began to stroke the thick head of his rod down my middle.

God, I loved how that felt and couldn't help but further push back against him. It was all exquisite and I showed him with my moans.

He was spurred on and encouraged and so in little time, he lowered his knees, positioned his dick at my entrance, and began to push in.

Immediately, every other thought about anything else was wiped out of my mind.

I was so tight that for a moment I wondered if he would be able to fit. The few guys I'd been with though never seemed to have this problem so it made me wonder if it was that I was too tight for him to fit or that he was too big.

Regardless and with his expert coaxing this quickly became a non-issue because soon he was in and my limbs went limp.

"Oh,.." I moaned aloud and threw my head back to rest against his shoulder.

It felt as though something that had been missing from inside me had finally been completely filled up from start to finish and I couldn't contain myself.

He kissed my shoulder sucked on my skin and I turned my head to reach for his lips. I needed to kiss him to somehow contain this because I'd never been filled up so thoroughly. I was stretched so tightly that I pulsed around his thick, hard, and long length and it made me want to see him lose control.

"You good?" he asked and I pushed against him. The feeling was exquisite but I needed him to move before I completely lost my mind.

"Fuck me," I pleaded and could feel the warmth of his breath at his quiet amusement.

Jeesh, I enjoyed everything about this man. From the way he looked to the way he smelled and spoke and acted. So much dominance and control and virility currently had all of its focus on me and it drove me wild.

He pulled out then slowly, purposefully and I held my breath for when he pushed back in.

My wall grazed the smoothness of his slick cock hungry and pulsing until he hit the end of me.

I moaned once again incredibly excited as his forehead briefly rested against my shoulder. Then he pulled out once again nearly to the end and then eased back in.

He did this over and over again and each time he went just a little bit faster.

I could see what he was doing now and this weakened me even further. By the time he couldn't hold back and his speed was cranked up to the highest frequency I was more or less a mumbling mess.

He fucked me so hard that the only thing keeping my body from slamming against the wall was the grip I had on the safety railing

My legs lifted off the ground over and over again but with his grip around my waist and on my ass I was held in place and secured.

" Fuck, you feel so good!" he swore into my ear as he fucked me impossibly faster.

My eyes rolled back into my head and my vision was completely lost. I could only feel now as I chanted his name over and over again. I leaned back to suck on the lobe of his ear and in return he kissed me. His hand moved toward my front to stroke my clit.

The added pressure was nothing short of pure torment. The best most wonderful kind. I loved it with every fiber of my being.

I wished it would go on forever. I wished I could just continue to feel the lust ripping through my veins and leaving me overheated and incoherent. It was just too damn good.

I'd never been fucked this way and my body didn't know how to process it and so much sooner than I'd like I was already coming. I didn't hold back. I screamed out his name at my release and he gripped me even tighter. I could feel the pain as well as his exertion because he didn't stop. He was so close I could feel it and so I tried my best to keep up with him as he fucked even harder and faster into me until in no time he was roaring out his release.

Warmth filled me and his hold became even tighter making me feel so completely owned and possessed by this man.

"Sophie," he called over and over again and though disappointing, this was at first easy to ignore. Eventually though and at the end it made me somewhat sad, that he truly didn't know who I was. I couldn't help it then as we both recovered and tried to catch our breaths wondering how my name would sound on his lips.

The way he'd called Sophie's name had been breathless and beautiful and it gave me goosebumps all over.

Still, I appreciated every moment of this so I turned around and wrapped my arms around him. I kissed him without holding back and it didn't take long before once again he was hard again. What I wanted more than anything else was to suck his cock and this was exactly what I told him.

His eyes widened slightly at the request but then he smiled and I was mesmerized.

"Sure," he said and pulled away from me. I instantly hated the loss. It was for a good means with a great need so I tucked away my emotions determined to enjoy this night without any hindrance whatsoever.

Chapter 19

Lucien

I truly couldn't recall the last time that I had my cock sucked.

Perhaps this was the celebration that was due for closing with Charles tonight, but the fact that she had asked I truly couldn't wait. Excitement coursed through me as I headed over to one of the pool benches and took a seat. I was completely naked and so was she but it didn't matter because I had paid for the work. No surveillance and no interruptions just the both of us fucking until we were exhausted and had to go to bed.

Judging by just how hard I had come, I didn't expect that there would be much sleeping for the both of us tonight.

We had agreed on one night while she had expressed an interest if I wasn't mistaken of perhaps more than one. At the time I hadn't given it much thought since I hadn't known how this was going to turn out. Perhaps it would have been a quick and unsatisfactorily release and thus I'd have had to cut my loss immediately before it caused any more damage. Therefore I had taken precautions. But now and as I poured the champagne into a glass and watched her head over to me I wondered if truly I could be satiated after just one night. I couldn't believe she was my assistant and that I had her within reach for so long yet I had not made a move.

The reminder came that she had been engaged till literally just the previous day so I nodded in self-consolation. There was no way I would have touched her when she belonged to another man. It made me wonder now as I watched her take the seat beside me why they had broken up. Who the fuck would have ended a relationship with someone like her?

She was beyond gorgeous... recently sassy but still of a calm and kind temperament and her body had just made me bust the hardest nut I'd had in years. She was the perfect woman if that could exist and so I found myself unable to stop staring at her.

"What?" she asked and I smiled

"Champagne?" I asked and she nodded.

"Yes, thank you," she replied.

I didn't bother using another glass because I had just eaten her out so what was a little intimacy in using the same glass? She apparently thought the same and had no qualms about it as well because she accepted the flute and nearly drained the entire glass.

I was amused.

"Thirsty I see," and she nodded.

She ran her hand through her hair and flipped it away from her face and something very close to affection stirred in the pit of my stomach for her.

She was just too beautiful and suddenly I found myself wanting to talk to her just a little bit more.

"This hairstyle suits you," I said and she blushed.

"Thank you," she replied and I nodded continuing to watch her. I moved the cart then over to her and it was a delight to watch her eyes light up as the board of food came a little closer. She picked up a grape, savored it, and then a bite of cheese and I watched it all.

"Want some?" she asked as salami followed and I nodded in agreement.

She picked up a grape once again and then turned to me.

She got up and I waited to see what she would do. There was clearly no need for any instructions so I leaned back against the recliner and had to check that it was sturdy enough to hold us both.

She weights absolutely nothing so when she sat astride me and settled her wet cunt across my stomach, my cock immediately began to swell once again with unbridled excitement.

She was fucking intoxicating.

She leaned down to kiss me, and I submitted fully. I savored the taste of the grape in her mouth, sweet and refreshing. I could kiss her for hours I realized as my hand began to caress her back.

I leaned backwards and reclined fully unable to relax while my entire body was being cranked up like a gear.

Her breasts... I couldn't get enough of plumping the voluminous mounds in my hands and suddenly I needed to be inside of her again. I had been excited for her to suck me off but not now. We had all night.

And so I grabbed my cock and it only took a few strokes for me to become as hard as granite once again.

"Fuck," she whispered as she watched me slowly jerk my length.

"That was what was inside of me?"

"It's going inside of you again," I said and she held on tight.

I guided her as she lifted her frame and then she lowered back down onto me.

I swore again as her walls gripped me so greedily and the slickness was so fucking exquisite. It was intensified now that we were on dry ground and my hand nearly raked up her back.

"Your cock," she gasped as she slanted her head to kiss me. "It's going to drive me fucking crazy."

I felt the exact same way and wanted to respond verbally as well but I couldn't quite find the words. She was already writhing and moving against me and I didn't want to distract myself. I wanted to watch her eyes so I kept my hands on her hips to stabilize her and keep her balanced.

"Let's see how well you ride," I said and the brightest most beautiful smile came to her face.

She bit into her bottom lip and my breath caught in my throat, "Fuck," I cursed.

I wondered then if the suspicion I had felt earlier was not that she suddenly felt like a different person, but at the fact that his woman was about to completely possess me in ways that I never knew were possible or could ever even imagine that'd I'd allow.

But here she was with her hand flattened against my

torso and her other gripping my knee as she stretched back to gyrate her hips with wild abandon.

I loved how she switched and alternated her movements. Sometimes she would rock against me and at other times she would let herself rise slightly upward and bounce on my rock-hard dick.

It was nearly overwhelming and even though my body was now overheated to the point of nearly being uncomfortable, I didn't want her to stop.

I rubbed her clit, and was unable to resist sending her juices into my mouth. I groaned as I savored it.

"Like how I taste?" she asked and I couldn't help but smile.

I loved it more than I could explain and so before I could stop myself I got up and switched positions.

I laid her across the recliner set one knee on the ground for balance and lifted her leg. I couldn't help first of all lowering to suck her cunt and she rewarded me with her cream.

"Fuck Lucien!" her back nearly arced off the surface.

She grabbed my hair and the pain was just what I needed.

I didn't stop her in any way. I wanted her to lose herself completely in my arms and if we both came away with a few bruises then it was what it was.

I ate her now even more hungrily than I previously had.

This was no longer a taste, no longer me testing the waters. I wanted to devour her so I pushed my tongue into her and thrust repeatedly.

Her grip grew tighter and her moans louder and still I

didn't let go. I sucked on her clit and then slid two fingers into her soaking wet cunt.

My pace at first was slow as I tried not to hurt her but the moment everything was clear and smooth I finger fucked her till she was nearly pulling away.

She gasped and cried out my name and nearly came. Just before she did, I pulled my fingers out and filled her hole with my cock. Everything was much rougher this time around because I couldn't control myself.

The way she gripped me was unreal but as I hooked her leg across my shoulder I watched the way she responded to me.

Her eyes fluttered open and shut constantly rolling into her sockets and then staring straight ahead as though she were in a trance. She gripped the seat behind her to keep herself somewhat grounded and I watched all of this from above her. Her breasts bounced as I fucked hard into her going even faster and she grabbed them, so overtaken with the pleasure that she pulled at the hardened peaks of her nipples and plumped the heavy mounds in her hands. She had such beautiful breasts that I wondered how and why she'd covered them up for this long with the outfits that she used to wear.

She leaned over then trying to suck on the sweet flesh and I was immensely thrilled at the sight. I wish I could have a picture of her in this way.

Her hair was stuck to her neck and skin from the moisture. Whether it was from the sweat of our exertion or the pool I didn't have a clue. Her make-up was still somehow intact and her lips a smeared pink but the flush of being so thoroughly fucked was all over her body.

I truly couldn't get enough of watching her but too soon it came to an end. The pressure gathered and built from the point at which we were joined and only intensified dangerously from there onward.

I threw my head back as I came and it was so hard that I almost couldn't catch my breath. I didn't hold back and neither did she and this time around it was as though we were for once perfectly synced because we came together.

Our voices rang out and echoed across the space and it was beautiful.

I collapsed onto her, unable to remain upright and she held me, her arms rubbing all across my overheated body.

My thighs were spasming, my cock still dripping semen deep into her and it was a while before either of us came back to our senses. We were still joined but I didn't want to pull out just yet. I could feel the wetness leaking from between us and it was so filthy that it turned me on once again.

I was too exhausted. I had barely slept all week after an impossible forty-eight hours. And so I decided then it was time to rest, I shut my eyes. Just for a few minutes, I told myself and as though she knew just how much I needed this, she held me. It was getting slightly chilly but the way she rubbed me so affectionately seemed to chase it all away. I was happy, extremely contented and I just couldn't wait to regain my energy and do it all over again.

Chapter 20
Scarlett

He fell asleep in my arms!

I couldn't believe it, but it happened so silently and discreetly that I almost didn't notice until I realized that his breathing had evened out. Mine had as well, and although I hadn't wanted to move because I loved the way he filled me, I didn't want him to pull out, his weight was nothing small to handle. Still, as I turned to watch his gorgeous peaceful face resting, something in my heart swelled and shifted.

He looked so at rest that I was almost envious, but I understood why he would need it. He had worked so hard these past few days and had slept very little, and then he'd fucked my brains out of my head twice in one go. I felt exhausted just thinking about it all, so I stroked his head in consolation. Regardless, I didn't trust this pool chair and its ability to handle both of our weights for too long so eventually, when it became too uncomfortable and concerning, I tried to move.

The instant I did, it was as though he hadn't been

sleeping deeply at all because I could feel his entire frame stiffen. And then he raised his head.

For a while, he seemed a bit disoriented, as though he didn't quite know where he was, who he was with, or the state that he was in. Soon enough though, he recovered and apologized.

I was surprised to hear his apology, but before I could think too much of it, he pulled out of me and rose to his feet. As a result, and for the first time that evening, I was gifted the full frontal view of his glorious cock. It was so fucking gorgeous that I could stare at it forever. His girth and length were seriously no joke, and given now that it was glistening so beautifully from our copulation, I truly wanted nothing more than to have it in my mouth.

"Still hungry?" I heard him ask, and when I looked up, I swallowed, feverish with anticipation. Without even waiting for permission, I leaned forward and with my hands on his hips, I pulled him a bit closer to me.

"You're such an insatiable woman," he said and I took it as a compliment because there was no way in hell I was going to act as though I didn't want him to come in my mouth.

He obliged, and his cock which was slightly hard from when he woke up, once again began to rise. I held it in my hands gently and then then I lifted my gaze to see that he was watching me.

"You're rich and you carry this around as well?" I asked and he smiled again.

"I'm the whole package." he joked and I was quite surprised to hear him show this gloaty side of himself.

He was the package, I wanted to say, but I truly didn't

want to inflate his ego too much so I ignored his comment altogether and focused solely on fisting him. I started slowly, mesmerized as I milked his slick, rigid length from the root to the tip, and the minute I was awarded my first dose of milky white pre-cum, I leaned forward and pulled the lush, flushed head into my mouth.

I sucked hard on the pink, leaking slit, pumping him hard and I could feel his body shudder as a result.

"Oh, fuck," he groaned aloud, slightly throwing his head back, and I loved the sight of the protruded bob of his larynx as it bobbed up and down his throat. He was so masculine and so virile that for the first time, I was truly fascinated about the difference between the sexes.

I wanted to close my lips around it, and I wanted to feel the hardness of his biceps and abdomen however I had no choice but to to be patient. We still had the rest of the night ahead of us and I was going to use that to enjoy every single part of his body, and as much as I wanted.

Hence this time around, the full subject of my attention was his cock and it was no small thrill.

Giving head wasn't my favorite thing to do, but with him, I enjoyed myself so much that I couldn't imagine stopping. His reactions were a joy to behold with the way such a powerful man such as himself sighed and moaned and scrunched up his face, very clearly and thoroughly affected.

I took him even deeper, all the way to the back of my throat until I was forced to pull away when it became too much. I continued though, refusing to stop for a moment and he grabbed onto my hair.

It hurt though he was somewhat gentle but I loved it

because, at the same time, it gave the pleasure a dangerous edge and made me feel so damn good.

I felt the pull in my clit as the roof of my mouth and the pad of my tongue held his cock tightly in place, bobbing my head back, licking him up and down until he cradled my face in his hands and began to pump his hips forward.

This was all for his pleasure and I loved that I could unravel him in this way just as he had to me. The feel of his cock thrusting and out of my mouth was so fucking sexy that I couldn't help but submit and allow him to use me in every way that he wanted.

It didn't take long for him to come once again. I pumped him harder and faster, sucking and rolling my tongue, and in no time all the muscles in his hips tensed.

He came then with a loud agonized groan, and it gave me so much pleasure to hear him and feel the trembling of his thighs underneath my hands.

The thick ropes sent down my throat slightly choked me but I didn't let a single drop of it go to waste.

I lapped his salty head clean, and then when our eyes met again, I picked up the last bit from the corner of my lips and rubbed it against my tongue.

"You're a fucking gorgeous woman do you know that?" he said and despite how hard I tried to not be moved by his compliment, I couldn't help the bright red flush that spread across my cheeks. I felt so appreciated and refreshed that I didn't know what to do with myself. Even standing to my feet made me wobbly but when he pulled me once again into his arms and kissed me, my entire body went limp.

"Ready to go back upstairs?" he asked and I nodded.

I wanted so badly to embrace him but he let go of me

quicker than I'd hoped so I couldn't try for it. I convinced myself as we began to gather and pack up our things that I didn't need to, but the fact that I couldn't just ask was one more thing that made me sad. I loved cuddling so much but there was a level of comfort and intimacy that was required for it to be wonderfully sweet and we didn't have that, at least not yet and probably never will. In my head, we were complete strangers but in Sophie's head and his as well they were probably the most familiar with each other. She spent more than 80% of her days and time with him so it was highly likely that he thought immensely fondly of her.

This is just for tonight, I reminded myself as we headed back to our suites. You're lucky that you've even gotten this much out of this I thought to myself.

Worse yet the annoying voice was actually right and so I pushed the slight tinge of unhappiness over my face away and refocused all my attention, solely on the present.

When we arrived on our floor I went to my room while he went to his, without a word I might add, I couldn't help but panic. This was not how this night was supposed to end. I wanted to be with him in more and several different ways but I couldn't exactly knock on his door and beg him to fuck me again within the space of two hours. Or could I?

Sighing, I returned to my room and took a shower. It was hot and soothing, but all I could think about was him; of how he had made me sore in places that hadn't been sore in so long, and how he made me feel things that I didn't think were even possible to feel from sex.

I was insistent now on wanting more and as I got out of the shower and began to towel dry myself, I was just about desperate enough to march over to his room to ask for it.

Too bad I was a coward because even after I threw on a robe and towel-dried my hair, I found myself staring at the door solely with the hope that he would knock.

True to expectation and reality, he did not. Still not wanting to fall asleep just yet, in case he did eventually knock I returned to the bathroom and couldn't look away from the gorgeous bathtub waiting for me.

I was no longer sticky and gross everywhere, but I did have the memories that he had stamped in my head to relive in warm water and bubbles so I immediately started to run myself one. I found some salt bath bombs and soon enough it was nearly bubbling over and ready for me. The flash-backs of him fucking me would for sure be haunting me for at least the next few days, so I shut my eyes as soon as I got in and relaxed my entire body.

Not long after, and unfortunately, my reminiscing was interrupted.

My phone started to ring then but thankfully I had brought it along with me so I didn't have to leave the tub soaking wet. I did ignore its ringing the first time but when it started again I had no choice but to place it against the wall and accept the call from none other than my twin.

"Video call?" she asked and I wondered what her problem was this time.

"No," I replied.

"You don't want to see me?" she asked.

"No need," I replied, but still I turned on the video function and she was able to see that I was in the bathtub surrounded by an insane amount of bubbles.

"Wow," she said. "You're truly enjoying yourself these days. Maybe I should have just stuck with my job for the week. If I had I'd be enjoying myself just like you and flying in private jets and soaking in bathtubs.

Her whining amused me, especially when I thought of all the ways her boss had bent me over and fucked me just barely an hour ago and I couldn't stop myself from blushing.

"Your cheeks are red," she noted. "That better be makeup and not that you have a wild story to tell me."

I knew why she was calling and what she wanted however I wasn't going to entertain her so easily.

I did however want to drink champagne and eat something and it reminded me of the charcuterie board that had been delivered to us. We'd barely even had any fill of it at all and it would have been the perfect snack for lounging like I currently was.

"What happened?" she eventually asked. "Are you getting ready to screw my boss or has it already happened?"

"You've become quite abrasive these days miss ma'am," I complained and she smiled.

It was sheepish and subtly apologetic so I decided to quench her curiosity and speak. I knew that she was just as curious as she was worried so I responded to allay her worries.

"We're done for now, although he said we had all night. I'm cleaning up."

All the color seemed to drain out of her face.

"What?"

I watched her, wondering why she was so surprised when we already discussed this.

"What is it?" I asked a bit nervous, and hoping this wouldn't truly upset her. "It's a problem isn't it?"

Talking about it was one thing but actually following through on it must feel different to her.

"Not really," she replied. "I'm just shocked. I mean, you too literally just met yesterday. I've known him for three years."

I nearly rolled my eyes.

"You were with Jerald."

"Still," she said. "You two really couldn't wait could you?"

I sighed then but had absolutely no regrets, especially since I was still literally floating on clouds.

"Tell me everything," she said. "How did it play out?"

Truly wanting to relive it out loud I nodded and lifted my gaze to think. Plus she was eventually going to pull it out of me.

"We went straight to a private pool here at the hotel," I said. "The water was warm, he's huge I came three times, and it was in several positions."

I returned my gaze to her then and found that her mouth was hanging wide open.

"What?" I asked

"I still can't believe it," she said. "I'd always thought he was quite stiff. But you, with Lucien Montgomery, several positions huh?"

"Is it really that shocking to you?" I asked however she remained thoroughly confused.

"Everything happening right now is thoroughly confusing to me," she said. "First of all, I can't get it out of my head that he thinks, or rather he knows you're you. Are you sure he doesn't know? Maybe he knows I have a twin and he's just pretending."

"That's insane," I said however she remained suspicious.

"Not as insane as him sleeping with me. I mean you after three years of absolutely nothing. Wait does that mean he's always had his eyes on me?"

"I asked him," I replied. "But he said that he'd never considered it because you were engaged. Now that you weren't though and he was quite familiar with you he felt as though he would prefer it and be more comfortable. Plus it does help as well that I dress like a wom-" I stopped myself in time. "I mean I dress quite interestingly."

"Interesting?" She said. "No honey you dress like a bougie thot while I dress like a lady."

Though we were joking this slightly burned so I couldn't help but shoot back at her. "Well your button-ups got you nowhere with him in three years but my low-rise tops got me rolling my eyes and humming for a couple of hours straight so I guess the bougie thot style is the way to go."

She narrowed her gaze at me, not in offense but as though she was almost convinced that I could be telling the truth.

"You're not lying or exaggerating are you?" she asked however it sounded more like a warning.

"Why would I?" I asked.

"To make me feel jealous. That has been your toxic trait from day one."

This made me laugh out loud because she was absolutely right however, another call came in and my heart nearly jumped out of my chest.

I'd thought it was Lucien. I was almost sure he was the one but when I realized it was a London number I relaxed.

I hung up with Sophie and answered the other call and received quite an unpleasant blow.

"I'm about to head over to the hotel you're staying at," Nancy said. "Where exactly are we meeting? The Bar? Outside? Inside? I wouldn't want us to remain there though because I have special plans for us tonight."

I listened to her continuously speak and truly didn't know how to respond.

Eventually though, and probably worried that I had a stroke or something she called my name.

"Scarlett?"

I was pulled out of my reverie then. I immediately wanted to cancel since I was enjoying the hell out of myself and was almost certain that sooner or later, and at some time during the night, Lucien would come calling again. When that happened I wanted to be available and waiting in my room rather than outside in a club or a bar with screaming Uni boys.

I hesitated because Nancy had been a close friend of mine and it had been so long since I had seen her as well as forever since I had come to London.

I had no clue when or if I'd be able to come back to London so I nodded and agreed to honor our plans.

"I'll be ready," I told her and got out of the tub.

She had gone through the trouble of finding a babysitter because she needed the night out as well and I wasn't going to disappoint her for any reason.

"Do you have a specific place in mind?" I asked. "If you do can you send me the address? I should be able to arrive there in about thirty minutes to an hour. That way you don't have to come over here first."

"An hour!" she exclaimed, I narrowed my eyes knowing her and knowing fully well that she was usually late for everything.

"Have you even left your home yet Nancy?" I asked and at the blatant accusation, she went silent. "You've forgotten that I know very well exactly what your *I'm heading over* means?"

She laughed at this. "You ask so many dumb questions," she said. "I see you're still a know-it-all all after all these years."

I ignored her attempt at intimidating me and shook my head. "I knew it," I said.

"Yes you did miss me and I'll send you an address."

"At least let me know what to wear," I said. "So I'll know how to dress appropriately."

"It'll be a restaurant and a lounge. High end. Don't worry it won't be some dingy and low-end bar. We're on a mission tonight."

"What kind of mission exactly?" I asked, knowing how she could sometimes get with her escapades.

"I'll tell you when you get here," she replied. "And don't worry it'll be fun."

"Got it," I replied, and the call came to an end. I was quick with drying off and in very little time I was slipping on a very dark red tube dress that hugged every inch of my curves and flattered my figure. I put on matching blood-red lipstick, blow-dried my hair, and was ready in no time.

My makeup was quick since it would be nighttime so barely half an hour later I was already heading down. I couldn't help but look at Lucien's door as I exited my room and started down the hallway. It was with eyes of longing, but I consoled myself as I waited for the elevators that there would be so many things to do with Nancy tonight. There was a lot besides Lucien Montgomery to look forward to. With the change in mindset, I was sure my time with Nancy tonight would be incredibly wonderful.

Once again as I strolled through the lobby feeling so gorgeous and confident, my eyes went to the seat Lucien had sat in earlier out of the way. I truly wished he could see me now. I wanted I realized to see the appreciation in his eyes and couldn't help but wonder just how good it would feel.

Chapter 21
Lucien

Our night hadn't yet come to an end. And so, even as I took a quick shower and headed straight to bed, I knew that at some point during the night, I was going to be knocking on her door once again. It was still quite early, barely eleven pm, yet in the past few days, it was as though I had lived several lifetimes, so I wasn't surprised at how easily I had fallen asleep on her.

The exertion had drained whatever strength was left in me, leaving me feeling as light as a feather. However, a little while later, I was rudely awakened by a phone call. When I grabbed the phone and checked the time, I realized that it was less than an hour since I had gone to bed and so it was extremely unpleasing to be awoken so suddenly.

When I realized that I didn't recognize the phone number, I had no choice but to answer because it could be an emergency of some sort somewhere.

"Hello Mr. Monthgomery," came the greeting and it was a deep voice probably belonging to a middle-aged man.

"Yes," I replied as I turned on the lamp by my nightstand. It bathed the entire room in a warm glow and for the first time, I looked toward the empty side of my bed and suddenly wished that I had someone to experience this with. I wasn't necessarily lonely but given the woman I'd been with earlier that evening, it was all my mind could conjure.

"Mr. Montgomery, this is Gregory Walters," the caller introduced himself; however, the name didn't ring any bell whatsoever.

"I work for Mr. Charles Nioly, and he instructed me to follow up with you on the collaboration with his brand. He looks forward to expanding the business to North America, and I will be the liaison between you both."

It was in times like this that I truly hated client business because what was so important about anything he just said that he couldn't just fucking wait to inform me the next day.

He soon informed me.

"I know it's pretty late, but I hear you might be returning to New York first thing tomorrow, and I myself will be flying out to Barcelona briefly. So if you have the time this evening, I hope that we can meet?"

I listened to his words more than ready to reject everything he had just proposed. However, when I cleared the fog in my mind and thought more logically, I realized it was a great idea because whatever the outcome of our discussion we could hit the ground running the moment we returned to New York.

"All right," I replied, getting up. "Where should we meet?"

"Do you know the Sabine in Soho?" He asked.

It didn't matter if I knew it because I had a personal driver who could get me there regardless, so I took down the address and got ready.

Since it was a night out, I went with something a little bit more casual: just a white linen dress shirt and tailored slacks. I sprayed on some cologne, put on some shoes, and was out of the door.

As I passed by her bedroom door, I couldn't help but pause. I wondered what she was up to and if she had fallen asleep. I wanted to knock but I was reluctant. I didn't want to sound desperate.

The car was waiting for me at the curb as I arrived, so I got in and we were on our way.

The restaurant and bar was quite high-end on the 10th floor of the Mondrian London at Sea Containers. The lights were dim, the music low and tasteful, and the host was ready to receive me at the door. Gregory also came over and we exchanged a handshake.

"Glad to finally meet you," he said.

"Likewise," I replied as we took our seats in the lounge. "I'm Charles Financial Adviser and he sent over your proposal a few months ago. We've been assessing it and now that the approval has begun, we can get started."

"What about the terms?" I asked. "The revenue share? Is that confirmed as well?"

"Well, we reached out multiple times for renegotiations, and you absolutely refused to change them. Unless now, you're being a bit more friendly?"

I smiled as I beckoned to the waiter to come over.

"Just confirming that we're on the same page because it still won't be changing. Which Charles knows, the profits will be astounding enough to make any of this inconse-quential."

"All right," he replied. "Let's talk briefly about your plans for expanding a few of the businesses. The first is the Casino in Atlantic City. He never actually set out to just build one. He has a whole plan of three he wants, but we haven't been able to reach this stage as of yet. Do we have the facilities to triple the income by the end of the year?"

I'd evaluated this intensely, so I had the exact answer he was looking for.

We continued speaking, and soon our drinks of whiskey were brought over.

I didn't want to eat anything amid such a meeting, so I kept my alcohol intake minimal and stayed alert.

Chapter 22
Scarlett

"What about those two?" Nancy asked.

It took me a while to turn around to see who she was talking about because I was not interested. We had been playing this game now for the better part of half an hour, and it was getting quite dull. Who knew that most men supposedly with money were not very attractive?

"Look," she slightly pinched my arm, and I smiled. Then I turned around to see who she was talking about.

It didn't take long for me to notice him. At first, I was sure that my eyes were playing a trick on me; however, his features and physique were unmistakable even in the dimly lit restaurant and bar.

"Holy shit," I swore and quickly turned back around.

"He's hot, isn't he? That's the first one we've seen so far, but I really don't think he's wealthy." she sighed and took a sip of her drink.

"Honestly, I didn't believe you when you said that billionaires hung out here, but now I do."

"Wait, what?" she asked. "Why didn't you believe me?"

"I don't know," I shrugged, "but you were right and they definitely do because that man is a billionaire."

"I don't know him," she stared even harder, she tried but failed to be discreet about it.

"That's because he's from the U.S. and he's my boss."

Her eyes nearly popped out of their sockets.

"He's your boss? If he is, then why are we here? You could have just given me his phone number or something?"

"And get fired? Absolutely not."

"You're right," she replied. "I said I was going to take you out for a night of fun, instead I dragged you over here to go wealthy husband shopping."

"This is more fun," I replied and couldn't put into words just how much I meant that.

It had been getting dull, but the moment I spotted him, every cell in my body came to life.

I was in awe but managed to contain myself. He had been on my mind every second since I'd left the hotel, and then here he was.

"So..." she asked, "Is there anything going on between you two? Can I shoot my shot?"

I was instantly on guard with this statement, which didn't make any sense whatsoever since he wasn't mine in any sense of the word, but perhaps he was for the night.

"No, nothing is going on between us," I replied.

"So I can go over? Please come with me? For once I actually have a chance at success since you're there, so you can introduce me as your friend."

I stared at her, and for a moment, I was sure that she was crazy. I would have easily done it the previous day.

Heck, even just a few hours earlier. But now, after he had eaten me out and fucked me several ways to Sunday was incredibly awkward.

But still, I wanted to see him, wanted him to know I was here for whatever reason, and unbeknownst to Nancy, this would actually be me using her. However, I didn't say a word. And so I nodded.

"Should we send a drink over?" she asked, and my brows lifted again. "It's either that or we go over you introduce me."

They seemed really deep in conversation, so I couldn't help but imagine they would be annoyed by the intrusion. I tried to make out the face of the man seated next to him, but I couldn't see him clearly or recognize him. Perhaps he was a friend? The best part was that he wasn't out with some woman, and this made me happier than I could explain.

"Send a drink over," I told her. "You're right, and it's safer. When the waiter goes to tell them, they'll look this way and decide if they're interested or if they're too busy to approach us."

She grabbed the menu then and instantly we got to work.

I didn't need to search for long because one of the benefits of being his assistant was I got a cheat sheet of everything that he liked, so I knew exactly what to look for.

"A bottle of Macallan Sherry Whiskey, twelve years please," I ordered from the waiter, and Nancy was surprised.

"An entire bottle?" she exclaimed. "That's quite pricey."

"You want to order something less expensive for them? This is already quite cheap even though it's almost 200 quid. But I can't spend more than that and anything less and they'll be severely unimpressed."

"You're right," she said.

I was quite nervous, but the arrow had already been shot and I couldn't take it back without looking like a complete buffoon. I kept speaking calmly with Nancy, knowing that in just a few minutes, he would know that I was here, and I truly wondered how he would respond. Would he acknowledge us or would he completely ignore it?

"I'll reimburse you soon," she said. "But can I say the drink is from me?" she asked, and I was amused by this.

"For sure," I replied. It wasn't exactly beneficial to me in this game we were playing, but I knew that if the message delivered was that the bottle was from me it would take the pressure off whatever distasteful repercussions that might come from this.

"It'll be delivered now, ma'am," the bartender informed me, and I nodded.

However, I couldn't look at him. I turned away while Nancy, on the other hand, crossed her legs, fluffed her curly hair, and got ready. I sighed then, and as I looked down at my arms, I truly couldn't believe that they were now trembling.

Chapter 23
Lucien

I wasn't happy about the intrusion, and at first, I didn't care to listen to the waiter's explanation of the delivery. But when he mentioned that the two ladies at the bar had sent it over, I was incredibly curious.

"Who?" Gregory asked, and my gaze followed the direction the waiter was indicating. One of the women waved coquettishly to us, but I didn't respond. I assessed her and was about to turn away, but there was something quite peculiar about the woman seated next to her.

"Tell them no thanks," Gregory replied, immensely amused. "We are more than capable of buying our own drinks."

I noticed as I watched the two women that the curly-haired one was trying to get the other to turn, but she didn't, and so I couldn't help but deliver another message to the waiter.

"Please tell them to come over for a brief greeting," I said.

The waiter looked at Gregory due to the conflicting

instructions while he turned to me in surprise. "I think it's more of a little prank or something," I replied. "The woman in red looks quite familiar. Plus, we could use a break and some entertainment."

"Oh, I didn't expect you to be the kind," Gregory commented excitedly. "And of course, sure. Definitely. Please invite the women to come over briefly," he told the waiter. "With emphasis on briefly."

The waiter smiled and went on his way.

I watched his every movement as he relayed the message to the woman, and excitedly the curly-haired one jumped up. Her friend, however, once again was extremely difficult to coax, but soon both women rose to their feet and began to head over to us.

She was unmistakable then. My eyes roved up and down her gorgeous body, and I almost couldn't believe that she was here. After all that we'd done, she really had the strength to get out of bed and come to a bar. They soon arrived, and this consideration was immediately wiped out of my mind, and I took her in. That red dress did something to her chest and hips that instantly made me rock hard.

My breathing came just a little bit harder as all the memories came flooding back, and then I finally lifted my gaze and met her eyes. I, however, didn't know how to approach this. Had she done this intentionally, or was this all the doing of her friend?

"Hello, Ladies," Gregory greeted them with a huge smile, and the curly-haired woman returned it.

"Hi, I'm Nancy," she answered in a sweet, song-like voice that, in my opinion, was much too coquettish and over the top.

My secretary, on the other hand, seemed to be a block of stone. It amused me slightly as I watched her because I truly couldn't tell if this was how she generally was or if this entire situation was more awkward than she could bear.

I looked at her friend, who was so enthusiastic about this, and wondered if she had been dragged into it against her will.

"And you, miss?" Gregory greeted her, but his tone was a bit condescending, which I didn't miss.

I turned to him, and when I returned to her, I almost laughed. Her brows were immediately furrowed into a frown, making her look just so adorable.

"I'm S-Sophie Turner," she greeted, and he held out his hand to offer her a handshake. She seemed reluctant to accept it, but eventually, she did, and so did her friend.

"Thank you very much for the generous gift," he said, and then he turned to me. "Still prefer to keep working or should we take a break with these lovely women?"

I looked at her, wondering what she truly wanted, and considered playing into this game. Eventually, I had no interest in whatever this was, so I turned to Gregory and responded.

"This is my assistant, Sophie," I told him. "And this is, I guess, a friend of yours?"

She seemed relieved at the introduction, and as her chest slightly rose and fell, my attention couldn't help but go to the fullness of the mounds.

"Oh! Your assistant?" Gregory was surprised.

"Yeah," I replied.

"So was this arranged by you two?"

"No," I replied as I reached forward to pick up my

liquor for a sip. "I guess it's a coincidence that we managed to meet here."

"It is," she replied. "And yes, this is my friend Nancy Graham. I was surprised to see you both here."

"Were you at the meeting earlier with Charles?" he asked, and she nodded. "Yes, I was."

"So, you're utterly familiar with this project as well. And you'll be working on it too?"

She glanced at me as she shifted her weight from one leg to the other.

"Well, I'm Mr. Montgomery's assistant, and regardless of what projects he's working on, I will undoubtedly be involved."

"Oh, you're absolutely right then," he said. "And you're extremely quick. I see why she's your assistant," he said and winked at me. I was instantly irritated by him. I wasn't even sure why; I just knew that suddenly I had no interest whatsoever in this interaction continuing.

"We'll be returning to our stools now," she said. "We just wanted to say hello."

She started to leave, then, but her friend grabbed her arm and stopped her.

I wondered who the woman was, especially since Sophie seemed somewhat uncomfortable. A former friend? Classmate? They could be the same age, but her friend was a little less petite, so maybe she was older.

"Oh, you don't want to stay for a little chit-chat with us?" Gregory asked. "Let's enjoy this bottle together. It's been quite a while since I was sent a gift by such a lovely woman."

This fucking man talked so damn much!

Her friend pulled her along, and they took the seats opposite us. I was directly across from Sophie and couldn't stop looking at her. She was so gorgeous, and it almost disturbed me to know that it took me so long to notice. Had I been blind all along? What else had I so conveniently missed?

Chapter 24

Scarlett

This had to be one of the top three most uncomfortable experiences of my life. I wasn't even sure what the problem was, but I guess Nancy was making it a bit too obvious just how excited she was about all of this, giving off the aura of ass-kissing and excessive interest. I wanted to remain aloof, especially since my—or rather Sophie's—boss was right here. I didn't know; I just didn't feel comfortable under the circumstances, especially now that I was sure he knew what her intentions were.

"Do you ladies want to eat something?" Gregory asked. "Since you bought the alcohol, we'll cover the meal. A very balanced exchange if you know what I mean."

Nancy was all smiles at this because, of course, she knew exactly what this meant. However, my distaste for the entire situation grew. I had already gotten my exchange. In fact, I was still owed some, and as a result, I couldn't help but slightly shift in my seat. That troublesome ache between my thighs had started again, and it was all thanks to the man directly across from me.

We barely touched underneath, but suddenly, I wanted to be seated next to him. This meant I had to make a decision—whether to play into this whole business or to be completely out of it. So, I picked up my phone and quietly sent him a message.

As I was typing, the waiter arrived, so I quickly sent it off and attended to the meal I wanted. He received it almost immediately; however, he took his time pulling his phone out to check, which made me somewhat salty. When he eventually did, I watched him read it and then he lifted his gaze to mine.

Me: I'm sorry if this makes you uncomfortable. We just wanted to say hello.

My heart pounded heavily against my chest for a few seconds, making it difficult to breathe. It made me realize and finally admit to myself that, to some extent, I truly did like this man. So far, no part of him had completely put me off, although there had been some slight abrasiveness and dickery, but even that kept things spicy.

I picked up my phone to reread the message I had sent him to distract myself and discourage questioning as Gregory began to ask Nancy a little bit about her life.

There was no way she would divulge that she had a kid, so as she blatantly lied that she was single, had never been married, or had no kids, I couldn't help but glance at her for a moment. It was amusing to me, but even more entertaining was Lucien's reply when it finally arrived.

Lucien: Is that true?

I lifted my gaze, but found, however, that his attention was on Nancy as he listened to her speak and drink.

I didn't want to play any games with him and had to remind myself that I could, to an extent, be as unhinged with him as I wanted to be since technically I wouldn't be working for him in a few days.

Me: We could leave.

Lucien: Why? This might actually turn out to be quite an interesting night.

I wanted to smile at his words, but given that he was so close to me and could see my every expression, I tried my very best to control myself.

Me: Alright, I'm down for making things interesting, but before I proceed, is it safe to assume that we're still within the period of our earlier arrangement?

Lucien: What earlier arrangement?

I grew quite frustrated. Of course, he would say this and respond this way. This was all part of the thrill of whatever this was to him.

I sighed then and quickly typed in another message.

Me: You're not my boss for the rest of tonight, are you?

At this, I watched him smile, and I was so mesmerized by it that I almost didn't notice he had sent a new message. The moment I did, I looked down and read what he had written

Lucien: I thought our agreement had been

duly handled after all we'd both delivered earlier.

Me: You said a night.

The moment I hit send, I immediately regretted it. I couldn't be this brazen. This would make things extremely difficult for Sophie after I left because she was not. To outsiders at least. To me, she was a complete monster.

Me: I understand. Our agreement has been settled.

I sent this and set my phone down, then gave my attention to Nancy and Gregory, who were interrogating her. I knew that it was only a matter of time before he turned his questions toward me. So, I tried to recall as much of Sophie after we started living apart as I could since I couldn't very well say anything contrary to what her boss already knew about her.

My phone lit up again, and this time around, I couldn't very well ignore him, so I picked it up and checked for what he had written.

Lucien: Are you wearing panties?

My eyes nearly popped out of my sockets. For a moment, I was reluctant to look up because I didn't know what to say. All in all, the situation just amused me. More than anything now, I just wanted to kiss him, to drown myself in his sweet and marvelous taste once again. Playing this game with him might significantly increase my chances of this, so I sent him a reply.

Me: Not for long.

Just as Gregory turned his attention to me to begin questioning, I rose to my feet.

"Excuse me," I said. "I'll be right back."

"I'll come with you," Nancy said, getting up as well, much to my annoyance.

I couldn't reject her even though she was the last person I wanted to join me because she was currently interrupting me, but I couldn't say this to her face, now could I?

"Hey, are you alright?" she asked. "You've been quiet."

I smiled at her as I stared at her reflection through the warmly lit mirror.

"He's my boss," I replied, "and that's a new client we just signed today. I have to behave myself."

"You're right," she said. "Of course. I'm sorry. I see now why this will be uncomfortable for you, and I'm not really sure I like this Greg guy. He seems very dangerous, and not in a good way, just in a slimy unpleasant way."

"I think you might be right," was all I said, and just like that, the conversation quickly shifted.

"What about your boss, though?" she asked.

"What about him?" I replied as I took my lipstick out and began to reapply it.

"My preference is most definitely inclined toward him and definitely not Gregory. So..." she lightly and playfully bumped my shoulder. "Is the coast clear?"

Despite how conflicted I felt about this question and my subsequent response, I tried to be as honest as I possibly could.

"Hmm..." I replied. "I can't really speak for him, so I'm not sure."

"But you're his personal assistant! If anyone would know, it would be you, right?"

"Yes, you're right," I said and turned to look at her.

"He definitely doesn't have a girlfriend, but you know how men are. He could have other people he's seeing on the side."

"So nothing serious then?" she asked, and I smiled and nodded.

"Definitely, nothing serious."

She smiled even more broadly then and continued to fix her hair.

I watched her quietly and the more I did the more sad I felt. I really couldn't help it.

"I feel like you didn't even really want to see me tonight," I said sadly, "after so many years apart I was hoping we could catch up."

At my words, she stopped as she contemplated my words and then she gave me an apologetic look. "I've been coming off that way, haven't I?" she said.

I simply smiled at her but the answer was unquestionable.

"I'm really sorry," she said. "It's been my only night out in months, and if you're around the women I hang out with at the programs, you'd understand. Being a single mom has been the absolute worst, and I've been in survival mode. They talk about going to places and bars like this to meet financially well-off men, and if it's not someone they can date, it might be someone they can exchange some sort of companionship for to get some financial compensation. I've been considering doing it for a while but I've been too afraid to ask any of them to come with me, but you... I guess I've always felt incredibly close and comfortable with you, so I thought this would be a great opportunity."

I completely understood her then and nodded. "You're

right, it is a great opportunity. Alright, I'll help you out. You can speak to both men, but I think you might have a better chance with Greg. From what I know of my boss, he really doesn't chase women frequently despite his wealth. He's the kind that's mainly focused on his work. As you can see, he's not even out now for social purposes; he's here because of business. Before this, he was fast asleep in the hotel."

"Oh, alright," she said.

"Plus, Gregory lives here in London, while Lucien is in New York. He might want someone close in proximity."

"I don't care," she said. "I'm more than ready to leave that dump, Luton. The crime rate is absolutely out of hand. I completely hate it there."

I understood her so I nodded and continued with fixing my hair and makeup.

I excused myself and entered the stall. I'd come in here with a purpose after all. I had been excited to engage in whatever play Lucien wanted, but after my conversation with Nancy, I didn't think I was up for it any longer. Still, I did as he had asked.

He had his eyes on me after we returned to our seats, and even Nancy herself began to notice. It was uncomfortable because, of course, he was expecting a response, and yet I was acting both deaf, blind, and dumb.

My phone lit up several times, yet I pretended to ignore it until eventually, he got fed up, and it was just as our food arrived.

"Sophie, come with me," he said and rose to his feet. Before I could inquire why this was necessary, he was already strolling majestically away. I looked at Nancy, who gave me a concerned look. She leaned over to whisper into my ear.

"Was I coming on too strong? Was I bothering him?"

I shook my head to assure her, and then I got up and followed.

Chapter 25
Lucien

I didn't understand the game she was playing, and it sure as hell wasn't interesting to me in any way.

I went straight to the bar and waited by it, and soon enough, she arrived with a slight smile on her face. My eyebrows furrowed, as I realized that she truly wasn't as hassle-free and naive as I had always imagined.

"What are you doing?" I asked as she tucked her hair behind her ear and folded her arms across her chest. Her posture was defensive, and I wondered what exactly she was being so defensive about.

"Nothing, sir," she replied as politely as she could, but I wasn't buying it.

"Is all of this one-sided?" I asked.

However, she didn't respond.

"Answer me," I said, and she opened her lips to speak, but no words came out. She glanced behind at our table to see those two watching us and then she sighed.

"I'm sorry," she said. "It's not one-sided, but there is a situation."

"What's the situation?" I asked and she sighed again.

"My friend's trying to see if she has a chance with you?"

At first, I was almost a hundred percent sure that I didn't hear her clearly. However, as she kept staring at me, waiting for a response, I leaned against the counter in complete disbelief.

"You're actually serious?" I asked, and she was reluctant to nod. But she didn't need to. I could see her understanding of how insane the statement she had just made to me was in her eyes.

However, for some reason, I wasn't offended. Instead, I was almost impressed by her audacity.

"You're pimping me out?" I asked, and her eyes widened in shock.

"What?" I waited, and she shook her head. "No. I mean, what? How could I do that?"

"We had an agreement that you're now reneging on fulfilling because you want to pass me off to your friend?"

This was exactly what it was, and said out loud it sounded absolutely wild.

"You know what," she said, "Please forget I said anything. I was kidding. I didn't mean a single word of what I said."

"And now you're lying directly to my face?" I asked, and she froze once again.

I was taunting her now, I realized, and at the myriad of emotions fleeting across her face, I realized just how much I enjoyed it. She was so expressive, more than I had ever realized before, and as I watched her try to free herself from this predicament, I realized that I liked her. It didn't come as any surprise to me, given that I had no complaints about her as a personal assistant for the past three years, but now, and especially after nearly losing ourselves in the swimming pool, I had no doubts in my mind that she was growing on me beyond our prior solely working relationship.

I, however, still had the gnawing suspicion that somewhere somehow she was different... something had changed, but I couldn't put my finger on it. There was no explanation for this, so I decided in the meantime to brush this out of my mind.

What was important now was the current moment and what I was going to do about her and her friend.

"This is what you are going to do to atone for your misdemeanor," I said. "Politely reject her on my behalf, and then you're going to go through dinner quickly. I don't intend to spend much further time in either of their company, so the moment you're done, feign some illness and I'll excuse myself as well so that I can escort you back to the hotel."

Chapter 26
Scarlett

I was a bit out of it as I returned to the table.

The wolf had gotten a phone call suddenly and was now unavailable. I had to return to the table somewhat sheepishly. It was very obvious that we had been talking about them, or perhaps they would assume that our discussion was about our current company and was therefore simply work-related.

This concerned me because I didn't want to come off as sneaky to Nancy so as I sat down, I focused on enjoying dinner and on thinking about how to use this to support my excuse of having to leave later on since I'd soon have to feign that I was sick and had to be immediately driven home.

I built up my courage and said what I was supposed to. "My apologies," I said to the others present at the table. "I haven't been feeling very well recently, so he was taking the chance to find out how I was."

This was an incredibly terrible lie as both people gave me peculiar glances, so I quickly added some more meat to it. "Amongst some other things," I added and they smiled in understanding.

After that, we all returned to our meal, but I couldn't help but notice that when Lucien was not around, it was a bit more difficult to hold a conversation between us three.

I was so done with this night or perhaps I was once again excited at the prospect of spending more time with him. He had said he would come back to the hotel with me, but whether it was simply to escape from this fiasco or because he had plans for us, I had absolutely no idea, and I had no intention of asking either.

Soon he returned to his seat as though absolutely nothing had happened.

In many ways, I felt slightly bullied by both of them and so even when Nancy leaned over to ask me what was wrong, I was almost reluctant to answer.

Eventually, I set down my fork and sent her a message so as not to seem ridiculous or manipulative with the men present.

Me: I'm not in trouble. He wants me to complete some work for him, so we're going to have to leave soon.

Her eyes popped wide open at my explanation.

Nancy: At this time? It's nearly midnight.

Me: It's a business trip.

Nancy: I thought we could go clubbing after.

I sent her a sad face emoji.

Through all of this, I avoided Lucien's gaze and finished my food.

He didn't rush me; instead, he engaged quite normally

with the rest of the group until I knew I had to comply or risk offending him, plus, and in all honesty, something in my mind told me that we for sure weren't going to be working, and I could barely wait.

"I'm sorry but I'm going to have to call it a night," I said.

Gregory smiled at me and then looked between me and Nancy.

"Do you need to leave as well?" he asked.

"Oh no, I have all night free." she shook her head.

I didn't miss his jeer, but truly I didn't care. I just wanted to be out of here, and so I rose to my feet.

"Do you want me to call my driver for you?" Gregory asked. "He can drive you back to your hotel."

"No, I'll take her," Lucien said, and before anyone could protest, he rose to his feet.

"It was great seeing you, Gregory," he said. "We'll catch up in New York?"

Brief and to the point.

"Sure," Gregory replied and got up to his feet.

"Nancy," I leaned forward to hug her.

"It was great seeing you again," I said.

She sent an apologetic gaze toward me. "I'm sorry," she mouthed, but I shook my head to dismiss the apology.

"Unnecessary," I said. "Say hi to your baby girl for me. Hopefully, I'll be back again soon to meet you both." I whispered into her ear. She nodded, and I smiled in response.

"Mr. Gregory," I sent him a smile, and he nodded and held out a hand.

"You're an extremely gorgeous woman, Miss Turner," he said. As his handshake lingered, I was very well aware that this was not in any way an offhand comment. He even stroked underneath my palm, and I wondered for a moment if anyone saw it. I didn't have the confidence to look, so I simply smiled and tried to pull away; however, he didn't budge so easily.

"I can't wait to see you in New York," he said. "I'll be there soon." I looked toward Lucien then and could see the slight annoyance in his expression.

He turned around and walked away, and I was finally able to pull my hand away so that I could leave.

It was awkward, and I guess it was easy to chalk it up to me just overthinking things, but that stroke in the middle of my palm had been intentional. I didn't know what it meant, but I was sure that it didn't exactly bode good news for me.

Still, I smiled at him and went on my way, but I couldn't help but feel slightly sorry for Sophie because he would be her problem to deal with.

As I followed my boss out, however, I had to wonder why I was so averse to Gregory. He wasn't old, but mature; he was good-looking and sophisticated. However, as we arrived outside the premises I watched Lucien pull out his phone to make a call and I completely understood.

His presence was formidable.

From everything I had learned about him so far, and from the way he had made me feel, every other advance from anyone else at this time tasted like bile in my mouth. It was absolutely ridiculous; but after the memory of him fucking me so deeply that I could feel the head of his cock all the way to the end of me, I couldn't even call myself out on his.

For now and for all intents and purposes, he was the one that I wanted and I was going to completely give into it.

Chapter 27
Lucien

I was pissed when my designated driver came around and immediately dismissed him. I wanted to be the one at the wheel. I moved around to get behind the driver's seat and noticed Sophie hadn't moved. I looked up at her wondering why she wasn't moving.

"Would you prefer I take a cab?" she asked.

I realized I was scowling at her. Relaxing my face, I approached her more politely.

"No," I replied. "I *can* drive."

She seemed a bit confused at this little joke, but it was the only conclusion I had come to, since most of the time she had worked with me, I'd barely ever driven myself anywhere. Thankfully, she accepted and pulled the door open.

I couldn't help but notice her skirt riding up her thighs as she slid onto the leather seat. I could feel myself harden against my zipper thinking about sliding my hand up the sensitive flesh of her inner thigh to find out if she obeyed me in removing her panties. Either way, I was in for a treat. I would punish her or reward her depending on what she did in that bathroom.

This girl was firmly under my skin. I just couldn't understand why I was feeling the things I was feeling. Wanting to continue this past tonight and her denial might drive me insane and that scared me in a way I wasn't ready to unpack.

Then when we went to leave the restaurant and George had held onto her hand I was feeling red hot jealousy. He had no right to touch her like that. I had lost myself and stormed out to the car needing the drive to cool my anger.

Shaking my head to clear the thoughts bouncing around, I continued driving quietly and tried to relax.

"I... uh..." she began by breaking the silence stretching out between us. I glanced at her and saw that, although she wanted to speak, she was very clearly hesitating.

I waited patiently letting her gather her thoughts. It wasn't like Sophie to fumble for words. It felt like it was taking forever to get back to the hotel. My thoughts were rampant with the things I wanted to do to her. Maybe she was feeling as anxious to get back as I was.

"I had asked if you wanted me to get a cab because you didn't seem very... I mean, you seem a bit upset."

"I'm not upset," I replied. My thoughts were bouncing from jealousy to raging lust for her.

"Not upset, per se," she said. "Just... I wasn't trying to pimp you out, as you put it."

"So you said earlier, and I have forgotten all about it. Why bring it up again?"

"Oh," she said, and I realized then that she might have just been trying to make conversation due to the silence. I was fine with the silence it helped me to think.

"Where did you meet that friend of yours?" I asked.

"We've known each other for a few years," she replied not really answering my question.

"She invited you out tonight?"

"Yes," she said sounding like she didn't really want to talk about it. I was fine with this as I didn't really want to think about her friend anymore either.

There was nothing left to say, and it made me wonder about our rapport when it didn't concern work outside of sex. I knew we worked well together, but what about everything else? She had always been a bit too bland and plain for my taste, but not anymore. Then again, it was as though her personality kept changing so I couldn't quite understand who I was dealing with.

I wondered if any of this mattered. Just a few days ago, I never gave her more than a moment's thought if it wasn't concerning work, and now she was running tracks through my mind.

Soon enough, we arrived back at the hotel and headed quietly toward the lobby. We were lucky because just then an elevator reached the ground floor and after the passengers disembarked, it was just us two that headed in. She went in front of me, and as a result, I couldn't take my eyes away from the shape of her figure. The dark red dress she had on hugged every curve and spread over her ass in such a way that it made my cock throb.

I knew what it felt like now, how soft and cushiony it

felt, and I wanted my cock gracing the space in between. The sight would be something for my memory, and as I leaned against the steel doors, I couldn't help but shut my eyes to imagine this.

Chapter 28
Scarlett

He was hard.

And it was not a little embarrassing bulge straining against his pants.

No, it was thick and heavy and for a moment it filled me with concern. What the fuck was he thinking about to make him so aroused?

I on the other hand was equally tormented because I was already soaking wet.

It had been from the first moment I laid eyes on him in the bar and every moment after that but with all the recent tension and the fact that we were heading to our rooms I was sure I would spontaneously combust if he even so much as touched me.

And there was the fact that I no longer had any underwear on. The space between my thighs was sticky and wet so I couldn't help but shift uncomfortable from time to time trying to soothe the ache.

He soon noticed. His eyes came open at my movements and then he glanced down to look at me.

"Are you okay?" he asked and I nodded. If he wasn't Sophie's boss and she needed a way to be able to still look him in the eye after this I would have told him exactly what was currently going through my head but I kept my mouth shut.

He had other plans.

"Come here," he said and I was a bit taken aback by the command and what was warranting it.

I wasn't afraid of him. His anger when we left the restaurant seemed to be gone. So, I complied.

Honestly, whatever he asked of me I would do. And so I went over and his hand wrapped around my waist pulling me the last few steps flush against him. I wanted to rub my body against him like a cat in heat but I refrained, barely.

I felt so fragile in this way, and it was almost intimidating. This was the part about this kind of intimacy that was always a challenge for me because in order for me to completely and wholly give myself over, I had to submit. My reaction to him made perfect sense to me. My heart was racing so hard that it felt like it wanted to rip out of my chest. As I stared into his gorgeous green eyes and his devastatingly handsome, gorgeously chiseled face, all I wanted to do was to submit to his virility, to his power, to the formidable man that he was in all realms.

He turned me around till my back was pressed against the elevator and then slowly, discreetly he began to lift my dress.

I was more excited than I was afraid. He curved his hands over my ass and grabbed it to shield me from any surveillance onlookers. He was big enough and much taller, so his frame covered mine too easily.

He didn't say a word as he continued to stare at me and it almost became too difficult to breathe.

The way he grabbed my ass and molded the plump mounds in his hands was amazing. I loved how they felt... how he made me feel. His touch was soft yet somewhat aggressive and with each second that passed by I felt my knees weakening.

I needed to kiss him. I stood on the tip of my toes, pleading... reaching.

At the corner of his lips, a somewhat arrogant smirk curved, but I didn't even give a fuck. He deserved it because I was leaking like a faucet. There was nothing sweet about the kiss. I had no intention or desire to be romantic. Instead, I wanted to devour and be devoured right back in return.

He was more than up to the task. He slid his tongue inside my mouth and sucked on mine, our dance was so sensual and so passionate that I couldn't get enough. And then he leaned even further down and grabbed me between my thighs.

He groaned into my mouth as his fingers slipped back and forth over my slick uncovered lips.

I couldn't help my needy moans as his fingers sank so smoothly into my soaking folds.

With the length of his middle finger, he stroked and rubbed on my clit and unbridled desire overwhelmed me like a wave.

I couldn't catch my breath as he switched between motion and pace, as though more than anything he enjoyed watching me hold on for dear life. And then he slid a finger inside of me, slowly, carefully, and I held my breath at the incredibly welcome intrusion.

I grabbed onto the railing while he leaned forward and buried his face in the crook of my neck. Somehow this felt so intimate and I loved every bit of it. Perhaps it was because we were in a confined space but whatever the reason was I was fucking having the time of my life. I spread my legs even wider giving him all the access he desired as he began to finger fuck me. He started off slow and then as though aware that we would soon be arriving on our floor his pace increased.

My spine turned to jelly at the onslaught of pleasure that wreaked through me but then he wrapped his arm around me to hold me in place and I shut my eyes in fevered excitement. He fingered me so hard and fast that my knees buckled and I completely lost my breath.

His strong arms held me up and my hand managed to find the back of his neck to hold on to.

This was so fucking unreal... all of it. The private jet, the mind-blowing sex, the gorgeous boss... I was thoroughly overwhelmed.

The ding from the elevator announced our arrival and he shifted to slip his foot in the door to stop it from closing all the way. With that taken care of he doubled down his efforts rubbing my clit till I was nearing completion and he didn't stop. Not until I was shuddering and my thighs were spasming. I came onto his hand and moaned so loud I was sure anyone in the hallway could hear.

He kissed me against my cheek and waited a few more seconds for me to recover and then he whispered into my ear.

"You good?" he asked as he stuck his middle finger in his mouth to suck clean. I was so enraptured I couldn't make a sound. He made me want to drop to my knees here in the elevator and suck on his cock the way he removed my juices from his finger. I wanted to get lost in him.

"Mhmm," I smiled and he moved away. I kept my grip on the railing and when I tried to take a step my legs wobbled on the stilettos I had on. It would be impossible to walk I did not doubt this so before he could realize what I was doing, I took my sandals off and staggered my way toward our doors.

Chapter 29
Lucien

I don't think I ever enjoyed being so intimate with a woman the way I loved it with her.

There was just something about her responsiveness to me that was so exhilarating and it brought my arousal to a fever pitch.

I enjoyed watching her, I realized as she basically wobbled toward our rooms.

I knew she needed help and previously I would have expected her to ask for it but this version of Sophie seemed to believe that she could lift the whole world with her bare hands. I was inclined to agree as I watched her arrive safely at her room and then begin to dig into her purse for her key card.

When she lost her hold on the purse altogether and it tumbled causing everything to spill out, I realized she wasn't quite as stable as she had purported.

She gazed down at the spilled contents as though in disbelief and then she looked up to meet my gaze as I arrived by her side.

I could see the frustration in her eyes, so before she lowered to gather everything I held her by the neck and kissed her. I just couldn't wait any longer, and neither could she because she wrapped her arms around my neck and sucked on my bottom lip. It was so fucking hot and I pinned her against the door and licked deep into her mouth.

The slide of our tongues against the other was hypnotic, and it all took me to a place that I never wanted to come back from.

By the time we parted, I could barely catch my breath as I looked at the lust radiating from her green eyes.

There was something wild in them yet gentle and sweet and it drew me to her like a moth to a flame. I felt exposed and took a step back and lowered to begin gathering her things. The purse had been tiny so there wasn't too much to retrieve. I picked up her cards, and her phone, then a small bottle. I bounced the bottle a couple of times in my palm as I rose to my feet and looked at her with my heart slamming against my ribs. My dick was throbbing at my zipper knowing where she wanted this evening to go. Her cheeks flamed as she watched the bottle bounce in my hand. She took a deep breath and met my gaze.

"I got in from a pharmacy before going to the restaurant."

I looked at the small transparent bottle of lube once again and nodded because things were about to get a bit more interesting.

"Open the door," I said as I handed her purse back minus the lube.

She headed into the room walking directly to the bathroom door and looked over her shoulder to me. I nodded and took a seat on the bed as I continued to stare at the bottle.

It took a few minutes of waiting before the door once again opened and staring at her to gauge her response I asked "Have you been fucked in the ass before?"

It was a very direct question and judging by the immediate pink flush of her cheeks maybe I could have been a bit more subtle in the way that I asked it. It didn't matter as the question was already out floating in the room.

I loved and appreciated her shyness and found it quite endearing but I grew impatient waiting for her to answer to my question.

"Have you?" I asked again and she leaned against the door to watch me.

Chapter 30
Scarlett

I was trying to act aloof and unaffected by his presence and everything he was doing to me, but it was way too difficult. I still couldn't walk right, but if I was to answer this awkward question, then I at least needed to look as nonchalant as possible. So, while depending on the door frame for support, even though I was acting like I didn't need it, I folded my arms across my chest and tried my best to stare him in the eyes.

I was going to respond and say the truth, but just as I opened my mouth to speak, I recalled that I had a twin sister who I was technically pretending to be and that even after I was gone, this man right here would think that what I was going to say was about her. My sexual escapade wasn't something I needed her to know about because even though we were identical twins, we didn't share that kind of rapport. I usually prefer to discuss things like this with friends, but with my sister, it was difficult because she was very vanilla and shy when it came to talking about sex making any conversation almost impossible.

"You don't have to answer if you don't want to," he said, and for a moment, I was glad for the reprieve. When his gaze turned disappointed, I decided there was no point in keeping this information to myself because if I did, I would be haunted by the fact he was probably assuming I was quite wild and even promiscuous.

It was none of his business whatsoever if this was indeed the case, but it bothered me that a wrong label would be ascribed to me, so I apologized to Sophie in my heart and replied.

"I haven't been..." damn. I began but yet couldn't continue with the brazen words I wanted to use.

I tried again, but the words still couldn't come out as smoothly as his had. It would probably sound more like a squeak, so I used something less hair-raising like a coward.

"Not really no," I replied, and internally I cringed.

"So you're curious?"

"I know what it feels like," I said, and his eyebrows slightly raised.

"Care to explain?"

I lifted my gaze to the ceiling and eventually found the words that I could say.

"Let's put it this way," I said. "Not all... c-cocks need to be real."

I definitely stuttered on that one, but as his brows seemed to rise even further, I figured that was the last thing on his mind. He kept watching me, and slowly, as his gaze narrowed, it seemed as though he was processing what I had said.

"So... toys?" he asked, and I couldn't help but smile. This was ultimately amusing because I couldn't understand how I was discussing this with my boss— I mean, Sophie's boss.

"Dildo," I said and he smiled as well. It was so beautiful and unexpected that my heart stopped dead in its tracks.

Since I'd met him and come to learn of his existence, I didn't think I had ever actually seen him fully and genuinely smile. Perhaps he had, but I hadn't noted it until now. His teeth were pearly white and perfectly straight making his gray eyes sparkle. I nearly couldn't breathe.

God, he was gorgeous. As I stared at him, I wondered if he knew this. He had to know, right? It wasn't truly impossible to look this way and not know it or at least not have heard of women chasing after him. I was internally becoming a complete mess. Still, I managed to compose myself to ask my next string of questions. Surprisingly, I was quite enjoying this conversation with him. The topic was wild, but I was sure that in his mind, as well as mine, we were both using it as a way and a reason to procrastinate. For me, it was because I wanted to extend the time we had together, as he had said it would probably not come again.

And so I decided not to hold back and let loose. "What about you?" I asked, and as soon as his face changed, I understood that I had probably just asked a really stupid question. He looked at me and then he cocked his head.

"Are you asking me if I've fucked someone in the ass or if I myself have been fucked in the ass before?"

At the very clear distinction, it was obvious, extremely obvious, which question I should follow; however, the little mischievous streak in me wanted to be just a tad bit playful. We had already come this far. But still, I tried my best to be as polite about it as possible.

"I assume the former is the case," I responded, and he smiled again.

"So you assume the former is the case, but you're also curious if the latter is also the case as well?" he inquired. I stared at him as he seemed to succinctly understand my mind, yet I couldn't quite bring myself to nod in response. And so, I diverted the question instead.

"You're my boss," I said. "I could never ask you that."

"Is that a fact?" he asked and rose to his feet.

I watched as his hands went to the buttons of his dress shirt and then he began to unbutton his shirt.

It was almost a struggle then to swallow but when I somehow managed to get the lump down my throat I returned my gaze to him.

"Yes," I said without even recalling the last question he had asked. What had he even asked me?

"The former is the case," he replied as he shrugged the shirt off and flung it aside.

He began to head toward me now, gorgeous intimidatingly built, and broad and I felt feeble; literally weak in my knees. I didn't dare move away from the door frame. Not till he arrived.

He didn't bother stopping or leaving room for me to breathe. It was as though he had no understanding whatsoever of the concept of personal space and wanted to be as close to me as possible.

He stared deep into my eyes and I tried my best to hold his gaze however the hard bulge of the front of his pants as well as the heat ricocheting off his body in waves was almost too much for me to bear. I needed to touch something... someone and it was him. I couldn't find the courage to hold on to him the way I wanted to. I instead held the side of his pants and hooked my fingers into the band.

His gaze lowered to them and then he embarrassed me outrightly without any response whatsoever.

"Still need support?" he asked.

He's your boss, he's your boss, I repeated in my mind over and over and as a result, I didn't even realize it when I shut my eyes. A few moments later I felt a hand hold my chin, gently warming and as a result, I opened my eyes and found he moved and his face was a mere few inches away from mine.

What are you thinking so hard about?" he asked, our noses slightly brushing against each other.

For a few seconds, absolutely nothing came to mind. Everything about him overwhelmed me to the point of incoherence, and so, in order to find a response, I had to lower my gaze to think.

"I keep having to remind myself that you're my boss," I replied. He lifted my chin once again, and before I could think another thought or say another word, he slanted his head and kissed me.

This taste, I was addicted to his taste, and it made me start to worry for the first time that when this was over, it would haunt me. Kissing Lucien Montgomery was heavenly. Like no one else, he knew how to be soft and gentle at the right time and how to be forceful on the other. He sucked on my lips and then soothed them with his tongue; he licked into my mouth with the most sensual, lush glides.

My hands moved from where they had been hooked in the side of his pants because I needed to hold onto him somehow, but all I met was his chest. So I lifted myself on the tip of my toes and boldly wrapped my arms around his shoulders. A few seconds after that, I was completely lifted off the ground. My legs had no choice but to wrap around his waist, causing my dress to ride all the way up, and by the end of it, I was practically naked. My sex grazed against his rock-hard abdomen, and I didn't hold back from writhing my hips, growing even wilder as the kiss became impossibly deeper.

I had never had sex this extensively before, and it made me wonder what kind of woman I'd be after tonight. Like a monkey, I refused to let him go, even when he pressed one knee to the bed, and this immensely amused me.

"We're gonna fall together," he said, but I just couldn't stop.

"Mn," I replied, but his smile eventually allowed him to pull away. He looked into my eyes then, and for a second, my heart squeezed in my chest. I wondered about who he really saw because it seemed as though something curious had flashed through his pupils, as though he could see that I wasn't Sophie. I was someone else.

This worried me, but at the same time, a certain hope and even thrill filled me at the thought that he could possibly realize that I wasn't my twin. "Let go," he said, and once again, I was smacked against the side of my head and pulled back to reality. I did and plopped down onto the bed. I was suddenly so exhausted and more than ready to hand over the complete reins to him, so I didn't say a word.

He pulled my dress up my body, and I helped pull it from my head. Afterwards, I was left wearing just my bra, and as I watched him take in my body, I realized that I no longer felt painfully self-conscious. It was the admiration I saw in his eyes and the appreciation. I could see and feel his desire for me in every way, and it left me heady with emotion. He began to kiss his way down my neck, and I shut my eyes to savor it all. His lips moved across my shoulders, my chest, to my breasts, as though he was intent on worshipping every part of me. I had no complaints. This, I could tell, would be slower but much more intense than before, and I shivered with excitement. There was time; we had time, and so I turned my brain off and gave in completely to the feeling.

Chapter 31

Lucien

Her complete submission to me was what I realized I loved the most about being so intimate with her. It was in the way she reacted and shuddered ever so slightly in my arms, as though she couldn't get enough and as though she couldn't contain the sensations coursing through her body. I wondered if this chemistry between us was because we had known each other for so long. Hence, there were little to no secrets, at least on my part. But I couldn't help but realize that I didn't know much about her. Beyond work and the services she efficiently provided for me, at least most of the time, I knew nothing else. And now, as I explored every part of her body, it was all I could think about.

My interest in every part of her was growing like a fire, and as a result, so was my restlessness. Somehow, I managed to tame it all and live in the moment despite the almost desperate urge to take a thousand premature steps in this new direction I was quickly discovering I absolutely loved.

My only hope now, though, was that later down the line, neither of us, for any reason, would regret it.

Lifting myself from the bed, I grabbed at the belt of my slacks and began to unfasten it. She opened her eyes then and stared up at me. Her dark, gorgeous hair was spread out across the white sheets, and her lips were plump and swollen from the kisses. As I undressed myself, a fierce possessiveness came over me. I never wanted her to be with anyone else, I realized, for any reason. It didn't mean I was ready for a relationship. I hadn't considered this in so long and didn't know if it was something that my current lifestyle could contain. But when I thought about the fact that she was my assistant and that our lives were more or less intertwined, I couldn't help but wonder if I had struck gold.

There were some things I needed to know, so after throwing my jeans aside and going to retrieve the small bottle of lube that had fallen out of her purse, I returned ready with my first intrusive question: "Why did you and your fiancé break up?" I asked as I lowered back onto the bed.

She seemed a little startled at this question, but before she could make too much of it, I kissed her once again and turned her around. She rested her head on the bed, and I couldn't help but appreciate the arc of her back and the smoothness and luster of her skin. She smelled divine, and I couldn't help but linger against it as I pressed kisses down the curve of her spine.

"I love your perfume," I couldn't help but comment, and I could feel her smile from beneath.

"Thank you, and I love yours as well. It has this tobacco and spicy feel that I adore. It's incredibly attractive."

This amused me because it was as though she was fishing for compliments. "You did well by purchasing it," I said. "I like it as well. I didn't care much at the beginning, but I've gotten quite used to it."

At this statement, I could feel her frame go momentarily stiff, and I wondered why. I was just kissing down the curve of her gorgeous ass and molding the mound in one hand, so I wondered if perhaps she was tensing due to the upcoming act.

"Are you alright?" I asked.

"Yeah, of course," and she loosened up once again.

"You know you can tell me to stop?" I asked, and she nodded.

"Keep going," she said, and I obliged.

I spread her legs apart, beginning from her soaked sex, and then I licked my way up to the crevice between her ass cheeks. She moaned and gasped lightly, and by the time I was coaxing her open with the lube, I could see the goose-bumps that had broken out all over her skin.

"Excited or worried?" I asked once more as I coated my cock as well.

"Definitely excited," she said. "It took a little getting used to at first, but after the awkward stage was passed, I think I've had my strongest orgasms from this. Well, strongest until earlier today."

This made me smile as I stroked my cock and began to nudge her opening with it. "You are the master of flattery," I said, and she rewarded me with a long, satisfied moan. I took my time, and by the time my head was in, I realized that she truly hadn't been kidding about being used to this.

"Alright?" I asked, and she nodded. I waited for her to use her voice to tell me what she wanted.

"Please don't stop," she managed to gasp, and I didn't need to be told twice. I could barely contain my excitement, but I forced myself to go slow, wanting all of this to last as long as possible. I inched forward with every passing second, and soon enough, I hit the end of her. Watching her hole encircle and grip my glistening length so tightly was almost enough to make me completely lose control.

"Ah, Lucien," she gasped. "Oh God, that feels good."

My eyes were shut as I savored the grip, and then without preamble, I began to move. The lure of this to me was possessing her in every possible way, and this indeed was the ultimate thrill. I wished, though, that she had one of her rubber friends as well because I wanted to bring her to the extreme brink and watch her fall spectacularly apart.

"If we ever get another go at this, then you're permitted to bring in one of your rubber friends," I replied. "I'd love nothing more than to watch every part of you be filled."

Despite how overtaken she was by pleasure and sensation, she still managed to respond. "That would be insane," she breathed. "And yes, definitely."

This made me smile, but all of that light-heartedness was soon completely wiped out as we were both sucked in even deeper into the throes of pleasure. Grabbing both cheeks of her ass, I lifted her hips lightly off the bed to fuck into her at just the right angle, and she was all too willing to comply. She was much louder in this position. She was so greedy for more, greedy for a faster pace that she eventually moved up to her knees and pleaded with me to give her even more.

"You're being too careful," she said. "I need... harder... make me forget my name... please."

Her pleas were their own set of aphrodisiacs to my ears, and I was more than willing to oblige this request. As soon as I slid into her again, I held nothing back. We changed positions several times, and by the time we both came to completion, she was a mumbling mess, and my vision was a complete blur.

Still, we could feel and sense each other as we collapsed side by side onto the bed. I could feel the heat ricocheting off her body as she tried to catch her breath, and the dampness all over was beautifully erotic. This was sure to bring our night to an end; however, I found that I couldn't leave. I couldn't see any reason to, so I just pulled her with me toward the pillows and wrapped her tightly in my arms. There was no protest as we both tried to recover and in very little time, we were both fast asleep.

Chapter 32
Scarlett

The next morning, I woke up to the sound of water running. This was the only thing I could compute. Everything seemed unfamiliar—the room I was in with its beige decor and accents, and the extremely soft and warm bed which felt nearly impossible to get out of.

The details of everything began to come to mind. I was in the Rotz Hotel in London, and I had fallen asleep in my boss's arms. I immediately sat up then, my eyes quite wide with wonder. Everything felt like a simulation, as though I was in this sort of unreal bubble that was about to burst at any time, and it made me quite scared.

The continued sound of running water drifted over once again, and it made me realize that he was in my shower. His room was next door, so most definitely he could have left to take a shower, but he'd preferred to use mine and I couldn't understand why. Perhaps it was because he felt lazy afterwards and didn't want to switch rooms, or perhaps it was because he wanted to see me, and taking a shower here was sure to wake me up.

"Well, mission accomplished." I wrapped the blanket around me like a toga and got up because I was reminded as well that I was his personal assistant and that I had work to do concerning our departure. He still hadn't given me any specific date, after all the business we came here to handle had been concluded. I needed to schedule our flight back with his jet, so I had to ask him if he was ready to go.

I considered, waiting until he was out, but after all we had done the previous evening, I didn't think it would be a problem. Still, I knocked as the water turned off, and a few seconds later, the door was pulled open.

It was all steam and virile male within, and for a few moments, I completely forgot what I had come here to ask him.

"Everything alright?" He asked, and my gaze went to his damp dark hair pushed away from his face.

"I, uh..." I began. "I just wanted to know your itinerary for the day and if you were going to fly back to New York or remain in London for a bit."

"Not stay here," he promptly replied. "It tends to immediately lose its charm if you do."

He headed out, and I felt the sheet I had thankfully but way too casually around myself start to slip. He was covered decently enough with a towel, and as I looked behind at the used shower, I couldn't help but lament the fact that I hadn't woken up early enough to join him in there.

"Alright, I'll get it arranged," I said. "What time should we be leaving? Sir?"

"Eleven," he replied, and I watched as he began to gather his clothes. It meant he had simply just showered here out of convenience. I thought he'd at least kiss me. I wanted him to at least kiss me, but this wasn't going to be the case, so I got my head out of the clouds and back to reality.

"Get ready," he said. "Meet me downstairs for breakfast?"

He turned, but I was staring at him so woefully and sadly that I didn't realize he was talking to me and waiting for a response.

"Sophie?" he called, and I was a bit startled by the strange name.

"Yeah?"

"Downstairs? Breakfast?"

"Of course, sir," I said, and the corners of his lips lifted slightly in a grin at me. I watched him exit the room and then sighed. I wanted to return to bed, but I knew if I did, it would be impossible to get up again, so I just found my purse to retrieve my phone and headed into the bathroom.

By the time I plugged it in and turned it on, I was quite startled to see the influx of messages that arrived, especially when I found out they were from Sophie and for several different reasons. She was usually so calm, but in my brief absence, she seemed to have had a mental breakdown, a panic attack, and an intervention as well. Then she had a resolution and, in the end, decided that threatening me for not responding to all of this was indeed the way to go.

Sighing, I read through all her messages as I sat on the toilet and began to address them.

Me: So after all this, you decided that villainy was the way to go?

She responded almost immediately, but this time with true concern.

Sophie: What happened to you? You completely went off the grid.

Me: My phone died.

Sophie: How the hell can your phone die when you're in a foreign country with your boss? How are you working?

Me: It was already midnight. Plus, I was with said boss. Trust me, whatever work needed to be done was done.

Sophie: Oh God! You two did it again, didn't you?

I didn't respond because it would just further enhance her mental spiral downward.

Sophie: Wow! Your silence says it all. Or are you no longer with your phone again? Like how does that even work?

Me: I need to shower and get ready to leave. We can talk when I get back.

Sophie: No, no, no! I have a lot of thoughts.

Me: Yes, you do, and I read them.

I giggled. She was too easy to get wound up.

Sophie: And you're not concerned? Jerald reached out to me again last night. He wanted to come over.

Me: And did you let him?

I already knew the answer because of course she did. There was no way she was going to be able to say no to him.

Sophie: Yes, I did.

Me: And…

Sophie: I don't know. He still doesn't seem to be in the right headspace.

Me: What exactly did he say?

Sophie: He wanted to know how I was faring, and he wanted to apologize.

Me: But he didn't want to repair your relationship?

Sophie: He didn't allude to that.

Me: So basically, he wanted free sex because he's gone out into the world and seen that it's not as easy as he'd been getting it earlier.

She didn't respond, and I got up.

Sophie: You're quite abrasive and judgmental for someone sleeping with my boss not even three days into the job.

Me: We know what we are. So no crime is being committed against anyone. Your ex-fiancé, on the other hand…

Sophie: Just stop, I don't want to get into it over text.

Me: Fine, I need to go anyway. There's too much to do in preparation to leave. Also, I need to contact the pilot.

Sophie: You have his details, right?

Me: Yeah, I do. I'll contact him now, as well

as the flight attendant. They're usually on standby when he goes on trips like this, right?

Sophie: Always.

Me: Alright, talk later.

Sophie: No, wait, one more thing, something occurred to me as well.

Me: What?

Sophie: Something extremely devastating and moronic.

I groaned, wondering why I had such a drama queen for a sister.

Me: What?

Sophie: How the hell am I going to explain the sudden change in my hair when I get back in a week?

She had a very valid point. We'd only thought of switching to my style not when it was time for her to come back and still have the same style.

Me: Uh... well he wont believe it was a wig. lol

Sophie: NOT FUNNY! I'm screwed, aren't I?

I couldn't help but laugh.

Me: Don't worry. We'll work something out. Best-case scenario you change your hair.

Sophie: And look like you?

Me: Looking like me got me your boss, and I do look like you naturally, unfortunately.

She sent me an angry emoji, and then finally, the texting for the morning came to an end.

Chapter 33
Lucien

I was looking forward to seeing her. She was a bit late, and although there hadn't been a set time to come down, I had expected her to be down early enough to join me for breakfast. But now, breakfast was done, and yet she was nowhere in sight. I was growing impatient, especially as we were set to leave in a few minutes, so I picked up my phone and called her.

"Hello, sir?" she greeted, her voice soft and airy through the receiver. I shut my eyes as I savored it.

"Where are you?" I asked. "Aren't we running late?"

"We aren't," she replied, "and I'm in the lobby. I came to pick up your room key so I could handle your luggage and cross-check your room for you."

"No need," I said. "It's already done. I'm down here with my luggage."

"Oh, alright. The breakfast bar?" she asked.

"Yes, the breakfast bar," I replied.

"Alright, sir, I'll be right there. Oh, I think I see you." I lifted my gaze then and found her indeed waving. Then, as though she realized what she was doing and deemed it inappropriate, she put her hand down and then began to walk over. I ended the call and put the phone away.

I tried not to watch her as she headed over, but it was impossible not to as I took in the high-waisted jeans that she had on, molded to her body, and the accompanying tight corset top, I couldn't help but appreciate just how gorgeous she was. The top had red roses and flowers on it, and her lips were painted a soft pink. Half of her hair was tied backwards, and all in all, she was almost breathtaking to behold.

She kept her expression stoic as she came over to me, but in the end, she let out a soft smile when our gazes eventually met.

"I'm sorry for keeping you waiting, sir," she said. "We can leave."

"Eat first," I said. "We still have time."

"Oh," she said and looked around. "Alright," she replied and left her luggage with me.

A little while later, she returned with a plate. It wasn't full, and I couldn't tell if it was because she was a picky eater or that she just wanted to be done as quickly as possible. On her plate were a sausage, some scrambled eggs, toast, and fruit, and that was it. I decided to refrain from encouraging her to eat more as there would be an in-flight meal on the plane, so there was no need to worry.

At the thought, I was struck with why I was worried. I'd never really given much thought to her well-being in the past, but now... and as I watched her, I realized that I cared. She wasn't just my assistant anymore, but someone whose welfare I was concerned about, and I didn't know how exactly to feel about this.

Our agreement had officially come to an end. Any further personal relations were not ideal; however, there was one question I needed an answer to. I was certain I had asked it the previous night, but I couldn't quite remember getting a response for it.

"Why did you and your fiancé break up?" I asked, and her fork stopped midway to her mouth. This, along with her startled expression, would have been quite amusing if I wasn't dead serious and intent on receiving an answer this time around.

"Uh..." she said as she lowered her hand and swallowed what she was already chewing. "You know," she said, "the usual differences."

"What exactly were they?" I asked, and she seemed reluctant to answer. I knew that I was being rather forceful, and so I decided to give her a break, but just before I turned away, she finally responded.

"He lost his mom a few months back," she said. I didn't see what that had to do with anything, and I waited for her to give me more context. Which didn't come.

"He couldn't lean on you?" I asked, and her brows shot up.

"Um... no," she said. "That wasn't it. He just... he felt a bit lost and needed to find his way."

At this, I frowned. "So you two will get back together?"

She stared at me as though contemplating her answer, and I found I held my breath as well, waiting. I truly wondered what she would say, and for the first time in a very long while, I realized just how nervous I was for a response.

Before she could give it either way, a phone began to ring. I didn't care.

I needed her to answer the questions, but then she moved her gaze from mine, and I realized that it was her phone.

"Hello," she answered and listened.

I closed the iPad I had been reading from and got ready to leave.

"Our car's here, sir," she said, and I nodded.

I guess it was for the best that our agreement had truly come to an end. I didn't want to lose her as a secretary by even considering taking things more deeply. We both had fun, but I accepted now that it was the end, so I adjusted my mentality appropriately. Afterwards, we were driven to the airport, and in little time, we were back in the air and on our way to New York. I'd slept wonderfully the previous night, much better than I had in a long time, and so I didn't need the additional rest. I did need the distance from her to rest and prepare myself to focus on immediately getting to work the moment we returned.

Chapter 34
Scarlett

I had never been more excited to get home before, but that was until I returned and opened my door. The apartment, in my haste to leave the previous day, had been turned into a complete dump, and so now I was left standing at the door and staring at a completely disgusting-looking space. I needed peace and quiet, and after going into my bedroom and seeing that the clutter was worse, I considered going to a hotel until I remembered that I had a twin who technically owed me. I set my things down in the living room, pulled out my phone, and dialed her.

"I need to sleep," I told her. "Come over and help me clean."

"What?" she asked. "And you're back!"

"Sophie, I'm serious."

"Just come here if your place is dirty. Lucky for you, I have time on my hands, so I've basically done nothing but clean."

I wasn't surprised this was her response, so I sighed, considered her offer, and was out of the door in no time. I took a cab straight to her place, and in less than an hour, I was knocking on a different door across the city. When she finally opened the door I realized how happy and eager I'd been to see her. All through our communication on the phone, she had seemed pretty fine to me, and even sometimes more chirpy and friendly than normal on account of all the free time I had bought her. But now, face to face, I realized that I could truly see how she was faring.

I studied her face and couldn't help but notice that she seemed a bit thinner than usual. I didn't know if that was on purpose or if it was just that she was forgetting to eat.

"Hello, whore?" she greeted, and just like that, I didn't give a fuck if she was going to starve herself to death; better that there was only one of us in this world than two. Her existence was already causing more problems than I wanted to handle. And so I threw my luggage at her and walked in.

"I want chicken soup," I told her and headed straight over to her bean bag by the corner. Her apartment was green and yellow and filled with soft colors. It was pleasing to the eye but much too girly for my taste. That white bean bag in the corner, however, was my favorite thing here. In short, it was even more comfortable than her bed, so I collapsed into it, grabbed her blanket, and pulled it over my head.

"Chicken soup," I repeated at the silence, knowing that she was just standing noisily and watching me.

"I'm not your assistant, ma'am," she whined even as I heard her go over to the kitchen, and so I smiled and took my bra off, wishing I had the strength to take my shoes and socks off as well.

I wasn't tired, but I had to sleep if only to forget just

how cold and awkward the plane ride with Lucien had been. He hadn't been warm but neither had he been impolite either and I knew enough about how guys could become distant after sleeping with you, but this... this bothered me a lot more than it should have. I didn't need to search too deeply for the reason because it was clear to me. He was handsome, rich, and fucked like a god – basically, a dream I never even imagined I had, until now.

"So," she called out from her kitchen. "How was London and my boss?"

I was a bit startled at hearing her call him her boss, even though that was exactly what he was to her.

"His name's Lucien," I said, and she glanced back at me.

"You're on a first-name basis with him now?"

I was surprised to hear this. "You aren't?"

"I mean, I am, but if I can avoid it, I don't call him by his name at all. And you'll find out if you try that this is incredibly easy."

She was right in that it wasn't very difficult to omit someone's name when trying to avoid the awkwardness of a title.

"So..." she said, pulling me back to the present. "How was it?"

"There's no new development from what I told you back in London," I replied.

She had her back to me, and the tap slightly ran to fill the can to make the soup for me. She dumped it into the pan and turned the stove on. Afterwards, she came over and sat on the couch right next to the bean bag.

A few seconds later, the blanket that I had buried myself under was being pulled away. I groaned, but knowing she wouldn't relent and she wanted some kind of reassurance, I turned and faced her.

"What is it?" I asked.

"Are you alright?" she asked, and I was a bit surprised at her question.

"What do you mean?"

"I know I've harassed you a lot these past few days. But I was thinking today about how you are suddenly thrust into all this for my sake. I know it's been very difficult and stressful, so I'm concerned if you're okay."

It wasn't strange hearing her concerned and caring because it was just in her personality, but it was a bit startling because she had been less of all of the above these last few days.

"I'm fine," I replied and shut my eyes once again. "You're the one that I should be asking."

"I'm fine," she replied. "It's just that my eyes are a bit clearer now."

"What do you mean?" I asked.

"The more time I spend with myself now, the more I realize that I truly neglected myself and my well-being for so long, and it just makes me feel so sad.

"You put him at the center of your world for too long, right?" I asked, and she sighed.

"I didn't put him there; time put him there. I was happy about it for a while, and I'm not complaining, but I just realized now how much of myself I'd ignored and thrown away just so that I could be who he thought he wanted. And then when he really needed someone, I guess he realized that what he had more or less molded me into wasn't what he needed. I just feel used and discarded, and I guess it's my fault for picking a weak man."

"It's not your fault," I told her. "You didn't choose a weak man. You chose someone that you loved, and he turned out to be weak. Why should any of the blame come on you for that?"

At this, she sighed and nodded. "I know," she said. "Some relationships work out and most just run their course, but in this case, it hurts. I'm doing better though, and when he came by yesterday, I was so angry that I was able to tell him no. He still didn't know what he wanted, but he thought I would be easy – the bastard – and so he came over."

"Complete..." I said but didn't complete the insult. She gave me a look, then she sighed.

"Now about you and my boss."

"Again?" I complained, and she smiled.

"Yes, again. Another reason for my crippling anxiety, and while I still cannot rest, is that you're setting the bar for a difficult arrangement that I don't necessarily want any part in by the time you leave."

"Yeah," I replied, my heart saddened as the reminder of the stark difference between the way we'd interacted the previous night and then later on the plane. "You don't have to worry about any of that. We're done. I mean, it's done."

She seemed quite concerned about this as well. "Did you two... was there a fight or something?"

"No, there wasn't," I replied. However, she didn't seem like she believed me, which was amusing. "There truly wasn't," I told her. "We agreed on one night, and we both stuck to that agreement, so now it's done."

"Oh, okay," she told me and looked toward our boiling chicken soup on the stove in the distance.

"You'll tell me, though, if there was any lingering awkwardness. I really don't want to return to work and have to find out the hard way that he can't look me in the eye any longer."

This made me laugh too loud. "Not Lucien," I replied. "Never him. He'll look you dead in the eye no matter what and never cower."

"Yeah, you're right," she said and got up. "You still haven't told me how we are going to resolve the issue about our hair being different."

"We still have a few more days," I told her. "We'll figure something out before then."

"Sure," she replied and returned to the kitchen.

Chapter 35
Lucien

There had never been quite a reason in all the years I'd been working for me to either dread or look forward to going to the office. No challenge had ever seemed insurmountable enough to cause me any sort of dread, but I did find that as I headed over today I felt both emotions strongly.

Unless I was the only one thinking of things more than was necessary, I couldn't help but wonder how we were going to navigate our way in the light of this new route in our relationship.

We'd seen every part of each other's body completely naked, fucked till we'd both fallen asleep in the other's arms and yet I was supposed to act like none of that mattered and simply just treat her as my personal assistant?

It was apparent to me now that my proposition had made absolutely no sense, even though back then, it seemed like a brilliant idea.

The thing is that I had ex-girlfriends in the past that I'd never had a problem with seeing or working with afterward, therefore this was the same logic and expectation I had applied for Sophie. I was frustrated by my sudden lack of emotional self-control.

She arrived late, which was unusual because she usually arrived before I got there. So when I headed past her desk and into my office and she was nowhere to be found, I was a bit surprised.

I continued with my morning until work officially began and I heard a knock on the door. I didn't respond but she knew to come in and the handle was pulled down and she walked in.

"Good morning, sir," she greeted softly as she headed over, and all I sent over was a nod that I hoped she'd catch.

"Schedule highlights for today," she said as she placed a clipboard containing my highlights by my side, and then she stood back for a moment.

I glanced at it to confirm that there were no surprises. However, one new item, in particular, caught my eye.

"We're meeting Gregory?" I asked and looked up then to meet her gaze.

I was struck by how familiar she seemed. First of all, she looked absolutely gorgeous as she usually did, but today it was as though she had softened everything about her. Her makeup was minimal and her cheeks flushed, as for attire she had on a light pink corseted top and a dark corduroy skirt that went all the way down past her knees to her calves.

I didn't need it to be shorter to appreciate her figure since the fabric was nearly glued to her skin, and the silhouette it formed reminded me of the exciting memories we shared.

"Yes, sir," I noted her response.

In an instant, I lost interest in the folder in my hand, so I leaned back against the chair to watch her.

"Is he coming over to the office? Have you communicated this with the investment team?"

"Yes, sir, I have," she replied. "However, from what I was able to gather, it didn't seem as though he would be coming to the office just yet."

"What do you mean?" I asked.

"He's suggested to have lunch together for a friendly discussion and a continuation of where you two stopped yesterday in London."

"Oh," I said, not surprised this was the route he was going to take.

There was something about him that I disliked. It always put me on edge, so at this announcement, I decided to work hand in hand with the team to ensure that there were no grounds for him to schedule another casual meeting like this again.

"Call him and change the meeting time to two," I replied. "Deny his request and make up some reason why. I have another client to attend to or something."

She looked at the schedule once again, as though wondering whether she had missed something, and I quickly explained.

"I want to bring his ego down a notch," I told her. "Otherwise, he will be a complete nightmare to work with, especially for the staff."

At this, she nodded, her lips slightly parting to form an 'oh' at the intentional strategy, and then she nodded.

I recalled that she had seemed particularly uncomfortable with Gregory the last time we had met, so I wanted to ask her if this remained the case.

I stopped myself because, as she turned around to leave, I reminded myself that this was something I would have never done before our little trip to London. It wasn't my duty to regulate the attention she received from a client; however, I made the promise to myself that if there were any unfortunate actions, then I would immediately step in.

Chapter 36
Scarlett

"Ugh," that damn Gregory, I couldn't help but mutter under my breath as I exited the office and returned to my desk. I'd thought by now that I would be able to see things a bit more neutrally and perhaps even realize that I had overreacted that night at the bar when he'd held my hand, however, I soon found that this was not the case at all.

Still, I continued with my work, which today was mainly occurring between floors as I had to work along with the investment team to ensure that all he needed for his meetings throughout the day was available. Just before noon, I was incredibly famished and hated to wait for a bit to eat when I realized that we would be leaving soon anyway to meet with Gregory. So, I simply munched on the leftover apple pie that Sophie had made the previous evening.

She may have broken up with Jerald, but I was so incredibly glad that regardless, his amazing baking skills had rubbed off on her because every single bite of the pie melted in my mouth in a way that nearly made my eyes roll into the back of my head.

I had decided to cut down on my eating so that I could get into my usual schedule of exercising, which I hadn't been able to do so far with the recent life changes and travel obligations. As I tasted this, I understood clearly now that the more contact I had with her, the more this would be a challenge.

With the pie in my mouth, I started pulling out my phone and immediately began to text her when suddenly the door to his office was opened and he stepped out. I looked up then and instantly rose to my feet, trying my best to halt my chewing in the process. His secretary smiled at me in amusement, and this reaction was what drew Lucien's attention to me, or so I thought.

He watched me as I licked my lips, and I wondered what he would say or if he would even say anything at all. To my surprise, however, he walked over to my desk, and his gaze looked down at the remaining piece of pie I had on my plate.

"Are you having this because we're having lunch late today?" He asked, and I nodded, but then I shook my head. "Not really. It's a snack that I would have had either way at some point; I'm just now getting the time."

"Oh," he said, and at his lingering gaze, I recalled that he hadn't eaten anything at all. Before I could stop myself, I offered it to him.

"Would you like to try some? It's pretty good and—"

I stopped myself midway. He gazed deeply into my eyes, and that sense of familiarity that I had already felt with him back in London seemed to come right back.

"And what?" he asked, wondering if this was normal at all, that he was questioning me further about this. I truly had expected him to reject me and be on his way.

"My sister ab-" I stopped myself once again. He cocked his head in wait, and true horror filled my eyes. "Um..." I wondered if it would be strange to him that I took away the sister bit and replaced it with myself. However, he soon solved this dilemma for me.

"Your sister what?" He asked, and I sighed internally. Fuck! Me and my big fucking mouth.

"My sister baked it fresh this morning," I said, and he nodded.

"Sure, I'd like to."

He held out his hand, and I handed over a piece. However, he didn't receive it. "I don't want to touch it," he said and instead leaned his head forward. My heart nearly collapsed in my chest. He was... asking me to feed it to him?

I stared at him in shock while he frowned, most definitely because I was wasting time. "Changed your mind?" he asked. "A small piece will do," he said, and I came back to my senses.

"Sure, sir," I added and slipped it into his mouth.

He took a bite, and then he chewed as though tasting wine, judging its taste. "It's good," he said. "But too sweet."

I didn't know what to say to this, so I nodded and returned the rest of it to my plate. "I'm heading to my apartment," he said. "Come with me."

"Oh," my eyes widened with alarm.

"Elena is back, and I want to see her before we head over to the meeting since I have some free time now."

I immediately panicked because I had no clue who

Elena was. "Oh, of course, sir," I said, shut the dessert box, and grabbed my purse.

When his car arrived and I got into the back seat with him, I immediately pulled out my phone from my purse and texted Sophie. My only desperate prayer was that she wouldn't be having a lazy afternoon nap or something and completely ignore my message.

Me: Who's Elena?!

I asked and put the phone away so he wouldn't see my screen by accident.

Ten minutes later, and just a few till we arrived at his apartment, she still hadn't responded. So, the moment we got out and began to head in, I stayed a little distance away from him and called her. It continuously rang, and it was just when we arrived in the elevator, and the doors shut close that she eventually picked up.

I was so furious, but I managed to keep my temper under wraps on account of the man who was right by my side. "Did you see my message?" I asked, however, by her loud yawn, it was very obvious to me that I had been right about her lazing away the afternoon when I dealt with pressure on all sides from her end.

"Um... yeah, of course, that's my boss's sister." she sighed.

I lowered my voice even further. "Anything I should know?" I asked.

"Um... yeah. We're definitely going to be caught now," she said, and my frown deepened.

"Aren't you a bit casual about that statement?" I grit my teeth, but she sounded amused. Truly amused.

"I'm friends with her like we're close. She's twenty now,

but we met when she was seventeen, so we kind of developed an affinity. You're awkward around people you meet for the first time, so if you act all bubbly and familiar with her, she's going to ask if something is wrong and then, of course, some references to our past conversations. She's currently studying engineering at UCLA and comes up here when she wants a reprieve with her brother."

Only some of this was useful information, but much more was needed. "And..?" I asked, grateful when the elevator dinged open, and Lucien stepped out. I stepped out as well but gave some space between me and him so that I could speak freely.

"What else?"

"Well, she loves books, novels, mostly romance, and I love them as well, so we usually catch up on whatever I've been reading whenever we meet.

"What?" I asked irritated. "People still read books? What about movies and shows and the rest?"

"You're so dull and condescending," she said, and I let out a sigh.

"Okay, give me a lowdown on what books are trending or what book have you read and would have recommended to her."

"Um, I haven't read in months," she said. "Depression at my impending breakup."

"So what do I tell her?"

"That should suffice." she said, "and it will prevent you from making mistakes. She'll ask about some changes she sees in you because she's very observant, and when she does, tell her that you just broke up with your fiancé and that you haven't been in the mood to read anything. She'll probably be the one, then, to recommend some stories to you, and when she does, please pay attention. I actually want to get back into reading now that I seemingly have all the time in the world."

At her words, I couldn't help but roll my eyes, but just as I did, my gaze met Lucien's. He frowned slightly at my expression, and I was immediately startled enough to yank the phone from my ear. I apologized unintelligibly as I arrived by the door with him wondering why he was waiting.

He stared at me, and I stared back, and I was so confused. All of this stress made me feel as though I was losing hair, and for a moment, I almost wanted to reach up to pull the falling strands I was sure to find off my scalp.

"The key?" He said. "You don't have my key card?"

My heart fell into my stomach. "Uh... no. I don't think so."

I instantly began to look into my purse, hoping that I would find it, and in my haste, once again all of its contents spilled from it. It spread all across the floor, and for a moment, I just shut my eyes, cursing Sophie all the way. This wasn't her fault, but I needed someone to blame or else I was going to go crazy.

"What's wrong with you these days?" I heard Lucien comment, however, he was quite close to my ear, so I turned. This brought our faces so close together that I was sure my nose brushed his.

We stilled then and looked at each other. However, my brain was completely blank; I couldn't think of anything to do or say after that. He stared at me, cocking his head, and then he smiled. His gaze, however, lowered to my lips, and I, for sure, didn't miss the hunger that I found in them. Suddenly, the lock of his apartment door seemed to shift, and just like that, the door was pulled open.

"Lucien!" A girl nearly half screamed, and he instantly shot up to his feet. Before my eyes, she jumped into his arms while I still remained on my knees on the carpet, watching them with awe. She placed a big fat kiss on his cheek, and then she turned her attention to me.

"Sophie," she squealed again, and almost afraid that she would do the same thing and also jump on me for a hug, I remained in my position on the floor.

"What are you doing?" she asked. "Why are you on the floor? Lucien, are you bullying her again?" He gave me one more glance, shook his head, and continued on his way into the apartment.

I watched him leave, and then all I could do was smile up at her.

"You can't say that to my boss. I think he pays me enough to bully me."

"Oh," she said, her eyes going across my face as though she didn't hear a single word of what I had just said. "You look different. Like very different."

I immediately lowered my gaze then and began to gather my things.

"It's the hair," I said and smiled at her. "How are you? How's UCLA?"

She frowned then as she cocked her head, and then she began to move around me as though studying me.

"Your voice is different, and your body? What happened? I saw you like a month ago."

"A lot has happened," I said and immediately moved

into the apartment, needing to get out from under her scrutiny.

She followed, but once again, my amazement at his apartment momentarily distracted me from my concern that she was seeing way too much of a difference between me and Sophie. The views were astounding, and as I watched Lucien head over to the refrigerator, I wondered how he ever left this place.

I turned around then to look at Elena, who was still looking at me, but this time around, she was smiling.

"What's new?" she asked as she headed over to the kitchen to join her brother.

I tried to watch them both and realized that, though they appeared casual, they were both just staring blatantly at me as though watching and assessing. It was very disconcerting.

"Nothing much," I realized. "Just busy as always."

"Lucien told me you two went to London yesterday, yet you couldn't even stay for an extra day to rest. I can't believe it. Did you at least get me a gift?"

"Uh..." I was extremely lost then, and her eyes narrowed at me, and then they widened. "You forgot my birthday?"

"Uh... holy shit."

At this, she laughed out loud, and when my gaze moved to Lucien, I thought for a moment that I saw the corner of his lips tilt as well.

"We only have a few more minutes," he said as he turned to his sister. "You can use the jet for five days. You'll be chaperoned by the flight attendant, and you must listen to him."

"For Pete's sake, I'm twenty years old, not fifteen. I don't need to be chaperoned."

"Whatever," he said. "I'm not sending your careless self off to an island in God knows where without security."

"Security?" she shrieked.

"Wait, you just said chaperone. Minimal watching by your flight attendant. Why the hell are you talking about security?

"If you want to go on your terms, then fly economy, but if you're leeching off me, then you have to stick to my rules."

"You're the worst," she muttered under her breath, and I couldn't help but smile. Elena, of course, didn't miss it. "See, Sophie thinks so."

Her brother ignored us both, but I nodded behind his back and agreed with her.

"I'll head up to open the safe for you. Remember to lock it when you're done. Your passport and emergency cash are in there."

"Sure," she said and smiled at him. He headed up the stairs then, and I watched him go. However, so much had happened within the space of just a few hours that I truly needed to sit down, so I headed over to the counter and took my seat.

She stared at me, a smile on her face. However, there was something in her smile that made me extremely nervous.

"So..." she said and I smiled back.

"So..."

"Read any interesting novels lately?"

"Not exactly"

"Are you alright?" I asked, and Elena, the devil, could barely hold in her laughter.

"Oh, I'm fine," she said. "I'm wonderful. My question is, what the hell are you doing here?"

I felt myself pale. "What do you know?" I whisper-shouted to her.

"That you're Scarlett, not Sophie. We're really close. I'm really offended that she thought she could pull one over on me."

"She isn't trying to pull one over on anybody; she just needed time, and she didn't want to disappoint Lucien with the deal they had coming up."

"So she deceived him instead by sending her gorgeous twin? I can't believe he thinks you're the same person. I noticed the difference instantly. All that money, and at the end of the day, he's still just a dense man."

This made me smile. "Please don't tell him; she'll be back in a few days. She just needs to rest."

"I won't tell him, but somehow he's going to find out. And even if he doesn't, someday eventually he's going to figure it out."

"I know," I sighed.

"Anyway, have fun," she said, "and you two really do look alike. She's showed me your photo before, and even then, it was uncanny. But seeing you in real life... I don't know whether to be jealous or terrified. I bet without any makeup on, I wouldn't even be able to tell you two apart."

"The hair," I said, and she nodded.

"Yeah, that. That's the dead giveaway."

I released a heavy breath then, and she smiled.

"Go ahead and enjoy yourself. Your secret's safe with

me until it no longer matters. Because it's just too good to keep to myself, so I'll give you a five-year warranty on my silence. And tell Sophie I'm really sorry about her broken engagement. You know that I'll call her. Or will the call go to you? You have her phone?"

"Yeah," she handed me her phone.

"Sophia!" Lucien suddenly yelled from the foyer, and I quickly input the number. I blew her a kiss on my way out and sent her a grateful look.

"I envy you," she called out. "How exciting."

For some reason, her comment made me smile. But when I reached the foyer and saw the angry look on her brother's face, I saw that there was absolutely nothing to smile about because he was pissed.

Chapter 37
Lucien

I truly didn't want to step too out of bounds and show overt concern for her, but I was beginning to become worried. She never used to be like this before. But now she was clumsy, easily startled, and just generally less put together than usual. She used to be so calm to be around, which was one of the reasons why I had worked so well with her for so long. But now, I found myself having to be the one to watch out for her, to be sure she didn't fall or break something.

For instance, now I was waiting for her in the car, and I didn't understand why.

I understood her close relationship with Elena, but this was no reason to delay our meeting. Eventually, she arrived and got into the back seat, and I turned my face away.

I let out a deep breath and understood I was ticked off. However, I didn't understand why. It wasn't just because she was clumsy, but I guess I also wasn't truly looking forward to seeing Gregory.

And as we got close to the restaurant, I had to admit that

I was also somewhat worried about her because of him. I'd seen the way he'd treated her that night and the eye he had for her, and I couldn't imagine he was setting up this lunch to simply discuss business. He wanted to see her again in a more casual setting, and I just happened to be in the way.

I couldn't help but glance at her as I wondered if she would even be able to protect herself.

As if noticing my gaze, she turned and we locked eyes. We both stared at each other. However, not willing to participate in a staring contest, I turned away and returned my focus to the road.

Soon enough, we arrived at the restaurant, and even though we still had about seven minutes to spare, Gregory was already seated and on the phone. The hostess directed us to our seats, and the moment he saw us, a huge smile spread across his face.

In the light of day, I realized he was much older than I had realized from our first meeting. I also realized that his excitement was solely directed at Sophie.

He rose to his feet and ended his call, offering out his hand for a handshake. I accepted and took my seat; however, when Sophie's turn came, he ignored her hand-shake altogether and instead opted for kissing her on the cheek. She accepted it, however, I watched her reaction, and her eyes were significantly lowered as she took her seat.

I looked at him then and truly hoped this meeting would not drag on.

"I'm in your city now," he said, and I nodded.

"Indeed you are."

"We're immediately ready to get back to work. I just

want to give you the chance to host me a welcome like I did with you."

"Sure," I replied, and he nodded awkwardly at me. Then he turned his attention to Sophie.

"We'll be taking a lot of trips to the casinos in Atlantic City as we work on this project together," he says. "You'll be escorting me, I presume?"

She stared at him, and then she gave me a look. I didn't want to step in because I was sure she knew how to protect herself, and sure enough, she didn't disappoint.

"Of course," she replied. "I go wherever Mr. Montgomery goes, so if he'll be in Atlantic City, then I will be there as well."

"What a great worker," he said. "Lucien, I might have to steal her from you."

I looked forward and grabbed the bottle of water that had been left for us. "We're on a first-name basis now?"

He seemed quite startled at this comment, but then he quickly recovered. His expression, however, darkened as he stared at me.

"Well, I am significantly older than you, and even all the money in the world cannot buy that," he said.

I didn't respond to this. Instead, I called the waiter over to come take our order.

"Sophie darling," he called in his mixed British accent, "what do you usually call your boss?"

"Mr. Montgomery," she replied, and he nodded. "Respectful. I guess I'll extend the same courtesy, then, if this is what you prefer."

"No need," I said. "We'll be working together extensively, so it's best to be comfortable with each other. You can call me Lucien, and I'll call you Gregory."

I could feel the frustration in his gaze and expression at this. However, I didn't owe him ease in any ramifications, so I ignored it and focused on the menu.

I ordered a salad with a turkey sandwich, and then I handed the menu over to the waiter. I turned then to watch Sophie, and I could see that she was a bit indecisive. I knew that she was looking at the exorbitant price, especially because she tended not to want to eat in situations like this. And so, I leaned forward and whispered in her ear.

"You haven't eaten anything besides some pie, have you? I'll cover the bill, so order whatever you like."

I pulled away then, and she stared at me, and then she smiled and nodded.

She made her order then and soon enough, the waiter was on his way.

"So," Gregory leaned forward, all smiles. "I've been to New York several times in the past, but I've never had the time to dilly-dally around. This time, though, I think I might be staying much longer to oversee the project with your company, Lucien. And I imagine it will be much more fun and eventful, seeing that for once I have utmostly favorable company."

Once again, he rested that creepy, distasteful smile on Sophie, and I could physically feel her shudder beside me.

Shaking my head, I leaned forward and began the meeting.

"What's your schedule like?" I asked. I brought Sophie along so that she could record our plans and know how to communicate this with the team. Then we can put something concrete in place and immediately get started on work.

"Right, right," he said and finally focused on his work.

We talked for over an hour about all the steps to be taken and our proposal for expanding the casinos and their current revenue. By the time we came up for air, once again with all the notes and plans recorded, an hour and a half had passed. We'd had a huge lunch, and it was making me sluggish. Sophie, though, I could see remained quite sharp.

Gregory, on the other hand, was beginning to act restless, and so I decided to bring it to an end.

"I have a meeting scheduled for four," I told him. "We can finish this conversation some other time if need be, and if not, if you have any inquiries or concerns, you can either reach my phone or you can stop by my office. I'll be available in both."

He pulled out his phone then from his pocket and nodded in agreement.

"Sure, what's your phone number again, please?" he asked, and I rattled it off to him.

And then he turned to Sophie and asked. "And your phone number?" he demanded. "In case I need to get in urgent contact with your boss, and he isn't available."

She smiled but hesitated. She seemingly still didn't know how to handle this, and so she suddenly set her napkin down and rose to her feet.

"Please pardon me. I'll be right back," she said to us both.

"Alright," he said, and I was left alone with Gregory.

Chapter 38
Scarlett

Finally! I exclaimed on my way to the bathroom.

The meeting had been long and arduous, and more than anything, I was glad for the reprieve. With the way it had started, I had been expecting things to completely go south from the beginning, but thankfully both men had soon put on their professional hats and focused on all the issues that were important at hand.

I, on the other hand, truly wanted to head home. It had been a very long day, and given that I was still somewhat jetlagged from the previous day's travel, I couldn't help but wish that I had some time away to just think and sleep. This arrangement with Sophie was only supposed to have lasted a week, but this week was beginning to feel like an entire year for me. I couldn't wait for it to be over, however, as Lucien came to mind, I found that I wasn't quite as eager for an end to all of this as I claimed.

And then we had Elena. I was still somewhat shocked by the fact that she had immediately smoked out our secret. I shouldn't have been realizing she knew we were twins.

More than ever, I felt so exposed, and I wanted to tell Sophie about it, but I was really concerned that she would worry. Elena, however, now had my phone number to call Sophie, and so I decided that it'd be better if she heard it from me than from Elena.

Sophie picked up almost immediately, which was rare. It was as though she'd been expecting my call, and so I couldn't help but feel afraid on her behalf.

"What is it?" I asked. However, to my surprise, she threw the question back at me.

"What do you mean by what is it? You were the one who called me."

"Oh," I said and nodded. "Yeah... um," I was relieved that it seemed as though she didn't know, and so I truly had to make the judgment now on whether to tell her at all. She was supposed to be resting, not getting unnecessarily worked up. Plus, Elena was on her way to her vacation in the Maldives, so my only hope was that she would be too busy enjoying herself in the waters to care about anything concerning me and Sophie until the week was done.

"Scar?" she called, and I smiled, watching my reflection in the huge restaurant mirror.

"Yeah," I replied. "Everything is fine."

"That's surprising."

"What do you mean?" I asked.

"You've met Elena, haven't you? She's very observant. She's going to notice even if the slightest thing is off."

My heart began pounding in my chest. "I met her, but not for very long. She was in a hurry to go on vacation, and so she didn't pay too much attention to me."

"Jeesh, that's such a relief," Sophie said. "A huge relief,

you have no idea. If there was any chance of this going bust, it would most definitely have to be because of Elena."

I swallowed then and turned away, ready to exit the bathroom.

"Anyway, I have to go now. We just finished the meeting with Gregory, or at least I hope it's finished. I want to go home. I'm so exhausted, and they've been talking forever."

I heard her smile through the phone. "That's the easy work with Lucien," she said. "The harder work is coming."

"Yeah," I nodded. "Alright, talk later."

"Bye," she said, and I couldn't help but note just how significantly more relaxed she seemed. It made me feel good that I had made the right decision, and so as I exited the bathroom to return to my seat, there was an extra spring in my step.

Until someone called my name.

I was immediately startled; however, I didn't turn around, the first time at least. And that was because, from the voice alone, I knew who it was. However, I tried my best to pretend like I had heard absolutely nothing and continued on my way.

"Sophie!" he called once again, and I stopped in my tracks. This hallway leading to the bathroom got dimmer the farther you went in, and even though it was daylight, there were no windows, so I knew that he had chosen the perfect spot to ambush me.

I turned around and released a deep sigh and soon found he had been leaning against the wall a little way from the women's bathroom, lying in wait for me.

I managed to work up a smile of surprise.

"Mr. Walters," I greeted. However, he didn't return the smile. Instead, his gaze was pretty dark, and for a moment, I was sure he was scowling at me, though I wasn't sure what exactly I had done to make him so angry.

I soon found out.

He leaned down to glance at his screen as he tapped some numbers in, and then he stretched his hand over to me, offering me his phone.

"What is it, sir?" I asked, and he stared into my eyes.

"Your phone number," he said calmly. Much too calm, and as a result, a cold shiver went down my spine.

"Um, I already have your contact details, sir," I told him, trying my best to play all of this so that it wouldn't escalate. Not just for my sake but for Lucien's sake as well and this project he had been working on for so long.

"Are you really going to keep acting dumb?" He asked with a crooked smile.

At this, mine immediately left my face. There was no point in pretending anymore because now, not only was I disgusted with him harassing me, but I was also incredibly annoyed.

And so I folded my arms across my chest and tried to seem as defiant and strong as possible. However, when his gaze lowered to my breasts, I realized this had been a bad move because my hands were sure to bunch them up. It was as though I was dangling a piece of meat in front of an already raging and ravenous animal. Instantly, I released my arms and instead kept them straight and glued to my side.

"How exactly am I acting dumb?" I asked, forcing him to respond to the question in his own words.

"You think I don't know what's happening between you

and your boss?" he said, and at this, my entire face fell. Nothing, absolutely nothing, could have prepared me for this accusation. And so he got the confirmation he needed while I was flat-out horrified and close to panic. But that only lasted a few seconds because there was no way he could have known this. He was just acting based on assumption and probability, and as a result, he was trying to use it to intimidate me. I'd had too many bosses in the past for me to fall for this nonsense, and so I stood my ground.

"I don't know what you're talking about, Gregory," I called him by his first name, adding as much steel and emphasis as I could in the tone of my voice, to show him that I wasn't for one moment moved by his antics.

"You really don't know?" he asked. "Alright. Once it's publicized on the internet that he's fucking around with his assistant we'll see what kind of blowback he gets. With all the possible risks it's surely enough to tank his reputation as someone who cannot separate business from pleasure. I'll also be sure to give my recommendation to Charles Nioly that he truly is too volatile to engage in this type of extensive investment. You might not know this, but what people like Charles invest in is not deeds but people. All I need to do to pull the string holding all of this together which can be done in one phone call. So what's it to be? Give me your phone number or watch me make the call?"

I stared at him. However, by the smile playing at the corners of his mouth, I could tell that he was gloating because he knew that somehow he had gotten to me. He had used the fear tactic brilliantly and, as a result, proved the relationship between myself and Lucien to an extent because if he was just my boss, my first thought should have been self-preservation above all else. But then here I was with the gears in my head desperately spinning as I tried to find a way out of this that would neither hurt me nor Lucien, or this deal for that matter. He truly had been working on it for the better part of the last two years, and knowing that it just might tank because of me was much more than I could bear.

"What's your point?" I asked. "I mean, what's your intention with any of this?"

"I'm not sure yet," he replied. "Maybe I'd like to get to know you better. Maybe I'd like the same kind of relationship you have with your boss. The possibilities are endless, but the bottom line of all of it is that I will treat you very, very, very well."

Bile rose in my throat as I stared at him and contemplated how to resolve this. If I called attention to this now, it was sure to blow up the deal. However, I really couldn't stomach this because regardless of the way I sliced it, this felt deeply like it was my fault. Maybe it was because of the way I dressed and looked. Maybe I was too provocative in my appearance because even Elena had pointed out that I was a bit more curvaceous than Sophie. Maybe this was what had caught this bastard's eyes, and so somehow I had to take responsibility for this. I gave this some thought and eventually made my decision.

I only had a few more days in this position, and after that, Sophie would take my place once again. She, I was sure, would know how to handle him, and perhaps his attraction to her would even wane since she was much less uptight than I was. If the harassment proceeded beyond this, we would know how to carefully resolve it. Maybe

Lucien would be able to contact his boss Charles, but before then, we would have to gather ironclad evidence that supported our claims and accusations. So I had to be patient, I had to endure, and I had to be smart about this.

In the end, I was able to form a decently set smile.

"That's no problem," I told him. "I doubt you can treat me well, but let's see how it goes. I hope you'll be able to surprise me."

He smiled at this, though his expression seemed even darker, and I input Sophie's number. This I was going to deal with by myself until I had the entire issue under control enough to pass the torch over to the next person.

Chapter 39

Lucien

It didn't occur to me that something was wrong until I eventually looked up from the report I was reading and noticed that both of them were gone. First, it had been Sophie who excused herself to the bathroom, and then later on at some point, Gregory had left as well, but I hadn't given it a second thought. I had been too occupied with what I was doing.

Now, however, I looked up and around the restaurant and couldn't help the sudden alarm that gripped me. I didn't think she would be in any physical danger here; Gregory wasn't that stupid, I hoped. But I didn't expect that if he did bump into her on the way, he wouldn't perhaps miss this chance to make his intentions known to her.

I contemplated for a moment about whether to step in or not. Would that be intruding? After all, she was technically free to see whoever she wanted, and if the advances were not wanted, then she could turn him down. All I needed in the end to make sure that she was safe was to remind her that if there was anything wrong that made her uncomfortable, then she was obligated to report it immediately to be dealt with.

I consoled myself with this, but as the moments passed and there were still no signs whatsoever of either of them returning, I rose to my feet. After setting the device down, I took off my jacket and started to head over to the restroom. Just before I exited the restaurant's floor, however, I realized that she was coming out. I stopped in my steps as I looked at her and didn't miss the sad and almost furious look she had on. She, however, didn't notice me until she was almost in my face, and instantly her expression turned to that of surprise.

"Lucien!" she called, and then she quickly corrected herself. I didn't miss her quickly looking over her shoulder.

"Sir, I mean," she smiled. "Are you going to the bathroom?"

I watched her closely, trying to read and understand her. However, before I could ask any further questions, my gaze moved to the man who was also emerging from the restroom area hallway. He was adjusting his suit, and for a moment, the sudden urge for me to drive my fist into his face arose.

However, I managed to control myself, thankfully because it wasn't exactly easy to harass her there. This was a very high-end establishment, and there were cameras everywhere, so mostly he had only tried to talk to her and was adjusting his clothes because he had gone to the bathroom.

"I'll be right back," I said as I moved past both of them and continued on my way to the restroom. In there, I was worried once again that I was leaving her with him, and I truly didn't like this. There had to be a better way to set my mind at ease, and so the moment I was done in the restroom, I pulled out my phone and called Felix.

"Sir?" he picked up almost immediately.

"Hey," I greeted. "I have something I need you to help me do urgently. " I said as I noted the time on my watch.

"Sure, sir," he said.

"I need the surveillance footage of the restroom area at Per Se, Ten Columbus Circle. "

"Okay," he said. "Timestamp, please?"

"Between three-fifteen and three-thirty pm."

"Okay, sir."

"Can you get this to me before the end of the day? It'll be difficult, but don't consider the expense. Just send the bill to me."

"I most definitely will, sir," he said. "Anything in particular I should be looking out for?"

"My personal assistant, Sophie. You know her, right?"

"Yes, sir, I do," he replied.

"Well, I'm currently working with a man called Gregory Walters from Charles Nioly's company. I want to see if between those frames there was any interaction between them, and if there was, I need to see exactly what it was. So make sure the footage is as clear as possible. I don't want any ambiguous clips or images."

"Understood. I'll contact you again before the end of the day," he said.

With this taken care of, I ended the call and put my phone away. Once again, I was exerting quite an intense level of concern for her, but I told myself that this wasn't the same type of mundane concern about her well-being. This was concerning the safety of my employee, and as her employer, especially as I was the one that brought her into contact with this particular douchebag of a client, it was my responsibility to ensure that she was safe. Otherwise, I and perhaps even my company would end up paying for the consequences at the end of the day.

After this, I returned to the restaurant, and as I did, I was sure to watch out for both of them. His eyes were on her while she, on the other hand, had picked up my iPad and was scrolling through. She was still speaking to him, I could tell, but was trying her hardest not to give him her attention and to discourage his advances in any way.

I could very clearly see from this distance how uncomfortable she was, and it made me wonder why she didn't immediately come to me with this. It was as though she didn't trust me, which I couldn't understand because we had worked together for so long. And there was also the fact we had been extremely intimate with each other, and for lack of a better word, we were more or less on good terms. So what was the problem? Why bear this annoyance alone?

This was the question I kept asking myself as I returned to the table, and afterwards, I couldn't bear to remain any longer. I sat with them for a little while, confirmed my suspicions, and then I stood up ready to leave. He did the same as well, and after shaking my hand, he tried to pull her in for a kiss on the cheek again, but she turned quickly with the excuse of packing up our things. I didn't miss his dark state directed at her. I also made sure that he was well aware that I didn't miss this, and when he eventually returned his gaze to mine, I could see that he was startled by the way that I was watching him.

I decided then that if she didn't have the courage, for whatever reason, to come to me about his unwanted advances, then there was nothing stopping me from confronting him about it.

"Sophie, go ahead and get Michael to bring the car around," I told her, and she met my gaze. Then she looked at Gregory, and I was sure she knew that I was going to interfere. She didn't seem happy about this either, which confused me, but she didn't say a word in protest. She nodded in agreement and made her way out of the restaurant.

"My assistant seems uncomfortable with your presence," I pointed out directly to him, refusing for any reason to mince my words. "Is there anything untoward I should know about?"

"Untoward?" he asked, acting dumb. "Uncomfortable? She told you that."

I was instantly irritated. "We've been seated here and interacting together for hours, so you've heard every word she's said to me, haven't you?"

"So, where are you getting that idea from?" he asked. "She seemed mighty fine to me."

"I know her," I said, "and therefore, her discomfort is very hard to miss."

"I know," he winked at him. "You're a lucky man."

I frowned instantly, wondering what he was talking about, and then a dark suspicion arose in the pit of my stomach. At the slight turning of my stomach, I understood his assumption and couldn't help but sigh. If that was what he thought... if he was indeed suspicious that I had been intimate with Sophie, then of course he would think that. To some extent, this made it easy since we were not in a relationship. And so I sighed and tried to control my temper.

"I don't know what you're referring to, but for the success of our collaboration, I hope you can refrain from making her uncomfortable. I don't know what it is you're doing, but it's casting a very dark shadow over this, and we have only just begun."

He was immediately offended.

"Mr. Montgomery, you've been quite abrasive and almost rude with me from the very first moment that we met," he said. "On account of Charles Nioly and this huge task he has assigned to me, I have been very lenient and patient, but everyone has their limits. Please, as we go forward, and if you want this to go forward, I will have to demand some level of respect from you and tolerate no further disrespect. I am not in any way, shape, or form making your personal assistant uncomfortable, and to even suggest that is a blatant and very dangerous accusation. Especially when you have no evidence whatsoever and are simply going on gut feeling. You're a man with vast wealth, so you should know just how deeply dangerous, legally speaking, this accusation is. You wouldn't want me out of the blue to claim she suffered some sort of emotional distress, would you? Please refrain from this kind of behavior in the future. I will pardon it now and let it slide, but I do not want to be embarrassed in this way again."

With that, and without waiting for my response or acknowledgment, he turned and went on his way.

I watched him leave, my blood boiling, but I knew I had

to be patient to paint the full picture of what was currently happening. The check was left for me to pay, perhaps for the inconvenience and distress I had caused him. After handling the bill, I walked out of the restaurant and headed over to the waiting Mercedes town car, Sophie was already seated and waiting for me at the back.

Chapter 40
Scarlett

Most of our car rides from the moment I started working for him had been quiet. But I had to say that this particular one was quieter than any I had experienced with him so far. We didn't say a single word or even look at each other, and it made me nervous to think that this was because of what he had noticed between me and Gregory. I didn't want him to notice anything, and I didn't realize how much I didn't want this until the possibility that he actually might arise. I wanted to take care of it without causing him any trouble, but now it was as though that ship had sailed, and I couldn't help from time to time sneaking looks his way.

However, he was turned toward the window, completely deep in thought. I realized that whenever we were being driven in the car, nothing was on. He didn't listen to music or the radio; rather, he went inside of himself to think and solely focused on staring outside. I could only imagine all the things that were constantly going through his head, as well as the myriad of employees that he had to deal with and handle daily. I managed most of this for him, and what amazed me the most was how he was able to compartmentalize it all so that they wouldn't overwhelm the other.

To me, he already had way too much on his plate, and I sincerely hated to think that my issues with that idiot would be another. Hence, I tried to bring up something light-hearted to distract him, hoping that it wouldn't annoy him.

"Sir, what do you want to have for dinner?" I asked as I pulled my phone out of my bag. "I'll make the arrangements now so there's no delay. Do you want it delivered to the office, or will you be heading home early?"

At first, he didn't reply, and I sighed. I waited, though, because I was certain that he would eventually speak.

"You're heading home early today?" he asked, and I was a bit surprised by the question. "Uh... no? I didn't think so. I mean, if you still need me, I can stay for as long as you need me."

My hypercriticism was not lost on me because I could very clearly remember nearly roasting Sophie for this very thing just a few days ago and now I was the one all too willing to offer myself up on a platter.

He turned then to glance at me, and I realized now more than earlier that anytime he looked at me, he stared deep into my eyes as though he were trying to understand me. I loved the attention and focus that he gave me, however on account of my fear that he would see more than I wanted him to, I couldn't say that I particularly liked or welcomed it. Afterwards, he returned his attention to staring out of the window, and I felt even more nervous internally.

To be honest I didn't want to think or even speak. All I

wanted was to be in a space with him where I didn't have to hide or hold back, just like we had been in London. And it made me wonder again if I could ask for a day just like we had. But I knew that this was impossible, and it frustrated me to no end. In particular, I wanted to kiss him, and as I shut my eyes, I couldn't stop imagining what it had felt like to have his tongue in my mouth when we were in London. It had been absolutely divine, and as the pangs of longing hit me once again at the pit of my stomach, I couldn't help stealing another look at him, wondering when and if I'd truly ever get to experience that again.

The fact was that right now, I would give anything, but I couldn't bring it up. And most importantly, I didn't think he would want me to. This would be crossing several lines that couldn't possibly be acceptable in our home country. Maybe in London, sure, where it was easy to forget, but not right here where it would be impossible to forget.

However, the thought of him bending me over that huge luxurious desk of his made me so overheated in his air-conditioned car that I couldn't stop myself from slightly throwing my head back to catch my breath. The way he fucked me at just the right angle and with such exertion that I felt it at the end of me and the reverberations gripped my body, it was perfect. He was perfect, and his cock... I wanted it so badly. In my mouth sucking him off, bringing him to his knees, watching him come all over me. He was such an alpha, and being able to weaken him in that way, no matter how brief, was a pleasure that not very many people got to experience. I relaxed now more and more as time passed, just how fortunate I was.

"Is Gregory Walters harassing you?" he asked, and my

eyes instantly shot open. I instantly went still, trying to process the question he had just asked.

Of course, he suspected it. It would have been quite daft for him not to notice my discomfort, but he was much too brilliant for that. However, I truly didn't want this to turn into anything at all.

"No," I replied simply.

His gaze narrowed at me, making me understand he did not believe me one bit. However, I didn't respond. Whether he believed me or not was his choice, but I didn't want to initiate his protection or ask for his help until and unless I was in danger.

Thankfully, he let it go, and soon enough, we returned to his office. We rode the rest of the way back to the office in silence, and through it all, I decided to put my encounter with Gregory out of my mind. Perhaps he was just taunting me, and perhaps he wouldn't even use my number to disturb me, and I was just blowing all of this out of proportion. Our collaboration would be long, so there was no need to worry.

With this thought, I was able to relax a bit more and continue with the rest of my day. As a result of refusing to admit any of the details to Lucien, I could see him grow significantly colder toward me. I couldn't understand it, and for a little while, it made me pissed. Eventually, I chalked it up to his frustration or concern for me, simply because that was what made me feel better. Not necessarily because it was true.

At this stage in my life, I was focusing on all the things that made me feel better and stronger, not the truth. The truth, I was coming to find, was absolute bullshit.

We kept working through the rest of the evening, and

when it was about seven, I was ready to kick him out of the office because what the fuck? The man was a workaholic, and I couldn't believe that this was what Sophie had to deal with.

As I brought what I hoped was the last stack of documents for him to sign for the day, I decided to try my hand at lightening the air between us a bit.

"You work so hard and spend so much time in the office. As a result, your apartment remains empty all the time. That's a little sad to me."

At first, he ignored me, and I felt quite embarrassed. But as I reviewed my statement, I realized that my comment might have read as rude.

"I mean, your apartment is so beautiful that's why I feel it's a bit sad."

My words faltered toward the end, especially as he glanced up from the document he was reading. After this, my mouth instantly zipped shut.

When he was done, however, and had closed the last folder to hand over to me, to my surprise, he responded.

"So if it wasn't a beautiful apartment, it wouldn't be sad?"

This made me smile because, once again, he was communicating with me like an actual human being.

"If you had seen my first apartment when I came to New York, then yes, you would have considered it extremely sad. If I still lived there, I'd sleep in the office. This place is much better, so I'd probably carve a little space under my desk and live here."

He continued to stare at me, and I quickly remembered

that this was my boss and the owner of this building I was speaking to, not my friend.

"I'm—I didn't mean I'd live here, not now. I have my place now. It's beautiful. I mean, not your kind of beautiful, that's out of this world—, it's in the skies, but mine... I mean-"

I faltered because he had leaned against his chair now and was staring up at me, listening as though intently. I knew he had to think this was senseless because nothing I was saying was even the least bit interesting. I was just rambling nervously, and he was very, very aware of this.

"Go on," he said after I shut my mouth, and I narrowed my gaze at him.

"No need," I replied with a smile, and he continued to watch me.

"I want you to continue," he said, "tell me exactly what your apartment looks like?"

At his words and his tone of voice, my heart skipped several beats because I knew that tone of voice. I knew what it insinuated and what it could mean, and just like that, I could no longer feel the floor underneath my feet.

I opened my mouth then to respond, but no sound came out, so I cleared my throat, looked away from him to get my bearings, and cleared my throat.

"I'm... it's, uh... " I started to describe my apartment, which had very minimal color, but when I recalled that I was supposed to be Sophie and that this might be a test of some sort, I growled inwardly and had no choice but to describe Sophie's apartment.

"It's, uh, quite feminine," I said, and that was putting it

lightly. To me, it was a cutesy apartment, and I liked it at times and at other times, I absolutely hated it.

"It's pink," I replied. "Green, yellow... colorful."

"Bright?" he asked, and I nodded.

"Yeah, but soft. There's no, like, reds or oranges... mainly pastels. Even the fridge is pink."

As I said this, he watched me and nodded, and I truly wondered what he would say afterwards. He simply watched me and then nodded. Just then, my phone began to ring, and I looked at the screen on the table. My heart leaped in my throat when I saw boldly the name that it rang, so I hurriedly picked up. However, it nearly flew out of my hands and right at my boss's face. Thankfully, I was able to catch it in time, and throughout it all, he just stared at me.

I immediately ended the call and slipped the phone into my pocket.

"Creep?" he asked, and my heart sank. Of course, he had seen it.

I nodded and smiled in response.

"Who's creep?" He asked, and I sighed.

"Um, my ex," I replied.

"Your ex-fiancé?" he asked, and I nodded, sincerely wondering why he was drilling me so hard now. He never usually seemed to care at all.

"You call your ex creep? On what grounds?" he asked. "I thought you two only broke up because of his inability to navigate his grief?"

"Well, because of that, he became creepy, hence why his name has been changed to creep in my mind."

I stared at him and watched as his expression darkened

toward me. He was sure I was lying, and there was no way I could convince him otherwise, so I didn't bother. What I knew was that I wasn't going to tell him about Gregory harassing and downright threatening me back at the restaurant.

"You can leave," he said since the documents he had to sign were done, and I nodded in response.

I felt immense relief as soon as I left his presence because more and more I was beginning to feel uncomfortable. He knew I was lying to him, I knew I was lying to him, and overall it all just seemed messy and ungenuine, and it was hurting me. I hated it. I had to endure because for now and the near future, there was no way to escape.

Chapter 41
Lucien

I hated that she was lying to me, and worse than that, I hated that I noticed. I didn't used to, but now I couldn't help it, and I just wished she would confide in me. Even though our relationship wasn't personal, I expected that due to the length of association we'd had so far, she would at least feel comfortable enough to reveal things to me that threatened her well-being when they came up. Unless Gregory had threatened her. But try as I might, I couldn't think of even a single thing that he could have used to successfully threaten her with. It made absolutely no sense to me.

I tried to get back to work but found I was too distracted, so after checking the time, I placed a call to Felix.

"What's the need of the day," I accused the moment he picked up. "Why don't I have any response yet?" I asked.

"My apologies, sir," he said. "I was just about to contact you to share what I have found."

"And what is it?" I asked. "Was there any interaction between them?"

"Yes, sir, there was," he replied. "From the timestamp of three-eighteen to three-nineteen pm. He was waiting for her outside of the bathroom when she got out, and then he called out to her. It took a while for her to respond, but eventually, she did, and they spoke for a bit."

"I nodded at this, and for the first time, I began to consider this from a different perspective. Was this even personal at all? Maybe he wasn't trying to woo her, but this was a business strategy of some sort. But again, I couldn't see the reason for this, as we were both partners. However, I had to be vigilant in every way, so I didn't leave any considerations out.

"Do you have the surveillance footage or pictures?" I asked.

"Yes, I do, sir," he replied. "That's why I was delayed. I saw all of these a while ago, but I needed to wait till now to collaborate with the security guy to hand it over."

"Alright," I said. "Send it over."

"Will do, sir," he replied, and the call came to an end.

A few minutes later, I received it on my phone. Immediately, I watched it and could confirm Felix's entire description of all that had taken place. I could see her reluctance, her annoyance, and fear. His bullying, his amusement. By the time I was done and had put the phone aside, I was so pissed that I almost didn't know what to do with myself.

All of this, and she was still keeping it to herself.

I thought of Gregory and thought of confronting him about this once again, yet something stopped me because it all felt too premature. Maybe their encounters wouldn't go beyond this. Maybe he was just showing her all this excitement simply because we had just begun and she was like a shiny new toy. And so maybe eventually, he would look away, and no fuss would be made.

These were all hopes I had at the back of my mind, but the fact that the reality could be worse, especially after I had seen the caller ID saved on her phone – 'creep', kept my gaze on the door to my office and kept my mind on her.

And so I called Felix back because I really couldn't bear to take a risk.

"I need additional surveillance, but this time around it will be on my assistant, Sophie Turner."

"Oh," he said, a bit startled at my request.

"When can you begin? Do you need her address?"

"No, sir," he replied, "and I'll get started on this now."

"Remain out of sight," I told him. "This will only be brief. I just need to ensure that she isn't being forced to do anything beyond her will. Only look out for the man we saw in the surveillance footage. Check if he comes anywhere close to her, and if they meet, and if this happens, inform me immediately."

"Yes, sir," he responded, and finally, I was able to breathe.

Scarlett

Suddenly, I didn't want to be alone. I had been looking forward all day to returning to my apartment and resting, but suddenly, all I could think about was Sophie's apartment and how much safer I would feel being there with her.

So, the moment I got out of the building, I hailed a taxi and went straight to her home in Chelsea.

On my way over, I received several messages from said creep. Most of which I ignored; this one, however, I had no choice but to respond to.

"I have a yacht decked and waiting to sail. Once again, I'm extending my invitation for you to join me for dinner. It's been twenty minutes without a response, so I will assume upon any further delays that you're reneging on our agreement to get to know each other better."

I looked at the message and felt a red-hot rage burning in my chest. If I went where he was, I was most definitely going to be in danger, and I could not and would not put myself at such a risk for anyone, even Lucien Montgomery. But still, I needed a way to defuse this situation, so I wondered what to do. I decided that his threats were worth nothing against the reality of real life, so I switched off my phone altogether and threw it into my bag.

I soon arrived at Sophie's home, and I didn't think I'd ever be so glad to not be alone. I was terrified, I realized, as I stood at her door knocking, and I hated this feeling. I hated the fact that Gregory was making me feel this way and that there was nothing I could do but bear it for the time being. It aggravated me to no end, but I didn't want it to ruin me, so I pushed it out of my mind and waited until she came over to open the door.

"What took you so long?" I immediately started complaining. However, just before I was about to step in, she stood in front of the door and shut it behind her.

I was startled and immediately alarmed, wondering if

something had gone wrong, but it soon turned out that this was not the case at all.

"What is it?" I asked, and she smiled at me. However, it was so guilty that I didn't even need to ask what was happening. It was written all over her face.

"Jerald's here, isn't he?" I asked, and she lowered her gaze.

"He wanted to talk," she said. "I'm hearing him out."

"Just talk?" I asked.

"Yes," she nodded.

I continued to stare at her, and then tears filled her eyes.

"I'm not over him, Scar," her voice lowered. "Throughout this week and in my anger, I've been searching for every reason to be, and I found a lot of them. But I've also found some very precious ones that are close to my heart. I just want to hear him out... to hear him explain to me what's going wrong in his head. He never did this before, but here he is now doing exactly what I had wished he'd done a week ago, and I don't know how to turn him away."

"So is the wedding back on now?" I asked, and she stared at me.

"I just... we just need time to figure things out."

I sighed then and softened my gaze at her because who was I to judge? I was the one who had slept with her boss and attracted a madman within the span of a few days.

"Space and time is what you wanted, and this is the reason we're doing all this, so of course, I'll give it to you. Speak to him, don't lose your head, and call me. Don't make any rash decisions without consulting me first."

She nodded then and leapt forward to hug me. I didn't physically return it because I was just too exhausted and annoyed at everything else. She moved away eventually and looked down at my purse.

"Why did you come here?" she asked. "I thought you were going straight home?"

"I was," I replied, "but I decided to come over here. I think it's because of that pie you baked earlier this morning. It was fucking delicious."

"Really?" she beamed, her face lit up like a bulb. "I still have some, want me to bring it out for you?"

My eyes widened at this. "I'm not even allowed to come into the apartment?"

"I just don't want any interference," she said, "and you two haven't ever really been on good terms, so I don't want him to close up."

"Jeesh, he's like some flower or clamshell."

"See what I mean," her expression darkened, and I rolled my eyes.

"Sure, whatever, bring out my apple pie, and don't tell him I said hi. Tell him he's an ass and he should get his head screwed on straight."

She gave me a look, and then she shut the door in my face and scurried into the apartment to retrieve my designated dessert for the night.

She came back and slid the pie through a crack in the door, mouthed, 'talk later, sorry,' and shut the door in my face.

I turned around and exited her building. I took a taxi one more time and stared at my phone, which was still shut off. I decided I was going to leave it this way until the following morning so as not to receive any missed calls. I was exhausted, and it dawned on me that would be my explanation.

I didn't care what his reaction to this would be; hopefully, he would sail off on that yacht, meet some misfortune, and never return. Furious, I shut my eyes and leaned against the seat for a much-needed rest. Eventually, I arrived home, and for the first time after I got in, I not only locked the door behind me but I double-checked, and dragged one of my kitchen island stools over. It was metal and heavy, so I was a bit more assured, but after staring at it, I wondered if my sofa would be more effective.

I decided I was being paranoid, and that there was no need for any of this. So, I headed over to the kitchen for some much-needed hydration. I drained the half bottle of water I found in the refrigerator and afterwards, shuffled over to the counter to start on the pie that Sophie had given to me. I wasn't going to eat dinner anyway, so I didn't bother controlling myself, plus the sweet taste was comforting.

I couldn't help but think of Lucien as I stood by the counter, deep in thought, until eventually, I carried the pie over and went ahead to settle in the living room. I turned on the television but kept the volume on mute, and in no time, and against my will, I was fast asleep.

Chapter 42
Lucien

"Have you found anything yet?" I asked as soon as I arrived home. I had just gotten into the elevator and had told myself that there was no need to check up on Felix or request any updates for the rest of the night. However, I found myself unable to hold back.

I didn't understand why I was worried, but I just needed him to at least confirm with me that he had found her, and for that reason, to be sure that he was up to the task, I had purposely refused to give him her address.

I knew her address from her files, so if he got this for a start, I would at least know he was up to the task. Otherwise, I had someone else in mind I could quickly assign the task to.

To my pleasure, however, he had a positive response for me.

"Yes, sir, I have. I followed after work, and she went to an apartment in Chelsea. But she didn't head in or, rather, she wasn't let in, and then afterwards, she returned to a different apartment in Soho."

I listened to his words and was immediately alarmed and concerned all in one.

I was also curious because nothing he had just said made any sense.

"What do you mean by she went to one apartment but wasn't let in, and then she went to another?" I asked.

"I think the second one she went to is her actual apartment," he said. "Because she has the keys for it and didn't have to knock or wait."

My frown deepened even further, as this, too, made absolutely no sense. So, I waited for him to explain. He didn't seem to have any, so I guessed the only way to find out was with time.

"Is she in danger?" I asked, and this time he had a response.

"She doesn't seem to be," he said. "She seemed quite familiar with the apartment she went into."

"She lives in Chelsea, not Soho," I informed him, and he processed this.

"Maybe she's temporarily staying with a friend. I'll confirm the discrepancy and find an explanation for it. Then, I'll let you know."

At his words, I hesitated because right now it seemed as though I was just unnecessarily prying into her life, and this was the last thing I wanted to do.

I just want to be sure that she is safe, and anything else makes me feel uncomfortable, as though I were crossing the line. So, I dish out a different set of instructions.

"No need," I replied. "Just follow her for the next few days to make sure she's safe and that Gregory Walters doesn't show up around her. After this is confirmed, then I guess we can bring this surveillance to a close. Anything else is completely unnecessary."

He seemed to hesitate in his response to this, but eventually, he agreed.

"Yes, sir," he said.

I put the phone away, then rested my head against the steel of the car doors. It had been such a hectic day, but I was usually used to them, so I couldn't help but wonder now why this particular one seemed to have drained me more than usual.

I returned to my apartment but could still feel the nervous energy plaguing my system. It was very clear to me now that unless I dispelled it somehow, I wouldn't be able to fall asleep tonight. So, as soon as I arrived, I took off my clothes, changed into gym wear, and went out for a run.

It was exhilarating, thus I didn't want to stop. But after running for forty-five minutes, I realized that it was a different kind of restlessness that I was trying to soothe. It was sexual energy stemming from my constant thoughts about her and subsequently the reminders of the night we had together back in London.

When I had to catch my breath, I stopped in the middle of the street and leaned against my knee. This was getting out of hand. It was clear to me now that I was out of control. However, I didn't know how to resolve it. Perhaps we could coexist as co-workers and yet continue with our sexual relationship? This, however, wasn't bound to end well, and she would definitely be the one at the end of the day getting the short end of the stick. Plus, I wasn't sure I wanted a relationship, or that I even had time for that kind of commitment. But I couldn't just sleep with her whenever I wanted to either. It was bound to get complicated without any labels whatsoever, just as it was right now. I already felt possessive of her, and so if we had that kind of relationship, I most definitely would want her to be exclusive with me, and it was only fair to me to provide her the same.

This was a dilemma I truly didn't know how to solve, but once again, I reminded myself of my still hopefully iron-clad discipline. I could push this away—all of this distraction—and focus solely on our work, just as we had before. I knew from the start that this was a risk, yet I had been willing to take it, and I had no regrets. But now, I had to find the perfect way to navigate it.

And so, I walked the rest of the way home, and the moment I got into the shower, I turned on the warm cascade and stood under it. I thought of her and tried to control my emotions, but it seemed as though the more I tried, the memories of being intimate with her haunted me. I remembered very vividly the erotic sight of her sex pulsing greedily around my cock, and it had been so intense that, in the present, my dick twitched in response. Desire swarmed me like a wave, and by the time I leaned against the tiled wall for support, I was so hard it almost hurt.

I couldn't hold myself back anymore and grabbed my dick, beginning to stroke it. It was too easy for me to recall how it had felt to have her mouth wrapped around it. I recalled the delight in her eyes and the enjoyment in her smile, making my grip harder and my movements faster. I could recall the last time I had masturbated for any reason, but now here I was, almost brutally bringing myself to completion. I was fucking enjoying every bit of it because one woman was in my mind.

I was excited, realizing that when I arrived at the office the next day, I was going to see her. Our relationship was different now, and I had to admit it. By dipping into the waters as I had, things would never be the same, and as pleasure overwhelmed me, and I threw my head back, her name falling from my lips, I decided that I didn't want it to go back to the way it was. I still wasn't sure how far we could go from here, but I promised myself one thing, and that was the fact that no matter what happened, and no matter the direction we both came to, whether one that was fortunate or unfortunate, she wouldn't, in any way, be left at a disadvantage. I would give in to her wishes at every point in time to ensure that neither she nor I ever viewed this as a mistake. I wanted it to be an experience that we could both look back on or perhaps even develop into something more.

The very thought was foreign to me, but it wasn't an impossibility. I had known her for so long, and I was comfortable with her. I enjoyed her company, and it was very easy for me to convince myself that if there was anyone I wanted to try a romantic partnership with, then it would be her. My only concern was that now that she had broken up with her fiancé, I might have been a rebound, and to her, I was nothing else. I was ready to face this as well. In short, at this point, I was ready to accept anything she requested as long as I got to be with her again. And with this, I eventually accepted that I was completely overtaken by her... by her beauty, appeal, charm, and wit. So, finally, I permitted myself to pursue this along with her and at her pace to see where it would lead. It was a risk, but finally, after so long, I couldn't help but feel slightly relieved that I was more than willing to take it.

Chapter 43
Scarlett

"There was something different about him the next day. I couldn't place my finger on it, until he called me into his office two hours before lunch.

"Have you had breakfast yet?" he asked, and I watched as he slipped his jacket back on.

"No," I replied almost distractedly as I watched his body with hunger.

He turned to face me, and I was forced to wake up from my lustful daydreaming.

"Let's go get something to eat," he said, and I was quite taken aback. This wasn't my first stint as a personal assistant. And so randomly going to eat with your assistant in the middle of the morning when meetings and obligations were scheduled in full was incredibly alarming.

However, he said it so casually and didn't seem too concerned with his schedule that I couldn't help but feel afraid.

"You... uh... you have a meeting with the investment team in a few minutes, sir," I reminded him.

"Isn't Gary here today?" he asked, and I nodded.

"He is, sir."

"Then tell him to handle it. And if there's a need for further input, then let me know when I get back, and I'll arrange another quick meeting with them for this evening."

I listened to his words and wondered if he had just said them for the sake of it or if he was being deliberate with his words because, from what he had just said, it was as though he didn't care he was skipping a meeting he needed to be at.

And so, to all of this, I truly didn't know the response to give.

"Um... sure, sir," I said, and our eyes met. "I'll go make the call."

He paused, and I gave his expression every single bit of scrutiny, yet I couldn't quite find anything to back up my belief that he was about to fire me over breakfast or whatever this sudden outing was.

I was exhausted and all of this worry and guessing put me in an even worse mood than the one I had been nursing all evening yesterday. I hated that I felt so worried and afraid, and so when I woke up this morning, everything just seemed bleak.

I couldn't give up now, and most importantly, I couldn't get fired, so I prepared myself to be able to say anything and plead the moment he even so much as brought up the suggestion.

Michael was waiting with the town car when we made it downstairs and we both climbed into the backseat.

"What do you want to eat?" he asked and pulled out his phone from his pocket. I turned to him, and at my widened eyes and expression, he seemed to also wonder what was wrong.

"Are you okay?" he asked, and I nodded albeit reluctantly, but what else was there to say?

"Are you? You're asking me to go eat with you and you're asking what I want rather than what you want even though you're my employer and I'm the employee?"

He ignored my question and turned to the front and told Michael where to go and the car moved into traffic.

I glanced over at my boss and found him staring out of the window with his hand on his chin and his gaze watchful.

I just felt so incredibly nervous and vulnerable, exposed, and I wondered why. It was making me overly emotional when there was truly no need to be, and at the end of the day, I understood that it was because I now care more than I'd ever expected to. I cared that the man beside me was about to fire me, not just because it was Sophie's job, but because just a few days earlier, we'd fallen asleep in each other's arms. It made me wonder how the hell he'd been able to convince himself and me that if we were intimate for just one night, everything else would return to normal because that was absolutely ridiculous and untrue.

There was no way in hell things were going to go back to normal, and being the extremely smart man that he was, he had probably realized this and was about to take rapid action. He couldn't even wait for the week to be over.

Sighing I couldn't keep from wringing my hands, and this is when he turned to face me.

"Are you alright?" he asked, and my eyes tightened shut because I truly wished that he wouldn't feign concern in this way when he was literally about to do something so evil. I thought of how to approach this. Could I convince him that there was no need to fire me because I wasn't actually Sophie and so he hadn't slept with his secretary, hence there was no reason to feel awkward about it or around me.

There were so many things to consider and actually quite several ways to resolve them, but I couldn't see a single way out of this that wouldn't cause me immense pain.

Regardless and not wanting to jump the gun, I remained quiet as I weighed my options and decided that unless he outrightly came to fire me, then I would simply observe. I had been a personal assistant for too long not to understand the power of saying less, so I remained as docile as possible until we got to the bistro. This wasn't a cheap place, but it wasn't too expensive either.

We found two seats that were empty because they didn't pay the staff nearly enough to show the guests to their table. We found a great seat by the window though, with only two seats, so we didn't have to worry about anyone joining us. But as I sat down and took in the view, I almost wished that someone would interrupt us and stop him from doing what he wanted to do.

"What do you want to eat?" he asked as he once again took off his jacket and draped it across the chair.

I looked up and saw the menu that he was handing over to me, and I was almost too afraid to accept it because somehow this all eerily felt as though I was willingly signing my death warrant. Still, I accepted the menu from him and took a quick perusal, but I didn't have to since I knew what I wanted. It was their most popular turkey, chicken, and beef sandwich, and there was just no need to go through more thought than was necessary, even though it was very likely that I would end up having it wrapped to go.

He ordered a basic chicken sandwich as though he didn't give it much thought, and once again, I was convinced of my suspicions. He was obviously distracted, and this was so unusual for someone like him.

Shutting my eyes, I pushed the menu aside after placing my order and leaned back against the chair.

"What's going on with you?"

He sounded sincere but I couldn't help but wonder if he was just trying to make small talk. He should just come out and say why he wanted to come here, and the moment he did, I would be ready to fight him back with whatever I could.

As I looked at him, I felt my heart shift in my chest, and I knew the last thing in the world I wanted was to fight him. So, I decided to be the first one to take the first step into stopping the blow. After all, when he landed his, it truly might be too late.

And so I straightened, squared my shoulders, and found my courage.

"Don't fire me," I said, and he had just been about to lift his cup of coffee to his lips.

"What?" he asked, his eyebrows nearly shooting up to his hairline.

I sighed. "I know what this is... at least I think I do, and I just want to let you know that truly there's no need for it. I know things haven't been as awkward-free as they were before London, but it's just because it's still new. I think we're doing pretty well. It's not uncomfortable for us to work together, at least it's not uncomfortable for me to work with you, and I hope it's the same for you. But if it's not, I assure you that it can be fixed, and with time, it will be as though nothing ever happened between us."

After my mini-mental breakdown, I found the courage to look at him, but as usual, I couldn't read his expression in any way. It was as though he was trying to slowly process all I had just said and had his full focus on me. I hated it. My stomach was churning, and I felt like I was going to faint. I released another deep breath and accepted the reality that I had cost Sophie her job, but it would be alright because I swore to find her a better one that offered even more pay.

"You think I brought you here to fire you?" he asked, and for a moment, I was stumped because that in no way was the response I was expecting. I mean, I expected, 'You're quite perceptive,' or 'You've always been able to read my mind,' but the accusation was thrown back in my face as though it weren't true. I couldn't even consider the possibility that it wasn't.

"Yeah," I replied, my eyes somewhat shifty.

However, as he continued to watch me, something began to tug at my heart because unless I was looking too hard, it felt as though the corners of his mouth were slightly curved in a smile.

"W-what?" I found myself stuttering.

His response was calm. "I didn't come here to fire you," he said, however, this was incredibly difficult to believe.

"Um... uh... okay. So why are we here then?" I looked around at the bistro in confusion.

"To eat, just like I said. I invite you out to eat, and you conclude that I'm going to fire you?"

I looked at him, and for a while, considered that maybe

this was a dream. I had fallen asleep on my desk, and I was being punished by thinking I was being fired. This was what was happening, right?

And so I shook my head slightly, and at this, he smiled.

"Relax, I know it's a bit strange that I'm coming out in the middle of my workday to eat, but I just want a slight change of environment. I can afford one hour today for a late breakfast. I don't have anything pressing, do I?"

He always had something pressing, I thought to myself. In short, his clearing off the hour for this meeting or whatever right now was at the cost of the very pressing meeting with the investment team that was supposed to have been held. But instead, here he was very clearly amused and taunting me.

"Uh... okay," I said, choosing now to completely shut my brain off since I couldn't make sense of anything that was happening. So all I could do was let it all pan out however it wanted, which was the plan from the very beginning.

Shaking my head, I picked at the napkin under my water glass to clear my head. This worked for a little while, and I was beginning to settle down, happy that he was ignoring this particular flight of lunacy. But then suddenly, he leaned forward and settled his hand on mine.

I was a bit taken aback at the move, but thankfully, I didn't pull my hand away. It was because, one, I was shocked, and second, his hand was warm, big, and strong against mine, and as my gaze lowered, I was mesmerized by how it completely covered mine. As a result, my heart skipped several beats, and this was in no way beneficial to my current state of mind.

I looked at him then, and this time around, he smiled.

He actually smiled, and I truly didn't know what to think or do with myself for that matter.

"Why are you nervous?" he asked.

Many thoughts and questions came to mind, which I thankfully shut down quickly and didn't voice out loud. Why are you touching me? Why are you watching my face? Why are you smiling at me? Please stop before I lose my head once again. I'm currently barely holding it together. Jeesh, I really couldn't wait for this week to be over, but at the same time, I stared as I realized that I was also dreading the end with all my heart. I loved spending time with him, loved admiring him, and I would give anything to have his dick in my mouth again just so I could see that gorgeous look on his face again.

However, because I was still somewhat sane and couldn't quite say any of these, I instead smiled and pulled my hand away from underneath his before I completely lost control of myself. To be honest, at this point, I was more concerned for his safety than mine.

Smiling, I couldn't stare at him like it seemed he wanted me to, I pulled out my phone and tried to reach Sophie. However, the little demon did not respond.

Shaking my head, I set the phone down, but when I returned my attention to him, I found that he too now had his gaze on his phone. This was so awkward, and I couldn't help it, but I began to feel a sense of responsibility for making this time fun for him because he never came out this way.

I had been thinking solely about myself, but I realized I needed to also be concerned about his enjoyment of the time we were sharing. After all, apart from everyone else working for him, he had chosen me to participate, and I deeply appreciated that.

But first, and because he was my boss, I still believed a part of him was not against firing me.

I cleared my throat, and though this didn't immediately draw his attention toward me, it did get him to put his phone away.

I had a smile ready for him when he noticed this and didn't quite reciprocate it, I immediately deflated. I didn't blame him; it looked painful and awkward at best. I didn't know how to ease into the lighter mood that I wanted to share with him so this outing would be enjoyable.

I didn't give up, though, so when his eyebrows raised as though asking me to explain the reason for drawing his attention, I had no choice but to speak.

"Has Elena ever dragged you along for her trips?" I asked.

He stared at me for a while, and then he slightly cocked his head, all without responding, and this was terrifying, to say the least, because suddenly I had just asked the questions that I was supposed to know the answer to.

"Why would she want me on any of her trips?" he asked.

This made perfect sense to me because no matter what, no matter the fact that he was not that much older than her and was still quite young, he was still her strict older brother and the last thing she wanted was for him to interfere with her college-aged friends. Both adults, sure, but there was a significant difference.

I nodded in response to this and gave up on speaking or saying anymore because sooner rather than later, I was sure to mess up and say something that I shouldn't have or that should have been unnecessary for me to say.

I completely gave up and began to look around like a lost sheep across the restaurant. For some reason, perhaps because this was a time of leisure and no work, Lucien was paying full attention to everything I did and said, and so he wasn't as willing as I would have expected to let this one slide.

"She specifically tells you to book her impromptu trips during times when I absolutely will not be able to go with her, so I won't rain on her parade." This sounded right and made perfect sense.

And once again, I had messed up, and so now all I could do was smile and act as though I was in complete agreement with him.

"Yeah," I replied. "Forget I said anything it was a dumb question."

To this, he nodded, and I was certain that this matter was done with, but he seemed hell-bent on getting me to expose myself in some way because he just kept asking questions.

"Why do you think it was a dumb question?" he asked, and almost instantly, I could see the true curiosity in his gaze. He wasn't being funny in any way but was truly trying to understand why I had made such an offhand statement.

"Uh..." I was now truly and officially confused by all the attention, by all the questions. If I wasn't going to get fired, then there was absolutely no doubt in my mind that he had discovered something I didn't know about because none of this was normal. And as I looked at him, my shoulders deflated because I really couldn't stand being this

constantly anxious anymore. It was emotionally and physically draining, and I wondered if now would be the best
time to take a leave until Sophie returned. After all, what
she didn't want to miss was seeing this deal with Charles
Nioly through, and now that it was done, there was really
no reason for me to be in the picture.

I looked at him and felt my heart wrench, and I couldn't
help but feel sad because I had been hoping to have more
days with him, but I really couldn't do this anymore. It was
difficult to speak and I understood why. It was too soon; the
sex had been out of this world amazing and I had never
been one for romantic ideations but I knew that if anyone in
the world could sweep me off my feet it would be him. And
he had. However I had to look away for my sanity because
perhaps I was seeing more than what was actually there,
and more likely, I was the one solely building this sand
castle in my head and with how ill-timed all of this was, I
couldn't imagine anything except a pathetic end. I was
almost sure I would never meet anyone of his caliber, who I
also had such explosive chemistry with, I was choosing to
look away for my own sanity. And so with a deep sigh, I
shut my eyes and straightened.

"I want to ask for something," I said.

He stared at me in that watchful, stripping gaze of his,
and then his eyes went to my wringing hands. I didn't even
realize just how nervous I was until my eyes lowered to
them, and I could see just how pale they had turned, so I
let go.

"What is it?" he asked, almost as though he knew
exactly what I was going to say.

"I think, uh... I'll need some time off. Not too long, just

a few days, until the weekend. I think with everything that's happened this week, I need the space to clear my head and recharge."

I stopped, hoping he would respond and say something, anything, to allay my worries, however, he didn't. He just continued to watch me, and for a moment, the sadness I was sure I saw in his eyes was heart-wrenching, but it made absolutely no sense. And yet, I felt it. I *felt* it and it made my heart flutter but I couldn't explain it.

There was something I could explain. "To be honest, I needed the time off earlier in the week, but I wanted to see this project through, especially since this was the final stage of concluding the proposal and taking him on as a client. But now that is said and done with, I think... I really need a little break."

Just then our food was delivered, and at first, upon the waiter's arrival, I was almost annoyed by his interruption. But when he lingered as he set down our sandwiches and ordered drinks, I realized that this was the perfect chance for a reprieve so that we could both process what I had just said.

Sophie was probably going to kill me for not being able to even last with Lucien for a week, but at this point, I didn't care. I just wanted to go back to my still manageable and emotionally stable life. It dawned on me now more than ever that I had been quite reckless, and I couldn't help but wonder if it was because I had been living Sophie's life and not mine. But then again, I felt as though I had been careful, yet everything seemed to have spiraled so wildly that I was now literally frightened for my life and job. No, I didn't expect that creep to hurt me, at least not physically, but the threat of being approached by him had kept me up all night and almost afraid to remain in my own home alone, and this was completely unacceptable.

"Alright," he said, and for a few seconds, I wondered if I had misheard him.

"A-alright?"

"Alright," he said. "You thought I was going to reject you? You have a lot of unused and accrued days, don't you?"

"Yes, I do," I replied and then nodded.

"You deserve the break. You've been through a lot this week, yet you remained available to me, and I don't take that lightly. I truly appreciate it. So take the rest of the week, and if you're able to arrange it with Larry, you can take as much time as you need to recover."

I was dumbfounded, relieved, and sad all at once. And so yet again all I could do was watch him. With every moment shared between us, the more I knew of his personality, the more my affection for him grew. The way he spoke and acted... the way he *fucked*. I couldn't get enough of him and I wondered if he felt even an iota of this regarding me in return.

Unfortunately, and as usual, he seemed unfazed as he picked up his sandwich and began eating. The rest of lunch wasn't awkward, per se, but it wasn't exactly filled with complete ease. I avoided his gaze, and he seemed to no longer be aware of my existence, which made me truly wonder what had gone wrong, or maybe this was how the employer-employee relationship between him and Sophie had always been. I didn't know what to compare it to because I had always had somewhat great relationships with my bosses since I picked companies with fun heads and business. Not, for instance, Lucien and his multimillion-dollar investments.

In the end, I wanted to fix this somehow, but I had to accept that I had been talking too much and doing way too much, and there was no need for that. And so, I remained silent and turned my attention toward wondering how I was going to break this news to Sophie. I hope she will under-stand. I knew she was trying to work things out with Jerald, but since, regardless of my presence or not, she still had the rest of the week off, or even more, like Lucien had proposed, then I didn't feel guilty at all.

Chapter 44
Lucien

Nothing was going according to plan. I wasn't nervous or anxious or panicked for that matter, I realized as I ate my lunch. I was just disappointed. For years I had given little thought to her presence in my life, but now that she was actively leaving, and even for long, suddenly I felt a little bit empty inside.

However, there was no way I was going to voice this, but I did want to ensure that the major issues were clarified before she left. And so, I'd start with the most important one.

"I know that Gregory Walters is harassing you," I replied.

At this, her brows shot up, her eyes slightly going wide as she stared at me, probably wondering how I got the information about this. I didn't need to tell her because she was quite familiar with Felix, and I didn't need to tell her either that I had paid substantial attention to this and retrieved the surveillance footage from Per Se. This was how I worked, and these were the things I did, and she was no stranger to arranging them for me.

She lowered her gaze then and tried to continue eating in silence, however, she seemed unable to do this, so she set her sandwich down and leaned back against the chair.

"This is normal," she replied. "Some employers will always think that women are fair game. He's one of those, but I know how to handle him and put him in his place."

"You do?" I asked, and she nodded. I was curious about this, even though for some reason I didn't expect her to tell me the truth.

"How exactly are you currently handling it?" I asked, and the ghost of a smile appeared at the corners of her lips. That smile, I realized, was something special. The room was relatively cool, but the moment she smiled, it was as though everything had warmed up in an instant.

"Well, now that I'm going on leave for a few days, it's not going to be incredibly difficult for me to handle him," she said. "All I need to do is keep my head low, and perhaps by next week, he will have forgotten about me."

Scarlett

"What exactly did he tell you?" he asked, as though he couldn't care less about anything I had just said.

"Well, he asked for my number when I went to the restroom, and I tried my best to get out of it."

"Did it work?" he asked, and I nodded, wondering where the light, one-hour brunch we had started had gone.

It made me wonder now if he actually came out for brunch, or if he just wanted to interrogate me in a more private setting. This, as well, made me unhappy, but he was a caring and responsible employer, which he truly didn't have to be, and so I had absolutely nothing to complain about.

"No," I finally responded. "I mean, yes, I gave him my number, but to my surprise, he's used it. I mean, he has used it."

At my words, his hands suddenly stopped moving, and then he looked up at me.

"He contacted you?"

"Last night," I replied but then stopped because once again, I wasn't listening to my advice. I had said that I wouldn't say a word until all of this was over so as not to alarm anyone or hurt Lucien's business. "It wasn't anything scary or uncomfortable," I said, and smiled, trying to play off my alarm. "He just wanted to invite me to dinner on some yacht. I declined, and that was it."

He watched me for a few more seconds, and then he continued eating.

"You're not concerned or worried by him?" he asked, and I shook my head.

"I'm not. I think he's harmless, and of course, if things became complicated and he became worrisome, then..." I stopped.

"Then what?" he asked. "I'll figure it out when that time comes."

At this, he resumed his meal, while I released a heavy sigh.

To my surprise, he wasn't done with his interrogation, and within a few minutes, the next loaded question came.

"Was the relationship we had in London something of a rebound for you?" he asked, and my entire frame went still.

I was almost afraid to meet his eyes because this question sounded incomplete, and two, I just couldn't.

I soon found that he wasn't going to say anymore or elaborate, and so I had to answer the question as plainly and unblemished as it had been asked.

"Maybe."

"And have you had more since then?" he asked, and I was taken aback, wondering where he could have possibly gotten this idea from. I started to respond but realized that this was quite private, so I didn't understand why he was asking like this at all.

"No, I have not," I replied with a smile. I was going to leave things at that, but I couldn't truly bear not adding some explanation, so I did.

"I didn't just hop from one guy to the next," I said, and our gazes met. "I mean, for the record, I got all I needed from you. And now I'm just going to focus on healing."

"What exactly did you need that you got from me?" he asked, and I almost sighed out loud trying to make my way through this minefield. This was supposed to be a relaxing brunch, but as I looked at him, I wondered why I even thought that was possible. He was purposeful in everything he did, so no, I was not surprised he was suddenly asking me all of these questions. Yes, he was my boss, but now I didn't want to be the one answering the questions, so I decided to ask one of my own.

"Since we're being a bit more personal, can I be personal too? I have some questions I want to ask."

He picked up his glass for a sip of his drink, and then he leaned against the chair in agreement. "Sure.. go ahead."

"You've been asking me a lot of questions since we sat down," I said. "That isn't very usual of you. At first, I thought you wanted to fire me, but since you've said that is not your intention, then I don't know what to think about any of this. It's a bit disconcerting."

He stared at me, and my heart began to race in my chest. This was the final leg. Whatever he said now in response would be the baseline, and I could only hope for my sake and Sophie's, it wouldn't be something crazy.

When he responded and told me in exact terms what his intention was, I was sure that right there on the spot, my heart stopped in my chest.

Chapter 45
Lucien

She looked like she had seen a ghost, and it truly would have been concerning to me if I wasn't so concerned that she would suddenly pass out.

"Are you alright?" I asked, and she shook her head.

"I-" she began but stopped. "You just-"

It sounded like she was having a stroke, so I calmly repeated what I had just told her. What I had decided on.

"Yes, I think we should continue with our arrangement. I want more days. Maybe even months until we both decide to bring the agreement to an end."

It took her another long while, but eventually, she responded. "I'm... sorry, I'm quite confused."

"You don't have to say yes," I said. "Your agreement or refusal doesn't affect our professional relationship in any way. I'm just putting it on the table that if you'd like more... I'd be willing to offer you more."

She still seemed shocked and I felt the same way. However, there was no going back now. I felt almost compelled at this point to see where all of this would lead.

In business, I was used to taking risks but all of it was calculated and based on solid facts and perhaps a pinch of intuition but now it seemed as though the entire sequence of events had flipped. Intuition seemed to be directing me in this case but whether this was accurate or that it was my libido, I couldn't tell. What I knew for sure at that moment was I couldn't bear not having her again. There would be consequences of course, but I was more than willing to face them for even one more night of completely losing myself with her.

"What exactly do you mean by more?" she asked.

"I don't want this in any way to be of any lesser benefit to you than it will be for me, and I know that if we go ahead with a solely sexual agreement, that might be the case in the end. So if that is not something you can or want to do, then I'm willing to offer a relationship."

She continued to watch me. "Like - an actual relationship?"

I nodded; however, she didn't seem relieved at all. She seemed thoroughly skeptical, but I remained patient, willing to set things straight as much as was needed for both her and myself. I wasn't completely clear on the terms, as this was very foreign territory for me, but as long as she was willing to converse with me and work things out, then I would be able to gain clarity.

"It doesn't..." she started again, and I listened. "It sounds a bit off," she said, and I cocked my head.

"What do you mean?"

She lifted her gaze to mine and soon replied with an explanation. "It sounds like you're telling me to take this as whatever I want to take this as."

I considered her words. "That is what I'm saying."

Her brows furrowed deep at this, and I wondered why.

"So it's not that you want a relationship, you just... technically want to sleep with me until you get bored. But you don't want me to feel bad about it, so you're permitting me to call it a relationship and perhaps to be the one to end it whenever I choose to not be at a disadvantage in any way?"

This sounded right to me and in alignment with my idea, so I nodded as well.

"Oh, wow," she said and lowered her head as though to compose herself. "Well, that absolutely cannot and will not work. Not only with me, by the way, but with every other reasonable thinking and feeling woman out there."

I wasn't in the least bit offended by her comment, but I was curious.

"Why?" I asked

"Because it's one-sided," she said. "I'm not saying that I need to be emotionally invested for this to work out, but I also don't want to feel like a charity case or something. I mean... this sounds like a business agreement."

"It's an agreement," I replied, and she continued to stare at me. I lifted my wrist to look at my watch because we were running out of time.

"It's an agreement," I said again. "And I want it to be as unemotional as possible, at least for a start. Things might get complicated after a while, but again, I'm saying that if it ever comes to that, then I'm willing and able to do everything in my power to ensure that you do not, for any reason, walk away with the shorter end of the stick."

She listened and then asked another question. "So... if I do accept, is it a given that I will lose my job?"

I wasn't going to concentrate on this, but now that she was being extremely direct about it, I addressed it head-on.

"To say I wasn't concerned that this would affect our working relationship would be extremely unrealistic," I said, and she nodded.

"Right, it most definitely will."

"Alright then... I know my stance, and so when and if that time comes, I will respond to yours as beneficially as possible."

"What if I don't want to lose this job at the end?" she said. "I've been working with you for a while now and that would be incredibly hurtful for me. I want to keep working with you for as long as I can."

This was endearing to hear, but now that I truly considered this, I realized that taking the initial step that we did in London was the problem. Yet, I couldn't quite label it all evil because it brought us to this moment we were currently in, and I wanted it. I preferred it.

And so, I straightened and told her exactly this.

"Sophie," I called. "I want you. But I've known you for a long time, and I'm hoping you've known me long enough as well to understand that I will have no issues whatsoever in accepting your refusal of this. We will continue working together, and this will no longer be brought up. I am more than capable of putting all of this aside so that we can move on. So all you need to do is tell me what you want or don't want, and I will respect it completely."

At this, she seemed about to speak, but the words didn't come out. She closed her mouth again.

"Alright," she said. "C-can I think about it?"

"Of course," I replied. "Take as long as you need."

Chapter 46
Scarlett

I only needed a few more days.

Just a few more days for all of this contemplation and confusion to be over. If I could just ignore his offer and lay low or as I had even gained permission for, disappear, then perhaps all would be well. I didn't have a few months with him, but Sophie did, and so if I even dared accept this offer in any way, then she would have to be the one to fulfill it, or the tensions between them would rise through the roof. He was probably not expecting the emotional turmoil this would bring, or perhaps he wasn't even aware, but no matter how tough someone was, the rude awakening was sure to come, and it was always bloody.

Maybe he was sure that he could control himself, but I sure as hell couldn't, especially because it was him. The fact that I was so elated by his offer and orchestrating ways to make it work in my mind was more than enough proof for me to understand just how much I liked him and just how much trouble I was potentially getting myself into.

There was just no one like him, and this is why I didn't

want to get too close to the fire because I was sure to get burnt. I also wanted the experience, and always there was a tiny sliver of hope that this could become more than we ever anticipated, but still, I wanted that experience. Because, judging from past experiences and encounters, all of this when stripped down to the bare minimum was a pursuit of passion the likes both of us hadn't experienced before.

It had been intense, sweet, and satisfying beyond either of our expectations and was now quite possibly the hardest thing to look away from.

And so, as I retreated to the office, I considered all of my options. I was so distracted and unsettled, especially because I had asked for the rest of the week off, and I had to handle this before the end of the day to give him a response. Or maybe this wasn't my focus? Maybe my focus was on discovering just how I could make this happen between us, so that rather than go home to my now suddenly distasteful, cold, and unpleasant apartment, I could go to his or wherever. But one thing was guaranteed: that I would be warm throughout the night and slightly out of my mind because I would be with him.

I was distracted with anticipation, dread, and confusion as I managed to keep my head together as I worked while also considering all the other possibilities. And at the end of the day, the only option that came to my mind that would enable me to accept this offer from him was to tell him the truth. That I wasn't Sophie. That I was instead Scarlett and that he had, in essence, never met me. But this was for sure to get Sophie instantly fired. My argument with myself, and one that I wished I had the guts to present to him, was that this wasn't a romantic arrangement between us either way, so there was no need to be too deeply hurt or offended by the deception. However, I had long learned that one of the most fragile things on earth was a man's ego, and so I deeply suspected that his annoyance would be more than enough to override this passion between us.

There was absolutely no way out that didn't involve some kind of loss. It was now a choice of which loss I could best part with. Costing Sophie her job was out of the question; however, there was one more option. Instead of taking the leave as I had planned, I could just hold on until the end of the week and indulge in him without restraints. Try my very best to get him out of my system so that at the end of the day, there would be no regrets, just great brief times and the sexiest memories to look back on.

And then, of course, there was the next best option of all; which was to ignore all of this and to stick to the original and solely professional agreement between the both of us. This one would completely be for Sophie's sake, and I was quite embarrassed that this wasn't my sole focus and concern.

Sighing, I continued to click away at my desk, barely paying any attention to anything until eventually, it was way past closing time, and I didn't even realize it. Lucien was still in his office after having completed a meeting and working away, and so ultimately, and once again, it was just us both. I didn't have a reason to go in, and he didn't have a reason to call me, and I hadn't made up my mind.

I truly didn't know what to do. I tried calling Sophie, but I didn't know how to tell her any of this. It wouldn't make sense. It would simply instigate her fury and make it look like I was emotionally out of control, but this was so far from the truth.

Eventually, every option was taken from me because suddenly the door to his office was pulled open. I nearly jumped out of my skin and was so embarrassed after the fact that I could barely look at him.

"Are you alright?" he asked, and I nodded.

"I am. Just uh... d-did you need anything?"

"No, I'm heading home," he said.

I looked at the time then and couldn't help but notice that this was much, much earlier than his usual time of clocking out for the day. I was a little unhappy and upset because I had hoped that there would be a little bit more time for me to figure out what I was going to do. However, it was as though there was truly no way out. He headed to the door then without a word, and I watched him go.

This would be the last time I saw him because there would be no reason for me to come in tomorrow. Absolutely none, and so I couldn't help the tears that stung my eyes. My heart twisted in my chest, but I couldn't say a word. He left the office, and I sank back down into my chair, but then I got up and began to pace.

I looked at his office door, and in the next second, I grabbed my things, shut off my computer, and was on my way. Thankfully, I met him at the elevators; however, he arrived just before I got there, so I could either hurry up to join in or call another. Just as I was contemplating what to do, his hand slammed against the steel door, and then his gorgeous face appeared.

"Aren't you coming?" he asked, and my only response to this was a resounding yes. It didn't even matter that he was just speaking about the elevator ride. I imagined it meant everything else and tried my very best to breathe.

The ride was longer than I had ever remembered it being, even though it was a private elevator. But through it all, I shut my eyes and savored the scent of his presence, knowing fully well that it might be the very last time.

And for that reason, I once again considered withdrawing my decision to take a leave starting the next day.

"Did you sort out your leave with Rosie?" he suddenly asked, and I was startled.

I looked at him, wondering who the heck Rosie was, and panicked that there was no way to find out because he was standing directly beside me.

I told myself to remain calm then because whoever she was, the fact remained that I hadn't seen her as of yet, so there was no point in lying about it and digging myself into a dark mess.

"No, not yet," I said and cleared my throat.

He turned to me, and I could see the surprise in his eyes. "You're going on leave, and you didn't sort it out with human resources?"

"Ah," my mouth almost fell open in realization. Rosie was probably the head of Human Resources.

"Um... I forgot," I said, and his eyebrows cocked up even further.

"You forgot?"

I wasn't exactly sure what was happening, but it sounded serious, so I turned away and kept to myself.

"Will you then be coming in tomorrow to handle it? I don't understand."

I didn't know either or understand anything, but what I

did know was I couldn't go a moment longer without soothing this now maddening ache for his touch. And so I turned to him and sighed.

"I don't know," I said. "At this moment, I really don't know anything, so it's making me quite confused all around."

"What exactly is making you confused?" he asked, this was the last thing I wanted to get into.

"I didn't go to Human Resources because I haven't made a decision yet from what we discussed earlier at brunch."

"Okay," he said, and I continued, allowing my head to guide me.

"I, uh... you're heading home now, right, or do you have an appointment?" I asked.

"You know my entire schedule," he pointed out. "You're in charge of my entire schedule."

He was right. That was a dumb question to ask.

"I think I may need to be convinced a little bit more," I said, and he cocked his head at me in wonder.

"Convinced?" he asked, and I nodded in response.

His eyes then seemed to sparkle with interest, but before we could say another word, we arrived at the ground floor, and the doors slid open. He ignored it and kept all his attention on me.

"And how exactly would you like to be convinced?" he asked.

"I'm not sure of this either," I said. "Maybe... you could give me some options."

He stared at me, and then he smiled and shook his head.

"I'm hungry," he said. "I want to eat. Do you want to eat as well?"

I couldn't help but smile at this. "You're inviting me?" I asked, and he nodded.

"We can talk more at the restaurant about what exactly you would require to be convinced, and I will see what I can do to make it happen."

Chapter 47
Lucien

I was glad to know that our day together wouldn't be coming to quite an abrupt end. For once I had been planning an early evening in and perhaps a movie or the news to take things a bit slow because just as she had told me she needed a break today I as well wanted to give myself one. It couldn't be for days like hers, but it was something I needed. I didn't want to go to a restaurant though. I wanted to make something myself. I didn't know how to orchestrate this without the invitation to my house meaning that I had other intentions. And so I remained silent, and not till I had collected my keys from Michael and was driving out off the premises with her in the front row did I even discuss dinner plans.

"Where do you want to eat?" I asked, but she didn't respond. I could tell she was thinking hard. Before either of us could speak, a call came in. I checked and after seeing that it was from Elena, I put it on speaker. In the next second, my sister's sweet voice rang out across the car.

"Luciennn," she called affectionately, though loudly, and I couldn't help but smile.

"What's up?" I asked. "I heard you're having the time of your life."

"Of course, you heard and the bodyguards you hired to stalk me also sent you some pictures of us in the plane, didn't they?"

This I didn't need to answer because she already knew, so I went right to the point. "What is it?" I asked, and she sighed.

"I was just thinking of you and the unbeatable oil pasta you usually make. My friend here is from Taiwan, so she claims to have made the original one with peanut butter and all, but I couldn't stop thinking about yours because it is much, much, much, much better. There's absolutely nothing comparable, I swear. And you know I'm not saying this as your sister; it just can't be believed."

This made me smile, and even though I didn't turn to look at Sophie, I could tell that she smiled as well.

"Anyway, just called to check up on you and to find out how things are going over there."

I was a little surprised by everything currently happening. By her call, and her show of concern. It was all very foreign and unusual. "Since when were you this concerned about me to call in the middle of your vacation?" I asked.

"Not concerned," she said airily. "We had pasta, I thought about yours, the end."

I smiled again. "I'm doing fine."

"And, uh... Sophie? You and Sophie are good?" I turned to her then and slightly cocked my head.

"Why are you asking that?" I asked.

"No reason," she said a bit too quickly, and I couldn't help but be suspicious. I also couldn't help but notice that Sophie as well had turned her face away and was now staring out her window, and it was almost as though she were trying to hide her expression from me. As a result, I suspected something foul at play here between the two women but couldn't possibly have any clue what it was.

"Sophie is fine, and so am I," I replied. "When are you coming back?"

"In two weeks," she replied, and I frowned.

"You're in consistent contact with Sophie, aren't you?" I asked. "Aren't you two friends? Shouldn't you know how she's doing? How come you're asking me?"

"Uh..." she seemed stumped, and I waited for her response. It soon came. "You're asking too many questions, Lucien," she said, and I shook my head because what else was I expecting?

"I'm going," I said. "By the way, Sophie's here with me. Do you want to say hi?"

"Uh..." A long silence followed. "Yikes, hi Sophie?" she said, and I truly wondered what this was about. They were much closer than this if I recall, especially because of that book-reading hobby that they both shared.

"Hi Elena," Sophie greeted, and I couldn't help sneaking a look at her beautiful face. Her features used to be much softer and rounder, but perhaps it was the change in hairstyle or the bolder her makeup looked, or perhaps every part of her changed since her breakup. She seemed sharper, more sophisticated, sexier... it was as though some magical dust had been sprayed over her, and just like that, she had become a different person.

Someone I couldn't get out of my head and someone I realized now that I wanted to spend intimate time with. I could picture it, both of us alone in my kitchen, talking. There was so much she already knew about me, yet so little I knew of her that wasn't concerning work or the credentials I needed to know to have offered her the job in the first place. She had been transferred. She was working for one of the sales managers, and then my assistant Lourdes needed to leave to attend to health matters of her daughter in Chicago, so Sophie had been sent up as a temp.

I remembered not being very impressed at first given how weak she'd looked, but a few months later I was comfortable with her. So many mistakes had been made; I had been impatient most of the time. But through it all, she'd taken it all in stride and adapted, and now she was damn near perfect. I just could have never imagined that perfection would extend to more aspects than I could have ever imagined.

"Well gotta go... you know relax on my vacation. Bye!" Elena hung up before either of us could even respond. I chucked because she was acting weird.

"How about..." I started as I neared the intersection of choice. It was either we went to a restaurant from here or I took her home with me. "How about I take you home?" I asked. "It's a purely platonic invitation, don't worry," I said. "It's just that now that Elena mentioned my pasta, I'm craving it. And aren't you the least bit curious to try it? She said it even beat the original."

At this, I saw a beautiful smile spread across her face as she considered this.

"Your kitchen is the most gorgeous kitchen I think I have ever seen," she said, and I nodded.

"That enough to convince you?"

"Yes, and the platonic promise, of course." I smiled but didn't respond to this because I had meant it. I wanted to get to know her a little bit better, and I was certain as a result that nowhere else would be better than the privacy of my home.

Chapter 48
Scarlett

The way life and my emotions fluctuated around him was insane. From being absolutely confused and certain that I was going to be saying goodbye to him forever, I was now somehow heading over to his home and about to cook dinner with him.

To say that I was excited would be an understatement. The nasty, nervous, and anxious feelings were still present though, but my excitement was more than enough to push them down just a little lower, and thus, I was well able to focus on the time ahead.

Soon, we arrived at his apartment, and although I had been here before, I just couldn't get used to how grand it all was. I promised myself then as he led me into the gorgeous foyer that someday soon after I began my law practice, I would ensure to get myself an apartment just like this. Perhaps in this very building, if by the end of all of this, we didn't fall out so badly that neither of us ever wanted anything to do with the other again.

"Make yourself at home," he said as soon as we got in

and then started to head up the stairs. I had no idea exactly what this entailed, and so I stared around, hoping he would come back. When five minutes passed and he still hadn't, I turned around then and headed over to the kitchen. The sight brought my mind back to Elena and how she almost exposed me the last time I was here.

Somewhere at the back of my mind, I was almost sure that she would tell her brother about us, so I had to say that I was quite surprised and almost impressed by the restraint that she had shown earlier. I know she didn't mean any harm whatsoever. Since she had found out, she had no doubt been bursting at the seams trying to keep it in and not tell Lucien, and it just made me shake my head.

She hadn't even gotten back from her destinations yet, and her attention was already divided and for some reason much more interested in my drama. Also, I had no clue what oil pasta was, and so while I waited for Lucien to rejoin his abandoned guest in the kitchen, I pulled up the recipe online and began to peruse through. It was quite easy to make, I found, and so I began to search around his kitchen to ensure that we had everything that we needed.

I found the spring onions, and the peanut butter, but couldn't find any peanuts, but that was okay. Then I found some meat as well, and everything that we needed. I was surprised to see it because from what I knew of him, he didn't eat at home much. This was not a question I could ask him because as his assistant, it was something I was supposed to know more than anyone else. And so before I made another huge blunder, I once again texted Sophie, and this time around, she replied.

Sophie: Hey, how's it going?

I stared at her message and truly couldn't help but shake my head. She was so unserious and had become lackadaisical, and it truly made me wonder if she even actually cared about her job anymore. So this was the first question I asked instead.

She called me immediately. "Why wouldn't I care about my job?" she asked. "Do you know how much we spent in getting this wedding together?"

I furrowed my brows and lowered my voice just in case Lucien suddenly came down the stairs and overheard me. "What wedding?" I asked suspiciously. "Please don't tell me it's back on after two days of being locked in your apartment together."

"We're just talking," she said, "and he hasn't been here. He left this morning."

"Hmm, hm," I replied and heard her smile through the receiver.

"Tell me truly though," she said. "Are there any issues?"

"None but... I was just looking to be careless, so if you are at the point where you can let the job go, then let me know."

"What the hell are you talking about?" she asked. "And what do you mean you are looking to be careless? Have things deteriorated even further between you two?"

I thought of Lucien's proposition earlier and Elena's call and shook my head because she had absolutely no idea. I stuck to my guns, though, about not telling her anything until I was nearly on fire, and thankfully, this wasn't something I had to worry about just yet.

"I'm fine, everything is fine."

"Where are you right now? Still at the office?"

I looked around the gorgeous apartment I was in and truly wondered what to tell her. The last thing I wanted to mention, even though I was dying to, was the fact that I was in Lucien's apartment and he was about to cook oil pasta for me, a dish I was sure was the only one he knew how to make and that he only made it for very few special people, and now I was one of them. Somewhat.

"Heading home now," I lied and shut my eyes, unhappy that I was lying to her but I truly couldn't get in a fight with her now that I was literally at the heart of the storm in Lucien's apartment.

"Oh, alright but it's pretty early though, isn't it?" she asked. "I know this is late for you, sorry about that, but Lucien is usually still at work this time."

"Yeah, I know but—" I paused then as I heard his footsteps descending the stairs. He was far enough, I was sure, for me to quickly wrap up my conversation with Sophia, but I couldn't take any chances. This type of apartment made me quite suspicious because it was so modern and state-of-the-art that I wouldn't be surprised if any words spoken in every corner somehow got transmitted to him. I had already said too much, and so I told her goodbye. "I'll call you later; I have to go now," I said, and before she could protest, I ended the call and put it away.

A few minutes later, he arrived, and I could see that he had pulled off his jacket and tie and pulled out his tails from his pants. He looked so different and casual from his usual office look that I felt mesmerized by watching him as he came over.

He looks so goddamn sexy, I thought, and at some point,

I was sure I physically started to drool because a weird expression came over his face.

"What is it?" he asked and I quickly came back to my senses. I had probably been staring at him as though he were something to eat.

"Um... nothing," I said. "Uh, I went ahead to check for ingredients, and it turns out you have all of them."

"Of course I do," he said, just as I realized that I had forgotten to clarify this with Sophie. I didn't bother making any commentary on this or asking him any questions because I was sure to expose myself, so I shut the hell up.

"Ready?" I asked, and he nodded just as he headed over to the refrigerator. I watched his eyes go down my body as he retrieved a bottle of water and twisted its cap open.

"You were told to make yourself at home," he said. "You can't be comfortable in those heels, right?"

He was right; they were killing me, but I figured I didn't have the right to complain since I was doing my best to look my best for him, especially tonight.

"I'm fine," I said. However, he didn't listen to me. He reached into a lower drawer and then retrieved a pair of house slippers. They looked so comfortable that I didn't even think to feign politeness and reject them.

"Thank you," I said and instantly replaced them with my torturous shoes. Instantly, I felt much shorter, lighter, and at ease, so I sent him a smile in gratitude.

"You can let your hair down as well," he said. "Pull out your blouse, whatever you need. Feel comfortable and grab whatever you want from the pantry or the wine rack."

I nodded as he spoke but didn't actively move to do any

of this. He, on the other hand, came over to the counter to inspect everything that I had just brought out.

"You know how to make oil pasta?" he asked as he looked at me, and for a moment, I was quite startled at the proximity.

"Sure," I said, momentarily losing my brain cells.

"Really?" he asked, and I realized then what I had just said.

"Oh no, I don't. Sorry, I wasn't thinking. What I wanted to say was that I checked the internet for the recipe when you went upstairs, so I got out all the ingredients listed as needed."

"That's good," he commented with a nod and then went over to wash his hands. I waited until he was done, and then I did the same, and throughout all this, my heart started to race. The room was airy and cool, but it was noticeably more difficult to breathe. I loved it, though. I loved my nerves frayed around him, and I loved the excitement that was bubbling in the pit of my stomach.

Earlier on, I was certain that I had been exhausted and hungry, but now I felt none of that. His scent permeated the space, and I just loved how he took the lead even here, as well, as though he were about to teach me.

"Help me dice," he asked then, and I was more than ready. I was assigned my chores, and provided with a knife and chopping board, and we stood side by side. It was silent, and I didn't mind. I loved it because it increased our aware- ness of the other, but pretty soon he turned to me curiously, and I looked back.

"Want me to put on some music?" he asked, and I was a bit surprised at that.

"You never listen to music even when we're in the car."

"Because those are working hours," he replied, and I nodded.

"Sure."

"What kind of music do you like?" he asked, but I shook my head.

"No preference, anything you choose should be fine."

"Well, you know I like slow jazz," he said as he pulled out his phone and began to press some buttons. A few seconds later, a soft melodious jazz tone filled the room. I loved it and almost shut my eyes to savor it, but I kept my attention on my cutting, lest I unintentionally include one of my fingers.

We continued to work in silence, but it wasn't awkward at all, at least to me, since I couldn't quite speak for him. How my mind processed this was that we couldn't technically have known each other for long, it almost felt like we had with the way we were in each other's presence.

"I'll get the pasta started," he said and turned around to head toward the stove, and I nodded. I watched him and grew even more excited when he headed over to the wine rack in the corner.

"Red or white?" he asked, and because I simply wanted something fruity and somewhat sweet, I asked for a white.

"Dry?" he asked, and I shook my head.

"If it's okay with you, I'd prefer something sweet," I said, and he nodded.

"Of course. I think I'd like that as well."

He brought a bottle and poured me a glass, and from the moment I tasted it, it felt as though I had gone to heaven. This was turning out to be such a special night. However, as

I sipped from my glass and watched him head over to the stove to check on the saucepan, I realized that I was somewhat holding back.

Perhaps it was best that tonight be my last with him. Perhaps it was best this didn't go on for longer than what we had right now, and so I imagined that this was the case. This was the only solution to my dilemma so far that ensured that no one got hurt, especially Sophie. So, I made my decision then that I wasn't going to be selfish. I wasn't going to hurt my sister's job by hanging on to Lucien for longer than I had promised, and I wasn't going to hurt Lucien by making him find out that he'd literally been with a complete stranger and not the secretary he had grown attached to for years.

I really didn't want to hurt myself because all of this could blow up dangerously, and if it did, I was in the center. Everyone else, for sure, would be in one pain or the other, but mine would, be incomparable.

And so I went over to him after he retrieved the pan he wanted to make the sauce with, and lightly brushed my hand down his arm. It was quite daring, but I reminded myself once again that this was our last night for real this time. He glanced at me, and my breathing caught at the sparkle I caught in his eyes.

"What is it?" he asked, but I shook my head. After roving his gaze across my face, he turned away, and a smile appeared at the corners of his lips. He knew exactly what I was doing, and what I wanted this to become, and my only hope was that he would accept and not reject me.

"I told you that my invitation was platonic."

I lowered my tone as I responded. "Well, what if I want

to change it?" I asked, and he looked at me. He leaned forward then and my eyes fluttered shut.

I had missed his taste and his kisses; however, when his lips connected with mine again, I was completely taken aback. It was warm and sweet, and perhaps it was the wine, but when his tongue began to stroke and glide against mine, all my brain could process was that this had to be the best kiss I had ever had. It was the perfect pace, slow and then fast, gentle and then heated. Through it all, his passion for me burned into my consciousness, yet he wasn't even touching me. He was already rock hard, and I needed the balance, so I swung my arms around his shoulders. I couldn't help but bring my crotch against his.

I wanted more; however, I didn't want to interrupt this moment between us, so I tried my best to control myself. It didn't work, but thankfully, he was generally a better person than I am, so he straightened and pulled away. My hands were already under his shirt, feeling the warmth and rock-hard strength of his skin, and my lips were already red and bruised in the best possible way.

It was difficult to catch my breath, but eventually, I was able to compose myself enough to be able to meet his gaze.

"Food first," he said. "We'll need the energy."

Something landed a kick in my gut at the words and it almost sent me to the floor. I would have indeed melted into a puddle, but I needed to show him that I was very well capable of controlling myself, and so I nodded, and with great reluctance, managed to pull away. I needed something to keep me busy, though, and so although I headed over to the counter to put things in order, I found myself just picking up my glass of wine and leaning against it to watch him.

His hair was gorgeous, I couldn't help but note. In the office, it was always short, slicked back, and away from his face, but right now, it was almost as though he had run a hand through it, and now it just looked messy.

I loved it, though. He looked so carefree and so breathtakingly handsome that I truly didn't know how to contain myself.

I did, however, want to know quite a bit more about him, however, I didn't know where to start. I didn't want to step into any traps either, but given that this would be my only chance, I went ahead but admonished myself to tread as carefully as possible.

"This is the only dish you cook, right?" I asked with the assumption that this was something of a shared knowledge between us, and thus he was free to correct me for 'forgetting.'

However, he didn't even seem to have noted the way I phrased the question. He just simply answered it.

"I can also make tiramisu," he said.

"Does it qualify as a meal though? That's a dessert?"

He glanced back at me as I said this, but I was too busy trying to recover from what had to be the sexiest thing I'd heard all day. But at the same time, the fact that he knew how to make it made me feel a little sour because it meant that he'd previously met with a woman in his life who maybe taught him.

And just like that, my smile deflated.

I tried to play it off, to act like I didn't care whatsoever; however, when he came over to me then with a wooden spoon stained with the sauce, I decided once again not to hold back.

I tasted it and was quite amazed by the outcome.

"That's great," I said, and he nodded.

"Dinner's almost ready. One thing I love the most about this dish is how everything can be done in one pan. I'll add some shrimp to it," he said and headed over to the refrigerator. He brought out some already-baked shrimp and plopped it in the pan, and I continued to watch until I couldn't keep my mouth shut anymore.

"The tiramisu," I said. "You learned how to make it for a previous girlfriend?"

"No," he replied, and it almost felt as though my spine was going to give out from the instant relief that I felt.

"I learned it for my mom's sake," he said. I was taken aback by this because I hadn't heard anything about his parents from Sophie. There were no pictures or mention of them, and so I paid even more attention now to everything he was saying.

I wanted to ask for more information, but I was sure this would be prying, especially since he wasn't offering any more. I sighed and concluded it.

"That is incredibly sweet," I said, and it was as though I had unlocked my access to more intimate conversation.

"Yeah," he replied. "She loved it a lot, but she wasn't allowed to eat it when she got sick, so I couldn't just buy generic ones for her. So I tried to make it as healthy as possible by switching out a few of the ingredients, and then I brought it to her. She always complained about the taste, but she never left a piece uneaten. Those were great days."

As he concluded this statement, I couldn't help but

admire him even more. If I could guess accurately, I would guess that his mother hadn't made it, and as he spoke fondly of her and referred to the days as great days, I truly admired him for it.

And so when the food was finally ready and he turned around to face me with the most gorgeous smile I'd ever seen, I headed over to him. He wrapped an arm around my waist as he looked down at the pan, and I did the same. My mouth watered, but above all, I wanted to watch him very closely and commit all of him to my memory, so I continued to watch him until eventually, he noticed. He leaned down then surprisingly, and once again, he was taking my lips with his.

I didn't want the food to go to waste and I wanted to know how it tasted. However, the longer he kissed me, the less I wanted to part away.

"I think we can have an entrée," I said when we broke away from the kiss.

Amused, he smiled, but before I could expect a response, he was kissing me once again, and I completely gave in. By the time we parted, all thoughts had been completely wiped away from my mind.

"Let's eat," he said so easily, so casually, while I had to reach for the counter to stabilize myself. He smiled as he watched me, but soon enough, I was able to take my seat on one of the island counters. He brought the plates over and joined me, and the aroma alone made me sigh.

The first bite was heavenly, so much better than I could have imagined, and immediately I understood Elena's compliment of him.

"This is amazing," I told him. "I'm pretty sure if you

wanted to learn about other recipes, you'd be amazing at them as well."

He smiled, and I watched as he rolled the noodles on his fork. He, however, didn't respond, but I was content with just watching him.

I knew he built all that he had now by himself, but the grace, dominance, and work ethic that he naturally exuded seemed to have been ingrained in him from birth.

He was like a drug, I realized as I stared at him. Everything about him seemed to be the perfect fit for all I had always wanted, and this just made me feel even sadder because how could I, against all odds, come so close to what I wanted, yet I couldn't have him?

"Eat before it gets cold," he urged, and he didn't have to ask me twice.

I was starving as I hadn't had anything to eat after that very charged and complicated brunch we had. Not much had been solved, but currently, with the warmth of the apartment, the stunning views, slow jazz, and this dream of a man, every single problem seemed so far away that they might have as well been nonexistent.

As we ate though, I thought about his words from earlier, about the proposition, and even though it sounded preposterous at the time, I couldn't quite get it out of my mind now. The longer I thought about it, the more, per se, it sounded even funnier. And so, I wanted to bring it up as we ate, but it seemed pointless.

A lot of things seemed pointless now that I had made the ultimate decision to leave. Him, his office... his bed... this one was going to hurt.

"What is it?" he asked without even looking at me, and I was somewhat startled.

"How did you know I was staring at you?" I smiled as I picked up my glass, and he shrugged his shoulders.

I couldn't help but smile, but then I decided to bring it up. "So, I was thinking about what you said earlier, your proposition, I mean. From what I interpreted, it seems as though you were saying that I could use you for as long as I want, or until I fly away, though I could break it up without feeling unhappy or used?"

"Yes," he said without missing a beat, and this made me smile even harder. "This is a dangerous proposition to give to women," I told him. "I've never really been worried for you, but now I am."

He smiled as he listened to me. "I'd never say that to any other woman," he said, and once again, my heart stopped in my chest. Thankfully, it soon restarted, but I couldn't help but shake my head as I watched him continue to eat, as though he had just destabilized me, which was so typical of him.

I resumed eating; however, just then, my phone began to ring. There was nothing to be nervous about, but since I was with him and it was technically Sophie's phone, I was always a bit nervous. I considered answering it in a different location, but that would make a big deal out of nothing, so I calmly grabbed my purse and retrieved it.

I suspected who the caller was. It was late at night, and I had basically ignored him the previous day, so this was to be expected. I delayed for as long as possible, rummaging through my bag before reaching it. By the time my hand closed around the device, the call had disconnected.

Relieved, and after confirming that my guess was right, I turned the phone off and put it away. This was the second time I was doing this, and it truly worried me that this would affect Lucien's business. After a few more minutes of contemplation, I turned the phone back on once more. I was leaving tonight, so I could handle him. There was no fear.

None of this, however, and fortunately, escaped Lucien's attention. "Are you leaving because Walters is harassing you?" he asked out of the blue, and again, I was startled by his observance and question.

As I stared at him, my brain was toasted for a few seconds, unable to put together a coherent answer, and it all served to make him even more suspicious. Eventually, I was able to get my mind working again, so I replied. "Oh, not at all," I said, however, he didn't respond.

He went silent, and I felt haunted by this fact, especially given that he had asked me about it earlier, and I had also lied to him about it. So, it was evidence that he was very suspicious or... my eyes widened. Could it be that Gregory had already expressed his interest to Lucien?

I turned to look at him, and he met my gaze. I wavered whether to bring it up, but I knew they had a meeting scheduled together for a visit to Atlantic City soon, and it would be while I was away, so I didn't want any lingering and unnecessary attention to be given to this.

"Did he, uh... did he say anything to you?" I asked.

I didn't expect him to respond to this exactly, but I was hoping that by his reaction, I would be able to gauge what had transpired. He was quiet for a little bit, and then eventually, he glanced at me and shook his head.

· · ·

Lucien

There was no reason to lie to her. But there was also no reason to tell her what I knew of his intentions, even though there were no explicit statements. And so I remained quiet. However, she kept talking about it, which confirmed to me even further that it weighed heavily on her mind.

"Little inconveniences like these crop up sometimes," she said, and I was almost amused at this.

"So you've said," I replied, and she nodded.

"A little flirting won't do anyone any harm, and it's not enough to make enemies with him and lose the contract in any way."

She watched me as she mentioned this, and I knew then that she was suspicious of my intentions to intervene. It was a fact that I had decided to draw back at first since no swords had been drawn yet, but I was more than ready at any time. And so I assured her as I rose to my feet.

"Alright," I replied and took my as well as hers to the sink. After washing my hands, I leaned against it and contemplated because I wanted her with every fiber of my being, but I was just so exhausted from a very long day. I didn't want her to leave either way and so as I turned around, I offered a simpler proposition.

"Are you heading home now?" I asked, and she took her time sipping her wine as she watched me, her eyes roving down my body. It caused excitement to course through me, but I did my best to keep my expression neutral.

"How about I spend the night?" she said, her gaze lowering. "Is that okay? Plus, it's quite late."

This was where this had been heading, and we both knew it, so I nodded. "I'll be upstairs taking a shower," I said, and she nodded.

I was exhausted, but as I walked into my shower and felt the warm cascade hit me, I realized that I had just the amount of energy needed to savor her before I went to bed. Plus, it would make for a more restful sleep. However, I didn't want to force her, so I remained in the stall and washed up.

A little while later, I heard the opening creak of the bathroom door and couldn't help my smile. I hadn't expected her to show up.

Yet here she was and I was so excited by the prospect that I instantly became hard. I waited patiently but when almost a minute passed and she hadn't joined me I turned to see her hooking her fingers into the thong she had on. She was watching me and as I took in her gorgeous body through the steam frosted on the glass, I couldn't look away,

She was so fucking gorgeous and as I watched her I found myself pushing the door open.

This seemed to encourage her because earlier on she had most definitely been hesitating. Now though and even though she looked at me more softly than she ever had, she seemed a little sad.

It was probably because she would be leaving the next morning for her little break I imagined and it made me sigh.

I was more than eager to have her but if she accepted our agreement then I didn't see why her not being in the office had to interrupt our relations.

Soon she was in my arms and as I shut the door behind

her and glued her warm soft skin to my body I almost sighed at the unbelievable pleasure of holding her so intimately.

I was usually never pushy but at this moment and as I leaned down to slide my tongue into her mouth I couldn't help but grab her ass as I pushed her against my cock, determined to ask for exactly what I wanted.

"Feel that?" I whispered to her and felt her whole body shudder as she grabbed onto me. "I know you're going on a break but it doesn't have to stop things between us. Come over, whenever you want, I'll give you a key."

She grinned, as she moved her body against mine, her arms going down my back. I grabbed her and found her soaking wet, and at her sweet gasp into my mouth, I knew that I truly couldn't let go of her.

This was one time in my life that I was willing to push just a bit further and so I wrapped my arms around her ass and lifted her till she was leaning against the glass. She wrapped her legs around me and in the next second, I watched my cock slide deeply into her. She was so tight and snug and given that we were in the extreme privacy of my bathroom stall I didn't hold back my moan and neither did she. It resounded within the stall and coupled with the steam and heat I felt I lost a bit of control over myself.

"Respond," I whispered into her ears. I knew I was pushing her, but rather than complain, she instead straightened from sucking hickeys onto my shoulders and wrapped her arms around me. Smiling, she kissed me and it was one of the sweetest I had ever received. This was a definite yes but for an extra measure she nodded after we parted and the joy that burst through me, was all that was needed to fill me up with the energy needed to fuck her the way she deserved.

She cried out and moaned and marked me with her nails and I loved every moment of it. The wet intimate sounds, the loud smacking of her ass against the glass, the taste of her on my tongue. I tried to go for as long as possible but by the time I had set her down and turned her around to fuck her from behind, it only took a few seconds for the both of us to have our legs quivering and coming. I flooded her with my seed and by then I had to hold onto her to keep her standing.

I couldn't plunge my cock into her any further I held onto her and kissed her without stopping. The steam and heat became too much to handle so we managed to wash up and she was soon curving into my arms, naked in bed with me and on the cool sheets.

We faced the breathtaking view of the city and as I leaned into the crook of her neck to inhale her scent which was a mixture of mine and hers I couldn't think of a more perfect moment to compare this to.

Chapter 49
Scarlett

Getting up from being with him the next morning had to be the hardest thing I had ever done. Especially as I rose to my feet and watched him sleep so peacefully that it nearly brought tears to my eyes. He looked so soft and peaceful, his long dark hair, which I realized was slightly wavy, brushed over his eyes.

I knew that he would immediately wake if I brushed the hair out of his eyes, and for a long moment, I was tempted to do so just to look into his eyes one more time. But I didn't have the courage to. I turned around to retrieve my clothes from where they had been discarded in the bathroom the previous night.

Things between us had always been somewhat explosive, albeit awkward. But this morning, as I looked out of the window of the taxi while riding back home, my heart ached because I knew that there had been something different. I couldn't quite place my hand on it, but even though our time together in the stall had been shorter than others, there had been something so raw about it. It was as though we had been stripped bare in the most intimate of ways, both figuratively and literally, and I didn't know what to do with myself.

Now, however, tears rolled down my face because although his proposal to continue with this made perfect sense, I understood then that this was the moment to stop. Going further, I would never be able to pull myself away from him until disaster struck in several ways, ways that myself and Sophia had been courting over the last week.

I was so remorseful now that we had deceived him and also filled with pain that he would look at me and think that he was looking at her. However, I knew what I was doing from the start. As I returned to my apartment, I wiped the tears from my face and reminded myself that the charade was over and that it was time to get back to my own life.

I tried going back to bed but, for some reason, felt too ill to do so. Plus, the second I shut my eyes, he was all I could think about. So, I got up instead and began to clean the entire apartment.

Sophie called a few times, but I didn't pick up. Eventually, my door was being rapped violently on. I was reluctant to open it; however, a few minutes later, she came barging in with her key. She found me by the counter washing the dishes I had abandoned there for a few days, and she seemed like she couldn't believe me. I wondered what the reason was, but when I simply looked away from the fury on her face, deciding I didn't care, I realized that I was somewhat sluggish and morose.

"What are you doing?" she asked. "Why aren't you at work?"

"I took a break yesterday, what do you mean?" I asked, and her face seemed to drop in shock.

"You're not done with the week yet," she said, but I ignored her and continued washing my dishes. I felt so exhausted and was sure that I had sufficiently tired myself out with all the cleaning and was ready to sleep for the rest of the day.

"You know what, I'm not even here because of that. I'm here because, yeah, you were going to take a leave, and yes, Lucien, for some reason, approved this, but you didn't even properly communicate this to Human Resources. Rosie had to find out this morning from the secretary that Lucien didn't have a personal assistant and had to bring someone over from the lower floors. Are you serious? How could you do that?"

I heard her, and as I realized the implication of what she was saying and how disorganized this would've made him, I lifted my head in shock. She seemed to sigh then, and she finally saw that I finally realized what I had done.

"Oh my God, I'm sorry," I said. "I hadn't made the decision yet to leave until late last night, so I couldn't talk to Human Resources on time."

"And so you just decided not to show up this morning?"

I remained silent because I couldn't tell her that I had spent the night in her boss's area and had assumed that somehow he would communicate this to Human Resources.

I just couldn't imagine going in once again to see him because if I did, I was sure that it would be too difficult to leave.

She went silent after this; however, I didn't know what to do beyond apologizing.

"I'm sorry," I said. However, she remained silent.

"You didn't even pick up your phone," she said. "Do you know how I found out?" she asked. "I just received a scathing email from Rosie asking me how, as the CEO's assistant, I could be so lackadaisical and sloppy."

I was getting completely exhausted by all of this scolding. I knew I had messed up, but I didn't want to hear any more about Lucien or that company any longer.

"Can you take over now?" I asked. "You can even go in and say that you just took a personal morning. You can start now, right?"

She looked at me as though she was completely hurt, and I held her gaze.

"You were so sloppy and lackadaisical about this. If this was your actual job and your reputation was on the line, you would have behaved better, wouldn't you?" she asked.

I could hear the anger and accusation in her voice, and although I knew that there was an element of truth in it, I knew as well that I busted my ass more than I would have if I was working for someone random because her reputation was what was at stake, and so I couldn't help but take offense to it.

I, however, couldn't argue with her, so I just rolled my eyes and returned to my chores.

"You're rolling your eyes?" she said. "Really? You're supposed to do this properly and hand the job back over to me properly as well. What the heck are you doing? If you knew you didn't want to attempt to help me properly from the beginning, then why did you? You just went over there and made a complete mess."

I stopped then and sighed and then turned to her.

"Can you get out?" I swore at her. 'I don't want to deal with you right now."

She gave me a murderous look, but she didn't argue any further. Instead, she turned around and would have slammed the door behind her if it wasn't so heavy.

Afterwards, I seemed to have lost my energy completely, so even though I wasn't done yet with my chores and my living room still looked a mess, I took off the gloves and went back to bed. This time around, as I shut my eyes, I didn't fight thinking about him.

I understood that it was fresh and that it would take a little while for me to get over all of this. I was certain that in a week at most, I would be perfectly fine, and that he would be nothing more than a distant memory.

Chapter 50
Lucien

I had never felt so distracted before. However, every time my door was knocked on and the new personal assistant that was brought in for the day came in, I didn't quite know how to contain myself. I kept staring at her, even though I didn't want to, until eventually, I just dismissed her. I could handle myself for the day, and despite Rosie's profuse apologies and unhappiness, I was glad for the reprieve. Plus, I needed to be on my own for the day anyway.

I wasn't even sure why I felt so restless and sad because even though we had both been nearly coherent the previous night enough to hear our agreement to our continued relations, a part of me wondered if I would ever see her again.

This made absolutely no sense, though, because I was aware of the reason why she wasn't in the office, and I had even scolded her lightly about not properly handing it over to Human Resources before her exit the previous day.

I knew she had eventually made her decision late at night and perhaps didn't want to come in to clarify it, but she could have called. She was much more thorough than this, and for a while, it made me wonder if she was alright.

After lunch, I picked up the phone and called her. I had been seated at my desk when I placed that call, but as soon as it started to ring, I understood that I was too nervous to sound as unbothered as I usually was. So, I rose to my feet and headed over to the windows.

She didn't pick up, and sadly, even after the line disconnected, I held the phone against my ear. After a deep sigh, I pulled it from my ear and contemplated calling again. However, just at the last moment, I stopped myself.

There was no need. I was certain, I had put an unnecessary amount of pressure on her the previous day by even suggesting it, and I didn't want to do that again. And since what I was most concerned about currently was the fact that she was safe, I called Felix instead. He picked up instantly, as though he was expecting my call, however, I didn't read into it.

"Sir," he greeted, and I nodded in response.

"Can you confirm quickly for me that Sophie is alright? She didn't come into work today, but I want to make sure that she's going about her day normally."

For a second, he was quiet, and I wondered why.

"Felix?" I called, and he soon responded.

"Um... sir, I've kept my eyes on her."

I had told him to lax a bit on this, but I knew that he knew her personally, so perhaps he wanted to be sure that she was alright.

"Is she alright?" I asked. "And after now, don't watch her anymore. I don't want to invade her privacy anymore."

"Alright sir, but are you aware that she has a twin sister?"

For the first few seconds, the words flew over my head as I turned around to return to my desk; however, just as I was seated, I understood what he was saying, and something seemed to strike my head with the force of an anvil. However, I wasn't exactly sure what it was and seemed unable to put actual words to it.

I thought hard, and he waited in silence until eventually, I gave up and decided to listen to what he had to say.

"No, I didn't know she had a twin sister. You saw them together?"

"This morning, sir," he replied. "She came in early from the old house I told you was in Chelsea. I mentioned to you earlier the last time that she went to the old house at first, and then came to this new one, and I didn't understand what the discrepancy was. So, I had someone keep an eye on her, and he finally reported to me that they were twins."

"Wait," I was immediately alarmed.

Truly, I was so stunned I didn't even know what to say. But most importantly, it was as though a million pieces that I couldn't quite understand where to place began to suddenly slot themselves into place in my head, and at the end of it, my eyes were open so wide that they nearly popped out of my sockets. There was a lot of explanation needed, but before all of that, there was one thing I had to confirm.

"The girl... the twin in Sophie's old house. What's the color of her hair and what length is it?"

"Sir," he said, and I shut my eyes because I already knew what he was going to say before he did.

"The girl in the original house is Sophie."

"And the one with the dark hair?"

"That's her twin sister," he replied, and something hurt and fiery began to burn in the pit of my stomach. I didn't know exactly what I felt or how to process this. At the end of the day, all I could do was instruct him to immediately head over to the office with the full details of his report.

Less than an hour later, he was seated before me with the folder in his hands as he narrated the details. However, I wasn't quite ready to open it up just yet. I wasn't even properly listening to him because my mind was in a dark place. One clear emotion that I could identify was anger, but at the same time, I was somewhat amused because I should have known. And then, a part of me as well was relieved because it meant that I hadn't been blind all of these years. From the very beginning, or more accurately, as I now knew from the beginning of this week, my attraction to her had been instant, and it was something that I had been unable to make sense of. But now that this thread had been revealed, everything felt connected, and I preferred this state of complete knowledge to be in the dark like I had been.

Finally, there was a part of me that knew it would be difficult to forgive her because I felt fooled. However, I couldn't understand why, and more than anything, I needed to know. And most importantly, how long had they been planning on continuing with this charade? Surely this hadn't just been something they had orchestrated for fun, right? I mean, there had to have been a purpose, and if there was, why had Scarlett, as I now knew her name to be, suddenly stopped coming today? Finally, as I pondered on this, I realized that I finally had a question I wanted to ask Felix, and so I lifted my gaze to his.

"Do you know why she stopped coming to work today?" I asked.

He opened his file then and began to flip through, but in the end, he as well didn't have an answer.

"We just discovered all of this this morning, so I have one of my men on it and building the details. But all that we have right now is what I've told you."

"Hm," I replied, nodding.

We both remained silent after this as I thought of what to do. Keeping quiet and acting like I didn't know anything seemed to be the best course of action. However, I knew that I would be too anxious to wait. My entire body, mind, and spirit were restless, and I knew that what I needed, beyond all else, was answers. And I knew just who to get them from.

"Call off your men from finding out more details," I told Felix, and he lifted his gaze at me, somewhat surprised.

"You don't want us to find the answers to the questions you have?" he asked, noting the glint of curiosity in his eyes.

"I do, but there's no need to search secretly when I can just ask Sophie."

His expression turned skeptical, and I knew exactly the reason for this.

"I know," I said. "You expect her to lie to me, but I don't think she will. There has to be an explanation for this entire charade, and I want to hear what she has to say."

He considered this for a few minutes and then offered an alternate suggestion. "Why don't I continue with my search, sir? As discreetly as possible, of course. This way, you'll have my report to use in corroborating whatever answers she gives to you."

I considered this, and eventually, I couldn't find a reason to reject it, so I nodded.

"How soon can you get back to me?"

"Within twenty-four hours, sir," he replied, and I agreed.

"Afterward," I told him. "You'll pay a visit to Sophie for me. And tell her that I want to meet with her."

"Certainly," he replied, and our plans were set in motion.

Chapter 51
Scarlett

By the time I woke up, the apartment had turned from daylight to nighttime. It was so dark that I wondered if there was any point in me even getting out of bed. However, when I realized it was just eight pm and I was starving, I eventually got out of bed and pushed my hair out of my eyes.

I remained silent for a little while as I tried to get my bearings, and a sinking feeling settled in the pit of my stomach as I realized all that had happened. It was a terrifying combination of dread, loss, and hurt. I pounded on my chest to somewhat alleviate what I could of it, but this was expectedly fruitless, so I got up and went off to shower. I felt so weak, yet I couldn't close my eyes or even linger in the stall because when I did, all I could think about was the previous night and the unbelievable way it had felt to be in his arms. It seemed as though the last week had been a year-long, so it was amazing to me that my entire world seemed to have shifted in the space of just a few days.

It made me so incredibly sad that by the time I exited

the bathroom, my entire body felt unstable. My weakness seemed to intensify, and when I finally sat down to decide what to order, I realized I didn't have the appetite for anything whatsoever. Then I considered just opening a bottle of wine and emptying it so I could go to sleep, or perhaps I could catch up on my classes. I stared at nothing as I considered this until eventually, I settled on the fact that what I needed was something sweet to chase away the bitterness I currently felt in my life. Sophie's sweet potato pastries came to mind, and I decided that what I wanted was to not be alone. Plus, we needed to talk anyway about how to seamlessly switch back to our own lives, and as I started to call her, at the last moment, I decided not to. Due to how upset she had been with me earlier, she was bound to be a tool on the phone and even refuse me to come over. But she was my twin sister, and if anyone had access to her, it was me. So, I picked up her house key and made my way out of the apartment.

I took a taxi and stared out of the window all the way through, unable, as a result, to stop thinking about the man who had this same habit. He listened to nothing on his commute, and didn't speak... all he did was hold his chin and think, and it was just one of the many things I realized that I liked about him.

Eventually, tired of keeping him in mind for my mental stability, I shook my head to dispel any further thoughts about him and pulled out my phone to begin searching for a new assistant job to fill up this one that I had just most definitely lost.

Eventually, I arrived at Sophie's apartment and didn't even bother knocking. Just as I turned the door key, however, I heard her call from inside. "That better be a burglar because if it's you, then just leave. I don't want to deal with you right now."

Rolling my eyes, I pushed the door all the way open and headed in. Just as expected, she was curled up on her sofa with a humongous blanket and with a tub of ice cream in her arms. She was watching Sex and the City, and as I noted the cozy, sweet-smelling apartment, I knew that I had made the right decision by coming over.

Immediately, I headed over to her and grabbed the blanket, and in no time, I was under the covers with her. She frowned deeply and almost tried to kick me out, but I refused to budge and got as comfortable as possible. Through it all, she glared at me until she finally accepted that I wasn't going anywhere. She watched me then, and when she finally noticed my droopy expression, she understood I wasn't okay.

"Here," she handed me her bottle of wine, and as I stared at the half-full bottle of wine she offered, I was amused.

"Why not just pour me a glass?" I asked.

"You look like you need more than a glass," she replied, and I didn't have any arguments whatsoever to counter this. And so, I took the bottle from her and took a healthy drink. I immediately felt better, but when I eyed the cookies on her plate, I immediately asked for more.

"Did you just bake those?" I asked as I held out my hand, and although reluctant, she handed one over to me.

"No," she replied. "I meant to, but I got exhausted, so I just used the store-bought mix that I already had."

"How is it?" I asked as I took a bite, and she didn't bother responding to me. Smiling, I tasted a bite, and it was just as heavenly as I had imagined. Coupled with the wine, I was beginning to feel so, so much better. She, however, only watched the show for a few more minutes before eventually muting it and turning to face me fully.

"Let's talk about things tomorrow," I told her before she could say a word. However, she refused.

"No," she said. "Things are quite a mess right now. In short, I was just about to call you or even come over again, but I was still pissed at you. We need to resolve everything that has gone wrong so that I can know where I stand because currently, it feels as though I am unemployed. In short, I'm a hundred percent sure I have been fired." Her rage flowed over me. "If he's even feeling half of what you're feeling right now, then maybe I won't be so easily dismissed."

"He approved me leaving the way I did," I groaned. "Unless you tell him he agreed with your twin and not you, then you have nothing to worry about."

"Hm," she said, and I wondered what she was thinking about. She soon explained.

"Do you think he knows?" she asked, and I was a bit surprised to hear this.

"If he did, would we be... I mean... would things be as calm as they currently are?"

"He doesn't throw tantrums when he's mad," she said. "Instead, he plots his revenge very slowly and carefully."

Her words made chills run down my back, but I tried my best to hide it as I asked, "What kind of revenge?"

"Well, right now, what I am almost a hundred percent sure of is the fact that the moment I go to work next, whenever that is, I will probably not even be let into the building. I would probably be given my dismissal letter at the reception and politely told to get the heck out."

"Why would you think he would do that if he doesn't know?"

"I don't know anything right now, Scar," she said. "All I'm focusing on at this moment is enjoying my evening, and you should do the same as well."

I followed her advice for a little while, but eventually, I couldn't help but speak again.

"You're not mad at me anymore?" I asked, my tone lowered and sheepish.

"Good assumption and a very sneaky way of framing the question," she said, and I almost laughed out loud. We were quite different generally speaking, but sometimes it was as though she read my mind.

I watched her for a few seconds and then decided to frame it the right way.

"Are you still mad at me, then?" I asked.

She hesitated in responding, but eventually, and without looking at me, she turned her face to the muted television screen as she spoke.

"I thought about it," she said, "and to be honest, I don't know why I was mad at you. I mean, you didn't do everything perfectly, but I was quite dramatic earlier. I was accusing you of sabotaging my job on purpose. That's insane."

I lowered my gaze as I processed her words.

"Sometimes it felt like that was what I did."

She turned to me, "Oh, you did ruin it alright, but not on purpose, hence why it's pointless to be mad at you."

I managed a sheepish smile.

"You look sad," she said. "Do you feel sad?"

I automatically wanted to lie, but at the last moment, I asked myself what was the point of that, and there was none.

"I was when I came here," I replied. "Immensely. But now not so much. Sugar and alcohol are the cure to everything."

She looked amused. "Tell me this," she said. "Honestly. Was it just a lust thing? Do you like him at all?"

Once again, I was given the option of lying, and I wanted to take it, but I needed to talk to someone, and better her than anyone else, so I nodded.

"Yeah, I like him a lot. That's why I had to stop."

"You didn't think you'd be able to leave if you kept going to the end?" she asked. "Why though? It was just a day or two left."

I considered her words and then released a heavy sigh. "He asked me to somewhat become exclusive with him," I said. "Yesterday." Saying it now sounded so strange to me because it felt as though all of this happened eons ago, however, it was just yesterday. I almost couldn't believe it.

Sophie couldn't believe what I was saying either because her eyes were somewhat agape as she stared at me.

"Really?" she asked, and I nodded. "What? Lucien Montgomery?"

"Does he have a secret girlfriend somewhere that no one knows about?" I joked. However, she replied bluntly.

"No, he does not, it's just that he's never really taken dating seriously, but now in so short a time, he wants to be exclusive with you? Like a real relationship."

I thought of explaining the rest of it to her, but there was no point, and so I kept it to myself.

"If..." she started. "If I wasn't coming back, and you were working for him, would you have agreed to it?" she asked.

And this question I didn't have to think about.

"Yes," I replied. "I would."

"So you held back because of me?"

"Not because of you," I replied, "but because of us. We deceived him majorly, and we should thank God if he doesn't eventually find us and chew the shit out of us, but that's by the way. The real issue is that if he finds out, he's sure to be mad and never want anything to do with any of us ever again.

"Yeah, right," she said, and then she sighed. "Let's stop talking about him," she said. "Whatever will be will be, or perhaps we can start trying to fix what we can tomorrow, but for now, I don't want to think about Lucien or his office."

"Sure, but we need to think about what we will do with the changed hair situation," I said, and she nodded.

"You're right. Damn, I wish you had just told him from the beginning that it was a wig. Now I have to cut my hair and dye it black. Absolutely not. I can't do that, so you're right, we need to think of a way to fix this problem."

I thought about what she was saying; however, I couldn't come up with any explanations.

"Maybe I should wear a dark wig instead?" She turned to me then to ask. "And then like in a month switch to my hair and say that I let it grow out and changed the hair color back."

"No one's hair grows that fast," I pointed out this very obvious fact to her.

"Well, what's he going to do? Question how fast my hair can grow?" she asked, and I shook my head.

"You're so salty today," I said, and she nodded.

"It was a very salty day. Also, weight gain," she said. "I started baking again this week to see if I could add a little more meat to my bones. Is it working?" she asked as she threw off the blanket from her body. However, she was wearing baggy home clothes and curved in an awkward position.

"I have no clue," I replied, "but I'll check later when you've gotten up."

"Sure," she said and threw the covers over her once again.

We both settled in to watch the series, yet we kept the television muted and turned on subtitles instead. And so the night drifted quite easily until just a few minutes before midnight, there was a knock on the door. I instantly knew it was her fiancé, and I couldn't help but be pissed at the interruption.

"Is that Jerald?" I asked. However, I realized that she was looking at the door as well and frowning deeply.

"Jerald left town on a business trip," she said. "Why would he be back here?"

She rose to her feet.

"Are you expecting anyone?" I asked, and she shook her head as she headed over to the door.

"Not this late."

I was curious as well, but not curious enough to turn to

watch the door as she answered it, so I kept my gaze on the screen until eventually I heard her speaking.

Her words were muted, so I didn't quite hear anything she was saying, but eventually, she shut the door, and then she just stood by it.

"What is it?" I asked.

"What's the time?" she replied, and I wondered why she was asking this. However, at the expression on her face, which was quite blank and even just a tad bit terrified, my heart jumped. I knew that there was something wrong, and my mind instantly went to Jerald.

"Is everything okay?" I asked.

"Is it midnight yet?" She asked, and I grabbed my phone.

"Twenty after," I replied, and she released a heavy sigh. Then she hit her hair and began to head over.

She stood before me and then she explained.

"That was Felix," she said; however, the name didn't ring a bell.

"You haven't met him so far, have you? It makes sense that you haven't; you were the one being investigated."

At my words, everything inside of me went still.

"What? Investigated? By who?"

Even as I asked these questions, I knew where and to whom it was all pointing. My heart was already beating so fast, and my stomach began to roil.

"Lucien," Sophie explained.

For the next full minute, I was struck speechless because I didn't know what to say, and then I became confused. Questions flooded my head, and I didn't even know which to address first.

"Why? I mean, did he know that I wasn't you?"

Despite my dread, a small part of me I realized was hopeful that all along he had realized the difference. That all along he knew.

"I don't know," she replied. "I don't know anything. All I know is that Felix said he wants to see me right now."

"Right now? In his home?"

"Office," she replied, and then she sighed.

"I'm probably going to get fired, but that's okay; I needed a change anyway."

This was a blow to my gut that left me unable to speak. Instead, I watched as she got ready until eventually, she was at the door.

"Should I take a taxi?" I asked, however, she shook her head.

"No, Felix came with a driver. They'll take me to him."

I wanted to apologize; however, the words didn't come out of my mouth.

"Tell him it was all my fault," I said, "that it had nothing to do with you."

"That's the lie that will probably ensure that he doesn't even want to speak to me. He probably already knows the truth if Felix is involved, so it's best I just come clean."

I nodded and she went on her way.

Chapter 52
Lucien

I had thought I would be able to wait. Truly, I wanted to see how all of this would play out to figure out what their original plan was, but I found myself unable to concentrate and unable to think of anything else besides... Scarlett. A lot of things had changed. First of all, it was so easy for me now to see her as a different person, to sort of separate her from Sophie, which was a relief, but then again, this came with an unsettling sense of dread because I now realized that more than ever she was a stranger to me.

There were a lot of things I had done with my guards completely down around her simply because I had thought her to be Sophie, but now that the truth had been revealed, I couldn't help but imagine that it was going to be much more difficult for me to be more relaxed around her. Or maybe it wouldn't?

All of these were the reasons why I wanted to see Sophie and her, but I didn't want to jump the gun. And so I found myself somewhat nervous when the knock I was waiting for finally came to the door. I didn't look up even as I was granted access, but when I eventually heard Felix's voice, I did and realized that he was alone.

"What happened?" I asked.

"Sophie's waiting outside, sir," he said. "But I just wanted to come in first to inform you that her sister was at the house when we asked Sophie to come with us."

I heard his words and understood their implications; however, I didn't bother asking him any further questions. Instead, I decided that I was going to direct it to her.

"Tell her to come in," I said, and he nodded.

A few minutes later the door was once again pushed open and my actual personal assistant came into the office. I thought I was ready, but when I finally saw her, all I could feel was amazed that I had been so dense. They looked alike, yes, but not enough to have fooled me. I just couldn't have imagined that there was anyone else with such an uncanny resemblance that could pass for her. But now, as I stared at the much smaller, petite brunette, conservative woman before me, I was almost embarrassed that I could have ever mistaken them. They didn't even sound the same, but I had brushed all of that off.

So many questions then flooded my mind, but eventually, as I stared at her, the most pressing at the moment floated to the top.

"Did she come with you?" I asked, and she finally found the courage to stare straight at me. Unlike her sister, however, I realized that she couldn't quite look me in the eyes, as had always been the case. She was a bit more reserved, quieter, shyer, and not aggressive at all. Yet, I had agreed, like Scarlett had urged, to chalk this all up to her developing a new personality overnight because her fiancé had broken up with her.

Once again, I felt like palming my face.

"No, sir, she didn't," Sophie replied, and I stared a bit more at her.

"Is she aware?" I asked and I hoped to God that she wouldn't lie to me. I felt relatively calm but I was still furious and offended, but I was still in a certain state of not knowing what to do. Whether to be lenient or whether to punish them harshly, however, how she responded to me from now on I realized would determine this and so I waited for Sophie to respond for her and her sister's sake. "Since things have come to this now, you should know better than to lie to me. I'm willing to listen to you now, but the moment you lie, things will become much, much worse for you and Scarlett."

I loved her name, I realized, as it sounded from my lips. And it was so befitting to her appearance and personality that I wondered if she had given herself the name because I couldn't have imagined that their parents would have been this clear about their differences from the very beginning.

"I understand, sir," she said, her voice low and contrite. "She is suspicious, especially since Felix came over to my apartment, but I haven't told her anything definite since I wasn't certain myself until I got here."

This sounds like the truth to me, so I accepted it. I watched her once again, and the same question came easily to me.

"Why?" I asked.

It took her a while, but eventually, and for what had to be the first time in probably forever, she stared boldly at me.

Her tone was strong, and even though I knew she was sorry I had found out, I was almost certain that she didn't regret that she had done this, and it somewhat annoyed me.

"I'm sorry, sir," she apologized first. "I'm really sorry. I never meant to orchestrate this, and I can assure you it wasn't for fun. It's just that... I didn't want to disappoint you. We had the meeting with Charles Nioly come up, and I knew just how hard you have worked toward it over the last two years. I didn't want to take the time off and force you to have to find someone who could assist you in the meantime. You'd have to catch them up to speed and explain things, and it was not an easy decision to make."

I understood what she was saying, and I appreciated it; however, I wasn't ready to just drop all of this and forgive her just yet, so I remained silent and continued listening.

"My, uh... it was true, my fiancé suddenly broke up with me and called our wedding off. This happened when I left early from work Monday and... I just... things had reached a breaking point and I didn't imagine that I could go on without a break. We've done things like this a few times in the past, even to our mom when we were younger, so I thought of it for a moment and made a bad call. I am deeply sorry."

I held my chin, and I shifted even more comfortably in my seat because this was getting more interesting than I could have anticipated.

"What exactly made you so sure that I was going to completely believe that she was you?" I asked, and she looked at me again.

"I wasn't sure. I was just a bit delirious at the time enough to try. It was a terrible call."

"You see it now as a terrible decision because you got caught?"

She shook her head.

"I knew it was a terrible decision from the beginning because I know just how much you value loyalty and how much you hate lies. I... I understand if you want to fire me because of this, but I want you to know that I would never have let it go on for long, and I didn't do it to cause you harm in any way. Things just got more..." She paused, but I understood exactly what she was saying and where she was going, and I couldn't help but feel a little bit uncomfortable that she was aware of how my relationship with her sister had turned sexual so rapidly while I thought she was the one. Facing the real person now, I had to admit that this was a bit difficult for me to swallow.

"What exit was the agreement between you two?" I asked. "I mean, how long was this supposed to go on for?"

"Just for the week." She replied. "I was sure I would be able to get my bearings back and recover within the time."

This made me frown.

"So if your arrangement was for the week, then why did she suddenly quit today?"

The room went silent now, and I watched closely because I couldn't tell if she didn't know the answer to give or if she was looking for a way to lie.

"Um," she eventually replied. "I'm not entirely sure about that, sir. She hasn't shared that with me yet."

"But you two were together when Felix arrived."

"Yes, but we decided to put away all talk about this for later on. Neither of us were in the best of moods."

I was reluctant to ask this, worried that it would reveal

to both me and Sophie the uncontrollable concern I felt at her words.

"Is she okay?" I asked. "Is she sick?"

"Not really," she replied. "We haven't talked about it. We were at odds as well because of how abruptly she had left earlier today."

I understood why she had left abruptly earlier this morning, but apparently, she hadn't told her sister about it.

"Are you two very close?" I asked. One would think it was a given that they were since they were twins, but I understood that this wasn't always the case.

"Before now, not very. We speak more on the phone than actually meeting up, but we've never been at odds."

I listened to her, and then I nodded. Truthfully, I didn't know how to go forward from here or what to do, and so I decided to give myself a few days to sit on it since my curiosity had been sated.

I wanted to see Scarlett, but I held back. I deeply suspected that more emotion than was needed would come into play if I didn't see her, but I couldn't trust myself to make the right call, and this was so strange to me. I'd always been able to compartmentalize emotions and distractions, but now and perhaps it was because of the late hour, it all just felt so muddled to me, and the last thing I wanted was to deal with anything. So ultimately, and since I had heard enough, I decided to dismiss her for the night.

"You can go," I told her. "I'll communicate my decisions about your position here with Human Resources, and they'll communicate with you on any necessary updates."

She was quiet for a long moment, and then she nodded,

her shoulders slightly slumped in defeat. Just before she left, however, there was one more request that I had.

"Give me your sister's phone number," I asked.

At first, she hesitated, but in the end, she headed over and I handed my phone over to her. She knew my password and all my details, so I didn't need to say a word as she inputted the phone number and then saved her contact.

"Goodnight, sir," she said, I didn't hear her. My attention now was completely on the new name that had been added to my contacts. I stared at the words and realized that I had been more intimate with this stranger than I had been with anyone else for as long as I could remember.

And yet, I had never called her by her name.

Chapter 53
Scarlett

The moment Sophie left to see Lucien, I knew I was going to throw up. I had somewhat staved it away all day and had chalked it up to my bad mood and annoyance with everything that seemed to be going wrong, most of which was of my own making. However, now I could no longer keep anything down or settle my nerves. I was anxious, sad, and furious all at once, and I didn't know how to contain any of it, not until Sophie called anyway.

I returned to the living room and sent her messages about how things were going. It was now almost two am and I had returned home, and yet there still hadn't been a word from her. Thankfully, she finally responded, and I was so relieved that I nearly dropped my phone.

I held my breath as I turned the screen around, praying in my heart that she wouldn't be fired. This was what I needed most above all else. I could take whatever punishment he dished out if only he would let her keep her job; otherwise, I would feel way too guilty.

I felt incredibly foolish now for worrying about this when I should have done so from the very beginning. I should have been more cautious, should have had a stronger will to enable me to resist Lucien, and yet I had lost, and Sophie was going to suffer as a result. I hurried to the sound of knocking at the door with all these swirling thoughts, it felt as though I was about to combust from the inside, and then somehow, it channeled into anger.

The moment I opened the door, I was ready to bring up this anger with her. However, just as it registered in my distracted brain that if she were here she would have her key, a burly man with a buzz cut straightened and spoke.

"Mr. Walters would like to see you," he said, and for the first few seconds, I was alarmed, and then I grew scared at his size.

"What?" I asked.

"Please follow me," he said, then without a word, and his voice made me understand that there was no room for defiance. If that didn't do the trick, the second suited hooded guard standing at the end of the hallway and watching me was more than enough to ensure my obedience. I knew exactly then who I was dealing with, however, I couldn't quite decide whether to be furious or scared about this forceful visit.

Eventually, I decided to comply because I didn't see how not doing so would grant me any peace for the rest of the night or fail to further complicate my life. And so I headed down as well, and a few minutes later, I saw the black town car waiting by the curb. I had no intention of entering, so I quickly went to the passenger side and knocked as loudly as I could manage without being outright rude.

The tinted glass soon rolled down, and inside was that man. I glared at him internally and was truly impressed by the smile I was able to curve my lips into externally. But with those two bodyguards who suddenly seemed to have disappeared, I wasn't going to risk being impolite to him.

"Hello," I greeted. However, he didn't respond. He continued to watch me, and I took the time to look around me to see if I could just walk away and be protected. However, it was too late, and there was almost no one around. And so I sighed and kept waiting.

"I detest being lied to, Miss Sophie," he said, and I honestly couldn't believe his words. I glared at him then, and it took all of my strength not to tell him to go screw himself.

"I wasn't feeling well... I'm still not feeling well. I didn't even go to work today, yet you wanted me to come hang out on a yacht?"

He listened to my words, and then he sighed.

"Get in then. I'm sure whatever's wrong with you, a little trip will make you feel better."

At this point, I was sure this was harassment, and that I could report it to someone, but now I didn't know who. He hadn't technically done anything wrong enough to warrant a visit to the police station, or maybe he had? But he was pestering me enough to be warned.

I thought of Lucien then, and it was as though all the pain and sadness I had managed to hold at bay from the morning came crashing down on me once again.

"I can't go on any boat right now," I told him. "I'll get seasick, and it's too late at night."

"I have my security in place to guard us," he said to me.

I could see in his eyes that he was set on this and that whatever he had planned for tonight was going to end up putting me in a compromising position. So there was no way in hell I was going to accept it. If he were to take me, he would have to take me kicking and screaming. Plus, I didn't work for Lucien anymore, so technically, he really could go screw himself.

"I don't want to," I said. "So respectfully, I decline."

"We're heading to Atlantic City," he said as I turned around, and I was almost amused because was that supposed to spike my interest. "I think it would be good for you to see one of the casinos we handed over to your company," he said. I smiled because what an idiot. The casino that our company manages. He was creating an alibi and dangling it in front of my face like a jeweled bait.

I ignored him, however. Just before I arrived at the entrance, the two men I had seen earlier came up to me and stood at a standstill. I was forced to stop and glare at them, and then I turned away to meet their amused boss in his car.

"You know, you forcefully take me to a place that I don't want to go, that legally constitutes kidnapping, and it's a serious offense."

He laughed at this. "How could it be kidnapping when we hit it off previously and then went out tonight to discuss work-related matters?"

"Please leave me alone," I told him. "I quit, so you can't use ruining this project to manipulate me. I don't give a damn."

"Get in the car," he growled, and I knew then that we would most likely not even get to Atlantic City. I might be assaulted in the car and dumped somewhere, so I immediately made a snap decision and made a beeline down the street.

However, I had only taken a few steps when I suddenly crashed into someone. Their chest was like a boulder, and they towered over me so immensely that I couldn't see anything beyond the dark coat and jacket.

I immediately started to fall backwards thanks to the impact, however, he reached out and caught my arm. I was immensely grateful then, but that quickly dissipated when I sensed that I was still in danger because this could as well be one of his goons.

And so I instantly began to move away, but then a familiar scent caught my nostrils.

I instantly went still then, and even if I wanted to leave, I couldn't. However, I was too nervous to look his way. My heart was pounding so hard in my chest that I felt as though I was going to be ill again, but eventually, when he called my name, I had no choice but to meet his eyes.

"Scarlett," he called, and my heart thundered in my chest. He didn't call me Sophie; he said my actual name for the very first time, and he was here at my apartment.

I tried my best to hold back, and when I finally met his gaze, I couldn't hide the moisture in them.

"Lucien," I called, and he watched me for a little bit, and then he looked at the car still waiting at the curb and the goons in the back.

"Are you alright?" He asked, and I nodded.

"Head upstairs to the apartment," he said. "I'll be right there."

I nodded and started to leave, but when I realized what this would result in, I caught his arm. I intended to stop him, however, he pulled his arm away from me almost as though I were some reptile.

I felt the rejection keenly but I understood. We were technically strangers; I mean, if he hadn't mistaken me for my sister, I might never have even been allowed access to the same room to be able to speak to him. And so I lowered my gaze, took a step back sheepishly, but thankfully still managed to say what I wanted to.

"There's no need; I mean, there's nothing wrong. He just wants a night out, and I refused."

He waited until I looked at him before he replied.

"He wants a night out so badly with you that you had to run to get away from him."

"This is going to ruin the deal," I told him, "and there is no point in it. I... I don't work for you."

He considered this, and then, to my surprise, he shifted from one leg to the other and then nodded. "You're right. You didn't work for me, so there is no point in taking my anger out on him. Still, head upstairs."

"Okay," I nodded, as I recited further emotional blows, but there was nothing more I could say or do. I headed over to my building, and before I even reached there, the men parted out of my way. I glared murderously at them, and in no time, I was returning to my apartment.

I would have thought that I would be so anxious to run up to safety and shut my door, but my legs suddenly felt as heavy as lead. Every step taken was almost excruciating because it felt as though I was walking away from him forever. Maybe I should have invited him to come up after he was done, I couldn't help but wonder. Would he... and why was he here? Had he come to see me?

Eventually, I arrived at my apartment and locked the door behind me. However, I couldn't leave. So I sat and waited and prayed that I would receive the knock that I wanted to hear more than anything in the entire world.

Chapter 54
Lucien

I didn't know what to do with both of them. On one hand, I wanted to hurt and get rid of them, but they were still attached to me in various ways. I watched her leave and then turned to the idiot in his car. If he had any sense, he would leave as well, but instead, he remained seated, waiting for me to reach him. The windows were already down, so I stared at him. And he stared back.

"Montgomery," he greeted. "Fancy seeing you here at your assistant's house past midnight."

I knew the angle he was trying to play and what he was getting at, but I realized I didn't even want to waste a second of my life speaking to him. "You'll hear from my lawyers," I said, and his face darkened.

"About what exactly?" he asked, but I turned around and walked away. The two men at the building's door instantly slinked away upon my arrival. I stopped for a moment to note their faces and then headed in. She lived on the third floor, so by the time I arrived, I had enough time to think about what I wanted to say to her. Or if I even wanted to talk to her at all.

I had passed by on my way home and luckily spotted her just in time. I had been sure that I had absolutely nothing to say to her and didn't want to see her, but the second I saw her run, my whole heart lurched. I was still in so much rage because I wanted to burn the skin off his bones, but I took deep breaths and focused on her. She was the one I had to address now, yet as I stared at her door, I still didn't know what to say.

I thought hard, and the opening of assuring her that she would be safe because I had eyes on her occurred to me, but I didn't care to do that. So in the end, I turned around and left. Just as I reached the first flight of stairs, I could hear her door creak open. I kept going but didn't hurry my steps, and just before I was out of sight, she spotted me.

"Hey," she called, and I stopped. She came out of the apartment then and hurried over, and I looked up to stare at her from across the space.

"You're leaving," she said, and I frowned. No kidding. I had the perfect comeback for that.

And you're a liar, I wanted to say, but I kept my thoughts to myself.

I stared at her then, and given that I had seen Sophie earlier, the difference was so stark now that I couldn't unsee it. And as a result, a mix of emotions surged within me—longing, anger, concern, loss... hope? I didn't know which was the accurate depiction of how I was supposed to feel at this moment about her and concerning all that had transpired between us, and it frustrated me to no end. I couldn't remember the last time I had been this indecisive about anything, and it made me even more annoyed to see her.

"Thank you for helping me," she said, and I watched her. Her face was scrubbed clean of any makeup and she had on baggy clothes. This way, she seemed so innocent, and my heart seemed to melt for her, but thankfully, I caught myself.

"You'll be safe," I told her. "So, don't worry. I'll keep surveillance on you until he is dealt with. My..." I paused as I quickly thought over what I wanted to say. It hadn't been put into effect yet, but I knew that the moment I mentioned it, it would be very difficult to take back. "My assistant will be in touch," I said, and she seemed to freeze.

"Your assistant?" she asked before I could take a single step further.

"Yes," I replied.

"So... does this mean that Sophie..."

I understood what she was asking, but I didn't feel like giving her the satisfaction of peace for the moment. "It's not your place to assume," I said.

She understood what I meant, and she nodded. "I know, and for the record, I didn't know things would turn out this way. She... she just didn't want to disappoint you by being unavailable, so I took her space for a few days."

Her words sounded crazy to me as they came out of her lips, confirming even further that anything done at this moment would be wrong. So I looked away and continued on my way.

"Please don't fire her," came the plea. However, I didn't stop, and to my surprise and horror, she came after me. By the time I had reached the platform connecting the two flights, she was bounding down and trying to catch up with me. Eventually, she did, but wisely, she maintained her distance.

"I'll do anything to ensure she keeps her job," she said. "Please. This means a lot to her, and... I was the one who took things too far."

I realized I didn't care about all of the explanations she was giving. There was one thing I needed to know. "Why did you suddenly quit today?" I asked. She seemed taken aback. "When I spoke to Sophie, she said that she doesn't know. So now I'm asking you."

She looked at me, then lowered her gaze and sighed.

"Tell the truth," I told her, but we both knew it was a warning going forward, however uncertain I was myself.

"Well," she began. "I only had a few days left with you and... because of what you were offering, it was getting difficult to say no."

"To say no to what exactly?" I asked, and she held my gaze.

"I wanted to continue being Sophie because of what you had proposed. I wanted to continue working for you, I wanted to continue as we were. I didn't want to leave, and I knew... I knew the longer I stayed, the more impossible it would be, and so I..."

"Allowed me to have one more intimate encounter with you and then disappeared. Just to be clear, that was your plan, right?"

I could very clearly and finally detect the hurt in my tone, which I now realized I had buried underneath everything else because I didn't want to admit, especially to myself, that in such a short while, not only had I been fooled, but I had cared enough to feel hurt by it. In a way, what she did felt like a betrayal because if Felix had never found out about her, then I would have never known. I would have continued to treat Sophie like she was her, and even when she rejected me and things got awkward, I would have never known.

"Was Sophie planning to take over with intimate relations with me as well?" I asked, and a pained expression came over her face.

"We're not insane," she said, and my eyebrows shot up.

"Is that right?"

She sighed then. "I'm sorry about what happened. Sophie was pissed as hell with me as well, and we were going to try to fix it, but from the beginning... it was never my intention. I didn't come on to you, this wasn't something I orchestrated to exploit you. You know how it happened. You approached me, and I couldn't say no."

This almost made me smile. "So it's my fault?" I asked, and instantly, she started to deny it, but then her expression changed, and she frowned. As a result, something inside me lit up in excitement.

This was the woman that I knew and had been enthralled by, and I honestly couldn't wait to hear the next words that would come out of her mouth. She enthralled me like no other, I realized, so I gave her my full attention.

"It was both our faults," she said. "And Sophie as well. But in my opinion, even though what we did was unsavory, neither of us did it to hurt you. She did it to ensure you got all the assistance you needed, and I... I, well, I couldn't say no to you. I liked you. I... I like you, and so... I have no regrets. So, don't punish her for something that we both did.

I hope you will consider this. I know that loyalty means a lot to you, and her intention wasn't to betray you. She just made a very emotional and silly mistake for a few days."

Afterwards, she went silent, and I didn't know what to say in response to this, but I was for sure not going to agree with her. So, I turned around and went on my way.

Chapter 55
Scarlett

Two *months later.*

"What's that?" Sophie asked. "Your fifth flute of the day?"

My eyes turned as I chugged down the sparkling liquid in the champagne glass. I frowned as I stared at my rude sister in the mirror but didn't respond as I finished the rest of the glass.

"Shut up and mind your business," I said as I put it away and then returned to fixing the bangs she had just complained about not being pronounced enough. We'd changed her hairstyle twice, wiped off her too-smoky makeup, and almost had to handle a mental breakdown because her dress was too tight.

Now she was fully dressed in her white gown for her wedding, and both my mom and I were suffering thanks to her anxiety but taking it all in stride. My mother was amused as she met our gaze through the mirror, but she was busy and on her phone. Before she returned to her screen, however, she shared a look with me, and I wondered what it was about.

I continued fixing Sophie's hair, but suddenly something occurred to me. As though she could read my mind, she looked up just then, and our gazes met again. "What?" I asked, but she shrugged.

"You two are making me even more nervous," Sophie said, and I wished I could tell her that she was nervous not because of us but because she wasn't sure of who she was getting married to, but it was too late.

"I need a nap," she said, and it almost made me laugh. But then the urge to go to the bathroom suddenly overrode this, so I set the curler down and turned around to leave.

"Bathroom?" my mom asked, and I nodded.

"I'll come with you. We'll be back in five minutes, Sophie," she said, and my sister nodded.

"Scar," she called out before I left. "Can I get a flat glass of that champagne you've been drinking? I need it."

"No," I replied. "I need you to be clear-headed throughout the day. Or else you're going to get drowsy and irritated. You do not know how to hold your alcohol."

She pouted in annoyance at me, but she just looked cute. So, myself and mom left, laughing.

We remained silent as we headed over to the bathroom, and it just made things even more awkward, especially since I didn't understand why they were awkward to begin with. When we got to the bathroom, it was more or less empty, so we took stalls next to each other.

It was quiet for a little while, although I was the only

one doing the peeing, and it sounded like she was just sitting there.

"Are you alright?" I asked, but she directed the question back to me.

"Are you?" she asked.

"What do you mean?" I said, but she didn't respond. Not until we both came out and met each other at the vanity.

I immediately looked away so that she wouldn't see how distraught I felt in my eyes. How forlorn I had been feeling for the past few weeks since I had found out. Or even earlier, since that night he had turned around and just walked away. One minute he was all I could think about, and in the next, it was almost as though he had never even existed.

Sophie had been put on punishment for a whole two weeks, and in that time, she had nearly lost hair wondering about her fate. To our relief, he had called her back to work, and although things had more or less gone back to normal, I had felt even more hopeless then.

Because no call whatsoever I understood was ever going to come to me. "You know he's going to be here, right?" she asked, but I didn't respond at first. I focused on washing my hands, but she didn't let it go.

"Is he?" I eventually asked and went over to dry. The noise drowned out whatever she wanted to say, but I couldn't avoid it or her any longer. "Mom, all of that happened months ago. And only for a few days, everyone and their mom has moved on. You, of course, should too."

She wasn't amused at this.

"If you have moved on, then why have you been so gloomy? Or you think we wouldn't notice the change?" I sighed, then turned to her. "Mom, I'm fine. He'll be here, yes, I'm a bit nervous, but we didn't know each other for long, and I keep hammering this into everyone's head, but no one's listening to me. I'll see him, I'll say hi, or maybe not. After all, he's just a wedding guest, and he's not my boss or anything, so please focus on the daughter who's getting married today and not the one who isn't?"

"Alright," she said. "I'll take your word for it, but what about your drinking? It's been at least six champagne flutes now, and I seriously wonder why you haven't collapsed yet." I gave her an incredulous look.

"It's six tiny flutes and I'm not Sophie." She narrowed her gaze at me.

"Is this just a one-time occurrence because you're nervous, or is this a habit of yours?"

At the immense concern on her face, I was amused.

"No, Mom, I'm not turning into an alcoholic, I just like this particular brand of sparkling cider, and I, of course, want to drink it from a champagne flute because why not?"

She seemed confused. Again, I leaned forward and blew my breath at her face. "No alcohol. For one, it's ten am, and secondly, in case you missed what I said the first time, it's sparkling cider. It's sweet, I'm starving, and it's available, so why not?"

"Oh," she said, and I watched as all her concerns drained away from her face. They, in turn, drained away from my heart, but I tried my best not to show it. "Alright then," she said. "You're fine, but Sophie's doesn't seem to be, so wait outside a while longer. I want to talk to her privately."

"Alright," I replied, more than grateful for the space and

reprieve. The wedding was starting anytime now, and most of the guests had already arrived. All the bridesmaids had long come and gone, and now it was the final moment, and it was just us three. I thought of going out to meet my dad, but I was sure to run into friends and relatives, and I needed the quiet anyway that I could get through the day.

No, I wasn't drinking champagne, but that wasn't because I didn't want to. All I wanted was an entire bottle of it, but I couldn't because I had something to hide. It was both fortunate and unfortunate, and it had sucked the soul out of me for the last few weeks ever since I had discovered it. And so all I could do was bide my time until I could eventually make up my mind on what to do, but every day that passed made things more difficult.

Perhaps, I wondered now to myself as I looked down the hallways if I had been waiting for this wedding all along. Perhaps I had been waiting to see him one more time so that I could decide on what to do. And so I was nervous and jittery and barely holding it together, and everyone, I was sure, could see through me. Sighing, I lowered my head just then, the door to the male bathroom pulled open. I had been standing by it, so I immediately straightened to give way to whoever had just exited since the hallway was so small.

"Sorry," I apologized; however, he didn't respond, so I was forced to lift my gaze then, cranky enough to just maybe call him an asshole for ignoring my politeness. However, as soon as my eyes set on the pair of gorgeous gray-gold speckled eyes that had haunted my dreams for the past several months, my heart stopped in my chest.

Chapter 56
Lucien

I had known that I was going to see her, and this, I had to admit, had deterred me from attending this wedding. But Sophie had my complete schedule as my assistant, so there was no way I could have lied to her in any way that I was unavailable.

Thankfully, though, Elena had been available, so she had agreed to come with me, and so here we were. If not at the church ceremony, I had expected to run into her at the reception, but now that she was here so early and standing in front of me, I had no idea what to say. She was in complete shock, I could see because her eyes were wide and her lips slightly parted.

She looked breathtaking, my brain instantly registered, but this was by the way. It wasn't a thought I could linger on, but the fact that I couldn't deny the ache and longing I felt as I looked at her was undeniable.

Before I could do what I had admonished myself not to, I turned and without a word continued on my way. Perhaps

I could have said hi, but I wasn't ready just yet to open up any unnecessary doors.

When I returned to the pew we were sitting on, however, I remained silent for a while before eventually speaking to Elena. "I've seen her," I told her, and she snapped her head to mine.

"What? Where?"

"Bathroom," I whispered, and her head instantly snapped toward the back of the church. Then she got up.

"I need to go to the bathroom; I'll be back in a bit," she said; however, I stopped her and frowned. "I'm just going to the bathroom," she pleaded. "It's best to do it before the ceremony starts, and it'll be starting anytime now." I kept my hard gaze on her, and eventually, she plopped back down onto her chair. "I would have just said hi, and who knows what else might have happened?"

"The 'what else might have happened' is precisely why I didn't want you to interfere."

"I wasn't trying to interfere," she said. "I was just trying to be nice and polite, plus I like her."

"You only met her once and joined her in deceiving me."

"It's been months, and you employed Sophie back. You need to have gotten over this whole deception debate with her."

I didn't respond.

"Please tell me you have," she said, but I ignored her. And thankfully, just then, the guests began to take their seats, indicating that the ceremony was about to begin.

I was more nervous than I wanted to admit or acknowledge, so I simply kept my expression neutral and took extra care to act as though I didn't give a damn in the whole wide world. Hopefully, it was effective because the doors were pulled open, and the procession began. The bridesmaids and, of course, the maid of honor, who was none other than Scarlett. I didn't bother taking my eyes off her because I knew she would do all she could to avoid my gaze. This was acceptable, so I took my fill of her.

Her hair was slicked back away from her face. It seemed a bit longer, but I had no idea how that had been pulled off. Her makeup, though, was set and pink, and she seemed flushed and so soft.

Watching her in this way, it became nearly impossible for me to forget how she had felt in my arms. The first month away from her had been easy; at least, that was what I had told myself. And then afterwards, it was a thought; my ability to keep telling myself this had been lost.

She popped into my mind at random times, but through it all, I fought it until I accepted that none of it was enough for me to start a relationship with her again, I allowed them in my mind and treated them as fond memories at best and cautionary moments at worst, dependent on my mood.

Now, however, and as I watched her, I wondered if the sadness and exhaustion I sensed from her were all in my head.

I was sure she had moved on as I had, but I couldn't help but agree with Elena in this, more about the fact that all of it was a shame. Our chemistry was undeniable, and I would give almost anything to experience that again. Sighing, I looked away and focused on the altar, and pretty soon, Sophie came in with her dad.

I watched her and couldn't help but imagine as well

how Scarlett would look in a white dress. Hers would be a bit more raunchier than Sophie's, who currently looked like a princess in a ball gown.

Suddenly, I received a nudge in the arm, and then I looked up to see that it was Elena trying to get my attention.

"What?" I mouthed, and she nudged my attention toward Scarlett at the altar once again. I was reluctant to look, but it was just in time to meet Scarlett's gaze. My heart lurched in my throat as we stared straight at each other, and then she turned away.

"She smiled at us," Elena said, and I released a heavy sigh.

Eventually, and during the ceremony, Elena nudged me on the arm again. "You really can't forgive her?" she asked, and I refused to respond to this.

Chapter 57
Scarlett

I needed to make a decision. The wedding was already over, and I knew that in very little time, he would be leaving. I had waited and hoped to see him here, wondering if, by some helpful twist of fate, we could reach some sort of understanding. I didn't even know what I was hoping for, but as I watched him throughout the ceremony, I understood that this was an instance where I wasn't going to wait for fate to cause a reconciliation on my behalf. Sure, I couldn't force Lucien's cooperation, but I could, to an extent, get his understanding. So, after emptying my sparkling cider, I rose to my feet, wishing to hell that I could drink alcohol of any sort. However, this was generally impossible, so I had to do this clear-headed.

I headed over to his table, which thankfully was empty as almost everyone else was on the dance floor. My legs were shaky, and I could feel all the perspiration I had somehow held at bay up till this moment began to appear on my skin and under my arms. I had to turn then to look toward Sophie's direction, and indeed, I found her watching me. For the first time in a very long while, I allowed my vulnerability to show as I asked her if I was making a mistake and if I should turn around. However, she smiled at me, softly, and kindly, and then she nodded.

She'd told me that after she returned to work, I was never mentioned. It was almost as though I had been completely erased from his mind and as though I had never existed. To an extent, and after this report, I had been certain then that I'd be able to do the same. But a few weeks later, I was pouring my guts out in the toilet bowl of a restaurant. At first, when I'd found out, I'd been shocked, but then I couldn't help but feel somewhat excited because the door that I thought was closed forever seemed to have been creaked open. Yet I had no way to burst through. Perhaps I never would, but now that I had seen him again, I was convinced that I didn't want to get rid of his baby.

He had to be the most gorgeous and excellent specimen of a man I had ever come across, and if his baby was the memento that was given to me of the fact that we had met and that we had been intimate, then I was ready to keep the baby. Taking a deep breath, I continued on my way toward the table, but just as I was approaching, two things happened.

First, I spotted Elena, who had been trailing around with one of our cousins on the dance floor, and started to head over to him. She seemed so happy and carefree, so it took a while for her to notice my approach, but the moment she did, she immediately did a three-hundred-and-sixty-degree turn and returned to the dance floor. Of course, Lucien was paying attention, so the moment she did this, his head turned in curiosity, and he finally noticed that I was heading his way.

I was forced to stop in my tracks because I almost expected him to rise to his feet to leave at my approach, but when after a few seconds had passed and he didn't, I was able to somewhat breathe easier. He didn't look away. Instead, he kept staring at me because it was now obvious I was heading toward him. I appreciated this consideration as well and managed somehow to keep one foot in front of the other as I approached. Still, my knees shook and my throat clogged with emotion. There was no doubt that tears were filling my eyes and at the most unfortunate moment they were probably going to fall and embarrass me beyond redemption but I couldn't help it. Three days after we'd met I was too afraid to call it what I now know it was. It felt right, it felt true, and it had made me crumble into pieces over the past month, over and over again. In that time I hadn't been able to stop myself from learning everything that was publicly available about him and with each moment that had passed I fell more in love with who he was. So now I knew that I was in trouble but the distance had kept me sane enough to not approach him. Now, however, I couldn't hold back any longer.

He was dressed immaculately in a pinstriped suit, but a bit more casual than usual. He had on a gorgeous pocket square, and his hair was slicked back, and my heart just wanted to tear out of my chest. Eventually, I arrived at his table, and he stared at me. I decided then, however, that I didn't want to talk in that location. I knew that everyone was probably busy dancing and didn't pay us any mind, but I couldn't stop myself from feeling that every eye in the room was on us, not even because of me but because of him. It was nearly impossible not to have noticed all the female attention he had received since he had arrived, but thankfully, for the most part, most of them had stayed away because they assumed that Elena was his girlfriend.

"Hello," I greeted as I arrived, and he nodded in response. "Can we, uh, talk?" I asked. For a second, he seemed as though he was going to reject me, and I couldn't risk it, so I explained further. "I, uh... have something to tell you," I said.

"Take a seat," he said, gesturing toward Elena's seat, but when I looked around, he understood my meaning and rose to his feet. I was so grateful that I almost cried, but I kept myself together, and we soon headed away from the venue. There was a gorgeous garden beyond with a little pond that we could stroll by, so we walked side by side through it until the people and the sounds and bustle from the wedding party were only a low hum in the distance.

Eventually, we came to a stop when we located the pond, and then turned around to face each other.

"What is it?" he asked, and I was immediately unhappy at his curt tone. However, I wasn't doing this to seek sympathy or anything for that matter from him. All I wanted was to inform him of the simple facts, and he could do whatever he wanted with the subsequent information.

I turned and watched him, and I was more certain than ever of the decision I had been leaning toward from the first moment I found out. It would be difficult, life would drastically change, but I was sure that I would never regret it. And so I didn't beat around the bush. Instead, I came right out with the words, and to my surprise, they flowed out much more easily than I had expected.

"I'm pregnant," I told him. Before this moment, I hadn't heard a single sound from around us, but now it was as though I could hear the tiny splashes from the water, the crickets, my breathing, his lack of anything. He seemed as though he had turned to stone at my words, so I didn't delay any further before he accused me of whatever was probably running through his head.

"Don't worry, I'm not here to ask for anything. I don't need anything from you; I'm more than capable of handling this myself. I just wanted to let you know. I debated for a while on whether to keep it or not, and I've decided to. You're welcome to be involved in his or her life, but whatever happens, you're obligated to nothing. I just wanted to let you know. That's all."

I didn't wait; I just turned around. But before I could leave, he caught my wrist. My chest constricted, making it nearly impossible to breathe, but I managed to hold my cool as I shut my eyes and tried to regulate my breathing.

"You're just going to drop a bomb like that and walk away?" he asked. I pulled my hand out of his hold and turned around then to face him.

"What do you want me to say? There's nothing to say. It's a fact, and being straightforward is the only way. No need for guesses or expectations or promises."

"When did you find out?" he asked, and I shut my eyes to think.

"About ten days ago," I replied. "So, a little over a week?"

"Why didn't you tell me immediately?" he asked.

"Well, I didn't exactly have such easy access to you."

"What about Sophie?" he cut me off.

"She doesn't interfere. Given our history, there's a clear line between all of this to her."

He listened, but I couldn't tell what he was thinking or feeling, so I decided to leave again, I didn't want it to be awkward if he stopped me once again.

"It was great seeing you," I told him, "Thanks for coming, and I hope you enjoy the rest of the party."

I continued on my way, and this time around, he truly didn't stop me.

It was what I had expected, what I had even almost hoped for, but regardless, it hurt so much that I had to wonder if I wasn't just lying to myself and asking for much less than I deserved. It didn't matter anyway because whether I was asking for too little or too much, I wasn't going to demand anything. I had laid down the cards, and it was up to him to do what he wanted. Whatever he chose, I promised myself that I would be more than alright. I would be great.

Chapter 58

Lucien

I had a decision to make. As I watched her leave, all I could think about was the fact that I understood what she was thinking. And when she said that she didn't need my help, I understood. I believed her. I realized as I took in her straight shoulders and back, brimming with confidence and guts, that she would like my input; it would make life better. However, she wasn't going to demand it because this wasn't why she had been intimate with me from the very beginning.

Although I'd considered every possible negative and positive about our time together, I'd never quite been able to shake off the feeling that perhaps some alternative and less-than-noble reason had been behind her involvement with me. And so now, I realized that I had more or less been waiting for the other shoe to drop, and indeed, now it had.

But to my surprise, I didn't feel defensive or angry. Instead... it felt as though whatever had been holding me back, a rope of the resistance around my hands, had finally been cut loose. And now, I could make the decision I actually wanted to make.

The last two months had plagued me with the kind of emotional turmoil that firstly I never knew was possible and secondly, I had completely failed in navigating. Yet I had refused to be impulsive so in the end I had remained in constant battle pushing my thoughts and memories about her to the back of my mind every time they popped up. I'd told myself that eventually I'd forget altogether but now, and after what she'd just told me, I allowed myself to admit that the last thing I ever wanted to do was forget.

Although a little while earlier, I had been planning to leave with Elena, now, as I returned to my table and saw her waiting, I decided to stay a little longer. I paid more attention to her family, her friends, and her parents; however, she was nowhere to be found. She had probably retreated and would most likely not be coming out again for the night. I was certain now that she had been prepared for me to give her nothing but wounds in regards to her news, and so had immediately retreated to lick them.

This made me sad, and more than anything, I wanted to send for her, to speak to her and to assure her that the outcome would most probably be good, but I didn't think she'd believe me. I believed me but I knew I'd need a bit of time to process and decide on the best way to proceed so eventually, I rose to my feet. After saying my goodbyes to Sophie and her family, I went on my way.

The ride home between me and Elena was quiet, but it was good because it gave me the time needed to think. When we were nearing the house, however, I turned and found her fast asleep with her mouth open. This made me smile as I watched her.

She had a blast, and that made me happy, but that was her personality. We had always been different in the sense that I found it very difficult to leave anything whatsoever to chance. I took risks but never really personal ones. But for the first time and with Scarlett, I wanted to take a chance.

I let this simmer in my heart and found with no surprise that after the initial surprise and dread had subsided, relief and excitement began to take its place. My blood began to hum through my body, and it was as though the turgid cold that had frozen me solid for as long as I could remember was beginning to melt. I felt alive and excited and couldn't believe how with the simple bit of information she gave to me, everything had started to take on a whole new meaning, and I loved it.

It didn't take me long to make a final decision, so the moment I got to the office the next day and on our way back from a meeting on a lower floor, I glanced at her sister walking by my side. They looked so alike, but now and in the light of my decision, I realized that I was more happy to have her working by my side like never before. Sure, the real thing wouldn't be available, but the ability to look at a close copy was quite thrilling.

"What's your sister up to?" I asked. I expected her to be startled, but I didn't expect the question to take quite a few seconds before it hit. And the moment it did, she turned to me with a wary surprise on her face.

She stared at me as though she didn't quite know how to respond, and I completely understood. She more than anyone else would be protective of her sister and twin.

"You don't have to respond as my assistant," I told her. "You can respond as her sister."

"Hm... what would that entail exactly?" she asked softly with a smile.

"You can have her best interest at hand, not mine, when speaking," I replied, and she made a soundless "ah" sound with her mouth. Regardless, it still took her until we arrived at the office for me to get a response.

"She just got a new job," she told me. "At Denver and Rail. This was about a week ago, and she's still in law school, so same old, same old."

I nodded at this and continued to my office.

Same old, same old indeed, but I needed to hear from her. I needed and wanted to hear every bit about her from her very mouth, so a little while later, I picked up my cell phone and headed over to the windows overlooking the city.

I couldn't count the countless times I had stood by this window thinking about her, wanting to call her but employing all of my will to ensure that I didn't.

It wasn't even that I was mad at her; it was the fact that I didn't understand why I wasn't.

I couldn't trust my willingness to be with her, regardless, and so all I could do was deprive myself until a reason that I couldn't turn away from came knocking.

Here it was, and the more I thought about it, the more gratitude I felt. I wanted to express this to her, but it was too soon, or perhaps it wasn't.

I no longer felt certain of much and was open to almost everything, and it was exhilarating, to say the least. So when the call finally connected and her sweet voice reached through the receiver, I couldn't help the warmth that spread all over my chest.

"It's Lucien," I greeted.

It took a few seconds, but eventually, she replied, and it made me realize just how nervous I was.

"I know," she replied, and I nodded.

"I heard you're working at Denver and Rail now," I said.

"Yeah," she replied, probably still wondering why I was calling her out of the blue.

"Personal assistant?" I asked.

"No," she replied. "I think I'm over that for now, at least. I'm a paralegal."

"Ah," I nodded. "It's more suitable considering your studies, right?"

She went briefly silent, and I understood why.

"Yes, it is," she replied.

"Can we meet? Lunchtime there is in about half an hour, right?"

"Um... I can't go for lunch today. There's a huge merger they're trying to close before the end of the day, so all hands are literally on deck."

"Hm," I thought about how to solve this problem.

"I know Denver personally. You might not be able to leave the facility, but if I stop by, can I get you alone for a few minutes?"

"A few minutes?" she asked.

"Yes," I replied.

"Um... if what you have to say will take just a few minutes, then I'd prefer we speak over the phone."

This made me smile.

"It's not that type of conversation," I said, and she considered it.

"Alright then, but I'd prefer we met at Late, it's a restaurant a few blocks away from the office. Do you know it?"

"I can find my way," I replied. "Want me to stop by your office to pick you up?" I asked.

"No need," she said. "And if possible, don't stop by the office altogether, please. I don't mean to be rude, but I have to try my best to stop you from getting me fired by speaking to Denver."

She was trying to make a joke, but it was so dark that I couldn't find it funny. This was one of the reasons why I needed to see her, and so I nodded either way.

"Alright," I replied, but she kept speaking.

"I mean, I'm not saying you're going to get me fired. I mean, you have good reason to, I guess, but just... you know what, ignore me; I was just trying to lighten the air, or whatever."

"Alright," I replied, and the call came to an abrupt end.

Chapter 59
Scarlett

I stared at myself in front of the bathroom mirror and truly considered ramming my face into the glass. It would shatter for sure, and I would be hurt, but it would be the fastest way to avoid this meeting with him. Sighing, I brushed dry hair across my shoulder and regretted not putting a bit more effort into my appearance today. Instead, my outfit was quite unflattering, my makeup barely evident.

It had been a rough morning, and my day's goal was to look decent enough to power through it, not to meet the almost cruel man that haunts every waking moment it. However, now he was available and asking me to meet, and I was terrified.

This meeting could go several ways. I could be threatened about the baby. He could want to force me to hand it over, or perhaps, and what I suspected would hurt even further, he was willing to accept some sort of joint custody arrangement and was meeting to hash out the details.

I would accept it because I wasn't going to put my pride before my child's welfare, but it just made me feel as though I was shrinking even further into my shell.

Sighing when my phone rang, I looked down and accepted that I had to get going. One of the firm's partners needed me, and I also had to find a way to be unavailable for half an hour to meet with Lucien.

It was much more difficult than I thought, but eventually, I was strolling out of the law office's building. However, I stood at the entrance, and before I hailed the cab to head over, I decided to call Sophie. She had sworn off any exchange of information between Lucien and me unless it was something alarming, mostly for my peace of mind, but now, this sudden request for a meetup could qualify as alarming, and I needed her to explain this to me.

However, just before the call connected, another one started to come in, and I frowned. I tried to cancel it; however, when I saw who was calling, my heart stopped in my chest.

I stared down at the phone, trying to stabilize my tone and emotions before I responded, especially since I had already embarrassed myself enough for one day. Eventually, though, none of that mattered when I eventually picked up, and he had a few simple but very terrifying words for me.

"I'm at the curb," he said, and my heart once again slammed against my chest.

I looked up, and indeed, just a little distance away from me was his waiting Mercedes. It was unmistakable, and through the tinted windows, I could almost see him watching me, and it immediately changed my entire demeanor. I straightened my shoulders, wiped off the expression from my face, and then I nodded and ended the call. I started to head toward it, and as I went, I wondered if I could ever be completely free around him the way I wanted to be.

Sighing, I walked as quickly as I could, concluding that it wouldn't matter anyway. Michael got out of his seat just then and I was a bit startled to see him opening the door for me. It was a bit unnecessary, but I thanked him anyway. His smile was gentle and kind, and I wondered if he knew about everything that had happened. He had to because there wouldn't otherwise be a reasonable explanation why he was picking a second Sophie up from a different office and wearing a different outfit from what he had probably seen her with earlier that morning.

I sent him an apologetic look and got in, and the door was shut behind me. It was like being put in a trance. The familiar atmosphere, the sweet intoxicating scent, the warm commanding presence. All I could send his way was a glance, and then I busied myself in putting myself together.

"How are you?" he asked, his deep, calm voice resounding through the car. It was quiet and felt intimate, but I couldn't tell if it was because everything about him always seemed amplified to me or if it was because his tone was just a bit higher than usual. Regardless, he sounded too close for comfort. I met his gaze again and nodded in response. We didn't say any further words and rode in silence until we arrived at the restaurant.

It was high-end but not alarmingly so. Definitely way out of my budget, but I wasn't about to take him somewhere cheap when this conversation was about to be difficult and most likely concerning my abilities in taking care of the child. Or maybe he wanted a DNA test as soon as he or she was born to commit to it in whatever way.

Just thinking about this made me frown, but I had to admit that it would be a reasonable request. So, I stopped my emotions from getting riled up. Instead, as soon as the waiter took our orders, I looked him straight in the eye and said what I wanted to.

"If you want a DNA test," I said, "I'm alright with you waiting until the baby is born before anything else. I have no problem whatsoever with this, so you don't have to push yourself into doing something that you don't really want to do. I mean what I said earlier at Sophie's wedding. I was just sharing information with you. I have no expectations."

After my statement, it almost felt as though it was just us two in the restaurant given how rapidly quiet everything became. He watched me, a somewhat darkened expression on his face, and I wondered what I had said wrong that had possibly gone over the line and offended him.

I wanted to ask; however, he wouldn't stop staring at me, so I spoke again.

"T-this is what you wanted to ask for, isn't it?" I asked.

He seemed to sigh then, and then his next words shocked the living daylights out of me.

"You don't think I care about you at all, do you?" he asked, and for a long moment, I was sure I was hallucinating. It was either this or that I didn't know how to respond to this question because I just kept staring at him.

"Scarlett," he called, and my heart nearly stopped.

At first, I wasn't sure why tears gathered in my eyes, but

soon enough, and as his expression somewhat softened, I understood why. He had only called me by my name once and it was a painful night to remember. It wasn't his fault, but I had half expected him to just call me Sophie like he always did, but now, it felt as though he was talking to me.

It took me a while to recover from this, and so I shook my head and lowered it until my emotions were back under control. There was no point in responding now. Afterwards, I simply just stared at him, and then, to my surprise, he got up and pulled his chair over until he was seated by my side. I had no idea what was happening and couldn't help but feel alarmed.

I was nervous and afraid, but beneath it all was an excitement that I couldn't explain. And then, to make things worse, he turned until I was forced to stare directly into his eyes. This was dangerous because in this state and with him, I definitely could not think straight.

Still, I managed to maintain my cool and listened to every single word he said like I depended on it.

"Things have been quite rocky between us, and so I understand why you wouldn't be quite sure what to think regarding me or maybe even assume the worst, but..."

I held my breath, and at his pause, I had to wonder if he was playing with me. And that was when I realized that as difficult as this felt for me, it felt the same way for him. He had always been straightforward in his manner of speech, seeming not to have a single fear in the world, but then here he was, and I could swear that I felt how awkward and nervous he was with every fiber of my being.

And so, before I could stop myself, my hand reached out to place my hand on his. I had no clue what that was intended to do, but I immediately took it off the moment I realized it and was starting to apologize. However, he took my hand and returned it to his.

I'm in love with you, I wanted to say with all of my heart as I watched him hold my hand. There was so much care and affection in his touch and my heart felt like it was about to burst.

"I didn't stay away from you for the past couple of months because I didn't care," he said. "I just... what I had with you, the way I feel with you, I've never experienced that before. And it came so fast and so suddenly that I couldn't trust it. I've always known the best things come with excruciating effort and with time but with you... it felt as though I had suddenly been presented with the whole world, yet it made absolutely no sense to me because it seemed to be too easy. When I thought you were Sophie," he said, "it made sense. I'd known her for years; you'd known me for years as well. And so with the new change, she seemed to have, I didn't doubt myself at all. But then I found out that was indeed you and a lot of my belief systems were shaken, especially in myself. Suddenly, I was wary when I hadn't been in such a long time, and I was somewhat confused and alarmed and, most importantly, felt like I couldn't trust anything, even what we had."

I could feel myself calming down because as he spoke to me now, I found myself becoming lighter. After all, I felt as though I understood exactly what he was saying to me. In short, it was as though I had thought this all along by now and assumed it as the explanation for his coldness, at least during the first few days, but I couldn't even fully accept it, and so I had brushed it to the corner of my mind.

But now that he was saying it right in front of me, I was almost afraid to breathe. His gaze lowered as he squeezed my hand in his.

"I care about you," he said. "Deeply. More than I can verbally express right now. And I know you might not be convinced of this, especially given how things have gone between us, but there is one thing that I want you to believe with all of your heart: that I am thrilled about our baby. I don't know how you feel about it, but to me, it feels like permission to chase what I feel with you. Because of this baby, I can throw my caution to the wind and throw away my reservations, and I..." he stared at me then and smiled.

"I'm out of words but... "

This made me smile, and I didn't even realize it until his gaze lowered to my lips, and I had to catch myself.

"I want to get to know you better," he said. "This was one of the things that pained me immensely these past months. I wanted to know everything about you, but I couldn't get past the mental barriers I had set for myself, holding me back. This has been a lifetime practice, but now... with you, I want to make the needed tweaks."

"I'm... Scarlett, I'm in love with you. And I just can't wait for it to grow even deeper. I want to go all in with you, and while I can't promise you the world, I can promise you my whole heart and unwavering commitment. Yes, your pregnancy is the knock I needed to accept this and come to my senses, but I also hope that you don't think it is the entire reason behind my fascination with you. You are the most gorgeous, breathtaking woman I have encountered in my life, and I do not want to spend another day not being able to call you mine. I won't put you under pressure in any way, but if you're willing to walk hand in hand with me so we can figure this out and perhaps make a dream of a family together, then I am more than willing to come along with you."

At this point, I was shaking, and I could feel it. First of all, this was more words than I had ever heard him speak, and secondly, I didn't think any words in the history of the world could ever sound sweeter.

I tried my best to hold back my tears but I couldn't and so when they fell I turned my face away.

I could feel his smile and he pulled me into his arms and for the first time, I rested easy in them. He was staring directly at me now and so I could say exactly what I wanted to say to him without beating around the bush.

"Lucien," I called and he stroked me gently.

"I... I know you already know this but ... I'm in love with you as well. The last two months have been the fucking hardest of my life." my voice cracked again as another bout of crying hit me but despite how much I resisted he was able to pull me away to look into my eyes.

He sighed then as he wiped the moisture off my cheeks.

"You were so close yet so far for many years. I can't believe what I needed to do much earlier was ask your sister if she had a twin and I would have met you."

This made me laugh out loud causing quite the startle around the restaurant.

But I didn't care. This was the happiest day in my life and I wasn't going to hold back from savoring and allowing myself to enjoy every single moment.

Smiling, I leaned away and in the most intimate way I could, I kissed him, and it was as though I had been brought back to life. It was a while before we pulled apart, and when we did and in answer to his very rare multitude of words, I only had a single one in response, but it carried the weight of both of our hearts.

"Yes."

Epilogue
Scarlett

"I can't believe you two," Sophie said.

This made me laugh because over the past hour, since we'd been here, she had mentioned this at least four times, and each time it just got funnier.

"You decide to wait until after the baby's born to give you both time to adjust to each other, yet two weeks after reconciling you just say *fuck that* and decide to get married?"

I didn't want to say the words. They were cringy at best, but as I turned around, taking in my reflection in the mirror, I couldn't help myself.

"What can I say? It was meant to be, I guess."

Sophie rolled her eyes from behind me as she moved through the rack of dresses, and it made me smile.

I smiled a lot these days. I just couldn't stop, and sometimes I had to pinch myself because never in my wildest dreams could I imagine that I could be this deliriously happy. But I was, and I loved every single moment of it.

"So, what do we think?" I asked as my hands brushed down the gorgeous pattern of the dress.

Sophie turned around to look at the wedding dress I had on, then she cocked her head.

"Fits like a glove," she said, and I nodded.

"Yes, it does."

"Sure you don't want something a bit flowing though?" she asked, holding up another dress.

It looked beautiful, but the one with small lace flowers attached to it made me want to change my mind. Eventually, I decided to try it on as well as two others, and then I was done forever.

"Nope, I'm exhausted," I said when the store attendant came out with another rack. But when yet another brought out a different charcuterie board with another bottle of sparkling cider, I was forced to reconsider.

"You're such a foodie," Sophie mocked with a smile, and I nodded as I headed over to a chaise lounge to relax. "We only have thirty minutes left, though. I have to return to the office."

"Alright," I replied and rushed my eating while more dresses were brought out for me to see. Eventually, Sophie came over to sit by my side and took off her shoes. I couldn't help but notice how exhausted she was as she yawned— not for the first time since we'd been here.

"How's work?" I asked. "I would have thought it'd be a lot easier and your workload would have reduced, given that you're no longer Lucien's assistant."

"Yeah, I hoped so too, but it turns out the marketing department staff might leave the office earlier than personal assistants, but they never actually sleep."

This made me laugh. "But you're enjoying it, though?"

"I love it—challenging but thrilling. It's what I've always wanted, and I just realize it more and more every single day."

I was incredibly happy to hear this but couldn't help but feel a bit worried now that she was no longer personally working with Lucien.

"Is his new assistant competent?" I asked, and she gave me a look.

"If he isn't, you want to apply for the job?"

"Why can't I?" I asked.

"Trust me, I'm probably just as attached to the position, so you can imagine how hard it was for me to let it go. But I assure you, James is extremely efficient and almost anal about his work, so your fiancé is being very well taken care of."

"Okay," I nodded and patted my stomach a bit.

"You're showing a bit now," she said, and I nodded.

"Not really. I think this is the food I just ate but by the time the wedding comes around next month, I might. It won't be very obvious in the dress will it?" I asked, and she smiled.

"You've settled on that dress?"

"No, but I'd like something fitting."

"Understood, and you're good. You look gorgeous."

We shared a smile, and a little while later, we left the store still undecided about the dress.

Michael was waiting for us at the curb. However, while I got in at the back, Sophie went over to the front to chat with him.

"Should I come up for a bit?" I asked when we finally arrived at Lucien's building and she got out.

"I'm not the one you should be asking," she said, and I nodded.

"Right. I have a few pictures from the store to show him as well, but I know how busy he usually is at this time."

"Right," she said. "Still, come up if you can. It'll be a surprise, plus it would be good for me to visit him and my old office again. You won't believe how impossible it is to see him now that I don't work directly for him anymore."

I felt a bit apologetic about this because even though I knew being involved with the marketing team was something she'd always wanted, I was also very well aware that ultimately her decision to leave was because of my relationship with Lucien.

We remained silent until we arrived in his office and I couldn't help but feel nervous. I could feel the smiles sent at Sophie and the curious ones given to me as we passed by some staff and it made me sigh.

"They know don't they?" I asked and she nodded.

"Of course, especially after I came back with my hair. I knew from the start that the hair was what was going to foil our plan."

"Well, I don't have any complaints. I couldn't have asked for a better ending."

"Neither could I," she said just as we arrived at the office.

The secretary was not at his desk but his new personal assistant James immediately looked up as we arrived, and for a short moment he was surprised as he looked between me and Sophie.

"Hey James," she greeted but it took him a while to respond. "This is my sister, Scarlett."

He nodded then, obviously completely aware of all that had transpired but still surprised.

"I knew you two looked alike but ..."

"I know," Sophie smiled. "It's uncanny."

I greeted him as well but just as I glanced at Lucien's door his eyes widened as though he had just realized something.

"Does he have guests?" I asked.

"Well..." he hesitated. "He's expecting some in the next few minutes."

"Oh how lucky," Sophie said. "So she can go in now?"

"Just a second," he said as he sat back down and picked up the phone.

"Sir?" he called and my heart began to race. We spent all of our time together after work and he had given me the sweetest kiss before leaving earlier that morning. Yet, I was still so wreaked with nerves at getting to see him. This was his empire and he was the king of it and I, his queen and there was nothing more exhilarating. I was so turned on that my clit began to throb.

James eventually put the phone down and then he nodded. "Please go in."

"Later Scar," Sophie said and turned around to leave but I was a bit surprised.

"You're leaving? Don't you want to go say hello together?"

She was amused. "He's my boss, not my fiancé."

"But he's your soon-to-be brother-in-law," I said but she shook her head.

"Not within these hours, and you were his assistant; you should know he doesn't like social visits during the day."

"Yeah, that's why I need you with me you were the one who suggested it."

"You don't need me. You're probably the only one he will accept to see socially right now."

Sighing, I nodded and she went on her way.

My nerves came back as I stared at his door for a second and then I knocked lightly and headed it.

I met him hard at work at his desk with his attention on the open file before him on the desk.

I stopped for a moment to admire him just as he signed a document and then the softest, most intimate smile spread across his lips at the sight of me.

It made him look like a dream, and for quite a while, I couldn't stop staring.

"Hey, beautiful," he said, and I headed over. A few seconds later, I was seated on his lap with his tongue in my mouth. It took a while for us to break away from that, and by the time we parted, I was out of breath but in the best way.

"I was expecting your pictures from the wedding store," he said, and I smiled guiltily.

"I know, I thought I was going to send them, but after seeing the dresses, I decided that I wanted to keep it a secret. I'll wait until the day for you to see me."

"Alright," he said. "But if you need any help-"

"I know," I replied.

I looked around the office and even though it was unfamiliar to me in a way it still felt a bit strange.

"Have you had lunch?" he asked.

"No," I replied. "I was about to stop to pick up some on my way back. Have you? Do you want to join me?"

I was immediately hopeful but he shook his head and refused.

"I have a meeting soon," he said and I recalled that his assistant had mentioned it.

"That's right," I said and got up from his lap.

Just then, a knock came to the door and his attention moved to it. He frowned silently and stared and this was somewhat peculiar so I couldn't help but be a bit startled. Then he got up and holding my hand in his, we walked together toward the door. Just before we arrived the door was pulled open and James came in. He seemed somewhat worried as his attention moved between me and his boss.

"They're here?" Lucien asked and he nodded.

"Yes, sir."

Lucien shook his head, and I wondered what was wrong but when we eventually headed out and arrived at the elevators I soon understood.

The elevators we were waiting for came open and a man and a woman dressed impeccably in suits appeared before us.

Huge, hearty smiles spread across their faces as they saw us and we all exchanged handshakes. I remained in slight shock through all of this because, of course, I knew who they were. He introduced me as his fiancé and they continued on their way toward his office.

"Eckhart and Guild?" I asked. "You have business with them? I thought your company had different lawyers?"

I caught myself then as I realized that I was bombarding

him with questions. I instantly stopped. "Sorry," I smiled in apology. "I got carried away."

He watched me and then he leaned forward to brush my hair over my shoulders. "I know you want to work with them," he said and my heart dropped into my stomach. For the longest time, I couldn't speak but eventually, I realized that my suspicion was right.

"So... they're not here because you have business with them as lawyers?"

"I do have business with them," he said calmly. However, he didn't say more and instead pulled me slightly closer to him. He stared into my eyes but when he started to lean down to kiss me I put up a hand gently against his face to stop it. This made him laugh.

"You're not doing what I think you're doing are you?"

"I didn't exactly want you to know about it," he said, and my mouth fell open. His assistant's nervousness finally made sense to me.

Once again my heart began to race as so many questions came to mind. I didn't know which to start with but when he glanced backward I knew that ultimately I had to go straight to the point.

"You're trying to put in a word for me so that they employ me eventually?"

"As soon as you're done with law school."

I was shocked.

"They only accept from Harvard."

"Not after I give them a chunk of my business."

My eyes misted but still, I had to state the obvious. "This is nepotism."

"I don't give a fuck," he said. "You've told me several

times that it has been your dream for the longest time to work for them but they'd never employ you. They'd better now."

I couldn't stop my smile.

"So... they'll guarantee it?"

"They'd better," he said and my heart couldn't stop dancing. He leaned forward once again to kiss me and I completely lost myself in it. His tongue stroked sensually against mine while I held onto him for dear life. Once again I was shaking with excitement all over and by the time we pulled away I was barely able to speak. But still, I ensured to say the words that I hoped he would never tire of hearing.

"I love you, Lucien," I said and he pressed one last kiss to my cheek. "I love you too, baby."

The End

Coming Soon... sample chapters
Enemy Boss

Chapter One
Maxine

The club is heaving, and I can feel the pounding of the bass echoing through my body. The air is hot and humid. and I gulp down the last bit of water in my bottle and put the bottle down on the narrow counter running along the wall.

I am not getting any cooler so I decide to go outside for a bit of air. I turn to tell Harriet, my best friend, that I am stepping outside for a moment and that I might actually call it a night, but she's joined at the mouth with a guy she's met earlier. I shake my head with a smile and decide to leave her to it. I'm sure between her and the other girls who are off somewhere in the club, they will be able to work out that I've gone home.

I start making my way towards the exit.

The club is jam packed and I have to squeeze between writhing, dancing bodies, and by the time I get to the exit,

I'm a whole lot more hot and bothered than I was on the dance floor. I make a promise to myself there and then that I won't come to a club if I'm stone cold sober ever again. The oppressive heat, the strangers being forced to stand too close to each other, and the incessant thump of the music are enjoyable when I'm drunk, but sober, they are awful. I wonder how any of the staff can stand to be there. I suppose it's slightly less packed behind the bar.

It is a relief to step outside. I take a long, deep breath of the cold air. I stand there until I feel goose bumps scurrying up and down my exposed arms. Crossing them in front of my body, I rub my upper arms, trying to get some warmth into them. My dress is cute; a barely there black bandage dress, but it really isn't suitable for the cold. Just like my heels aren't suitable for the concrete steps leading down from the club's door.

I start making my way down the steps carefully. Holding on tightly to the metal railing despite how cold it is against my hand. I look down, concentrating on my feet. What sort of idiot designs a place where people wear heels and drink alcohol to have concrete steps to get in and out?

I'm about halfway to the bottom when I feel my ankle roll.

I grab for the railing with my spare hand as my knees bend and I fall towards the unforgiving jutting edges of the steps. I don't hit the those gray stairs though. Instead, warm, strong hands catch and hold me until I manage to regain my footing. I look up, ready to thank my savior, but the words are stolen from my mouth.

I just look at him, my words momentarily lost, drinking in the sight of him.

He has tanned skin which perfectly complements the deep brown of his eyes. His hair is cropped short and for a second, I imagine running my hand over the silky strands. I imagine my hand moving lower, running over his arms and chest, which I can see through his t-shirt are muscular.

One side of his mouth curls up in a mocking smile and I realize I have been staring. I feel my cheeks flush and immediately I feel awkward, which brings on a surge of unreasonable anger inside me. As though it's somehow this stranger's fault that I was staring at him like a lost puppy.

"Thank you," I say huffily, self-consciously pulling down the edges of my dress.

"You're welcome," he says, but he doesn't move. His voice is low and gravelly, and I feel a shiver of desire go through me at the sound of it. I ignore the feeling and continue to frown at him. He's still so close I can feel the heat coming off his body... and he still wearing that irritatingly knowing smile on his face.

"Well?" I demand. "Are you going to get out of my way?"

He casually glances over his shoulder at the rest of the steps.

"Do you think you can make it that far unassisted?" he asks, unperturbed by my shocking rudeness.

"I'm not drunk you know," I blurt out.

"I didn't say you were," he replies, looking even more amused.

God he's annoying. And hot. Annoyingly hot.

"You implied I can't walk down a flight of stairs on my own," I say.

"Ah but I wasn't basing that conclusion off how much

you may or may not have had to drink. I was basing that off the fact you have already almost fallen once and you're not quite half way down the stairs yet."

I know he's just teasing me, and I can't really argue his point either because he's right. Drunk I might not be, but my ankle is throbbing slightly, and my heels are too high. I have a feeling I will turn the ankle again before I reach the bottom of the stairs. Even so I can't give him the satisfaction of being right.

"Thank you again for catching me, but I assure you I am perfectly capable of getting down the rest of the stairs," I say firmly.

The smirk on the man's mouth becomes more of a grin as he waves his hand in the direction of the bottom of the stairs.

"Be my guest," he says.

He steps back enough to allow me space to move past him, but he makes no effort to carry on up the stairs towards the club. He watches me and I turn back to look him.

"Well?" he says.

"Go on then," I mutter grumpily.

"You go on. Looks like you're the one with something to prove."

I can hardly admit that I don't think I can make it the rest of the way down without hurting myself after I have been so adamant that I am just fine. I take a steadying breath and move down a step. So far, so good. I move down another one, but as soon as my already weak ankle hits the ground, pain flares up and my ankle rolls again. I don't even have time to grab for the railing with my spare hand this time before the sexy stranger's big warm hands are on me.

He stops me from falling, but instead of letting go of me, he lifts me into the air and throws me over his shoulder in a rather undignified fireman's lift.

"Put me down this instant," I demand, one hand thumping against his back and the other desperately trying to make sure I am not flashing my ass to the people coming and going from the club, some of whom are laughing at my predicament.

"Your ass is fine," the man says. "In more ways than one."

I ignore his strange compliment just like he ignores my command for him to put me down. I keep thumping weakly on his back as he moves down the steps, but the truth is, it's at best a token protest. It's good to get to the bottom of the stairs without further hurting my ankle and yes, I admit it, it feels good to be on his man's shoulder, his arm around my legs. I like the strength of him, the way I feel safe propped high up here. I like the warm, masculine smell of him too. Very nice. Very, very nice.

We reach the bottom of the stairs, and he slaps one hand against my ass. I yelp in indignation rather than any pain as he sets me back on my feet.

"Now we're acquainted, I should introduce myself. I'm Cullen," he says.

"Max," I reply. "Do you always spank people within seconds of meeting them?"

"Only if they've been naughty," Cullen says, laughter twinkling in his eyes.

I swallow hard, his words leaving me speechless and despite myself, I'm wet and turned on. He probably sees my discomfort, but he has no idea how much I liked his words.

"I'm joking Max, relax," he says.

I feel a bit silly, and I smile, forcing myself to stop showing myself up. He's not flirting with me. He's just trying to lighten the moment. "I much prefer my girls to be naughty. I would never punish them for that."

Ok, maybe he is flirting with me.

"Well, I hate to disappoint you, but I'm most definitely a good girl," I say.

"Obviously," he says. "Because every good girl can be found falling out of a club at two am."

"Ok, I agree that wasn't my finest moment," I say, smiling. "But I really am sober. That's what makes it worse. If I was drunk, I probably wouldn't have fallen."

Cullen chuckles. "Or if you did, you wouldn't have cared."

"Exactly," I agree.

"You're leaving early. Is it bad in there?" he asks, jerking his head in the direction of the club.

"It's bouncing, but when you're sober, it's awful. Too full, too loud, and way too sticky."

"With a recommendation like that, I think I'll give it a miss. Come on."

He starts to walk but I don't follow him. I'm not his little toy to boss around. He looks back over his shoulder at me.

"What?" he asks. "Are you waiting for me to carry you again?"

He starts back towards me, and I shake my head, knowing that he will actually pick me up.

"No," I say. I lift one of my feet up and slip my shoe off. "Just getting rid of these."

I slip the other one off and walk towards him, my shoes

dangling from one hand. He's walking in the direction of the taxi rank anyway so I may as well walk with him as walk alone. I tell myself that's the only reason I am following him, the only reason I am still talking to him.

We are about half way to the taxi rank, crossing the parking lot for the club and the restaurants and bars that line the street alongside it, when he puts his hand in his pocket and pulls out a car key. He presses the fob and a sleek Audi beeps into life. Cullen veers away from me and heads for the car.

"See you around," I say.

He frowns at me.

"Playing games Max?" he asks.

I shake my head. "No game. I'm fine. I'll get a cab."

"Yeah?"

I know I should put my foot down here and go and get a cab, but there's something about Cullen, something intriguing. His very presence pulls me in and makes me want to spend more time with him. I will be honest – what most people would call charm is coming off to me as arrogance, like he thinks he only has to say the word and I will follow his instructions. But he's not wrong. There is something in his tone that is both commanding and also soft, like he isn't giving me an order, but explaining a foregone conclusion.

"Yeah," I confirm. "I just want to get a cab, go home, and wash my feet."

"Are you worried I'll kill us both? I've come straight from the office and Scout's honor, not a drop of alcohol has passed these lips."

I looked at his lips. If he's an axe murderer, he is one hell of a gorgeous one. I hadn't even thought of his sobriety

403

and that is bad. I should have. But I do feel reassured knowing he hasn't had a drink. And not because of his driving skills. But because it means this flirting thing isn't one sided between sober me and drunk him. He's as sober as I am and he's not holding back.

"It's not that," I say slowly. "My mother told me not to get in cars with strangers."

"Really?" Cullen asks with another of those damned sexy grins. "And do you always do what your mom tells you to do?"

I do what I've *never* done before. I shake my head and start walking towards his car.

"Nope," I say as I open the passenger side door and get into the car.

Cullen gets into the driver's seat and pulls on his seatbelt. I like that. It tells me that despite his arrogance, there was still a part of him that wasn't sure if I was going to follow his orders or not. As Cullen watches me, I put my heels back on. He's still looking at me when I finish.

"What?" I ask, looking back at him.

"Put your seatbelt on," he says.

"Aww... are you worried about me?" I tease.

"I'm worried you might crack the windshield if you hit it," he says expressionlessly.

I can't help but laugh softly as I put my seat belt on. "Well, we can't have that can we."

He shakes his head, puts the car into gear and pulls off. He leaves the parking lot, turning right. He needed to turn left to get to my place and I tell him so. He grins at me, a grin so full of lust that I feel my whole body tighten. Between my legs an incessant throb begins.

"Isn't it time we stopped pretending you are going anywhere but back to my place?" he says.

The good natured flirting has been replaced with an intense sexual air that leaves me feeling breathless and I just nod because to even try to resist him at this point would be futile and I don't trust my voice to come out sounding even.

"Good," he says.

He puts his hand on my knee, and I feel tingles spread up my leg and to my pussy. It takes everything I have not to squirm on the seat. If he can make me feel like that with his hand on my knee, what is he going to be able to do with his hand further up? With his mouth? With his cock in me? A rush of warm lust floods me and I glance at Cullen. His eyes are on the road, but that smirk is completely gone, and I think maybe he felt it too where his hand touches me.

When he has to take his hand away to switch gears, I miss his touch. When he has changed them, but his hand goes back to the steering wheel, it is hard to hide my disappointment, although I think I manage it, because he would be grinning like a Cheshire cat if he knew how much taking away his touch had affected me.

We don't speak much for the rest of the drive, but I keep glancing at him out of the corner of my eye, and several times, I catch him looking at me too. The air is charged with lust, and in my fevered brain I feel as if I can almost see sparks flying around in the air. I've never felt anything like this before, and certainly not this quickly.

If someone had told me I was going to meet a guy and go home with him within five minutes of that meeting, I would have told them they were crazy. Yet here I am. And the strangest part is that it doesn't feel wrong and although I am a bit nervous, I'm more nervous that I might say or do something stupid rather than being nervous because I am going home with a stranger.

Finally, he turns the car off the road and down a driveway. He stops outside of a garage, but he makes no effort to open the garage door. He cuts the engine and I realize he's leaving the car there. I look up at the house as we get out of his car. It's a massive house, the front painted white, with a wrap-around porch. The garden is nicely kept as is the front of the house.

We get to the front door and he unlocks it and steps in, gesturing for me to follow him inside. I do and he closes the door and locks it. Then he smiles at me. A slow, sexy smile that turns my insides to jelly.

"Do you want to pretend you're here for the tour, or do you want to go upstairs and have the best orgasm you've ever had?"

He's very arrogant, very self assured. They aren't traits I generally like in a man, but Cullen pulls them off. I look up at his face, my mouth suddenly dry, my chest heaving.

"The ... the second one," I stutter.

"Wise choice," he says.

Pre-order here:
Enemy Boss

About the Author

Thank you so much for reading!
If you have enjoyed the book and would like to leave a
precious review for me, please kindly do so here:

Confessing To The CEO

Please click on the link below to receive info about my latest
releases and giveaways.
NEVER MISS A THING

Or
come say 'hello' here:

Also by Iona Rose